STOLEN MOMENTS

STOLEN MOMENTS

Rosie Harris

This first world hardcover edition published 2013
in Great Britain and in the USA by
SEVERN HOUSE PUBLISHERS LTD of
19 Cedar Road, Sutton, Surrey, England, SM2 5DA.
First published 1991 in mass market format only under the
title Sighing for the Moon and pseudonym Rose Glendower.

British Library Cataloguing in Publication Data

Harris, Rosie, 1925- author.
  Stolen moments. -- New edition.
  1. Wales--Social conditions--19th century--Fiction.
  2. Chartism--Fiction. 3. Great Britain--History--
  Victoria, 1837-1901--Fiction. 4. Love stories.
  I. Title
  823.9'2-dc23

ISBN-13: 978-0-7278-8326-1   (cased)

All Severn House titles are printed on acid-free paper.

Severn House Publishers support The Forest Stewardship Council ™ [FSC™],
the leading international forest certification organisation. All our titles that
are printed on FSC certified paper carry the FSC logo.

Printed and bound in Great Britain by
TJ International, Padstow, Cornwall.

To my Husband, Ken

'What's in a name? That which we call a rose
By any other name would smell as sweet.'

ROMEO & JULIET Act 11 Sc 11

1

1838

'I'm going to be a Nanny . . . a Nanny . . . a Nanny. . . .'

Cheeks flushed, Kate Stacey paused to get her breath back before opening the garden gate to Bramble Cottage. Eager to impart her news, she had run non-stop from the end of the lane, her skirts held high so that they wouldn't be marked by the grass which was still damp from a sudden April shower.

She straightened her straw bonnet, impatiently pushing back the escaping black ringlets beneath the white brim before retying the ribbons. Then she smoothed down the long full skirt of her cornflower blue cambric dress, that exactly matched the colour of her eyes. It was the first time she had worn it and she knew it flattered her slim figure, cinching her waistline in the style so much in favour since the young Queen Victoria had come to the throne.

Her once-a-month Sunday afternoon visit home was a long-standing ritual. The moment her grandmother heard the click of the gate, she would pour boiling water from the big iron kettle, that stood bubbling away on the trivet in front of the open fire, on to the leaves already carefully measured into the best flower-patterned teapot.

Still breathless, Kate caught her lower lip between her teeth apprehensively. Now that the moment had come to tell her grandmother her news she wondered if she should have asked her advice first before taking such a momentous decision. Grandmother had, after all, brought her up and been a mother to her.

It was too late to think of that now, she reminded herself. She'd already given her answer so there was no going back.

'Hello! I'm home,' she called as she pushed open the cottage door.

'Come on in, m'lovey. It's all ready.'

Sunday tea with home-made jam and pickles, and a freshly baked cake, were spread out on a lace-edged tablecloth. Uncle Charlie, scrubbed, shaved and wearing a striped flannel shirt was sitting at the table waiting to tuck in.

Kate hugged and kissed the old lady, bursting to tell them her news but anxious to choose the right moment.

'Stand back then and let's have a good look at 'ee. That's a new dress you'm wearin'.' Her grandmother fingered the material between thumb and finger. 'A proper lady 'ee looks in that and no mistake,' she murmured, smoothing the velvet ribbon trimming and touching the tiny pearl buttons down the front of the bodice.

'I've some special news for you, Gran,' Kate exclaimed brightly as her grandmother began to pour the tea. 'I'm changing my job, I'm going to become a Nanny.'

'A Nanny? What's that when it's at home?' Mabel Stacey frowned. Her face, wrinkled as a walnut under her lace-frilled Sunday mob cap, wore a puzzled expression.

'Be it looking after goats,' guffawed Charlie, spearing a hunk of cheese with his knife and taking a bite from it before dropping the rest on to his plate.

Kate looked at her uncle in exasperation. It would have been so much easier to tell her grandmother on her own.

'Well, go on then, bain't 'ee goin' to tell us what this nannying business be all about,' he jibed when Kate remained tight-lipped and silent.

Charlie was an avid gossip and she knew he savoured each new item almost as much as he did the home-made relish he was ladling on to his bread.

'Yes, m'lovey,' her grandmother pressed, sipping her tea with satisfaction, 'tell us all about it then.'

2

'It's looking after children,' Kate explained, her voice edged with irritation as she saw the mindless grin that spread over Charlie's face.

'Has schoolmaster from Mere been filling your head up wi' a load of nonsense again?'

'Of course not! I've not seen sight nor sound of him since I left there four years back.'

'Just because 'im made 'ee a Monitor at school it don't mean you'm cut out for that sort of job,' her grandmother warned sharply.

'I know that!'

''Tidden possible for 'ee to be a governess, not wi'out qualifications,' the old lady persisted.

'More's the pity!' Kate tossed her head pertly, her blue eyes flashing, a blush staining her cheeks. 'Schoolmaster Barnes said I had a good head for learning and if I'd stayed on at school . . .'

'You mean you'm goin' to be a nursemaid then, do 'ee?' her grandmother interrupted.

'Wipin' babies' bums, cleaning up sick, feedin' 'em pap and walkin' the floor wi' 'em when they'm teethin'. Mug's game that, if you asks me,' Charlie Stacey guffawed, jabbing out a pickled onion from the jar in front of him and munching it noisily.

'If you'll shut your trap, Charlie, and listen a minute I'll tell you both what I mean,' Kate exclaimed heatedly.

'Go on then, we'm all ears.'

At that moment she hated him so much she wanted to hit out at him but she knew better than to try. Just one of his huge ham-like hands could imprison both of hers, and her slim frame was powerless against his brawny strength. His strength was the talk of the King's Head pub. It was rumoured that Charlie had once picked up Farmer Eden's bull by the horns, swung it round and dropped it over a hedge into the next field. And having seen the effortless way he swung churns of milk up on to a cart, she didn't doubt the truth of that story for one minute.

3

'All brawn and no brains,' she thought cynically as she watched the great mountain of flesh that spilled over the top of his corduroy trousers wobbling uncontrollably as he shook with laughter. It was a pity he hadn't been sent off to Australia like the farm labourers from Tolpuddle. She'd seen him waving a pitchfork and trying to incite others to join in the riots, but no one had taken any notice.

'Poor old Charlie,' they said. 'Silly old fool's been on the scrumpy. Means well, but 'ee don't know what he's doing.'

'Take no notice of his moidering, m'lovey,' her grandmother said placidly, ignoring Charlie's snorts of laughter. 'Just 'ee tell us what this nannying business be all about.'

'It's looking after children who are too old to have either a nurse or a governess, Gran.'

'Just carin' for 'em and lookin' after their clothes?'

'And going for walks with them and keeping them company. Sort of taking the place of their mother when she's too busy to be with them.'

'What'll folks wi' money think of next,' Mabel Stacey sniffed.

'I'd a thought they'd need a grow'd woman to mother 'em, not a chit of a girl who's barely eighteen,' Charlie said derisively.

'What's wrong with being eighteen?' Kate demanded. 'A lot of girls my age are married with children of their own.'

'Got too much to say for 'emselves, thinks them's gro'd up but 'em aint,' he snarled.

'The new Queen was only eighteen when she came to the throne,' Kate told him defiantly. 'If people think she's old enough to be on the Throne of England, then I'm old enough to be a Nanny.'

''Tidden the same thing, m'lovey.'

''Er don't have to do anything 'cept sit there,' spluttered Charlie, his mouth full of one of his mother's fruit scones. 'She've got Ministers to do all the work.'

4

'She'm just a figurehead.'

'And us don't know as if 'er's any good at it yet,' he added wiping the crumbs away with the back of his hand.

'That sort of talk's disrespectful and ain't fitting at Sunday tea-table, Charlie, so 'ee stay quiet and listen to what Kate has to tell us,' his mother told him disapprovingly.

'Well, that's it!' Kate shrugged as she helped herself to a piece of cake.

'There's no children nowadays up at The Manor, m'lovey,' frowned Mabel Stacey. 'Master George has children of 'is own.'

'It's his two girls I am going to be Nanny to,' Kate said quickly.

'You'm moving away . . . to Bramwood Hall?' asked the old woman in a querulous voice.

'It's not all that far away, only a couple of miles.'

''E'd be a lot better off staying at The Manor,' Charlie told her.

'I've been there ever since I was fourteen.'

'And come next fall they'll make 'ee Parlour Maid. Just think o' that!'

'I don't want to be a skivvy, waiting on folks at The Manor forever!'

'Be able to wear one of them little lace caps,' grinned Charlie.

'Two afternoons a month off . . . and more money. What more could 'ee want! Charlie's right, m'lovey. Lookin' after Master George's two girls won't get 'ee anywhere. In next to no time they'll be off to Finishing School, or else married, and where will that leave 'ee?'

'But Gran,' Kate's blue eyes shone with enthusiasm, 'it's a chance to better myself!' She pushed the dark tendrils of hair back from her face, her finely boned chin lifted proudly.

'That'll happen when you'm made parlourmaid.'

'At Bramwood Hall I won't be sharing an attic with the rest of the servants. I'll have a room all to myself and I'll be called Miss Stacey.'

'And that David Owen spends a lot of time at Bramwood Hall,' Charlie added slyly. 'Fanny 'im, don't 'ee!'

'Shut your face!' Trembling with anger, Kate glared at her uncle.

'I see'd 'ee an' him only t'other week,' he leered.

Her breath caught audibly in her throat, her face paled, then flamed.

'Too busy the two o' 'ee to notice I. . . .'

'If you must know,' she spat, 'the reason I so badly want this job as a Nanny, and the chance to get right away from The Manor, is because I'm fed up of being spied on.'

'Ah, well, perhaps then it'll be for the best,' Uncle Charlie said, shifting uneasily in his chair.

'There's folks around here, who I won't mention by name, that I can't abide,' she added darkly.

Perspiration gleamed along the top of his upper lip. As he wiped it away with the back of his hand, Kate smiled to herself. He wouldn't say anything more against her idea. He was too scared that she might tell on him.

Some said her Uncle Charlie was just a bit simple, but she knew he was sly, lecherous and sadistic. She hadn't trusted him since she'd caught him watching her through a chink in the outside privy when she was about twelve. When she'd threatened to tell her grandmother he had twisted her arm behind her back until her shoulder cracked and the pain brought tears to her eyes.

She had suspected for quite some time that he still spied on her. Now, she was more than ever sure that the rustlings in the bushes, when she and David Owen met in the summerhouse, wasn't a rabbit, or some other wild creature, but her Uncle Charlie watching them.

Kate found that convincing her grandmother that she was doing the right thing in going to Bramwood Hall was not easy. Though she was riddled with rheumatism, her body shrunken beneath the dark brown dress, Mabel

Stacey's brain was sharp and Kate found it hard to placate her.

'I'll be able to come and visit you more often, every fortnight I'll get a whole day off. I'll have a room all to myself! And there will be a maid to wait on me and the girls,' she told her grandmother over and over again.

'Since 'ee've already made your mind up, let's hope it all works out for the best,' Mabel Stacey sighed at last. She closed her eyes, leaning back in her chair as if too tired to argue the matter any further.

'That's right, Gran, I have,' Kate said stubbornly. 'And it will be for the best, I know it will,' she added, kneeling beside the old lady's chair and tenderly holding one of her grandmother's gnarled hands against her face.

2

Life had changed for Kate from the moment she had first seen David Owen.

It had been a bright, frosty morning and she'd been sent to fetch kindling from the barn. On her way back across the yard she'd stepped on a patch of ice, losing her balance and her pile of wood. Knowing how Cook would scold if she took too long she'd scrambled to her feet, and in spite of the pain from her twisted ankle, struggled to pick up the scattered sticks.

'Here, let me help.'

The sound of a man's voice had startled her. Before she could protest he had collected up the wood and she'd been too embarrassed to speak as he'd piled it into her sackcloth apron.

For days afterwards the man's voice had haunted her and she'd walked round in a dream, remembering his brown eyes and the firm pressure of his hands when they'd briefly touched hers.

'What's the matter, Kate?' asked Phoebe Mullins. 'I've spoken to you twice and you've not answered. Be you in love?'

'Course she is,' giggled Carrie Withers, the other girl who shared the attic room with them. 'She'm in a trance half the time!'

'Tell us 'is name, then,' pressed Pheobe.

'I don't know it,' sighed Kate, 'but he's the handsomest man I've ever seen.'

They listened wide-eyed as she related her adventure.

'So do either of you know who he is?' she asked hopefully.

They stared at her blankly.

'We never get above stairs any more than you do. Lucy Parsons might know though, being Parlourmaid. She must have heard them call him by name when she's been serving meals.'

'None of your business who he is, Kate Stacey,' Lucy told her primly. 'Anyway, I'm not supposed to talk about anything I might hear.'

'Go on, tell me his name. You must know it.'

'Just remember your place, Miss,' reprimanded Cook. 'We don't stand for no gossiping about our betters. You'd best remember that if you are hoping to take over from Lucy when she leaves to be wed next autumn.'

'I wasn't gossiping about him, I only wanted to know what his name was because . . .'

'It's no concern of yours who visits Lord and Lady Sherwood,' interrupted Cook sharply. She folded her arms over the spotless white apron that covered her ample figure, her black gimlet eyes boring into Kate's. 'Do you understand? We don't want no hoity-toity sulks either,' she added sharply when she saw Kate biting her lower lip to stop herself answering back.

Kate still hadn't been able to put the man from her thoughts. Each night, after the candle had been snuffed out, she would lie there in the darkness remembering every detail about him.

Her memory was so vivid that she could almost touch the thick dark hair and side-whiskers. Or run a finger over the well-shaped brows that framed his warm brown eyes. She remembered his broad shoulders, the strong jawline, the swing of the dark cape that had topped his boxcoat with its smooth velvet revers and the well-cut trousers of black cloth fastened with straps beneath his shiny black boots.

As he came alive in her mind, his voice would ring in her ears. Not like the slow, buttery burr of the cottagers, or the sharp cultured tones of the Sherwoods, but mellow and musical. A voice that was as deep and rich as his colouring, yet as firm as the set of his square chin.

9

She thought about him so much that on her next Sunday off, when she left The Manor and found him leaning on the stile by the lane, she wondered if she was dreaming.

'Good afternoon, Kate.'

She smiled at him shyly from under her grey poke bonnet, afraid to speak in case it shattered the illusion.

'I see your ankle is quite recovered.'

'Yes . . . thank you.' Colour rushed to her cheeks as he glanced down at her feet.

'Is this your afternoon off?'

'Yes, sir.'

'And you're on your way home?'

'I'm going to visit my grandmother at Bramble Cottage and have tea with her.'

'Then, since the sun is shining, and it's such a perfect day for a stroll, I'll accompany you, if I may, for part of the way.'

As they walked side by side in silence, she felt both elated and uneasy, conscious of the drabness of her dark blue dress and thick grey shawl alongside his elegant clothes.

She kept glancing sideways to see if he was still there, not completely sure if she was dreaming or not. Yet the swish of his silver-topped walking cane, as he cleared away the undergrowth that covered the path in places, was real enough.

Her walk from The Manor took on a new significance.

Never had the early snowdrops looked so pure and white, the sky more blue, the clouds more fluffy. The leafless trees, pencilled against the sky, were beginning to show their buds. Blackbirds and robins darted from bush to bush, seeking out likely nesting places.

Her heart bursting with joy, she began to murmur aloud a poem she had learnt at school.

> 'When wintry weather's all a-done,
> An' brooks do sparkle in the zun,

An' naisy-builden rooks do vlee
Wi' sticks toward their elem tree;
When birds do zing, an we can zee
Upon the boughs the buds o' spring—'

'Then I'm as happy as a king.'

Kate looked at her companion sharply as he spoke the next line.

'That's one of my favourite poems, too,' he smiled.

'It was taught to me by Schoolmaster Barnes from Mere.'

'And written by him, too. Did you know that?'

'Yes,' she admitted shyly. 'He wrote lots more that I know by heart.'

'Since I have been at University I have read every word William Barnes has ever written,' he told her, solemnly.

'University!' Her eyes widened in amazement. 'Are you a teacher?'

'No. I've been studying at Oxford University, though, for many years. I've sometimes thought I'd like to be a teacher.'

'Oh, so would I,' she gasped. Then, blushing at her own temerity, added quickly, 'I thought you'd come to live at The Manor.'

'No, I was merely paying a duty call the morning I bumped into you. I was staying at Bramwood Hall.'

'Oh! You're a friend of Sir George Sherwood.'

'I'm his brother-in-law. I often come and visit them during my vacations. My name's David Owen. You can call me David.'

'I daren't call you that!' exclaimed Kate aghast.

'Of course you can. If we are going to be friends then you must call me David and I shall call you Kate.'

'Cook would skin me alive if she heard me call you that!'

'Then we must make sure she never does.'

'However can we do that?' Kate asked in confusion.

11

David's smile widened. Then he patted her hand and placed a warning finger across his lips.

She had been half an hour late arriving at her grandmother's cottage that day. And had started back for The Manor ten minutes early.

She hadn't been disappointed. David Owen had been waiting in the lane to walk with her, just as he had promised.

They met often after that. Snatched moments. Brief encounters. She never knew when or where he might appear. Sometimes they could only smile at each other from a distance but it was enough to set her heart thudding.

On her birthday, David had given her a slim, leatherbound volume of William Barnes' poetry. She treasured it greatly, wrapping it in tissue paper and keeping it hidden at the bottom of her clothes box. Each night before she put out her candle, she would read one of the poems. And before she closed the cover, she would study the inscription written on the fly-leaf: 'For my dear friend Kate.' And it was signed 'David'.

Those words meant even more to her than the poetry.

It was David's idea that she should move to Bramwood Hall.

'My sister needs someone to look after their two girls, Beth and Mary,' he told her.

'As a lady's maid?'

'No . . . I don't think they're old enough yet for a personal maid,' he frowned.

'You mean as a governess?'

'No, not exactly. She's looking for a Nanny . . . a sort of companion for them. It's a position that would suit you.'

At first, she dismissed the idea as being beyond her capabilities and therefore utterly impossible.

'I'd jump at the chance, but I've no training for such work,' she told David ruefully.

'You don't need any,' he assured her.

'Are you quite certain about that?'

'Positive. I've already spoken to Helen and she is quite agreeable to taking you on.'

'Oh, David!' Delight left her speechless.

'It will be a chance for us to spend more time together. Bramwood Hall is like a second home to me.'

'And where is your first home?' she asked, curious to know more about him.

'In Wales.' His mouth tightened, a nerve twitched along his jawline and it seemed to her that the question had annoyed him in some way.

The idea of becoming a Nanny, to break free from the drudgery of domestic service, excited her. It was the sort of opportunity she had so often dreamed about. She wanted to get on and better herself, she wanted so much more out of life than Phoebe Mullins or Carrie Withers did.

They were content to serve in their appointed role, just as parson told them they should, but she wasn't. She didn't want to end up marrying a farm labourer, struggling to make ends meet.

William Barnes had opened her eyes to the power of words and learning. He'd fired her ambition to be a teacher and someday, she was determined, she'd achieve that goal.

She knew she'd been fortunate to have been able to stay at school until she was fourteen. At the time, though, her grandmother's insistence that since she could read and write fluently the time had come to put away her books had seemed unreasonable. Now she was older, she understood better her grand-mother's concern that she should be able to earn a living.

She often wondered if life would have been different if she had not been an orphan. Her father had been killed at Peterloo and her mother had died when she was very small, so she had never known either of them.

Perhaps her parents would have listened to School-master Barnes' suggestion that she should stay on as a pupil teacher, Kate thought wistfully. By now she would have been fully qualified, perhaps even in charge of a village school.

Whenever she asked her grandmother about them the old lady was evasive and made it plain it was something she didn't want to talk about.

'Don't you worry your head about the past, m'lovey,' she would answer and then change the subject to other things.

She'd tried asking Uncle Charlie but he would always shake his grizzled head and tell her to ask her grandmother.

When she'd started work at The Manor she'd refused to be fobbed off and insisted her grandmother should tell her about them.

'Nothing to tell 'ee. She were in service in Mere. Your father were killed at Peterloo afore 'ee were born, so 'er brought you back to live wi' me. 'Er didn't live all that long after. Just a couple of years. Died of a broken 'eart, I reckon.'

Kate had tried once more after that to persuade her grandmother to talk about them but without much success.

'One thing I will tell 'ee, m'lovey, you'm the spittin' image of your mother 'cept she were a bit plumper. Tall though, wi' jet dark hair and eyes like blue speedwell, same as your'n. It's been like having my little Annie with me all over again, you bein' around the place.'

It was a Saturday morning in July when Uncle Charlie called at Bramwood Hall to tell Kate that her grandmother had died in her sleep almost a week before, and had been buried that morning.

Kate was supervising a game of croquet between Mary and Beth, fascinated by their skilful manoeuvres, and the elegant way they both used their mallets to hit the ball neatly through the hoop.

She felt a great sense of pleasure in their company. Both girls had accepted her wholeheartedly, intrigued by the novelty of a Nanny, feeling it was so much more sophisticated than having a Nurse and less restrictive than a Governess.

Kate had been concerned to discover that she was only a few years older than Beth, worried in case the girls would not respect her authority, but those fears had soon vanished. Fourteen-year-old Beth was a sweet-natured girl and Mary, two years younger, followed her sister's lead in everything.

They had their mother's looks and nature, fair and placid, with round faces and hazel eyes. They were eager to be friendly and always obedient when it was necessary for her to exercise discipline.

Such occasions were rare indeed. For most of the time she supervised their reading and music practice, helped them with their sewing and embroidery, and escorted them on walks. She shared the girls' passion for reading and the Sherwoods' extensive library was a treasure-house of poetry, biography and history books.

When she first arrived at Bramwood Hall a year ago Kate knew nothing of games like tennis and croquet.

Beth and Mary soon instructed her in the rudimentary rules so that she could partner them or act as umpire. David sometimes joined them and then all four played tennis, with more vigour than skill, until they all collapsed, exhausted, into wicker chairs.

As she summoned Polly to bring them ice-cold lemonade, Kate was sharply aware of her own changed circumstances. Her new mode of life seemed to be one of unending leisure.

She wondered how long it could last.

Charlie's news momentarily stunned her.

'Why didn't you let me know she was ill,' she demanded.

''Er didn't feel ill, leastways not so as 'er mentioned to me,' he told her, passing his hand over his chin.

'Didn't she say anything at all?'

'No. Went off up to bed same as usual. Next mornin' when I came in for breakfast I knew somethin' was up because the table was bare and there was no fire in the grate. I called but 'er didn't answer and so I went up to 'er bedroom and there 'er was . . . dead.'

'Why didn't you send for me then?'

'Not much point. Doctor said 'er was a gonner.'

'I should have been there to help see to things.'

'I had 'er laid out and fetched undertaker.'

'And even then you didn't think to let me know so that I could be at her funeral,' Kate snapped angrily.

'Didn't see the sense of it . . . you bein' a woman.'

'I should have been there,' argued Kate, stubbornly.

'Men's job to do the buryin'. 'Twas all over tidy and quick. No fuss.'

Kate stared at her uncle in exasperation. His great florid face was red and sweating, his small pale eyes watching her shrewdly. She had never hated him more than at that moment.

Her grandmother had meant so much to her. She'd been mother and father, confidante and friend. She may have looked old and wrinkled on the outside but Kate

16

knew her heart was warm, her mind sharp, and that she was full of loving wisdom. No one could ever replace her.

Not to have been there when she was dying, not to have had the opportunity to pay her last respects by attending her funeral and laying flowers on her coffin, was a cruel blow.

''Ere, I brought these over for 'ee,' muttered Charlie, thrusting a bundle into Kate's hands. 'Thought as how 'ee'd like that shawl as a kind of keepsake, seein' as 'ow it be made from goat's hair and you bein' a Nanny,' he guffawed.

'Thank you, Charlie!' Tears filled Kate's eyes as she pressed the blue cashmere shawl to her cheek. It had been her grandmother's most treasured possession, worn only on special occasions.

'T'other stuff she'd put to one side wi' your name on it,' he said, handing her a small parcel.

Inside, wrapped in tissue-paper, was a gold-rimmed cameo brooch, the only piece of jewellery Mabel Stacey had owned, and a framed painting of a young woman in her twenties.

Kate gasped. It was like looking into a mirror. She noticed that over her mother's shoulders was draped the same blue cashmere shawl that she was holding in her hands.

'Thank you, Charlie. It was good of you to bring them.' With the back of her hand she brushed away the tears that misted her eyes.

'Well, 'er wanted 'ee to have 'em. Put 'em on one side ready after your last visit. Must 'a sensed 'er were goin'.'

'Yes. I wish I'd known.'

''Ad a good innin's, mind. Close on eighty.' He shook his grizzled head.

'I should have been with her. . . .'

'I've cleared the old cottage out. Movin' in wi' Widow Greenslade over to Kilmington.'

'You're doing what?'

17

Kate's exclamation of surprise seemed to ruffle him.

"Tidden no good stayin' on at Bramble Cottage, now, be it? 'Tidn't as though you'm ever likely to come a visitin'.'

'No.' She gave him a long, cool stare. 'No, that's true.'

'Well then, I've done what I thought best. You've got your bits and pieces so I'll be on me way. Don't suppose our paths 'ull cross again. You'm nicely set up 'ere by the looks of things,' he muttered, his slack lips twisting into a sneer.

Kate was so engrossed in her own private world after Charlie left that she was unaware anything was amiss until she heard Sir George's voice raised in anger.

'What is the meaning of this?'

She looked up startled, to find him towering over her, his face red with anger.

'How dare you permit Beth and Mary to behave in such a manner.'

'But . . .'

'I want no excuses for your laxity. Daydreaming when you should have been supervising my daughters.'

'It wasn't Kate's fault, Papa,' Beth protested.

Outraged, he ordered them indoors.

After the storm died down and both girls had dried their tears, Kate learned that Beth had missed the ball and caught Mary on the ankle with her croquet mallet. Their father had overheard their unladylike expressions as he approached the house on his way from the stables.

'We didn't see Papa, he was hidden from sight by the yew hedge,' explained Beth.

'I only called Beth a pig,' grumbled Mary.

'And hit me with your mallet!'

'You squealed before I touched you.'

Complying with Sir George's instructions, Kate kept them confined to the conservatory for the rest of the day. Subdued after his lecture on their behaviour, they spent the time reading. Kate, too, sat with a book open on her lap but she wasn't reading, she was remembering the past, and how much she was going to miss her grandmother. Now there was no one who really cared about her . . . except David.

Closing her book, she thought ahead to dinner. David would be facing her across the imposing mahogany table with its crisp white napery, gleaming silver and sparkling glassware. It was another reason why Beth and Mary's indiscretions had been so unfortunate. Sir George, outraged by their behaviour, had forbidden them to come down to dinner.

Kate regretted the whole incident but put the matter from her mind as she escorted the girls upstairs. She left them to entertain themselves while she changed into her new spotted pink muslin dress. It had once been Lady Helen's and she'd had to take in the bodice to make it fit. Studying the result of her handiwork in the cheval mirror she was conscious of how it emphasized her waist. The neck had been very low cut so from a sense of modesty she'd added a muslin tucker. The result was extremely flattering, she decided, as she twirled, admiring the drape of the skirt.

Sitting in front of her pretty, chintz-draped dressing table she began to unpin her hair, releasing it from the formal chignon and letting it fall in a dark cascade on to her shoulders. With long, sweeping movements, she brushed it back from her brow and twisted it into ringlets so that it framed her face in the same style as in her mother's portrait.

She waited patiently for the girls' meal to arrive. She knew Cook would send it up in advance of serving dinner since both maids would be needed to wait at table. Once Beth and Mary were settled she could go downstairs. She might even have the opportunity to talk to David before they all sat down at table, she thought hopefully.

Polly's arrival, puffing under a heavy tray, cut short Kate's musings.

'Dinner for three,' Polly announced, dumping the tray on the table with a clatter. 'Cook was told to dish everything straight out on to plates and not to trouble with any tureens.'

'I think there is some mistake, Polly,' Kate told her. 'You should have brought up only two meals.'

'No, Miss.' Polly's grin widened. 'Sir George told Cook to send up three. He said you was to have yours up here along with the girls.' She eyed Kate's dress and her carefully styled hair with a smirk. 'I heard him say it, Miss!'

'Very well, Polly, then you may leave the three,' Kate said coolly.

'And Cook said you was to make sure that all of you ate every bit 'cos you won't be getting no dessert.' She grinned cheekily as she deftly laid out a knife and fork beside each plate.

Kate felt furious but bit the inside of her cheek to stop herself saying anything further, knowing that every word would be relayed back to the kitchen and gloated over. It had never entered her mind that she would be expected to share Beth and Mary's punishment. Her cheeks burned with anger over such humiliating treatment. She suspected that Sir George was subtly reminding her of her place.

Of late, he had remarked several times in her hearing that David was becoming a much more frequent visitor to Bramwood Hall, and there had been no mistaking his implication.

Kate sighed. How would it all end?

It was all very well for David to say that his sister accepted their friendship, but to someone in Lady Helen's position there was a distinct class divide between employees and family.

From what she had overheard during her first few weeks at Bramwood Hall, Kate knew that Sir George had not approved of her appointment.

'Hifalutin nonsense, my dear. If the girls are too old for a nurse then a governess would have been a much more satisfactory arrangement,' he had said abruptly when Lady Helen had explained Kate's presence.

'They already have an excellent visiting tutor,' Helen had told him, spiritedly.

'Then why do we require the services of a Nanny?'

'They need someone to take charge when I am not free to be with them.'

'Humph! And where was she nannying before she came to us?'

'She is here on David's introduction.'

'You mean you've taken her on without references?'

'Schoolmaster Barnes from Mere speaks very highly of her. And so, too, does your mother, so let's give her a chance to prove her measure.'

Sensing his disapproval, Kate had done her best to fulfil her new role but for the first few weeks it had been far from easy. She had no real place at Bramwood Hall. The servants resented her because she enjoyed privileges they didn't. The family weren't sure whether to include her at family meals like a governess, or confine her to the nursery wing and let her take her meals there with the two girls the same as Nursie had done.

Eventually, a compromise was achieved. The old nursery was converted into a sitting room. Kate and the girls took their breakfast and lunch there and dined with Sir George and Lady Helen only when there were no guests present.

David was considered to be one of the family, and his frequent visits were the highlights in Kate's new life.

Whenever he visited Bramwood Hall, he sought Kate out, anxious to know if she was happy in her new surroundings. During dinner he would go out of his way to include her in the general conversation, asking her opinion or inviting her comments on all manner of topics.

Now, not being allowed to join them for dinner was a crushing rebuff for Kate.

Too angry to eat, she walked over to the window, waiting for the girls to finish their meal, scheming how she might meet David, determined that he should hear the truth about what had happened.

Polly regarded Kate's untouched plate with raised eyebrows when she came to clear away. After she'd left, Kate told Beth and Mary to go to their rooms and read until it was time for bed. Their protests died on their lips as they saw the angry set of her face.

Draping the blue cashmere shawl around her shoulders, Kate went out on to the landing. She paused at the top of the great curving staircase, listening to make sure the meal had ended and the servants had withdrawn to the kitchen before descending.

As she went out into the garden, she could see the lights were still on in the dining room and wondered how long David and Sir George would sit there, smoking their cigars and drinking port. She pulled the cashmere shawl more closely round her shoulders. Already the evening air was chill.

At the sound of a man's step on the gravel pathway, Kate took refuge in the summerhouse. She was barely inside before she heard David softly calling her name and his broad frame filled the doorway. He was stylishly dressed in slim-fitting trousers and a dark frock coat set off by a white stock, and a red and grey striped waistcoat.

'Why were you not at dinner?' he asked anxiously.

She explained about the girls' misdemeanour and their punishment.

'Such nonsense,' David laughed derisively. 'You should have sent yours back and come on down to the dining room.'

'I hardly think Sir George would have made me very welcome since he seemed to blame me for the girls' unladylike behaviour,' she replied sharply.

'Helen was so evasive when I asked where you were that I thought you must be unwell,' he told her.

'How did you manage to get away?'

'I told George I wanted a breath of fresh air. Helen guessed my intentions so she discouraged him from accompanying me.'

'You'd better not stay out too long or Sir George may come looking for you,' Kate said looking over her shoulder nervously.

'It might be more sensible if we took our walk in the sunken garden,' David suggested.

As they descended the stone steps from the terrace, into a section that had been laid out in Italian style, David placed his arm lightly about Kate's waist as though to assist her. When they reached the bottom level she was conscious that he made no attempt to remove it.

Blissfully, they sauntered between the sweet-smelling flower beds, the high-riding moon shedding a silvery glow around them. The night air was soft on their faces, and with David's body so close to her own, Kate no longer felt cold.

'You are looking very lovely tonight,' David murmured, lightly fingering her cashmere shawl. 'Is this new?'

In a subdued voice she told him about her grandmother.

'It was because I'd only just heard the news that I was so inattentive and left the girls to their own devices for a few minutes,' she said, a catch in her voice.

'Did you explain that to George?' frowned David.

'No. I didn't have the opportunity.'

'You must tell Helen. She will understand. Now, just forget all about it,' he murmured, drawing her into his arms.

'David, we mustn't,' she stiffened, pulling back. Her concern that they might not be able to meet was now replaced by fear that they might be discovered together.

'You must know how I feel about you, Kate!' His breath was warm on her face, his voice harsh with emotion. He was holding her so tightly that she could barely breathe.

Her love for him had long been a secret joy, something she cherished. To know that his feelings reciprocated hers brought happiness greater than anything she'd ever known. Her mind was in a whirl. She'd been aware David held her in high regard when he'd arranged for her to work at Bramwood Hall, but his admission of love sent her senses soaring.

As he held her more tightly against his strong body, Kate melted into his embrace and when his lips found hers she didn't even pretend to struggle. This was the fulfilment of her most secret dreams, the most wonderful moment in her entire life.

She closed her eyes as wave after wave of emotion washed over her. Her fingers traced the outline of his face and brow, tangling in the silky softness of his thick dark hair, as she tried to convince herself that this really was happening and was not just some figment of her imagination.

'Kate, my sweetest darling,' David breathed before his lips once more covered hers. She felt his hands moving over her shoulders, his strong fingers pressing against the flesh of her forearms. Her breasts rose and fell rapidly, taut against her gown, until their bodies seemed to fuse together as one.

She trembled in response to his touch. As one hand cupped her breast, she was aware that the pressure was making her nipples harden, so that she felt sure he must feel the erect nubs against his palm.

'You feel as I do,' he whispered hoarsely. 'Kate, we belong to each other.'

'It's sighing for the moon, David,' she protested. 'It cannot be. . .'

'Hush! I will not listen to such talk,' David admonished.

As his lips sought hers again, her heart pounded. Her response to his kisses became as passionate as his own. All her grandmother's warnings when she had first left home to work at The Manor flooded her mind.

His arm still around her, he led her to a secluded corner of the Italian garden where elm trees formed a natural arbour. As he drew her down beside him on to the soft, mossy grass, common sense warned her she was taking a grave risk in becoming so deeply involved with David Owen. Yet she knew she wanted him as fiercely as he wanted her. This was the moment she'd dreamed of: her grandmother's warnings were forgotten.

The intensity of David's passion thrilled her, yet at the same time bewildered her. He was Lady Helen's brother, in a totally different class to her, yet she was confident that he wasn't just taking advantage of her innocence.

Had he merely wished to satisfy his lust, then he would have done that long ago, she told herself. There had been ample opportunity during their secret meetings in the deserted lanes around The Manor. Instead, he'd treated her as an equal, insisted she should call him by his first name, acted like a real friend. Their walks together, their shared interest in William Barnes' poetry, his genuine concern for her well-being were as considerate as though he was courting her.

Her fingers flexed in the softness of his hair as his lips trailed kisses of fire over her throat and neck. When she felt him unbuttoning the bodice of her dress, and slipping it off her shoulders so that his lips could caress the flesh beneath, her whole body trembled in response.

David, seeing her aroused, covered her mouth with his, stifling her mild protests, exciting her to an even greater degree of ecstasy until, discarding the last remnants of caution, she surrendered to his lovemaking. Strange, wonderful sensations, as intoxicating as heady wine, brought shattering satisfaction.

She looked up at the leafy canopy above them, the linked branches making a tracery against the heavens.

There was no breeze; it was as if a great stillness covered their world.

Suddenly she shivered. The moon had scudded behind a cloud and there was an ominous quality about the darkening summer sky. Something she couldn't put into words filled her with foreboding.

Early morning sunshine streaming into her bedroom wakened Kate. For a few moments she lay with half-closed eyes enjoying its brightness, letting her thoughts wander. It never ceased to amaze her how everything had turned out so well for her at Bramwood Hall, just as David had predicted.

She felt a flush of colour staining her cheeks as the mere thought of his name brought the events of the previous evening flooding back. Had she been foolish to give way to him, she wondered anxiously. Was she inviting heartbreak?

From the moment of her arrival at Bramwood Hall it had been made blatantly clear that he was already destined for another. Beth and Mary talked of little else. Sometimes Kate felt like screaming, or boxing their ears, or both. Anything to stop them chattering away like two magpies about David's future prospects.

To make matters worse, his chosen bride-to-be, Penelope Vaughan, sounded such an ideal match. As an only child, Penelope would inherit the vast estates her father owned at Tretower, on the north bank of the Usk in South Wales. In due course, she would bring to the marriage both considerable wealth and important tracts of land.

Kate pushed the matter to the back of her mind as she suddenly realized that it was Sunday and that David was still at Bramwood Hall. Her eagerness to look her very best when they met at church lent speed to her actions.

A half-smile played on her lips as she took a dress of white lawn, sprigged with tiny mauve violets, from her wardrobe. She held it at arm's length to admire it. It was a dress she loved. As she laid it out on the bed, along with a wide-brimmed bonnet, lilac gloves and a matching parasol, she thought of how David's eyes would light up when he saw her later in the morning.

As soon as Beth and Mary finished their breakfast she told them to get ready for church.

'Do we have to wear two petticoats?' Beth protested, 'it's going to be a stiflingly hot day.'

'I don't know why we have to go to church, anyway,' Mary sighed, 'the service is always so tiresome. I would much rather stay in the garden and play croquet.'

'Croquet is banned, as you well know, and likely to remain so for quite some time to come,' Kate reminded her severely. 'And anyway, Mary, you should know better than to speak of such things on the Sabbath.'

'Yes, Kate,' Mary agreed demurely. 'Though why it is wrong to enjoy oneself on a Sunday is something I will never understand,' she added, wistfully.

Helen's entrance, while she was helping Beth to fasten the tiny buttons down the back of her dress, startled Kate. It was so unusual for Helen to visit them that she suspected something was wrong. One look at Helen's face confirmed her fears.

'Are you ready to leave for church, Kate?' Helen asked anxiously.

'Why, yes . . .'

'Hurry!' Helen gave her a little push towards the door.

'What is wrong?'

'It is important that David speaks to you on your own. Leave by the kitchen door and make sure Sir George doesn't see you. David is waiting with the trap at the far end of the drive.'

'What about the girls . . .?'

'I'll take them to church with us. Go on . . . hurry,' she urged impatiently.

Her heart thudding, Kate tied the strings of her bonnet, picked up her gloves and parasol, and did as Helen instructed. As she reached the end of the gravel driveway she saw the trap a few yards further down the road and hurried towards it. David reached out a hand to help her up, then he picked up the reins and drove at a spanking pace towards Ingham Bray village.

For a brief moment, just to be sitting alongside David on such a glorious summer morning filled her with happiness. The sun was already high, climbing between puff-balls of scudding white clouds. The hedgerows, filled with lacy meadowsweet, dog-roses and honeysuckle, gave off a heady perfume. The roads were empty and it was as if they had the whole world to themselves.

As they passed through the village many of the cottagers were already in their gardens. Women sitting in the sunshine, shelling peas or scraping potatoes in readiness for the midday meal. The younger children, aprons over their Sunday best clothes to protect them until it was time for church, played contentedly.

David remained silent until they had driven through the village, then he took her hand, holding it against his thigh. As she felt the tenseness of his muscles beneath her palm she looked anxiously up at him.

'I wanted this chance to speak to you alone, Kate. There may not be an opportunity later in the day as I am leaving Bramwood Hall directly after luncheon.'

As she studied his profile, the firm set of his jaw, the tenseness round his dark eyes, the furrow that ridged his brow, her concern grew.

David pulled suddenly on the reins and the trap swung to the left down a narrow lane. When they came to a halt at the bottom, alongside a weir, the roar in Kate's ears was not just from the water cascading through the sluice gate and falling in a shower of white foam on to the river bed below, but an inner turmoil of knowing that something was desperately wrong. This unplanned ride together must, she was sure, be the fore-runner of bad news. She waited anxiously.

'You are so lovely, Kate,' he murmured, turning towards her, cupping her face in his hands, his dark eyes studying it as if trying to commit to memory every detail of her features. With his thumb, he gently outlined the curve of her mouth, the proud tilt of her chin, the dark brows that swept wide over her blue eyes. 'You've meant a great deal to me, Kate,' he murmured.

'Why are you going away?'

As she looked into David's dark eyes she saw her own face mirrored in them.

'My father has sent for me.'

'You mean you are returning to Wales?'

'Yes. I'm afraid so.'

Kate felt stunned by his news. Fear gripped her. Had he known he would be leaving in the morning when he had made love to her the previous evening, she wondered.

All the rumours she had overheard about David and Penelope Vaughan sang in Kate's head.

'You will keep in touch, David?' she asked tremulously.

'If you have any messages for me then give them to Helen to pass on.'

'But why can't I write to you direct?'

'It would be inadvisable.' He turned away, unwilling to meet her questioning eyes.

She bit her lip, debating whether to stay silent or not. To speak out might antagonize him, yet she couldn't endure the suspicions that gnawed like mice at the wainscoting of her mind. If their act of love had meant anything at all then surely she had the right to know the truth.

'Is it because you . . . you are going to marry Penelope Vaughan?'

The question sounded outrageous and she found the tense silence that followed alarming.

'You've been listening to servants' gossip,' he said sharply, avoiding her eyes.

'No!' She shook her head. 'My informants were Beth and Mary. They talked of little else when I first arrived here. Is it true, David?'

'My father hopes for such a liaison,' he said evasively.

'And you, David?'

'Kate, my dearest, you know the secret of my heart.'

Capturing her wrist, holding her hand between both of his, he raised it to his face. She felt his sideburns prickle against her fingers as his lips pressed against her palm. Of its own volition, her other hand moved upwards until her fingers were entangled in the thick softness of his dark hair, and she was pulling his face down to her own.

As David enfolded her in his arms, the trap rocked precariously. Startled, the grey mare reared up so that it seemed the trap would overturn. David jumped down to pacify the animal. Releasing it from between the shafts he tethered it to a tree, where it could graze the grass.

As he helped Kate from the trap, David picked up the plaid rug from the seat. Escorting her to a secluded spot a short distance away, he spread the rug on the ground for them to sit on.

With his arms around her, the thunder of the weir in the background, the drone of insects all around them and the birds singing in the trees overhead, Kate felt once more transported into a realm of fantasy.

As his lips trailed a string of kisses over her throat she pulled away. She had to know the truth. She would not be fobbed off with vague statements and improbable dreams.

She'd known when they made love that she was risking her reputation. She knew only too well that many of the young gentry took advantage of girls in their family's employ as if it was their given right. They notched it up as a pleasurable experience, with no thought as to the possible consequences. If the girl became pregnant she was the one to bear the stigma of being no better than she should be.

David wasn't like that. He hadn't ravished or raped her. Their relationship had developed over many months, grown out of a deep regard for each other. She had wanted him to make love to her.

31

'Tell me what is happening, David,' she demanded. 'Why you have suddenly reached this decision. Has it anything to do with Sir George.'

'No, of course not,' he said hastily, then he shrugged helplessly. 'It has in a way,' he admitted.

'Go on!'

'I think perhaps I have outgrown my welcome at Bramwood Hall. I suppose I have been a rather frequent visitor since you arrived.'

'Has Lady Helen complained?'

'No, she has encouraged it. In fact, my sister has grown increasingly fond of you since you joined the household,' he added with a warm smile.

'Sir George hasn't! He isn't even sure that I am the right influence on his daughters,' Kate retorted bitingly.

'My brother-in-law has very rigid opinions and obviously objects to our friendship.'

'If he has asked your father to summon you home in order to separate us, then surely you can refuse,' she said bluntly.

'That is the damnable part of it. Unless I comply, my allowance will be stopped. My father feels it is time I shouldered my responsibilities,' he explained with a shrug. 'It seems there have been a great many problems of late and he feels I should be there helping to deal with them.'

'What sort of problems?'

'You would hardly understand. Discontent among the miners over their working conditions. My father is hoping that I can dissuade the men from joining the Rebeccas, a trade union which is part of the Chartist movement.'

'But why should they listen to you when you have no experience of such things?' Kate asked in amazement. 'Surely it is a question of improving conditions, not just talking?'

'Look, Kate, you can't possibly comprehend these matters, not even my sister does and she was brought up in Wales. . . .'

32

'Oh, but I do, David!' She suppressed a shudder. 'I know all about the terrible conditions the miners and their families have to endure. Women stripped to the waist, crawling on all fours like animals, dragging heavy trucks of coal . . .'

'Kate, where did you hear such things,' interrupted David in shocked tones.

'I read about them when I worked at The Manor.'

'Read about them?' he looked puzzled.

Her seriousness vanished into a grin.

'You remember how I used to have to light the morning fires for Cook . . . you should do since we first met when you helped collect up the kindling I dropped when I slipped over one morning.'

'What has that to do with it?'

'The newspapers were always sent down to the kitchen after Lord and Lady Sherwood had finished with them and it was one of my jobs to roll them up into spills ready to start the fires. Sometimes I could hardly believe what was written there.'

'Kate, really! I . . .'

'In the towns, streets full of rubbish and the gutters running with filth. I read once that the smells were so foul that even in the hottest weather people had to keep their windows shut because of the stench and fear of the plague. I read about young children working ten hours a day in factories. And there was a report of one poor girl whose hair caught in the driving belt of one of the machines and her entire scalp was torn off, and another . . .'

'That will do, Kate! You obviously scoured the printed page for the most sensational reports you could find,' he frowned. 'I will not be dealing with anything like that, merely persuading the men who work for my father that it is not in their interest to join a trade union.'

'And what if they won't listen to you? Will they be deported to Australia like those farm labourers from Tolpuddle were four or five years back?'

'This is no time to talk of such unpleasant matters.'

His lips sought hers and as she returned his kiss with a passion that equalled his own, her anger that there was so much injustice in the world was forgotten. All that mattered was their love for each other.

The thought that they were to be parted filled her with dismay. Once more she pressed him to tell her when he hoped to return so that at least she would have something to look forward to. It was the vague uncertainty that she found so hard to bear.

'How can I know until I find out what is required of me?' he said diffidently.

'Then promise you'll write to me, David,' she begged, her eyes bright with unshed tears.

'I've already told you it is out of the question!' he exclaimed tetchily. 'I will try and keep in touch through Helen but we must be discreet. You understand?'

She felt defeated. Had she read too much into his kisses, caresses and tender words of love? she wondered. Once again it seemed she was sighing for the moon.

5

As he was driven away from Bramwood Hall, David Owen looked back with mixed feelings at the three figures waving goodbye to him.

He was sorry to be leaving. Helen, because she was several years older than he, had taken his mother's place in his life and, as he had once told Kate, he thought of Bramwood Hall as his second home.

He felt a moment's unease as the carriage reached the curve in the drive, knowing that any moment now the house would be hidden from view. He was surprised that only Helen and the two girls had come to see him off and wondered why Kate had not joined them. He had hoped that he would have the opportunity to remind her how important it was to be discreet about what had taken place between them. It was unfortunate she had heard gossip linking his name with Penelope Vaughan. Women could be so unpredictable when assailed by jealousy.

He congratulated himself on how skilfully he had handled their parting. There had been no recriminations, no tears, simply a plea that he should keep in touch. It had been flattering to know she was so taken by him, since he was fond of her and had enjoyed her company over the past months.

Her suggestion that they should correspond with each other was out of the question, of course. He could imagine his father's reaction if he chanced to intercept a letter from her. Or George's if he wrote to Kate under cover of correspondence to Helen.

He sometimes felt that George resented the special affinity between himself and Helen and only tolerated him out of politeness and was glad to see him leave. They certainly had very few interests in common.

George was a dyed-in-the-wool country gentleman with a strong preference for open air activities: horses, hunting and shooting. He had no time for the arts and although there was an extensive library at Bramwood Hall, George rarely read anything other than official documents relating to his estates and his daily copy of *The Times*. David suspected that George regarded him as a dilettante, looking upon his love of literature and extended studies at University as effete.

They were exact opposites in looks as well as taste. George had a heavy-jowled, florid face. His shaggy speckled eyebrows almost hid his watery, light-blue eyes. His sandy coloured hair was brushed to one side over a high forehead. Beneath his thin-lipped mouth, the lower half of his face was covered by a speckled beard.

David considered George to be boorish, callous, bigoted and pompous particularly in the way he treated his staff and family.

Over the years, he had seen Helen change from a high-spirited, carefree girl into a woman whose life was ruled by her overbearing husband. He could remember when her fair hair had flowed free and, light of foot, she would race him along the river bank near their home in Wales. Now she was a plump, staid figure, her hair parted down the middle and drawn back into a bun. She had lost her sparkle, her hazel eyes had an anxious look and her manner was hesitant as if she was afraid of saying or doing the wrong thing.

It wasn't so much the fact that she had two daughters who were almost ready to leave the schoolroom that gave her such a matronly look, as her subdued manner. Sometimes she seemed to be almost afraid to express an opinion. Yet he could remember, in the days before she was married, how she would argue vociferously, priding herself on her individuality. David was sure that behind her apparent placid exterior his sister still held strong views about many things but was scared to voice them.

Although Helen never complained, David was sure she wasn't happy. The shadow that darkened her hazel eyes when George raised his voice in anger, her concern when either of the girls irritated their father in any small way, her unease if a meal was a few minutes late, or one of the maids made some slight mistake when serving at table, were not those of a happy, confident woman in charge of her own domain.

Their father had considered her marriage to George Sherwood a brilliant one because George had a title and was also extremely wealthy. Loss of personal liberty seemed a high price to pay for social standing, thought David. This was the main reason why he absented himself so often from his home in Wales. He found the constant pressure for him to marry Penelope Vaughan and produce an heir quite unbearable.

He didn't want to lose freedom of thought and action as Helen had done. Her so-called brilliant marriage had brought her under the domination of a bigoted, overbearing tyrant; a man who was similar in many ways to their own father.

David felt sure one of the reasons Helen always made him so welcome was because she understood why he was reluctant to bow to their father's wishes. Marrying Penelope Vaughan meant he would become involved in her family's iron works as well as his father's coal mining. He knew coal and iron were both essential to industry but the methods used to obtain them appalled him.

He recalled his first visit to a colliery when he'd been about ten. He and his father had arrived at the mining offices just as a shift was ending. The miners, coated in thick black dust, their faces white smudges, their eyes gleaming slits screwed up against the dazzle of daylight, had stumbled from the lift cages that had winched them up from the bowels of the earth.

They had looked like strange animals as they stood there swaying and gulping in fresh air, before staggering away to the terraced cottages that ringed the lower slopes of the nearby mountain.

Even worse was when he had been taken underground. Not by his father. Tudor ap Owen preferred to delegate such menial tasks. Perri Jenkins had been his guide. Perri had worked underground since he was seven. A twisted, wizened little man, with a coal-pocked face and one arm missing below the elbow, he had survived four explosions and two cave-ins.

'Lucky, see,' he told David. 'That's why they're putting you in my care!' His coal-grained face had creased into a smile. 'Like a cat, see. I've got nine lives, I suppose. Come on, then, into the cage with you.'

The jolting drop to the floor of the mine had churned David's stomach. Shaking with fear, he had followed the hunch-backed little man along the narrow, coal-dark, underground tunnel for almost a mile, before they reached the seam where half-naked men, women and children, their bodies streaked with sweat and dust, were working.

Kate's words had brought all this back and reminded him of the grim realities of the life that lay ahead.

While he had been at Oxford his time had been fully occupied with studying and pursuing his literary interests. There had been papers to be prepared for debating societies, discussion groups or poetry readings. There had been fellow students, dons and professors to entertain, visits to the theatre, lectures to attend and a thousand-and-one other enjoyable activities to fill his days and nights.

Since meeting Kate he had spent his vacations at Bramwood Hall. There in the idyllic Wiltshire country-side, with Helen and her two girls, it was easy to put the less pleasant memories of life in the South Wales coalfields from his mind.

Now it was all coming back.

Once again he was being haunted by the memory of women, stripped to the waist, hauling trucks through passageways and tunnels so low that it was impossible for them to stand up. Men streaked with sweat, crouched down, hewing and chipping at the shiny seams of black gold, knowing that an unlucky blow could bring thousands of tons crashing down, smothering them in putrid dust, entombing their bodies for ever. Young children, their faces pitted with coal-induced scabs, scrabbling to fill the trucks with the smaller lumps of second-grade coal, or leading the pit ponies that lived permanently underground in the semi-darkness, and which were used to haul the larger trucks.

Given the choice, David would never have returned to such an industry. He would have much preferred to surround himself with books and involve himself in the academic world where he could compose poetry or write essays.

He thought enviously of the idyllic life William Barnes led, running his small school in the Chantry House behind the church at Mere. Free to think, free to write his poetry, free to enjoy the rustic beauty around him. There were no man-made scars, no blackened pit workings, no great chimneys belching smoke in that corner of Wiltshire. The only industry there was the linen factory at Lords Mead Mill. Men and women went into service or worked on the land as farm labourers. Their hours were long and their pay low but at least they breathed good clean air.

He took one last look back at Bramwood Hall as the carriage reached the final curve in the drive, wondering when he would see it again. As he did so, he saw Kate standing slightly apart from the Sherwood family, a slim figure in a neat blue dress, her dark head held proudly.

Sweet Kate. He would miss her company. She was different from most servant girls. She had benefited greatly from the schooling she'd received from William Barnes. Her soft, low voice, had an unusual refinement.

She was polite without being obsequious. Yet she was not without spirit.

He had wanted her from the moment he'd seen her at The Manor. Persuading Helen to engage her as a Nanny had been a brilliant stroke, he thought smugly.

For him, seducing her had not been mere sport as it was with so many of his contemporaries. He couldn't stand the thought of raping a girl, not even a servant. Had he stayed on at Bramwood Hall he would have enjoyed continuing his relationship with Kate.

Now, with Bramwood Hall behind him and out of sight he viewed the matter more pragmatically. Perhaps one day, if he was ever in a position to be able to afford to do so, he would set her up in an apartment somewhere so that he could visit her whenever he wished.

The vision pleased him but he wondered how Kate would react to such an idea. She would certainly enjoy the independence of no longer being at other people's beck and call. But what of the moral implications, he wondered. Despite her fierce pride and self-confidence, would Kate be content with a clandestine affair or would she expect the security of marriage?

Compared to Kate's slim shapeliness, Penelope Vaughan was unattractive, he thought pessimistically. Her features were as bold as those of a man. She had a strong chin, a deep forehead and a thin, determined mouth. Her green eyes were shrewd and she had a temper to match the fieriness of her red hair.

From childhood she had been spoiled, her slightest whim indulged and, like George Sherwood, she enjoyed active outdoor pursuits.

He sighed. There was little chance of escaping from marriage with Penelope Vaughan because the outcome would be so advantageous to both their families. The large tracts of land owned by the Vaughans contained valuable seams of coal and they were anxious for its potential to be fully exploited. A marriage that united the two families was the most satisfactory method of consolidating such an arrangement.

He was being sacrificed in the same way that Helen had been. Power was of paramount importance to his father and meant far more than their individual happiness.

Arrangements for Helen's marriage to George Sherwood had been made by their father without any consultation at all with Helen. She had been inconsolable when she was told about it and had shut herself up in her room refusing to eat or talk to anyone. Tudor ap Owen had remained adamant.

David would never forget the day when he had tried to speak up for Helen, to explain to his father that she didn't love George Sherwood and shouldn't be forced into marrying him.

'What does an eight-year-old know about such matters!'

'Helen doesn't even like George Sherwood.'

'Poppycock!'

'Helen wants to stay here with us.'

'She told you that?'

'I know she does. That's why she's crying.'

His father had ridiculed him.

'It's not fair to make her go and live with George Sherwood. He's old and ugly,' David had protested.

'You've said quite enough,' thundered his father.

'But . . .'

'Go back up to the schoolroom and stay there. Stop trying to interfere in matters you are too young to understand.'

David would never forget the scene that followed. In defiance, he had gone to Helen's room. His father had followed him and had ranted and raved before locking him in his own bedroom.

'You'll stay there until I give you permission to come out,' he ordered. 'And don't attempt to speak to your sister again.'

41

The following week he had been sent away to boarding school. To his surprise, once he was over the strangeness of being away from home, he found he enjoyed it there. Not only did he have the opportunity to study but he was encouraged to do so. He chose friends who were more interested in poetry and learning than in boisterous games.

The next time he had seen Helen, she had been walking down the aisle of their church on the arm of her new husband, Sir George Sherwood.

He could still remember the look of triumph on his father's face as he addressed the guests at the reception; his overbearing smugness because the deal had been successfully completed. Now, he was sure, his father was planning to treat him in exactly the same ruthless manner as he had Helen; without any consideration for his feelings.

It was his turn to obey.

6

Bramwood Hall seemed desolate after David departed.

The weather had turned damp and chilly and neither of the girls wished to venture out of doors. Feeling restless, Kate walked to the end of the drive and back on her own one mid-morning. She felt dispirited, as if part of her very soul had been dragged from her and transported she knew not where.

It was with considerable effort she carried out her duties for the rest of the day, trying to make herself amenable although her thoughts were far away.

There was nothing unusual in the fact that Sir George barely acknowledged her when they met at dinner. He had never shown any real warmth since the day she had arrived and the incident over the croquet squabble between Beth and Mary had not improved matters.

What did worry Kate, however, was that Helen also seemed cool and distant. She hesitated to ask what was the matter because she had the uneasy feeling that she wouldn't like Helen's reply.

A week later she had her answer.

She had just returned from a leisurely walk with Beth and Mary when Polly informed her that Sir George wished to see her in the library.

Puzzled, Kate removed her bonnet and passed her hands over her hair to smooth it into place.

'Master's asked for you twice already, he'll be in a right tizzy if you don't look sharp,' Polly warned.

Sir George was sitting at the leather-topped desk with his back to the long windows that looked out over the front lawn. His face was inscrutable as he told her to sit,

43

nodding towards a chair strategically placed so that she would be facing him.

Her heart thudded as she saw his hand was resting on a white envelope and she wondered if it was a letter for her from David. If so, she thought, panic rising like bile in her throat, what was Sir George doing with it? David had made her promise to send messages only through Helen and he would do likewise. Had Sir George intercepted one of his letters containing a message for her? she wondered. Was this why Helen seemed to be under some sort of strain?

Kate tried to control her fears as she studied Sir George's face. He was the complete opposite to David. No one could ever have termed him handsome, she thought critically. The heavy jowls, the watery eyes, the scant, tow-coloured hair brushed to one side revealing a high, dominant forehead and shaggy brows. His thick lips had an unpleasant downward droop, the corners disappearing into his speckled beard.

'I'm terminating your appointment as Nanny,' he barked, leaning back in his chair and watching her reaction from beneath hooded lids.

'But why . . . what have I done wrong?'

'It should never have been made in the first place . . . not without my foreknowledge,' he added pompously.

For a moment Kate was unable to comprehend what he had said. Then, slowly, the colour drained from her face only to come rushing back as a tide of fury swept through her. He'd waited until David was well out of the way before delivering this blow, she thought angrily, because he knew David would have spoken out in her defence.

'This,' Sir George went on, indicating the white envelope on the desk, 'is payment in lieu of notice. You will find it is most generous. There is also a reference for when you find yourself a new position.'

Kate clenched her lower lip between her teeth to hold her temper in check. If Sir George had thought the spat he had overheard between Beth and Mary a couple of months ago had been unladylike, he would think what she was ready to hurl at him was positively obscene, she thought grimly.

'You may go and pack your things,' he ordered.

'You want me to leave right away!'

'Richards is waiting to convey you and your belongings to your home.'

Stunned, as she realized the full implication of the situation she was now in, Kate desperately tried to think clearly but her mind was in a jumble. She had sensed the changed atmosphere over the past few days but she'd had no idea what it was leading up to. She had even tried to tell herself that it was all in her imagination and that her sense of unease was because she was missing David so much.

Now she understood Helen's reticence. She must have known, or at least suspected, that Sir George intended to dismiss her.

'I want you out of the house within the hour. Understood?'

She took a deep breath, determined not to let him see her anguish. She met his challenging gaze in proud silence. Let him assume she was arrogant or insolent, his opinion no longer mattered to her.

'I forbid you to speak to Beth or Mary. I shall acquaint them of what has happened in due course,' he added.

His words added to her resentment. Being dismissed was one thing, but to be sent away without the chance of saying goodbye cut her to the quick. And she needed to see Helen to find out where she could contact David.

'How do you intend to explain to them that you dismissed me for no reason whatsoever, may I ask?' she said pertly, her blue eyes flaring.

'That will do!' A film of sweat glistened on Sir George's upper lip.

'You can hardly tell them the truth . . . that you are dismissing me because you don't like me.'

'After such comments, Miss Stacey, I am more than ever convinced that I am doing the right thing. What my mother, or my wife's brother, could have been thinking about when they recommended you as being suitable to look after two young, impressionable girls, I really can't imagine. However, that is now in the past.'

'That's really what all this is about, isn't it?' Kate exclaimed furiously. 'You didn't like it because you weren't consulted when I was appointed as Nanny. You like to think your opinion is the only one that counts in this house.'

'There is no need to be impertinent!'

'And you certainly don't like the idea of me sitting at the same table as you. You've made that abundantly clear.'

'That will do. I should have sent you packing months ago. I dread to think what radical ideas you may have instilled into my daughters.'

Maintaining a dignified silence, Kate rose to her feet. Squaring her slim shoulders, tilting her chin proudly in the air, she smoothed down the skirt of her dark blue dress.

'I wish to speak to Lady Helen before I leave.'

'No!'

'I can't just walk away and leave all the clothes she has given me hanging in the closet . . .'

'Take them!'

'Without her permission?'

'They would only be burned,' he snapped.

'I must speak to her,' Kate insisted stubbornly.

'No! I forbid it. Here,' he held out the envelope. 'I want you gone within the hour.'

She reached out to take it but he held it slightly out of her reach.

'Remember now, you are not to speak to my daughters or anyone else in the house,' he rasped as her fingers curled round the envelope. 'The carriage will be ready in exactly one hour.'

For one desperate moment, Kate wondered if she dare ask Sir George where she could contact David. Then as she saw the thin, ugly smile snake across his face she knew

46

it would not only be a waste of time but would add to his sense of power over her.

'I'm glad you are being sensible about this, Kate Stacey.' His eyes narrowed speculatively. 'With your looks and youth I am sure you will find some other opening more suitable for your talents,' he added with a derisory sneer.

Sensible! Outwardly she may appear calm, but inwardly she was in turmoil. If only there was someone she could confide in, she thought desperately. In the old days she would have turned to her grandmother, but now there was no one . . . not even David.

Struggling to control her tears, she went upstairs to her room. Standing at the window, staring out over the smooth lawns to the woods in the distance, she ached for David.

Her grandmother's cautionary words when she had first said she intended to move to Bramwood Hall, rang in her head.

''Tidden the sort of place for you, m'lovey. Stay where you are at The Manor. Remember your place in life.'

But what was her place in life? Again a mixture of anger and frustration seethed through her. She certainly didn't intend becoming a servant again, doing menial chores for other people for the rest of her life.

A plan bubbled in her mind.

Schoolmaster Barnes had said she was quick to learn so perhaps she could live on the money she'd just been given while she trained to be a teacher!

Her hopes rose like autumn leaves in a high wind.

It might mean the start of a whole new way of life, she thought excitedly. She'd go and see Schoolmaster Barnes right away. He and his wife Julia might even let her lodge with them. She would help out with their little ones as well as studying every minute of the day. Help out in the schoolroom as well if he would let her.

Her heart lightened.

47

Losing her job as a Nanny no longer seemed such a tragedy. She had always wanted to become a teacher but like so many of her aspirations it had seemed like sighing for the moon.

'Them sort of jobs is not for the likes of 'ee, m'lovey,' her grandmother had always warned.

She hadn't argued with her because she knew her Gran believed the parson when he said everyone had their allotted place in the scheme of things. And in her grandmother's eyes, Kate knew, she was destined to be a servant.

She had never believed it, though. And now she had tasted the power of telling others what to do, instead of having them giving her orders, she never wanted to be a servant again.

Becoming a Nanny, even though it wasn't in the same class as being a Governess, since they were mostly educated gentlefolk forced by reduced family circumstances to find work, had been the first step up. Whatever happened now she was determined not to slip back down again. Her life at Bramwood Hall had given her a new sense of self-esteem.

She'd enjoyed being called Miss Stacey, having servants at hand to clear away after her and do her bidding, being accepted almost as an equal by Lady Helen.

She would never forget the look of astonishment on her grandmother's face the first time she had told her that she had sat at the same table for dinner as Lady Helen and Sir George, David Owen, Beth and Mary.

'Oh bless my soul, what an ordeal! Weren't 'ee struck dumb and frightened out of your wits?' her grandmother had exclaimed.

She hadn't been, of course, because David had been there, sitting facing her, smiling encouragement, making sure she was included in the general conversation.

She came back to earth with a jolt as she opened the closet doors and saw all the clothes Helen had given her.

Dresses which she had painstakingly altered in order to look pretty for David.

She laid them out on the bed, together with their matching bonnets and gloves. Then she took down the canvas bag she had brought her own few things in and wondered how she was ever going to get them all into it.

She stood there, reluctant to leave behind any of them because of the memories they held for her. A sound in the passage outside made her look up. The door opened and Helen, her face flushed with exertion, dragged a small tin trunk into the room.

'I thought you might need this for your packing, Kate.'

'Helen! So you do know. . . .

'I have just been told . . . I am so sorry. . . .'

'Why am I being dismissed?' Kate struggled to keep her voice steady.

'It has nothing to do with me, Kate.'

'Then why . . .?'

'I've loved having you here and the girls have never been happier.'

'Is it because of my friendship with David?'

'I'm afraid so! My father heard and . . .'

'Who told him . . . Sir George?'

'My father has other plans for David. You see . . .' Helen hesitated, a flush of embarrassment creeping over her face.

'I know!'

'You've heard Beth and Mary talking between themselves?'

'They say David is expected to marry someone called Penelope Vaughan.'

'It has been agreed since they were young children,' Helen admitted almost apologetically.

'Childhood sweethearts, do you mean?'

'No! It's all to do with land and property and business interests.'

'A marriage of convenience,' sighed Kate. 'Poor David!'

'It will be a loveless marriage and I know only too well what that will mean. Has David given you his address . . .?' Her voice trailed away as Kate shook her head emphatically.

'He said I was to send messages only through you.'

'Oh, my dear! I will do my best to let him know what has happened, but don't count too great a store by it since it may not be possible.'

'Sir George reads all your letters?'

'Of course. And anything I write to David may be intercepted by my father.'

'What am I to do?' Kate's blue eyes welled with tears, her lower lip trembled. 'I love him so much,' she breathed, her voice barely a whisper.

'I do understand,' murmured Helen sympathetically.

'Promise you will tell him the truth about why I left.'

'Of course! It may be some while before I see him. My father will not wish him to come here again.'

'But surely David doesn't have to comply!'

'Family loyalty has been instilled in him since he was in the nursery,' Helen sighed, her round face sad.

'He dictates your lives?'

'He always has done. Of late, because he has allowed David a degree of freedom, I thought he was becoming more lenient in his advancing years.'

'It would seem you were mistaken,' Kate said bitterly.

'I'm afraid so.' She smiled weakly. 'What of you, what are your plans?'

'I'm going to see Schoolmaster Barnes at Mere. He once told me I should train to be a teacher so I'm hoping that now he will help me become one. I'm hoping that he and his wife will let me stay with them for a while and look after their children.'

'Are you sure about all this, Kate. They have no idea you are coming, remember.'

'I shall just have to hope for the best then, won't I,' Kate said sharply, with a defiant toss of her head.

50

'Oh, Kate! I feel so anxious for you. If only David were still here. . . .'

'If he was, then Sir George wouldn't have turned me out, now would he!' Kate retorted with sour amusement.

She turned away and began to fold the clothes laid out on the bed, packing them into the tin box. Helen's kindness made her feel even more bitter about being dismissed from Bramwood Hall. She wished Helen had not voiced aloud her doubts that Schoolmaster Barnes might not be able to help her.

'Take this, Kate,' Helen murmured, handing her a piece of paper.

'What is it?' She studied the scrap of paper eagerly, hoping it was David's address. 'Who is Myfanwy Edwards?'

'She's a dear friend whom I grew up with in Wales. If things don't work out for you in Mere then go to her.'

'You mean for help?' frowned Kate.

'Yes. Her younger boy is about nine and Myfanwy has been unwell ever since he was born; she'll take you as a Nanny, I am sure. You'll like her, Kate.'

'And will you let David know he can find me either at Mere or at this address?'

'Of course I will. At the first opportunity I get.'

'Thank you, Helen.' Kate's eyes misted again with tears.

'Goodbye . . . and good luck.' Helen took Kate's hands in her own, and leaning forward kissed her cheek. Suddenly, they were in each other's arms, hugging as if they were already sisters.

Kate felt her heart lighten. Knowing she had Helen's approval over David lessened the hurt of being dismissed so abruptly.

51

7

Lady Helen Sherwood made a rapid inspection of the bedroom to make sure Kate had left none of her possessions behind.

It was a pleasant room, furnished in a style more suitable for a house guest than a servant. But then, she reflected, Kate had not been a servant in the recognized sense. The post of Nanny had carried with it a great many privileges that even the highest ranking servant would neither expect nor be given.

Kate had never taken advantage of the fact that she had full control over Beth and Mary most of the time. Indeed, she had handled the situation extremely well, Helen mused. As a result they had regarded her almost as a member of the family.

Perhaps that had been a mistake, Helen sighed. Such familiarity had brought Kate into contact with David far too frequently. It was easy to see that he was taken by her. The look of pleasure on his face when she entered the room, the alacrity with which he opened doors for her, or held her chair at dinner, went beyond mere courtesy.

Dear David! To her he had always been rather special. The twelve-year age gap between them meant that she had been a surrogate mother to him as well as a sister.

She had watched him grow from babyhood, through lanky boyhood into a handsome, broad-shouldered man. Now he towered over her so that she was forced to tip back her head to meet the warm brown eyes that twinkled above the straight nose, or to see the teasing smile soften his Byronic features. He was such a romantic figure with his dark hair waving to his collar that it was no wonder Kate had fallen for his charms.

Even as a boy he had been sensitive as well as clever; eager to learn and absorbed by fine words. She could remember his passion for reciting poetry or reading aloud. It had been soothing to listen to him; his deep, gentle voice had always had the power to banish her feelings of tiredness or depression.

Now, in view of what had happened, she was assailed with guilt.

Perhaps she should not have encouraged him to visit Bramwood Hall so often but her own life had become increasingly dull. She'd welcomed his company. David's wit, ready laughter and sensitive understanding had brightened her days and made her existence more bearable.

Helen wondered if she was partly to blame for the estrangement between David and Penelope Vaughan. Were his long absences, because he spent his vacations at Bramwood Hall instead of returning home, partly to blame for the rift, she wondered.

She had never felt they were suited. Penelope was so deeply involved with her horses. Riding and hunting were all she seemed to think about or could discuss with any enthusiasm. She was so brawny and muscular that she made David appear almost effeminate by comparison.

No wonder David had been captivated by Kate, Helen thought fondly, remembering the girl's graceful, slender figure, her warm smile and her enthusiasm in everything that was happening.

She'd found Kate such a stimulating companion that probably she had spent far more time with her than was customary, Helen reflected. It had pleased her to give Kate gowns she had tired of, or which no longer fitted, and watch her deftly adapt them to her own trim shape. Kate's exclamations of delight as she pirouetted in front of the cheval mirror admiring the results had been a reward in themselves.

Beth and Mary had both benefited from Kate's dress sense. She had shown them how to choose the most flattering colours and fabrics, how to coordinate their outfits, even to selecting the right colour ribbon for their hair and to making an overskirt of cascading frills for their parasol in the same material as their gown.

Under Kate's guidance they had learned how to wash and starch the most delicate lace and how to take care of their bonnets by making sure the crowns were either stuffed with soft paper or perched on polished wooden blocks before being stored away on the closet shelves in individual bandboxes.

Her advice had indeed transformed them both into elegant young ladies, poised and self-assured.

Helen hoped that Schoolmaster Barnes would have an opening for her in his school. Kate would find teaching a most fulfilling occupation, of that she was sure. She had both patience and skill; Beth and Mary had both profited from her coaching with their reading and writing.

It was one more thing that Kate had in common with David, Helen mused. She walked over to the window to catch a last glimpse of Kate as she crossed the yard to the carriage waiting to take her away from Bramwood Hall.

David had told her on several occasions that he had no interest whatsoever in the coal and iron industry their father had built up. He considered digging out coal from the bowels of the earth to be a form of vandalism. The slag heaps that scarred the mountainsides he regarded as desecration. He rated every underground explosion, or cave-in, as Nature's reprisal, though he grieved for the men involved.

Coal was the lifeblood of their father's empire and he regarded David's attitude as a passing whim, something he would grow out of once he left University and began to take an active part in the day-to-day running of their enterprise.

For all his mild manner and academic tendencies, Helen knew David could be as stubborn as their father and his future troubled her greatly. If he did not conform he might find himself disinherited. Tudor Ap Owen was not a man to compromise.

She had always been in awe of her father and obedient to his wishes. Dominated by him. He had not even consulted her when he arranged her marriage to Sir George Sherwood.

'He is so much older than I,' she had protested. Like David, she had a strong romantic streak and her dreams had been of a handsome, considerate husband. Sir George Sherwood was neither of these things.

'It's an excellent match,' he told her sternly.

'I have never given marriage a thought, I am happy enough here with you, Papa.'

'You are turned twenty . . . well past marriageable age,' he had snapped irritably, his light brown eyes sharp and direct.

'My days are fully occupied caring for David.'

'I'm sending David away to school.'

'Oh Papa! He will be so unhappy.'

'He needs toughening up. To be with boys of his own age.'

'He doesn't enjoy outdoor pursuits.'

'He spends far too much of his time reading and dreaming. One day he will be running my companies and he'll need a sharp mind when he's in competition with men like Hanbury, Sir John Guest and Crawshay Bailey.'

'I don't think he really wants to be a coalmaster. . . .'

'Silence, daughter!' His pointed beard stabbing the air, her father had cut short her words. 'My mind is made up. Your marriage to Sir George Sherwood will take place just as soon as everything can be arranged.'

Her plea not to be forced into marrying a man she didn't know, a man who was only ten years younger than her father, fell on deaf ears. She knew he was desirable in her father's estimation because he was titled, exceedingly rich and owned extensive estates in Wiltshire, but she thought him a pompous boor. She wanted to be courted with loving, tender words, not treated as a saleable commodity.

Her loveless marriage had proved to be even more of an ordeal than she had envisaged. Having mastered the complexities of household management at Bramwood Hall she had looked forward to entertaining but Sir George preferred to dine alone at home, except when his parents visited. His business deals were conducted at his Club or in the Estate office, so Helen found her social life almost non-existent.

Her romantic dreams of marriage had been shattered on her wedding night. There had been no tender words or chaste kisses. Sir George had taken his conjugal rights as a matter of course and she had submitted meekly. After the births of Beth and Mary he had ceased to trouble her, a state of affairs she accepted with relief.

The warm affection she'd witnessed between David and Kate had served to remind her of all that she had missed. Even though she knew her father would not approve, she had gone out of her way to smooth their path. It would be such a joy to have Kate as a sister-in-law rather than the formidable Penelope.

She had hoped George would not notice what was going on. When he had told her he intended visiting her father, and refused to take her and the girls with him, she should have realized what was happening.

No sooner had he returned from Wales than David had been summoned home.

She didn't for one moment believe her father needed David to deal with a dispute at Fforbrecon. For as long as she could remember he had employed an agent to handle that sort of thing.

In her mind's eye, Helen could see him dressed in his smartly cut frock coat over striped black trousers, his shiny calfskin boots planted astride so that his portly figure was as steady as a rock.

'Never bandy words with working men,' he would declare in ringing tones.

'Make the bullets but let other people fire them, that way you stay superior,' had always been his maxim.

'An unseen force has hidden strength. I am their Coalmaster. The Owner! Someone they hold in awe. If I allowed them to be on speaking terms with me then they would no longer fear and respect me. Familiarity breeds contempt!'

These were the standard statements he used in any argument and she had always known that it was pointless to dispute them. Would David be as tolerant as she, she wondered, especially when he discovered it was all part of his father's strategy to separate him and Kate.

Helen watched as Richards, the groom, strapped Kate's trunk on to the back of the carriage. She saw Kate turn and look up at the house, raising a hand in farewell, but she didn't wave back. Screened by the lace curtains she waited until Richards took his seat and picked up the reins.

As the carriage began to move forward, Helen wiped away a tear. She felt as if she had failed both Kate and David.

Once she was sure that Richards couldn't see what she was doing, Kate opened the white envelope. The reference was written on thick crested paper and she gave it only a cursory glance, knowing that it would be couched in favourable terms.

Apart from the silly incident over the girls squabbling on the croquet lawn there was no way in which Sir George could have found fault with her work, she thought proudly.

Folding up the reference, she put it back inside the envelope and tipped out the remaining contents. Her fingers trembled as she counted the coins.

The ten separate shillings were her month's wages, but in addition there were twenty-five gold sovereigns.

She had never handled so much money in her life.

Kate counted the coins again, then wrapped them in a handkerchief and put them into her reticule. She was still marvelling over her considerable fortune when the carriage drew up alongside the Guildhall in Mere.

'I said I wanted Chantry House, not the Square,' she told Richards haughtily as he opened the carriage door.

'Master wants me to collect some stuff from John Walton's and they'm right here.'

'Chantry House is only just down the road,' she retorted sharply.

'You'm not getting me down them narrow lanes,'

'It's not a narrow lane. Folks manage to get their carriages down there when they go to church on Sundays and turn round again with no bother at all.'

'Well, that's as may be but I'm not going down there!'

Unstrapping her tin trunk he thumped it down in the roadway.

'And don't threaten me that you'll tell the Master since I knows you b'ain't coming back to Bramwood Hall ever again,' he told her waspishly as he climbed back up on his seat.

Gathering up the reins, he swung the carriage round and clattered across the square to the side road that led to John Walton's emporium.

Tying the flowing strings of her blue bonnet firmly beneath her chin so that it wouldn't blow off, Kate stared after him resentfully. Then she picked up her canvas bag in one hand and the straps of the tin trunk in the other. It was a struggle. By the time she reached Chantry House she was feeling hot and bothered and her arms ached.

A middle-aged woman wearing a dark green bombazine dress, trimmed with a white lace collar, answered the door. Her steel grey hair was strained back into a bun. She didn't look like a servant, Kate thought as she asked for William Barnes.

'The Barnes's moved a long time past.'

'Away from Mere?'

'Gone to Dorchester and opened a school there so I've heard tell.'

'Oh . . . no one told me.'

'Are you a relative of theirs then?' the woman asked, seeing the look of dismay on Kate's face.

'Not a relative . . . just a friend.'

'Indeed! Well, they've been gone from here this two years. Funny they never let you know if you're a friend of theirs.'

'I . . . I've been away.'

'Thinking of staying with them, were you?' the woman persisted, looking down at the trunk and bag at Kate's feet.

'No!' Quickly Kate regained her composure. 'I just thought I would pay them a visit.'

'And brought all your belongings along with you,' smiled the woman thinly.

'I've only just arrived in Mere. I shall be staying at The Ship overnight.'

'Is that so?' The woman looked at her hot, dishevelled state disbelievingly.

'I wanted to say goodbye to them because I'm off to live in Wales.'

'Well, I never did!'

'Yes, I'll be leaving first thing in the morning,' Kate embroidered. 'I've got a seat booked on the stage coach.'

I can afford to stay at The Ship, with a room to myself just like one of the gentry, Kate told herself, remembering the sovereigns tucked away safely in her reticule.

She retraced her steps to the Square. When she reached there she checked to make sure that the Sherwood carriage wasn't still outside Walton's. She didn't want Richards to see her going into The Ship in case he told everyone at Bramwood Hall that she'd gone there looking for work.

And tomorrow morning I'll take a seat on the first stage coach going towards South Wales, she determined.

8

September dusk was gathering as the stage-coach from Monmouth lumbered through the Afon Lwyd valley.

Sitting high up on the brightly painted coach, wedged between a farmer and a frock-coated lawyer, Kate Stacey was taking a keen interest in the countryside. They had just passed the magnificent ruins of Raglan Castle, and as she caught fleeting glimpses of the waters of the Afon Lwyd and River Usk, knew they could not be far from her setting down point in Abergavenny.

She shivered. The mountains in the distance were swathed in dark clouds as if a storm was brewing and she hoped she would be able to reach her final destination, Machen Mawr, before it broke.

She hoped Myfanwy Edwards would be like Helen, in nature if not in looks. Ever since leaving Mere, she had been building up pictures of Machen Mawr, hoping it would be a gracious country home, similar to Bramwood Hall. Since there was only one child, Mathew, to look after she might even be given a sitting room as well as her own bedroom.

She wondered what Morgan Edwards would be like. He sounded important. Helen had described him as an ironmaster.

What she had so far seen of South Wales had confused her. Helen had talked of the air being aromatic with wild flowers and mountain plants, of sheep grazing on the mountainside, women spinning in their cottages, but the landscape that had met her eyes since entering Wales had gradually become more and more industrialized.

The mountains that rose to the north were bare and scarred, as though their green skin of grass had been scraped from them, and on their lower slopes were row upon row of tight-packed terraced houses. Tiered up one row behind the other, it seemed that the smoke from one row of chimneys must go straight into the doorways and windows of the row higher up. And smoke there was, plenty of it, billowing upwards like a thick fog.

In the distance, silhouetted against the darkening sky, were man-made hills of black slag and coal dust. Atop them strange contraptions rose into the sky, giant wheels with ropes and pulleys dangling from them. One of her travelling companions told her that was the winding gear belonging to the coal mines.

It was such an alien world that as the coach pulled into The Angel Kate was tempted for a brief moment to turn straight round and go back to Wiltshire. She drew in her breath sharply, remembering how much of her precious money she had already spent journeying from Mere to Bristol, where she had been forced to stay overnight, from there to Monmouth where she had again changed coaches, and knew she had no choice but to stay.

Stiff from her long hours of travel, she followed the rest of the passengers into the inn.

'Machen Mawr? Oh dear me, no! Nothing going that way,' the landlord told her when she asked about transport for the rest of her journey.

'So what do I do?'

'Most people walk!'

'I can hardly do that with all my luggage.'

'Visiting there, are you?'

'Yes. It's somewhere near Nantyglo.'

'Oh, I knows where it is all right!' He looked at her keenly, his dark eyes raking over her, studying her fine clothes with interest.

'So how do I get there?'

'If you took a room here for the night I might be able to find someone to take you there in the morning.'

'What will it cost me?'

'Two shillings for a bed and another shilling for a good hot supper and a fine cooked breakfast.'

Kate shook her head slowly. She was tempted but she had already spent more of her money than she intended.

'That's for a bed to yourself,' the landlord went on. 'If you are willing to share then it would only be a shilling.' His eyes narrowed as he looked her up and down. 'Or even less . . .'

'I want to get there as quickly as possible.'

'Visiting the Edwards family, are you?'

Kate nodded, refusing to be drawn into any explanation.

'Well,' he scratched his head, 'there's only one person likely to take you and that's Dai the Milk. He's got a cart, see. Take your luggage and all, like.'

'Where can I find him?'

'He'll be in here any minute for his ale. Why don't you take a glass of something while you wait?'

Dai the Milk proved reluctant.

'Horse is tired, see,' he protested. 'Just finished for the day and needs her rest. We both have to be back on the road at daybreak.'

'I'll pay you well.'

Again Dai the Milk hesitated.

'Just you, is it?' He pursed his lips in concentration.

'And my luggage.'

'To the Edwards' place, you say.'

'To Machen Mawr.'

'Urgent, like, is it?'

When Kate nodded, he drained his glass and slapped it down on the counter. 'Wait here then and I'll rouse old Betti. She won't like it, mind you.'

Kate sat by the window that overlooked the street, nervously twisting her handkerchief, wondering if he would come back.

As soon as she heard the clatter of hooves on the cobbles outside she was on her feet. Her heart sank at the sight of the conveyance. It was a high-sided float, holding three milk churns, with a single plank seat for the driver.

She would have done better to have heeded the landlord's advice and stayed where she was for the night, she thought apprehensively, as Dai the Milk loaded her tin box and canvas bag on to his cart. In the morning, she could have left her belongings at the inn and walked to Machen Mawr. It had been the landlord demanding two shillings for a bed and another shilling for supper and breakfast that had deterred her.

The drive was nerve-wracking. The road was rough, and she was jostled and bumped on her hard wooden seat until she felt bruised all over and again she wondered if she had acted too hastily. Arriving in the dark on a milk float was not the sort of first impression she had intended. Who would believe that she was Miss Kate Stacey, Nanny to Lady Helen Sherwood's two daughters. Myfanwy Edwards might even refuse to see her!

By the time they reached Machen Mawr her nerves were stretched to screaming point.

As she counted out the fare demanded by Dai the Milk, she debated whether to ask him to wait until she was sure she was welcome. Before she could do so he unceremoniously dumped her belongings on the front doorstep, turned his float around, and disappeared into the darkness.

The house loomed darkly but she was heartened to see lights at several windows. Summoning up her courage she tugged on the bell pull.

The jangling died away but there was no sound of approaching footsteps. She reached up and banged loudly with the iron knocker and waited in trepidation. When nothing happened she hammered yet again.

After what seemed an interminable time the door opened. The middle-aged man who stood there, holding a candleholder aloft, was wide-shouldered yet thin and wiry with a heavy thatch of dark hair and a square-trimmed beard. He didn't look like a servant, yet, from the carelessness of his dress, she didn't think he could be the master of the house.

'May I speak to Mrs Myfanwy Edwards,' she demanded, holding herself stiffly, hoping he wouldn't notice that she was shaking with fear.

There was a long silence. The man's eyes were like two glow-worms as they reflected the light from the candle.

'Mrs Myfanwy Edwards,' Kate repeated. 'I've been sent by a friend of hers, Lady Helen Sherwood . . .'

'You'd better step inside,' the man said curtly.

For a moment she felt dubious, not sure even if she was at the right house. As she hesitated, a thin, pale-faced boy came running down the hall. He stopped short at the sight of her, then timidly started to inch backwards, one foot at a time.

'Mathew? Are you Mathew Edwards?' Kate asked.

The boy nodded, his brown eyes wide with surprise that a complete stranger should know his name.

'Come along in. The night air's not good for the boy,' the man ordered impatiently. 'He's not been well. An attack of asthma, or so the doctor said.'

'Oh, I'm sorry.' Kate looked down at her luggage, then picking up her canvas bag she stepped over the tin trunk, and into the hallway.

'Follow the boy, I'll bring the rest of your belongings,' the man told her, placing the candle down on an oak chest that stood against one wall in the hallway.

The room Mathew took her into was spacious with a lofty ceiling and two large windows. Kate glanced around, feeling uneasy. Although everything in the room was of the very best, the room had an air of neglect.

The Axminster carpet, patterned in shades of red and gold, was of the richest quality. The red, flocked wall-coverings echoed the same colour theme. Two elaborate chandeliers, with magnificently wrought candle-holders, were supplemented by oil lamps strategically placed around the room. The gold velvet drapes had been carefully chosen to complement the upholstery but they were drawn in a lopsided manner, the tie-backs hanging untidily.

Kate's fingers itched to straighten them, plump up the cushions and straighten the antimacassars.

The ornaments on the mantelshelf, as well as on the side tables and rosewood chiffonier, were badly arranged. Coal had spilled out of the grate on to the hearth and lay smouldering beneath the fire irons.

She turned her attention to Mathew and was shocked by the frayed cuffs of his velveteen jacket and the missing buttons. His hair was tousled and he had a pale, washed-out look. His eyes were red-rimmed as if from crying.

'You are Morgan Edwards?' she questioned the man who had followed them into the room and stood looking at her, one of his hands resting heavily on the boy's shoulder.

'That's right.' His voice was clipped.

'Then I have the correct house,' she said, attempting a smile.

His lean face remained set.

'I have been working as Nanny to Lady Helen Sherwood's two girls and . . .'

'Who sent you?'

Some sixth sense told her that all was not well at Machen Mawr. It was not just that the opulence of the furnishings and decor was at odds with their unkempt state but Morgan Edwards seemed to be under some sort of strain.

'Lady Helen. She thought you might like to engage me in a similar situation for your son Mathew.'

'There must be some mistake. . . .'

'I have an excellent reference from Sir George Sherwood,' she interrupted, taking the document from her reticule and holding it out.

She waited uneasily, knowing she had put her case badly. The man's inscrutable stare had unnerved her, making her feel at a disadvantage.

She studied him covertly as he read her reference. He, too, looked in need of care. His jacket was stained and his cuffs frayed. And why had he been the one to open the door, she wondered. Surely a house of this size would merit servants to do that sort of thing.

His next words stunned her back to the present.

'My wife died several months ago. I should have informed Lady Sherwood but Mathew has been ill and such matters have not received my attention.'

'I'm so sorry . . . I don't know what to say . . . Lady Helen had no idea, of course, or . . .'

'I have no need of a governess. Mathew attends school in Pontypool.'

'I'm not a governess,' Kate told him, quickly. 'A Nanny isn't a nurse, either,' she hurried on before he could speak. 'A Nanny is someone who deputizes for the child's mother.'

'It's a pity Lady Sherwood didn't write and ask me first,' he frowned. 'Or, perhaps she did. . . .' He ran a hand through his thick dark hair so that it stood up spiky around his brow. 'So many things have gone awry since Myfanwy died.'

'I'm sorry to have troubled you . . .' her voice trailed off as she saw that Mathew was leaning against his father as if for support, his breath coming in short, laboured gasps.

'Mathew doesn't seem well . . . shouldn't he be in bed?' she asked, her voice full of concern.

'He was just on his way upstairs when we heard you at the door and it frightened him. He gets asthma attacks when he's worried or tense,' Morgan Edwards stated uneasily.

'Would you like me to take him up to bed?' she suggested, holding out her hand to the child.

Mathew hesitated for a moment, his dark eyes studying her face solemnly. She held her breath, aware that this could be a turning point. If Mathew accepted her offer she had a feeling that she might, after all, be asked to stay.

The boy looked questioningly at his father but Morgan Edwards' face gave no clue of what he was thinking.

Kate waited anxiously, as Mathew's mute gaze travelled from one to the other of them. His raucous breathing was the only sound in the room. Slow and laboured, each breath was a conscious effort as his narrow chest lifted and fell.

She wondered what thoughts lay hidden behind the troubled brown eyes and marvelled that this puny, white-faced boy had the power to decide her fate.

Kate was quite sure that if Mathew spurned her suggestion then no amount of persuasion on her part would convince Morgan Edwards that she was needed at Machen Mawr.

She wanted to stay. Not simply because she had nowhere else to go but because she felt concerned about the boy's welfare. Remembering her own sadness and sense of loss after her grandmother had died, her heart went out to him.

The dark shadows beneath Mathew's eyes told of sleepless nights, of fear and loneliness, and she longed to be able to comfort him.

She couldn't envisage this grim-faced man holding the boy in his arms, wiping away his tears, calming his fears, or helping to ease his sense of loss with consoling words.

'All right.' Shyly, Mathew slipped his hand in Kate's. 'Come on then, show me where to go.'

'Will you tell me a story?'

'Of course!'

'And stay in my room until I go to sleep?'

'Yes, if you want me to.'

For the first time since she had arrived at the house she saw him smile. His breathing eased as they left the room together.

'Take your bag upstairs with you. I'll bring up the trunk and show you which will be your room,' Morgan Edwards ordered abruptly. 'We'll settle the details of your employment after you've put Mathew to bed.'

9

Long after Kate had gone to bed, Morgan Edwards remained in the drawing room staring into the dying embers of the fire, brooding over the strangeness of Fate, and wondering if her chance arrival might be the start of better things.

A thin, wiry man, his broad muscular shoulders made him appear shorter than he really was. He had a long face, with deepset dark eyes hooded by heavy dark brows. His wide mouth above the square-cut beard was thin-lipped, giving his face a perpetually grim look.

Perhaps a substitute mother was exactly what Mathew needed, he mused. He was such a namby-pamby weakling with his pale, narrow face, and spindly legs and arms, that at times he felt ashamed to think he had sired him. More like a girl than a boy with his meek manners and whispering voice.

Mathew had been sickly from the day he was born, Morgan thought gloomily. He'd hoped that when the boy started school he would improve but he was still afraid of the dark, and preferred to sit reading rather than be out of doors.

Myfanwy's long illness hadn't helped. Mathew had haunted her like a shadow, sitting beside her holding her hand for hours at a time, as if willing her not to leave him.

Morgan had expected hysterics when he'd told Mathew that she had died but the boy had said nothing, barely shed a tear. Two days later, he'd had his first asthma attack. The bouts had recurred with increasing intensity at intervals ever since. The slightest shock or upset seemed to trigger off an attack which sometimes lasted for hours.

He'd thought Mathew was all set for one tonight but Kate Stacey seemed to have nipped it in the bud. It was as if her presence, and the tone of her voice, had quelled his fears and restored his self-confidence.

Morgan got up and poured himself a whisky.

He felt vaguely uneasy that a complete stranger could walk into his house and have more effect on his son than he had. It went against the grain. He liked to be the one in control of any situation he was involved in.

It was just another sign that he was losing his touch, he thought bitterly. Since Myfanwy had died his entire life had fallen to pieces. Their social life had declined slowly over the years but now it was non-existent.

And that wasn't all. They no longer began each day with family prayers. Nor did Mathew attend Dr Howell's school regularly, he reflected irritably. More often than not he'd stay home claiming he wasn't feeling well, but Morgan knew that once he had driven away, Mathew would creep down to the kitchen to be with Mrs Price.

For all that, Mathew seemed to manage to keep up with his learning. He could read and cipher with the best of them. Yet regular schooling was necessary. The boy was much too introverted. He needed companionship and organized exercise to put some colour into his cheeks.

At one time Morgan had felt so guilty about the situation that he'd tried spending more time with Mathew, even taking him walking. The result had been disastrous! He'd never forget the time they had been half-way up Sugar Loaf Mountain and Mathew had started one of his asthma attacks.

They'd been marooned on the mountainside with no one to help. Morgan shuddered, remembering how Mathew had struggled for breath, his lips blue, each gulp of air rasping and laboured.

He'd been petrified Mathew was going to die and had carried the boy back down the mountain and into Abergavenny. By the time they reached there he, too, was puffing and wheezing as though he was the one with asthma.

Mathew had taken a long time to recover from his ordeal and afterwards seemed even more fragile. Watching him stare listlessly out of a window, or toying with his food, Morgan sometimes wondered if it would have been better if the child had not pulled through since he got so little enjoyment from life.

Mathew didn't even have any feel for horses!

Brynmor had ridden since he was three and was as much at home on a horse as he was on his own two feet. Not so Mathew. The sight of a horse, or one whiff of the stables, and he was coughing and wheezing like an old man of ninety.

It was something to do with animal hair, according to the specialist he'd taken him to in Newport. A complete load of rubbish as far as Morgan was concerned. More likely the boy was frightened of the beasts, he thought cynically.

He'd never been afraid of anything in his life. Even as a small child he would face the fiercest ram with impunity.

The boy was sickly, there was no doubt about that. Perhaps the arrival of this woman, who called herself a Nanny, would have some good effect. She seemed too young to have had much experience but he was prepared to give her a trial since Helen Sherwood had sent her along.

Helen's name had stirred memories long forgotten. His thoughts went back to when he was in his twenties, and Helen and Myfanwy younger even than that.

He remembered Helen, round-faced and fair with gentle hazel eyes. Myfanwy had been her opposite in colouring. Her hair had been dark and straight, framing her oval face. She'd had such a proud look, haughty almost. He sighed; so very different to how she looked just before she died.

It had been a happy release; her illness had taken its toll of them both.

70

Long before the end came he'd reached a stage where any feelings he had for her had withered under the strain. But was it an illness? He'd asked himself that question a hundred times or more. The doctor had never been able to attribute any specific cause for her gradual decline. It was as if she wasted away because she'd lost the will to live. And that seemed unbelievable when she had so much to enjoy. Wealth, a lavish home, servants to wait on her and a carriage to ride out in as well as her own horse.

Brynmor had been almost ten when Myfanwy had found herself pregnant again. They'd given up all hope of another child by then and right from the moment she knew she'd seemed to resent what was happening.

She'd carried well but the birth had been long and arduous. For weeks afterwards she'd remained in bed, barely moving, refusing to see any visitors and showing hardly any interest in the baby.

She made no attempt to feed him and although they'd hired a wet nurse, Mathew still didn't thrive as he should.

With a semi-invalid wife and a puny, mewling baby in the house he had spent more and more time at work and stayed away from home as much as he could. Most other men would have done the same, Morgan reasoned silently.

Looking back, he wondered if, had he behaved differently, been more conciliatory, it would have altered the way things had turned out. Given the right encouragement, Myfanwy might have regained her strength and interest in life. And Mathew might have become a sturdy, healthy child like his elder brother.

A smile twisted Morgan's thin lips as he thought of Brynmor. Now there was a son to be proud of!

Nineteen, and a head for business matters like a man of thirty. He was a chip off the old block and no mistake. Brynmor had inherited his own aptitude for hard work coupled with his grandfather's shrewdness.

71

He had to admit that at times Brynmor could be ruthless.

Determined, that was what the boy was. Look at the way he had devoted himself to finding out about the powders and lacquers used for japanning. Nothing but the best in materials and technique would do for the trays and tableware made at his factory. Night after night, long after the men had left, Brynmor worked on, determined to perfect a method that would make his Japanware the very best.

It was a pity Brynmor had involved himself with the running of 'Tommy Shops', Morgan thought irritably. There was something evil about them in his opinion. Unlike most of the other ironmasters and owners in Ebbw Vale he didn't approve of them. And he had told Brynmor so on more than one occasion.

'Setting up shops and letting your employees buy on credit sounds benevolent enough until you look at the prices you are going to charge,' he told Brynmor.

'They expect to pay a bit more if they're getting it on tick!'

'What you're asking is daylight robbery.'

'It's the usual percentage.'

'It works out double what they would pay in the normal way.'

'And interest on top of that!'

Yet the workers fell for it. Being able to get credit was the attraction. Most of them were bad managers of money and their wives were even worse.

Brynmor made sure there were no bad debts outstanding by deducting what was owed straight from each man's wages before he handed over their pay.

'Poor dabs!' argued Morgan. 'It means some of them only take home a few shillings at the end of the week! The rest's already been spent in the Tommy Shop.'

'Where would they be without their bit of tick, tell me that?' argued Brynmor.

'It's not right to encourage them to spend their wages

before they get them.'

'The men count on being able to get their baccy and a nip of whisky or rum from one of my shops even when they haven't a penny piece in their pockets.'

'Think of their families.'

'I do. Where would their wives be if they couldn't get meat, cheese, bread and flour on tick? They'd starve, that's what they'd do, and all their snivelling children along with them.'

'It's a form of slavery,' Morgan protested.

'Nonsense. I'm being philanthropic,' laughed Brynmor.

'They're working to pay what they owe you before they even start to earn the next week's money. They're up to their eyeballs in debt all the time.'

'And that's what keeps them loyal and makes such good workers out of them,' scoffed Brynmor.

Morgan didn't like it.

Taller than him by a head, and with shoulders just as broad, Brynmor had stood there young and confident, his broad face shining with satisfaction.

He might be clever but he could be cruel and vicious Morgan reflected, remembering the way Brynmor's mouth had twisted in a sardonic grin. Took after his grandfather on his mother's side, all right.

Old Rhys Carew had been a hard man. One of the greatest ironmasters of his day, he'd enslaved his workers and exploited them. At Brynmawr, he'd built an entire village, close enough to his foundries that the men had no excuse for not hearing the bell that clanged ten minutes before the start of their shifts.

Many times as a young boy, Morgan himself had run from his home at the far end of one of the terraces, eating a bread-and-dripping butty as he went, so as not to be late.

He thought back to the day he had been made foreman.

'Been watching you, boyo, and I can see that you have the feel for the iron,' old Carew had told him. 'You may

73

be a bit on the young side but you've got the makings of a leader.'

He had towered over him, a formidable figure in a black broadcloth jacket and trousers and striped alpaca waistcoat. A thick silver watch chain strained across his enormous paunch. His six foot of rolling fat swayed powerfully.

And that had been his first step on the ladder. There had been no turning back after that even if he had wanted to do so. Rhys Carew had no sons of his own and he'd more or less adopted Morgan. He had forced success on him, even to the point of dictating that he should marry Myfanwy.

Morgan could hardly remember his life before then in the tiny terraced house where he'd slept in the same bed as his three step-brothers. After making him foreman, Rhys Carew arranged for him to move into respectable lodgings just outside Beaufort at the head of the valleys. Six months later he had been put in charge of the ironworks there.

Myfanwy had been Rhys Carew's only child, his most cherished possession. Morgan remembered how honoured he'd felt the first time he'd been detailed to escort her to a public function.

Her friends had giggled behind their fans knowing he worked for her father. The only one who had not done so was Helen ap Owen. She and Myfanwy had been friends all their lives and in those days seemed inseparable.

He'd liked Helen. She'd been a sweet, friendly girl, easier to get on with than Myfanwy. Her father, Tudor ap Owen, owned Fforbrecon, the biggest colliery in Ebbw Vale, and supplied Rhys Carew with coal for his blast furnaces.

Tudor ap Owen lived at Llwynowen, a magnificent mansion midway between Blaenafon and Govilon. Not all his fortune came from coal. Some came from the herds of black cattle that grazed the estate and the sheep that roamed freely over the Blorenge Mountain.

It was after Helen married Sir George Sherwood that the close friendship between her and Myfanwy waned.

Tudor ap Owen had been puffed up with pride because his daughter was the first of the two girls to marry and that her future husband had a title as well as a country estate in Wiltshire.

Not to be outdone, Rhys Carew had announced his own daughter's forthcoming marriage . . . to the man he'd put in charge of his ironworks.

Neither union had been a love match.

Morgan had been in awe of Myfanwy and well aware that she considered herself far superior to him. He'd known it wouldn't be easy living up to her standards. She'd been determined to educate him to her fine ways, insisting it was necessary if he was to take his proper place alongside her in local society.

There had been some gruelling moments but by the time they walked down the aisle his behaviour was impeccable. He'd even learned to tolerate George Sherwood's company without batting an eyelid.

When Helen was first married she corresponded regularly with Myfanwy. He was never shown the letters but he gathered from what Myfanwy told him that George Sherwood was something of a martinet. Helen's new life in Wiltshire was not the romantic bed of roses she'd dreamed it would be.

On the rare occasions when Helen came home to see her father, Myfanwy visited her. Sir George Sherwood didn't approve of his wife making social calls without him. Afterwards Myfanwy always expressed concern about the way Helen had changed. She had become so subdued and formal that even Myfanwy felt uncomfortable in her company.

The rivalry between Tudor ap Owen and Rhys Carew had flared anew when Myfanwy's son was born. Tudor ap Owen waited impatiently for a grandson of his own and only thinly disguised his disappointment when Helen gave birth to a daughter. After the arrival of Helen's second baby, also a girl, Tudor had discouraged her from visiting him. Instead, he focused his attention on his son, David, who was several years younger than Helen and still at school.

By now, David must be finished at University, mused Morgan. He wondered if he was as bigoted and over-bearing as George Sherwood, now that his head was crammed full of fancy theories. If so, he'd probably exploit the workforce the same as his father had done and not know one man from the next. To him they would be as indistinguishable as pit ponies.

Perhaps it was because he came from humble beginnings himself, thought Morgan, as he poured himself a whisky, that he took such an interest in the men who worked for him. If they had a problem he wanted to know about it. A man couldn't do his job to the best of his ability if he was worried. That much he knew from personal experience!

Some said if he'd spent as much time bothering about his own affairs as he did about those of the men he employed, then his wife would be alive today. He had tried. He'd been more than willing to do everything in his power to get her well again but she'd shut him out. There had been an invisible barrier between them. He often wondered if it had been because of his humble background, if she felt she'd been sacrificed in order that Rhys Carew could ensure his precious ironworks were handed on to the only man he could trust to run it in the same way as he had.

He'd proved himself many times over, Morgan thought confidently. He'd been the one to persuade Rhys Carew that they should have their own colliery at Blaina and not rely on Tudor ap Owen for their supply of coal. It had caused a rift between the two men but economically it had been a great success.

He got up and poured himself another whisky, and stirred the glowing nest of coal in the grate with the toe of his boot.

As the flames shot up, firing the soot at the back of the chimney with a thousand sparks, it brought back memories of the great blast furnaces and the fierce competition he'd been up against from Joseph and Crawshay Bailey, the most ruthless and successful of the Ebbw Vale ironmasters.

All that was in the past. Joseph had retired some ten years ago and Crawshay was no threat to him these days.

He wished Rhys Carew was still alive to see how he'd achieved everything he'd set out to do and how he was now numbered amongst the greatest Ironmasters in South Wales.

10

When she woke next morning the first thing Kate resolved to do was to take stock of her new surroundings. She was pleasantly surprised to find that in daylight Machen Mawr was a much grander house than she had first thought it to be.

Built of warm red brick, it had contrasting Bath stone at its corners and a slate roof. The six bay windows on the ground floor were all mullioned with elaborate cartouches above them; the long, narrow, upper windows had swags beneath them. Barley-sugar columns flanked the enormous oak door.

The forecourt was divided from the roadway by a set of splendid wrought-iron gates. On the other side of the house, a further sweep of drive led to the stables and garden.

Inside, Machen Mawr was equally impressive.

All the main downstairs rooms were panelled and the ceilings decorated with intricate plasterwork. If everywhere had been in pristine condition, floors swept and polished, furniture gleaming, ledges and ornaments dusted, it would have been magnificent, but to Kate's critical eye there was a general air of slackness. It was as if the cleaning had been rushed, carried out indifferently by someone who knew that nobody would take the trouble to check it.

The previous evening, Morgan Williams had implied that he would expect her to oversee the running of his home as well as look after Mathew, which was why she felt it was necessary to explore her surroundings in such detail.

In one room, Kate stopped to admire an impressive

collection of exquisitely japanned trays and boxes that were artistically displayed in a glass-fronted cabinet. She noted with surprise that these really did look cherished and that the cabinet gleamed from regular polishing.

As she wandered through the house, Kate found her first impressions confirmed. The furnishings were expensive and bore the hallmark of good taste but the niceties that turned mere rooms into a home were lacking. It was as if no one ever used the rooms or had any interest in the things in them.

Kate left visiting the kitchen until last.

'You'll have to handle Mrs Price with kid gloves,' Morgan Edwards had warned. 'She's been Cook-Housekeeper here since the day we moved in. Doted on my wife. Broke her heart when Myfanwy died.'

She found that, unlike the rest of the house, the kitchen had an air of warmth and friendliness.

The array of china and glassware spaced out on the impressive Welsh dresser sparkled. Copper cooking pots gleamed. The open range had been newly black-leaded. The steel fender and trivet, that stood on the freshly whitened hearth, shone like silver.

Mrs Price was making bread, her arms bare to the elbow as she kneaded dough in a brown earthenware bowl. Mathew was kneeling on a wooden chair, at the other end of the scrubbed pine table, spooning up a bowl of porridge.

She acknowledged Kate's greeting with a stiff nod of her grey head, her dark eyes wary as she studied the slim young stranger from top to toe.

She certainly looked respectable, she thought with relief, noting the neatness of Kate's grey dress, the demure white lace collar, white stockings and canvas boots. There was no guile in the cornflower-blue eyes that met hers and the sweetness of her smile would win the stoniest heart. A trifle too pretty, perhaps, Mrs Price decided, noticing that although Kate's black hair was pulled back in a knot in the nape of her neck, wispy tendrils had escaped, and tiny ringlets framed her face.

It had come as a shock when the Master had told her what had happened. She couldn't for the life of her imagine what sort of young woman would be traipsing round the countryside after dark, knocking on doors of people she'd never met. And then staying in a strange house without even being sure there were other womenfolk sleeping there.

Her immediate thoughts had been that the girl must be a right young hussy, bold as brass and no better than she should be.

Now, faced with this sedate young woman whose voice had a gentle West-Country burr, she felt nonplussed.

Still, looks weren't everything, Mrs Price told herself. She wasn't going to be fooled by a pretty face. She'd wait a while before passing judgement. Sweet and pretty she might seem but it could be a different story when she'd settled in and started imposing her will and making all manner of changes.

'So this is where you are, Mathew,' Kate chuckled. 'Having breakfast by the kitchen fire.'

'It's warm down here, and that old nursery is cold until Glynis gets round to lighting the fire. And she hasn't the time to carry coals up there first thing in the morning. Too many other jobs to be done, see,' Mrs Price said defensively.

'A very sensible arrangement,' agreed Kate mildly.

'Mathew spends a lot of his time down here with me. Lonely for the boy all on his own in a great barn of a place like this,' Mrs Price added challengingly.

'Well, we'll soon find plenty to occupy his time now,' Kate told her, turning to smile at Mathew who kept his head down and attacked his bowl of porridge ferociously.

'Not had a lot of schooling, poor little lamb, him being weakly and everything,' Mrs Price explained. 'Bright as a button though, aren't you, Mathew? Going to be like Brynmor one of these days,' she added fondly.

'Brynmor?'

'His brother,' explained Mrs Price. 'You've not met Brynmor yet, of course.'

'He lives here?'

'Indeed he does! He comes home today, doesn't he, Mathew? Been down to London on business this past week. All that way and him only nineteen!'

'I see. He works for his father, does he?'

'Gracious me, no!' Mrs Price exclaimed. 'Runs his own business in Pontypool, does Brynmor.'

'And what sort of business is that?'

'Makes Japanware, does Master Brynmor. Very clever he is at it, see. His new methods have outsmarted all the others doing such work. He has the very finest painters working for him. Wonderful designs and patterns in his range. People from all over the world send orders for his Japanware,' she added, her eyes shining, her hostility forgotten in her fulsome praise.

'Well then, Mathew, if you are going to be as clever as your brother perhaps you should be off to school.'

'He's not too well,' Mrs Price said sharply.

'Really. What's the matter, Mathew?'

'Been at home all week with a nasty cough. I've kept him busy helping me here in the warm,' Mrs Price replied for him.

'Come on,' Kate held out her hand. 'If you're not going to school, how about showing me round Machen Mawr? There are so many passages and corridors, I keep getting lost.'

Eyes shining at his reprieve, Mathew looked anxiously at Mrs Price to make sure she approved.

'Off you go then, Mathew. I'll send Glynis to find you at mid-morning with a glass of milk and a bakestone?'

'Yes, please!' he grinned widely at her.

'And what about you, Miss. Would you prefer coffee?'

'That sounds most acceptable, Mrs Price,' agreed Kate, smiling her thanks as she steered Mathew out of the kitchen.

81

By the end of the morning, Kate and Mathew were firm friends.

After he had shown her over the house they wandered across to the stables where Dai Jenkins and his son Twm were tending a handsome chestnut stallion with white markings, and a placid grey cob that Mathew told her was used for the trap.

Mathew looked sheepish when she showed surprise that he didn't have a pony to ride, and hurried her along to the kitchen garden where Huw Parry was lifting potatoes and storing them in a straw-lined pit for winter use.

Morgan Edwards surprised everyone by arriving home for his luncheon. Flustered, Mrs Price offered to lay out a dish of cold meats for him in the dining room.

'I'll take my meal with Mathew and Miss Stacey in the morning room, and share whatever they are having,' he told her.

Kate judged from Mathew's nervousness that it was a rare occasion for him to eat with his father. Tentatively she enquired if they all dined together in the evening.

'The two girls and I always joined Sir George and Lady Helen unless they were entertaining,' Kate told him.

Morgan Edwards was silent for a moment as he gave the matter further thought. He was surprised that George Sherwood would sit at table with a servant but if such an arrangement was good enough for George Sherwood, then it suited him.

'Mathew has never come down to dinner in the past but I suppose that's no reason why he should not do so from now on,' he observed.

'What time do you dine?'

'Promptly at seven.'

'Very good. I'll make sure we are both there on time.'

'I'll explain the new arrangement to Mrs Price on my way out,' he said, pushing back his chair and rising from the table.

'Perhaps you and Mathew should take a drive out this afternoon, Miss Stacey,' he suggested, pausing at the door.

'Thank you. I would like that.'

'You can't get lost as there's only one main road. Mathew can point out our ironworks and coal mines. You'll find it very different from Wiltshire. Best to see it for yourself before you decide whether or not you want to stay.'

'Oh, but I am sure,' Kate told him quickly, her eyes darkening with sudden alarm in case he was thinking of changing his mind about her appointment.

'You need to be quite sure.'

'I've thought over all the things you mentioned last night, Mr Edwards.'

'And you are prepared to oversee the household as I asked?'

'Providing the ordering of provisions and the supervising of the kitchen remains in Mrs Price's hands.'

'I wouldn't want it any other way.' He took a briar pipe from his pocket and proceeded to fill it with tobacco from a leather pouch.

'Then can I take it everything is settled?'

'Brynmor will be home by dinner time. Perhaps you should meet him first.'

'There's no need . . . I've already made my mind up.'

'Go and take that drive,' he ordered abruptly. 'Do young Mathew good to get some fresh air in his lungs.'

Mathew watched anxiously as Dai Jenkins harnessed Gryg, the grey cob, between the shafts of the trap for their outing. He fidgeted uneasily until Kate took the reins, and as he climbed up beside her she was aware that he was biting his lips nervously.

As they drove out of the wrought-iron gates of Machen Mawr, Kate saw that the Valley resembled an immense basin, the sides formed by mountains. The one that loomed up to their right ran along the skyline. Her interest quickened. She recalled David telling her that his home was ringed by mountains. Had he been speaking of these, she wondered.

She listened attentively as Mathew pointed out the scattered white farmhouses, telling her who lived in each one of them. She felt disappointed that he didn't mention the name Owen, until common sense told her that David's family would live in a much grander house than any they could see dotted about in the valley and that it would probably be shielded from open view by trees.

As they approached Nantyglo, Kate looked around her in disbelief. She had never seen anything like it in her life. Row upon row of tiny terraced houses stretched like strings of beads around the lower slopes of the hillsides.

The mountain towering up behind them seemed to block out the rest of the world. A pall of smoke, that almost obscured the sun, rose from the conglomeration of sheds and chimneys at the foot of the hillside.

Long before they reached the ironworks, she was aware of the brown, unpleasant dust that permeated the air. As they drew nearer, they passed towering heaps of cinders that gave off acrid fumes, streams of molten metal, and enormous furnaces that glowed fiercely, sending up a myriad of sparks that turned the sky red.

Kate suppressed a shudder; the hair on the nape of her neck rose as their ears were assailed by the thundering noise of hammers and all kinds of other dreadful sounds. An immense wheel, impelled round with incredible velocity by a steam engine, astounded her. It was a hell hole. The malodorous fumes that stung her nostrils were like something from a dark satanic pit. She understood why there was unrest among men who had to work in such conditions and why they formed unions to try and improve their lot.

They drove on quickly. When she turned to look back, the great black towers were belching out smoke and flames from their tops and it looked as if the mountains were on fire.

Although she felt she had witnessed enough horror for one day, curiosity made her agree to Mathew's suggestion to visit one of his father's coal mines before they went home. One coal mine would be very like another, she told herself, and it would bring her just that little bit closer to David if she knew what was involved.

Half an hour later she reined the trap to a standstill. They were high on a hill looking down on the scene of activity at the pit head where a great wheel turned and coal spewed up from out of the ground. As they watched, a group of miners were brought up from the bowels of the earth. Small, hunched figures, they climbed wearily from the cage, their faces and clothes black with coal dust. The whites of their eyes gleamed as they blinked in the bright daylight.

'Papa took me down one of his mines once,' Mathew told her.

'Did you have to wear helmets?'

'Yes. We put them on before we climbed into the cage.'

'And then you were lowered underground.'

'Yes.' He shuddered. 'We went down ever so deep.'

'That doesn't sound a very pleasant experience!'

'It was horrible! I could hardly breathe. When the cage stopped we were in complete darkness except for the light from the candles fixed in the front of our helmets.'

'What happened then?'

'We walked along a narrow tunnel. I kept slipping and falling and every time I stood up I banged my head.'

The excitement suddenly went out of his voice and Kate heard the tremor that replaced it as he said, 'I thought all the time that I was going to choke, it was so difficult to breathe down there. It was the same sort of feeling that I get when I'm going to have one of my attacks.'

'You make it sound very frightening,' Kate shuddered.

'I thought about it for weeks afterwards,' Mathew told her gloomily.

'And was that when you started having asthma attacks?'

'No.' He gave a deep sigh.

'So when did those start?'

'After they put Mama in her coffin. I thought she must feel the same as I did when I went underground, all shut in and unable to breathe.'

'And was that when the attacks started?'

Mathew nodded, his face ashen.

'I was choking for breath, just like when I went down the pit. I called out for Mama but she didn't come.' He choked back a sob. 'I thought I was dead, too, because no matter how hard I tried I couldn't get any air.'

Kate looked down at the small, pinched face and her heart ached. Unsure what to say, she reached out and took the boy's hand and gave it a reassuring squeeze. She wondered if David felt fear when he was forced to go underground.

'Have you ever heard of Fforbrecon Colliery, Mathew?' she asked.

'Why do you want to know?'

'I thought it might be close by.'

'I think it's near Blaenafon, over the other side of the Blorenge Mountain.'

'A friend . . . someone I once met, told me about it. I thought it was somewhere around here.'

'Does your friend work there?'

'I'm not sure. Have you ever heard of anyone called David Owen?' she asked, her heart thundering.

'No.' Mathew shook his head. 'Is that why you came here . . . to find him?' he asked with a child's sharp intuition.

'No . . . not really. I just wondered . . .'

'Are you going away again when you do? Please stay,' he begged. 'You must! If you go away then I'll have no one again,' he added piteously, his eyes filling with tears.

'Nonsense!' Kate told him briskly. 'You have your father and brother. And Mrs Price? She cares about you very much.'

'Papa hasn't much time for me. I think he is ashamed of me because I'm not like Brynmor.'

'But you will be . . . when you are older.'

As she spoke, Kate saw fear darken the boy's eyes.

'I never want to be like Brynmor,' Mathew told her fervently, panic in his voice, his chest rising with the force of his statement.

'Why ever not?' asked Kate, remembering the empathy between Mary and Beth and the way Mary had aped her elder sister, striving to emulate her in everything she did.

'Wait until you meet Brynmor,' he told her darkly. 'I hate him . . . I'm afraid of him,' he added in a whisper.

'Why is that?'

He bit his lip and seemed reluctant to talk about it, so she picked up the reins and turned the trap towards Machen Mawr, wondering what the problem could be.

11

Knowing that it was the first time Mathew had joined his father and brother for dinner, Kate surmised he must be feeling nervous so she went along to his bedroom to make sure that he was dressed properly for the occasion.

'Do I look all right, Kate?' he asked anxiously.

He had put on a pair of black and white check trousers and a tight-fitting bottle-green jacket over a plain white shirt. He'd made a brave attempt to fasten his black silk tie but had only succeeded in achieving a rumpled, one-sided bow.

With deft fingers, Kate adjusted it for him.

'That's fine, Mathew.'

As she stood back to admire the finished result she noticed that his bony wrists extended a good two inches past the cuffs of his jacket and his trousers barely covered the top of his boots.

She said nothing. The evening was going to prove enough of an ordeal for him without making him feel self-conscious. She made a mental note, though, to check the clothes he wore to school and make sure they fitted him.

'Right! Are we ready to go down, then?'

'Yes!' He ran a hand over his flattened-down hair and clamped his top teeth over his lower lip to stop it trembling.

'You look pretty,' he murmured shyly as Kate stopped to check her own appearance in the mirror.

'Why, thank you!'

She had chosen a silk and velvet dress in two shades of blue, nipped in at the waist, the skirt full and long. The velvet was the same colour as her eyes, or so Helen had told her when she had given her the dress.

'It's one of my favourites,' Helen had smiled, 'but I've put on so much weight I can barely squeeze into it.'

Kate had thought it the most beautiful dress she had ever seen and had spent several evenings altering it to fit. This was the first time she had worn it and she wondered whether perhaps it was just a little too grand. She was, she reminded herself, merely an employee and the dress made her look more like the lady of the house.

'Your hair looks prettier all loose and curly,' Mathew broke into her reverie.

Kate lifted up the black ringlets from the nape of her neck, studying the effect with pleasure. Letting them fall back, so that they gleamed like sable against the whiteness of her shoulders, she wished her grandmother could see her now and know how well she had done for herself.

It was fortunate that Mathew had taken to her so readily.

Morgan Edwards seemed to be completely at a loss on how to cope with Mathew. It seemed strange that a man who employed servants and any number of workmen didn't understand the needs of a child.

He had seemed so relieved when she'd explained that a Nanny was neither a Nurse nor a Governess but someone who deputized for the child's mother, that she was sure if she had refused to undertake any other duties he would still have wanted her to stay simply to look after Mathew.

She hadn't been too sure about agreeing to oversee the running of his home. She had complied because it gave her undisputed power should the housekeeper be resentful of her appointment. Yet she had been lucky on that score, too. Just the mention of Lady Helen's name and she had immediately found favour with Mrs Price.

Mrs Price had known Helen as a girl, seen her grow up alongside Myfanwy, and held her in high regard. Kate wondered what she ought to tell Mrs Price if she asked why she had left Bramwood Hall. Certainly not the truth! Perhaps it would be best if she said that Helen's two girls were being sent away to school, she decided.

Providing she left Mrs Price to deal with kitchen matters in her own way, Kate was quite sure they could become the best of friends.

'Come on.' Taking Mathew's hand she prepared to face the final hurdle: meeting Brynmor.

Morgan and Brynmor were already seated at the table when Kate and Mathew entered the dining room.

Kate studied Brynmor with interest. He was heavily built and looked older than his nineteen years. He was dressed in the very latest fashion, black trousers fastened under the instep with straps and a dark blue tail coat. A frilled white shirt was visible under his blue and red striped silk waistcoat and his bow tie was in matching red silk.

He had inherited dark hair and eyes, a prominent nose and square chin from Morgan, but his mouth was full-lipped and sensuous. His thick hair grew down to meet the side-whiskers below his ears. Coupled with swarthy skin, and heavy dark brows, this gave him a saturnine appearance.

Kate was acutely aware of the way Mathew tensed as they entered the room. His face looked pinched and ashen. For a moment she thought he was about to turn tail and run.

'What are you doing down here dressed up like a young jackanapes,' Brynmor commented, studying his young brother with a contemptuous smile. 'Shouldn't you be in the nursery?'

'Papa said I could come down to dinner with Kate,' Mathew answered in a tight, strained voice.

'Kate is it!' His calculating gaze sent a shiver through her. It was as if he was divesting her of every stitch of clothing and appraising what he saw beneath.

His hand as he shook hers, after Morgan had formally introduced them, was hot and clammy. She was conscious of the pressure of his fingers as they encompassed her own and that he held her hand for far longer than was necessary.

Instinctively, she shared Mathew's dislike of Brynmor.

Morgan indicated where she was to sit, facing Mathew. Brynmor sat at the far end of the table and Kate was relieved to find she was partially hidden from his view by the vase of pink roses that decorated the table.

Conversation during dinner was stilted.

As Brynmor boasted of his visit to London, where his Japanware had been received with enthusiasm, and his plans for future expansion, Kate suspected that he was trying to impress her.

Mathew picked nervously at his food. He seemed to be dismayed by the array of heavy silver cutlery. As each course was served, he waited until Kate picked up the correct knife, fork or spoon from alongside her own plate and then selected matching ones. She discouraged him from drinking the wine and suggested to his father that Glynis should bring him a glass of water.

It was a relief when the meal ended, even though she had enjoyed the food prepared by Mrs Price. Everything had been of the best quality. Delicately flavoured consommé, sole in Hollandaise sauce, lamb cutlets and vegetables, followed by sherry trifle decorated with thick cream.

When the meal ended, Brynmor and Morgan retired to the library to sort out various documents concerning one of the business transactions they had been discussing during dinner. Kate went through into the drawing room with Mathew. A fire had been lit and a multibranched candelabra cast a soft glow over the handsome furnishings.

Conscious that Mathew had been virtually ignored during dinner, Kate encouraged him to talk about his interests. At first he was reluctant to do so, preferring to lie on the floor and bury his face in the shaggy coat of

Danni, the black and white sheepdog, that lay stretched out in front of the fire.

'Can you play, Mathew?' she asked, walking over to the pianoforte and experimentally depressing one or two keys.

'Not very well.'

'Show me.'

'I haven't played for a long time.'

'Come on, play for me,' insisted Kate.

'I don't want to.'

'Please, while we are on our own.'

'I'm out of practice.'

'Play just one piece for me, Mathew.'

After considerable persuasion, he did as she asked, and although she had no ear for music, Kate could tell that his fingering was not very accomplished. When he came to the end of his piece, she wondered whether she should praise or criticize his efforts.

The arrival of Brynmor made a decision unnecessary.

The moment he came through the door, Mathew slid from the stool and returned to playing with the dog.

Brynmor paused just inside the door, his eyes narrowing as he surveyed the scene. Without speaking, he walked over to the fireplace and with the toe of his polished boot roughly parted the boy and dog. Then, with a well-aimed kick, he sent the dog howling into a corner.

'You!' Fists flailing, Mathew lashed out at his brother, ineffectually pummelling the thick-set thighs that stretched the black broadcloth trousers to capacity.

'Mathew!'

Although she sympathized with his reasons and would have preferred not to interfere, Kate felt she couldn't condone such bad behaviour.

'Don't worry on my behalf, I can control him,' Brynmor said coolly He seized the child's wrists in a cruel grasp and swung him up in the air. Mathew screamed as he left the ground. He struggled to free himself by striking out with his feet, but Brynmor held him at a sufficient distance to make contact impossible.

Kate felt her blood run cold as Mathew yelled and struggled, and she saw his face twist with agony. She was reminded vividly of the way she had suffered as a child at the hands of her Uncle Charlie. Brynmor was exercising the same brutal strength, and deriving pleasure from inflicting pain on his hapless victim.

'Put Mathew down this minute!'

Surprised by her tone, Brynmor released his hold.

Mathew thudded to the floor and lay there completely winded. Kate helped him to his feet and used her handkerchief to dry his tears. She could hear his breath rasping as his chest heaved painfully.

Flushed with fury she rounded on Brynmor.

'Have you any idea what such treatment can do to a child like Mathew,' she berated him hotly.

'Liven him up?' His dark eyes stared venomously.

'You're forgetting his precarious state of health,' she retorted scathingly.

'Nonsense!' A sneer twisted his face. 'Namby pamby little bugger's managed to hoodwink you already.'

'On the contrary, he has convinced me that he's in need of care and affection. Unless he is treated sympathetically his asthma attacks will increase both in number and severity,' she flared. 'Anyone with a grain of common sense would understand that,' she added contemptuously.

'Well, well! Who would have thought that such a demure young lady could be such a hell-cat,' he gibed. He licked his full red lips as if amused. His stance, legs set wide apart, chin thrust out, eyes bold and challenging, was masculine and aggressive.

Kate turned away, shaking with anger.

It was obvious to her that this wasn't the first time that Mathew had been the butt of his elder brother's savage bullying. From the look on Brynmor's face she knew he was challenging her to stop him.

It was clear why Mathew was so anxious for her to stay on at Machen Mawr. He wanted someone to protect him from Brynmor.

'If you ever touch him again I shall complain to your father and acquaint him with what you are doing,' she told Brynmor furiously, her colour rising.

'Will you, indeed!'

As Brynmor crossed the room to where she stood, Kate felt frozen to the spot, afraid he was going to assault her as he had his brother. She could smell his powerful body odour, feel the heat emanating from him, but she clenched her hands until the nails dug deep into her palms and stood her ground.

'I most certainly shall,' she retorted, her eyes icy as they met his.

'I don't like being threatened,' he snarled.

'Then you'd better behave yourself.'

'And you'd better remember your place . . . Nanny!'

'Come Mathew, it's late, time you were in bed.' Keeping her head high and her back very straight, Kate walked over to the door and held it open. Ignoring Brynmor, she escorted Mathew upstairs, her hand resting comfortingly on his shoulder.

'Will you come and say goodnight to me after I'm in bed?' he asked hopefully.

'Of course,' promised Kate as she set the candle down on top of the chest of drawers.

'You will come back?'

'In five minutes?'

She stood by the window in her own room, staring out into the autumn darkness, trying to calm the turbulence within her as she waited for Mathew to get ready for bed. Brynmor was a bully. Morgan Edwards must know this but obviously was not prepared to do anything about it. Perhaps he regarded it as being manly! He certainly seemed to hold his elder son in high esteem. She suddenly remembered his words: 'Wait until you have met Brynmor before making up your mind about staying.'

94

Now there was something ominous about them.

She looked round the well-appointed bedroom, with its floral carpet, velvet drapes and four-poster bed. She had never known such luxury! It was almost as large as Lady Helen's bedroom at Bramwood Hall. To give all this up, before she had managed to find David, would be very rash, she decided, wrestling with her own conflicting thoughts.

The only drawback was Brynmor. But then, nothing was ever perfect, she reminded herself, so it was no good sighing for the moon. All she had to do was avoid him as much as possible. He was a sadistic bully, the same as her Uncle Charlie, and she had managed to handle him. The secret was not to let bullies know how frightened you were. That was where Mathew failed. The poor child was petrified. Brynmor knew this and used it to his own advantage. She had seen the same vicious gleam in Charlie's eyes when he was tormenting someone weaker than himself.

She shivered. She'd always made allowances for Charlie because he was simple. Brynmor was astute and shrewd which probably meant that he could be even more devious and cruel. She was sure he wasn't used to being defied and for that reason alone he would try to retaliate in some way.

If Brynmor worked in Pontypool, and he was as industrious as his father and Mrs Price claimed, then he must be away from the house a great deal of the time, Kate consoled herself. With any luck, he would forget all about their spat and in future she would take care to avoid him and make sure Mathew did as well.

Hopefully he would leave them both alone now that he knew she wasn't frightened of him, she reasoned. Bullies like Brynmor only kept up their tirade when they knew they had power over their victim.

More than likely it was the way he treated his workmen, believing they dare not retaliate for fear of dismissal and then was surprised when they rose up in revolt.

With a sigh she remembered that the reason David had been called home was because of trouble at Fforbrecon colliery. Probably it was all settled and he was back at Bramwood Hall, she thought, as she went to say goodnight to Mathew.

Mathew was in bed, lying hunched up on his knees, his face buried in the pillow.

'You can't be very comfortable like that,' Kate murmured as she straightened the bedclothes.

'I'm all right.'

'Lie down straight and see if you can touch the bottom of the bed with your toes. It will make you grow taller!'

'I don't want to.'

Slowly he straightened out in the bed.

'Why are you crying, Mathew?' asked Kate when she caught sight of his tear-stained face.

'I thought you'd forgotten about coming back,' he sniffed with a muffled sob.

'I was waiting for you to undress.'

'I've been in bed for ages.'

He sounded so forlorn that her heart went out to him. Her doubts about staying were wiped from her mind as she smoothed his brow and calmed him.

Kate sat by Mathew's bed for almost half an hour, holding his hand and talking to him until he finally fell asleep. Gently she released his fingers from her own and tucked in the bedclothes round his thin little body before extinguishing the candle and tiptoeing away to her own bed.

12

Olwen Price took an immediate liking to Kate Stacey.

'There's nice it is to have another woman around the place,' she remarked to Glynis over and over again. 'The change in that young Mathew is a joy to see.'

'You said she was nothing but an upstart when she first came here,' Glynis reminded her.

She thought Kate looked just like the picture on the chocolate box the Mistress had given her the Christmas before she had died. The chocolates had lasted only until the New Year but the painting on the cover of a beautiful girl, with jet black ringlets falling on to her milk-white shoulders, had entranced Glynis and she had treasured the box ever since.

'I admit I was taken aback at first,' Mrs Price agreed primly.

'You mean her coming right out of the blue without a word of warning.'

'That and arriving in the middle of the night.'

'Bit of a shock, like!'

'It took a bit of getting used to, I must admit.'

'She's nice though,' murmured Glynis.

'She'll do,' Mrs Price admitted grudgingly.

Kate's arrival had needed some getting used to. Mrs Price had been struggling for ages to keep the place going, with only Glynis and Sara, the daily woman, as regular helpers, and then suddenly Kate Stacey had appeared and started organizing everything as if she was in charge!

Anyone who could bring a spot of happiness into young Mathew's life was acceptable as far as she was concerned. It had broken her heart to see the way he had taken his mother's death. No amount of tempting him with his favourite foods seemed to make any difference to his flagging spirits. It had been as if he was wasting away before their eyes.

Since Kate Stacey had been in the house there had been a tremendous change for the better. Mathew's appetite was still poor for a young boy but at least he was attempting to eat what was on his plate instead of pushing it to one side and leaving it. He was more cheerful, too. Once or twice she had actually heard him laughing. And he didn't mope around the house as he had done. Nor did he spend as much time in her kitchen.

She missed his company but it was good to see him riding out in the trap or being taken for a walk. When they returned his eyes would be bright and there would be a spring in his step and colour in his cheeks.

He'd never be half the man his brother was, of course, but then Brynmor was cast from a different mould.

Brynmor might have his father's dark eyes and hair but for all that he took after his maternal grandfather.

Olwen Price could remember the first time she had ever seen Rhys Carew. She had been almost thirteen when she'd started work at Pwll-du. He'd been a formidable-looking man with his full set of whiskers and piercing dark eyes. She had never seen anyone so broad in the shoulders. And he'd had a great paunch to match. Rhys Carew was Master and expected to be obeyed. When he roared out an order everyone jumped.

He'd thought the world of his daughter. That was why when Myfanwy had married Morgan Edwards he had insisted that she should accompany her to Machen Mawr.

'I know I can rely on you, Olwen Price, to see my Myfanwy is properly looked after,' he had boomed, his hand on her shoulder. 'It will be a home for the rest of your life.'

As a young, lonely widow, having lost her husband Llewellyn at the Battle of Waterloo four years earlier, she had complied.

She had performed her duties loyally. She would defy anyone to say different. She had nursed Myfanwy through both her pregnancies and been at her side when she was dying. She had done everything in her power to make her life as easy as possible.

'Myfanwy was a proud beauty when she was a girl,' Mrs Price confided in Kate as they sat in her parlour enjoying a cup of tea. 'She had big brown eyes, thick lashes and dark, glossy hair. And she had the most perfect oval face you've ever seen. Just like a cameo.'

'So it was after Mathew was born that she went into a decline?'

'That's right. She never really picked up after her lying-in. Lost all her looks. Her hair went lank and her face became haggard,' Mrs Price sighed as she refilled their cups.

'Was Mathew a troublesome baby?'

'I suppose that had a lot to do with it. He was difficult over feeding and cried such a lot at night that he kept the whole house awake. It seemed to wear her down. The slightest exertion tired her out and she spent more and more time resting in her room. Sometimes she'd stay there all day!'

Enjoying a cup of tea together each afternoon became a regular practice and Mrs Price confided more and more in Kate as their friendship strengthened.

Kate learned that because Myfanwy was so often indisposed, more and more responsibility had fallen on Mrs Price. She learned of the subterfuges Mrs Price had resorted to in her attempt to keep from Myfanwy even the slightest whisper of anything that might upset her.

Because of Brynmor it had been difficult.

'Brynmor was a problem from the moment he could walk,' Mrs Price explained, shaking her grey head regretfully.

'In what way?'

'Whatever he demanded he was given.'

'Spoilt and indulged!'

'He grew up thinking he owned the world. At fifteen he was the terror of the neighbourhood.' She paused and wiped the corner of her eye with her apron. 'Perhaps if I hadn't tried to shield him, matters would have been nipped in the bud, but I couldn't bear to think how upset my Miss Myfanwy would be if she ever heard of the scrapes he got himself into.'

Kate's attention was captured. For the moment she forgot that she was waiting for the chance to ask Olwen Price about Myfanwy's friend Helen and whether she had known Helen's brother, David.

'Covering up for Brynmor led him to believe that I was willing to condone anything he might do,' Mrs Price confided.

'You probably were, up to a point.'

'I suppose so, but I drew the line when he started pestering the girls who worked here. As soon as I found out what was going on I refused to have any young maids living in. For their own sakes, you understand!'

'So what happened?'

'They soon grew tired of the long walk night and morning, especially in winter when it was dark and the roads icy or snow-bound. One by one they left, until in the end it was difficult to run things properly.'

'Glynis lives in, doesn't she?' Kate murmured.

'Well, yes, but that's different.'

'Oh?' Kate's eyebrows rose questioningly.

'She's my niece, see. And she's not too bright.' Olwen Price tapped her head significantly.

'That's very sad!'

'I put it down to the fact that my sister was in her forties when Glynis was born,' explained Mrs Price.

'And her mother died when she was born?'

'Oh no! Glynis was going on fourteen when her mother died. There was no one but me to look after her so I thought that as she was strong and healthy, she might as well come and help out here as go anywhere else.'

100

'Where you could keep an eye on her!'

'Indeed!'

'And you've had no problems from Brynmor?'

'She sleeps in the room right next to mine on the top floor where I know she's safe.'

As the weather had turned dull and drizzly, Kate took to spending more and more time with Olwen Price, encouraging her to reminisce, hoping she would talk about Myfanwy's childhood and perhaps mention Helen and David at the same time. Mostly, though, Olwen Price talked about what it had been like at Machen Mawr after Myfanwy had died.

'It was as if a lamp had gone out,' Olwen Price said sadly. 'The place wasn't the same. The Master had no interest in what was happening in the house. As long as his meals were on the table and there was a clean change of clothes to hand, that was all that mattered.'

'But surely he was concerned about Mathew?'

'At first. He even took him out and about, but it didn't last.'

'Mathew seems to be frightened of him.'

'He's happiest when he's here in the kitchen with me. Likes to talk about his mother, see, and his father can't put up with that.'

'And Brynmor? Did he grieve?'

'Not really! He was too busy learning all there was to know about japanning. He went off to Pontypool most days. People felt sorry for him, knowing he had just lost his mother, so they were willing to answer his questions. Some even offered him a job. He'd only stay a few weeks though and then he'd move on. Folks thought he was restless because he was grieving. It wasn't that at all. He was studying their methods, see! He used to make notes about the different ways they did things. Back here, he'd be up in his room carrying out all sorts of tests. You should have seen the mess he made! Nasty smells, too! He hated it when I cleared any of it away!' She sighed expressively. 'It paid off, mind you! In the end

101

he knew more about japanning than any of them. Then he persuaded his father to set him up on his own.'

'And has it worked out well?'

'Indeed it has! His achievements have been outstanding.'

'You mean he runs his own business?'

'It's as if he's combined the flair of old Rhys Carew with that of his father plus a spark of genius of his own,' Mrs Price exclaimed.

Kate's interest quickened at the mention of Rhys Carew's name. She was far more interested in hearing about him than she was about Brynmor and encouraged Mrs Price to talk about the past.

She even offered to do some of the mending when she learned it was the job Mrs Price disliked most.

'We can talk while I'm working,' she smiled, sitting by the kitchen window. 'Tell me more about Rhys Carew,' she invited as she deftly replaced the buttons on one of Mathew's shirts.

'Myfanwy's father. Well, he was one of the greatest ironmasters in Blaenafon. A very forward-thinking man. Do you know, he was one of the first to use coal instead of wood to fuel his ironworks.'

She paused, pushing aside the apple pie she was making and sitting down in one of the high-backed wooden armchairs.

'Those were great days, I can tell you.'

'Was he a good boss?'

'Men were proud to work for him.'

'And you say that Morgan Edwards once worked for him?' asked Kate, picking up another shirt to mend.

'Indeed, he did!' Olwen Price's eyes misted with tears. 'I can remember when Morgan Edwards hadn't two halfpennies to rub together. Lived in a terrace house no better than the one I was brought up in.'

'Really?'

'Rhys Carew was quick to spot that he had a feeling for the iron, see. Encouraged him. Made him foreman.

102

Treated him like the son he never had. Worked him hard, mind you, but look at his reward! In next to no time, when most young men of his age were still serving their time, Morgan Edwards was in charge and running things.'

'And then he met Myfanwy and fell in love with her,' Kate added dreamily.

'There's lovely you make it sound,' Mrs Price sighed.

'Why? Wasn't it like that?'

'People thought Rhys Carew was out of his mind marrying his lovely Myfanwy off to a man who worked for him. Rhys Carew ignored them all. It was what he wanted.'

'The two most precious things in his life, his ironworks and his daughter, united.'

'Mind you,' Olwen sighed, overcome by nostalgia, 'it wasn't all plain sailing. Morgan Edwards had a lot to learn.'

'You mean before he fitted in socially.'

'And in business. There was fierce competition. The most famous ironworks in South Wales, you see, are right here on our own doorstep. As long ago as 1827 they had seven of the biggest blast furnaces ever seen.'

'Those must be the ones I saw my first day here,' Kate shuddered, recalling the odorous fumes and the huge glowing furnaces.

'They belong to a pair of Yorkshiremen: Joseph Bailey and his younger brother, Crawshay. A ruthless pair, I can tell you! In my opinion, the only good thing they've ever done was to build a tramway that connects the ironworks at Nantyglo with the canal at Llanfoist. And they constructed that more for their own benefit than anyone else's. Out to make a fortune those two, see!'

'Those furnaces were what I have always imagined hell must be like!' affirmed Kate.

'Lots of the men who have to work there would agree with that,' Mrs Price admitted, 'especially those who work for the Baileys.'

'They aren't popular?'

'Most of the men hate them. Crawshay and his brother know this and that is why they built those two monstrous stone towers up behind their house. You must have noticed them. If ever there is trouble brewing at their works in Nantyglo they can take refuge there, see!'

'And have they ever had to use them?' Kate asked, biting off an end of cotton.

'Many times! The "Scotch Cattle" used to go on the rampage around there!'

'The what!'

'Bands of men dressed up in the skins and horns of animals. They would tear through Nantyglo terrorizing any men they decided were blacklegs. Mind you, we didn't have any trouble of that sort around Blaenafon. Rhys Carew would never had stood for it.'

'The men who worked for Rhys Carew liked him, did they?' asked Kate.

'Some did, some didn't. They had to admit, though, he was always ready to listen to ways of improving things. Like renting his workers a plot of land so that they could build themselves cottages.'

'That sounds a wonderful idea.'

'It was. Put to him by Robert Owen. Within ten years the place had grown into a tidy-sized village. Lovely it was with all the trees. Folks had gardens where they could grow their own vegetables and there was a big village green shaded by oaks and beeches. He built them a market-house that could also be used as a chapel and it had a fine burial ground laid out beside it.'

'Was Robert Owen Lady Helen's father?' questioned Kate, her pulse racing at the mere mention of the name Owen.

'Oh bless you, no! The Owen I'm talking about came from Montgomeryshire. He was full of ideas to try and get better conditions for the workers, but none of them seem to meet with much success. The last time I heard of him he was trying to get all the workers to form a co-operative. I don't know what difference he thinks it will make. Workers is workers and bosses is bosses. Always has been and always will be.'

'Some bosses are better to work for than others,' Kate said mildly.

'And some folks work better than others,' rejoined Olwen Price, 'so how can you expect the good ones to throw their lot in with those who couldn't care less?'

Kate picked up her sewing again, listening with only half an ear to what Mrs Price was saying. It was David's family she was interested in, but it was some time before Mrs Price got back on to that subject.

When she did, it was as if a dam had burst.

Everything Kate had longed to hear seemed to pour from her lips.

'My word, Tudor ap Owen would be taken aback if he heard his name linked with that Robert Owen,' she said at last.

'Tudor ap Owen, that's Helen's father?'

'Yes, and a man of high standing around these parts. One of the real gentry, wealthy and highly respected. He owns Fforbrecon and he farms as well. Acres and acres of land he has around Govilon. Most of the sheep you see on Blorenge belongs to him.'

'He must be getting on in years now.'

'Outlived old Rhys Carew! I suppose Miss Helen's young brother, David, will step into his shoes when . . .'

'Did you know David?' Kate interrupted, trying to quell the excitement in her voice.

'No!' Mrs Price shook her head. 'He was just a child when Miss Myfanwy married Master. He'll be grown up by now, of course.'

'He used to visit Lady Helen quite frequently when I was at Bramwood Hall,' Kate told her, eager to talk about David.

'There now! I don't suppose I would know him if I fell over him.'

105

Kate sensed Mrs Price was not really interested in David but that no longer mattered. She had already told her enough to give her hope. Knowing Fforbrecon colliery was close by, she could plan what to do next, confident that she and David would meet again before very long.

13

During her first weeks at Machen Mawr, Kate spent most of her time with Mathew. He flourished from her undivided attention, striving to please her in whatever work or pastime she suggested.

On fine days, they walked a great deal, exploring the nearby countryside with its strident contrasts of green valleys and pit-scarred mountains. When it rained, they read together or he played the pianoforte and the regular practice improved his skill considerably.

Once Mathew went back to school, Kate looked for other ways to occupy her day. He left the house just after eight each morning to ride with his father into Brynmawr to Dr Howell's academy and it was almost six in the evening before he returned home. When she learned from Mrs Price that no spring cleaning had been undertaken, Kate felt this omission should be rectified even though it was now September.

Her years of training as scullery maid at The Manor had given her a thorough grounding in the right way of doing things. With Morgan Edwards' permission she arranged for Mrs Price to hire some additional daily help and she made sure they all accounted for themselves well.

Kate supervised as curtains were taken down and washed, carpets lifted, taken outside and hung over the clothes line where they were thoroughly beaten. Upholstery was brushed and sponged, wooden furniture polished, ornaments washed and put back on newly polished shelves.

On fine days the windows were opened wide to let in fresh air. Soon the house had a sparkle and freshness that was apparent to even the least discerning eye.

Determined to reorganize the running of Machen Mawr, she studied the general routine, comparing it with the way things had been done at Bramwood Hall. When she was ready to make changes she introduced them gradually, talking them through with Mrs Price, securing her approval and winning the older woman's support.

Morgan Edwards seemed well satisfied with the way things were turning out. He frequently praised Kate on the smooth running of his home. It was a long time since a woman had graced his table, and he found himself looking forward to his evening meal and the chance to talk to her.

There were exceptions to the air of contentment that otherwise seemed to pervade.

When Brynmor was at home the atmosphere underwent a subtle change. Mathew became edgy and would dissolve into tears at the slightest provocation and frequently this made Morgan irritable and impatient.

For her part, Kate sensed that Brynmor was watching her, waiting to strike.

On the surface he was polite, but whenever she chanced to glance at him there was a calculating gleam in his small, dark eyes and a curious, leering twist to his thick lips.

She avoided him as much as possible. When he invited her to visit his works and see for herself the wondrous process he had perfected for Japanware, she declined, saying that she was too busy reorganizing things at Machen Mawr, an excuse that sounded feeble even to her own ears.

Once the novelty of her new situation wore off a little, Kate began to lie awake at night in her four-poster bed, fretting for news of David. She considered writing to Helen but was afraid Sir George might intercept her letter.

If only she knew how far it was from Machen Mawr to David's home. Morgan Edwards or Mrs Price would be able to tell her, of course, but some inner caution kept her from mentioning her close friendship with David.

Kate went hot and cold at the thought that David might agree to marriage with Penelope Vaughan. Surely he wouldn't take such a step . . . not now! Not after they had lain in each other's arms, and he had told her how much he loved her and whispered sweet words of endearment. He must know she wouldn't have given herself to him so completely unless she believed his feelings for her were as deep as her own for him. He had been her first and only lover.

No one would ever take his place.

Some nights, when her need for David became intolerable, she envisaged leaving Machen Mawr and making her way to the valley that lay between Coity and Blorenge to see if she could find Fforbrecon colliery.

In her fantasy, she could almost feel his arms around her, hear his exclamation of delight when she arrived so unexpectedly. He would declare his love, kiss her tenderly, and promise that they'd never be parted again.

Then he would introduce her to his father and announce they were to be married. There would be no awkward questions about her background or where they had met, just welcoming smiles and joyous acceptance.

To banish such thoughts, Kate concentrated on the changes she was making at Machen Mawr.

'Every day there seems to be another innovation,' puffed Olwen Price. 'The years I've been working in this kitchen and never thought to change things,' she added as they took a well-earned rest.

'If you don't like the new arrangement we can always move everything back as it was.'

'Oh, no! It makes the place look better as it is now.'

'I think you'll find it easier when you're cooking.'

'Bound to do so. I can reach everything so much easier.'

'And you won't be standing with your back to the range when you're making pastry on the table.'

'That's true. So me and Glynis won't bump into each other all the time when she is stirring something over the fire.'

'You'll be able to see if any of the pans are about to boil over without having to turn round.'

Every room in the house benefited from Kate's attention to detail. She became so absorbed in these changes that at first she failed to notice how quiet and withdrawn Mathew had become. When she did, she dismissed it as being fatigue after his long days at school.

Tired out herself after her exertions, Kate slept heavily until one night she was woken by someone tugging at the bedcovers. It was Mathew and he was sobbing uncontrollably.

Sitting up in bed, she gathered him in her arms, soothing him with whispered admonishments, trying to discover the reason he was so upset.

It was some time before he was coherent enough to tell her that he'd had a bad nightmare. Only then did she learn that he was being teased and bullied at school.

Knowing how timid and nervous he was, her heart ached for him. She held his trembling body close until his sobbing ceased and the convulsive shudders that wracked him finally eased. He was cold and shivering so she wrapped the blanket and quilt around him, cuddling him until he was asleep. As she lay there wondering if it would waken him if she carried him back to his own bed, she drifted off to sleep herself.

When the early morning household sounds roused her, she realized that Mathew was still cradled in her arms. Without comment, she sent him back to his own room to get dressed.

Two nights later he repeated his middle of the night visit.

'I've had another nightmare, Kate.'

'It's over now you're awake,' she told him, trying to calm his fears.

'It'll come again when I close my eyes, I know it will,' he sobbed.

'No, it won't.'

'Can I come into your bed,' he begged. 'I'm cold.'

'Only for a minute or two, then.'

She held him close until his sobs abated.

'Off to your own bed now, Mathew.'

'Must I . . .'

'Come along and I'll tuck you in.'

Half an hour later, Kate was aware that he had crept back into her bed again. Still half asleep, she let him stay.

They were awakened next morning by Brynmor. He had entered the room very quietly and was standing by the side of the bed before Kate realized he was there.

'What are you doing here?' She sat up with a gasp of alarm.

Aware that Brynmor's gaze was fixed on the open neck of her nightdress, she pulled the sheet high up to her chin, her face flushing with embarrassment.

'So this is what you get up to,' he leered, his dark eyes gleaming as he looked down at Mathew still curled up asleep. 'Does my father know what is going on?' he queried, raising his dark brows questioningly.

'Mathew had a nightmare, he needed comforting,' she told him sharply.

'Lots of us get nightmares!' He ran the tip of his tongue over his thick lips. 'It's an interesting cure.'

'Get out . . . you had no right coming in here in the first place,' she ordered, her voice quivering with anger.

'When neither you nor Mathew came down to breakfast I came to find out why,' he told her, watching her reaction. 'It is almost nine o'clock.'

'I don't believe you!' Kate stared at him in dismay. She was usually sitting down to breakfast by half-past seven.

'It's quite true!' His eyes narrowed. 'Fortunately for you, my father left early this morning and asked me to take Mathew to school.' He dragged the cowering child

111

from under the covers and, placing the toe of his boot against the small of Mathew's back, sent him crashing through the doorway.

Kate bit the inside of her cheek, struggling to control her anger at his vicious treatment of Mathew.

'Finding you cosseting him in your bed is hardly the sort of behaviour I expected from a Nanny,' he taunted with arrogant amusement.

'Mathew was frightened . . . he needed reassurance.'

Even as she made the explanation, Kate felt resentment rising inside her. There was nothing for her to make excuses about, she had done nothing wrong. And, even if she had overstepped her role as Nanny, there was no need for her to account for her actions to Brynmor. He wasn't her employer.

Morgan Edwards had hired her to look after Mathew and to take his mother's place. Taking a child into her own bed to try and allay his fears after a bad nightmare was exactly what any mother would have done in the circumstances, Kate told herself.

Brynmor was out to make trouble for her, but she couldn't understand why. Surely he couldn't be jealous of Mathew! The child was puny and undersized for his age, fraught with nerves and no match at all for a brother who was ten years older and already a businessman in his own right.

'Mathew was frightened,' she repeated, her voice firm, her shoulders squared, her dark head held proudly.

'I get frightened, too,' Brynmor answered in a soft, insidious tone. Leaning forward he seized her wrist in a vice-like grip.

Kate tried to pull free but his hand clenched tighter until she was squirming with pain.

'Next time I'm frightened, can I creep into your bed?' he asked suggestively.

'Get out of my room and stay away from me or I'll tell your father,' Kate stormed, her blue eyes blazing, her anger so roused that it overcame her fear of him.

'If you do then I shall tell him about Mathew being in here and see that he is whipped!'

'Don't be ridiculous! Your father wouldn't punish him.'

'Are you sure? My father wants Mathew to grow up strong and resilient. The thought of him coming crying to you would make him very angry. Whipping turns a weakling into a man . . . or didn't you know that?'

'You are wrong . . . quite wrong! In Mathew's case it would probably bring on an asthma attack.'

'A fine excuse!'

'Don't you realize he is still missing his mother . . .' she paused, fighting back the sour taste in her throat as she became aware that Brynmor was regarding her with a contemptuous smile. She felt the flush rising in her cheeks as she realized she was letting him provoke her and saw the mocking gleam in his dark eyes.

'I hope you can remember all that when the time comes,' he warned.

'When what time comes?' She regarded him blankly, unable to understand the direction his mind was taking. He stood there, a tall, domineering young buck, one hand behind his back, the thumb of the other tucked inside the pocket of his striped red and blue silk waistcoat. The scented oil he had used to control his thick, dark hair and mutton-chop whiskers wafted towards her, sweetly sickening. She noticed that his smooth-fitting black jacket with its long, wide lapels, had been padded to emphasize the width of his shoulders. His black trousers were so tightly tailored that they outlined the shape of his thighs. Even his cravat was flamboyant. He had fastened it in a Duke knot and then weighted the end of it to ensure it hung in a precise line.

As she became aware of what a dandy Brynmor was, so her fear of him ebbed away. There was no cause for her to feel guilty over what had happened. She had been hired to be a mother substitute, she told herself again, and

113

she was doing nothing wrong in reassuring and comforting Mathew.

'You deserve to be reprimanded for this,' he persisted. He licked his full lips. 'I know the punishment I should like to see meted out.'

She saw him for what he was, a polished version of her Uncle Charlie. All men are brothers stripped of their frock coats and finery, she thought scornfully. He was cunning and wily as Charlie had been and from now on she would be on her guard.

'I wish to get dressed, Brynmor,' she stated icily.

'Am I stopping you?' He grinned sardonically.

'I can hardly do so while you are still in my bedroom.'

He gave a deprecating shrug and turned towards the door.

Kate waited until she was quite sure he had gone before she threw back the covers and slid out of bed. Her legs felt like jelly as she crossed the room and locked the door.

The incident troubled her for the rest of the day.

Mathew, too, seemed subdued when he returned home from school. Kate wondered whether she should talk to him about what had happened that morning or whether it was better to say nothing and treat it as something of no consequence. So much depended on what Brynmor told his father.

When she learned that Brynmor would not be home for dinner that evening, because he was attending a meeting in Newport, Kate decided to put the matter out of her mind.

Later, when she went up to say goodnight to Mathew, he kept his eyes tightly closed, pretending to be asleep. She sat down on the side of his bed, stroking his hair, wishing he would talk to her. She wanted to assure him that he had done nothing wrong and that he shouldn't be upset by anything Brynmor had said.

Since he refused to converse with her she began talking in a low, gentle voice, hoping that some of the things she

114

said would make sense to him and help soothe away his fears.

Before she went to bed herself, Kate went along to Mathew's room again. As she tucked him in she sensed he was not asleep. As she closed his bedroom door, she heard a muffled sob and it took every vestige of self-control not to go back, gather him up in her arms and carry him to her bed.

Kate had no idea how long she had been asleep when she woke to the sound of her bedroom door being opened. She lay still, thinking that it was probably better if she let Mathew think she was asleep.

The bed creaked as a body slid beneath the covers.

Suddenly she was fully awake, her skin crawling with fear. It wasn't Mathew who had climbed into her bed!

Before she could utter a sound a hand was clamped over her mouth.

'Not who you thought it was, eh!' Brynmor sniggered.

Kate struggled violently but she was no match for his strength.

'Now it's your turn to have a nightmare!'

Keeping one hand over her mouth, he ripped her nightdress from the throat downwards and she shuddered as he groped at her. As she started to cry out, he whipped the pillow from beneath her head and crushed it down on her face. She struggled desperately but he held it there until she was almost suffocated, until all the flight had gone from her.

She lay limp and inert after he removed it, too weak to fight him off as he squeezed and fondled her, invading every crevice of her body.

His mouth savagely covered hers, silencing her feeble moans. His sexual appetite was voracious and unhealthy and she felt sick with horror at the things he did.

She wanted to die.

When he left just before dawn, her entire body was bruised, battered and bleeding, her mind dazed with shame at the way she had been treated.

14

A million thoughts whirled round in Kate's mind as she stood by the bedroom window staring out across the valley to where countless chimney stacks rent the glowing sky, their smoke a yellowish grey pall against the red backcloth. On the skyline, she could see the great winding wheels of the coal mines, the slag heaps alongside them desecrating the hillsides like enormous warts.

What sort of place was this, she shuddered. Men, women and children descending into the bowels of the earth every day of their lives, seldom seeing the sun or feeling the wind and rain on their faces.

Entire families slaving in the intense heat of furnaces where a splash of molten metal could sear and disfigure or maim them for life. Men labouring in such a fierce glare that it blinded them. Children who could barely walk and talk being taken into these hell-holes to work, older children and women being used like animals to drag heavy carts.

Was it any wonder if they grew up to be sadists, with minds as twisted as their bodies.

Yet Brynmor had not been raised like that, she reminded herself.

The vile things that he had done to her would remain for ever in her memory. She felt so humiliated and disgraced that she wanted to hide from the world. Even take her own life if that was necessary.

She looked round the room wondering how she could achieve such an outcome. When she had been a child she had heard her grandmother talking about a woman who had tried to end her life by drinking poison. All it had done was to make her violently sick and leave her permanently weak in the head.

Uncle Charlie had told her about a man who had hanged himself from a tree with a length of rope. 'Swung there in the wind just like a scarecrow,' he'd told her over and over again. It had frightened her so much that for weeks afterwards she had peered up into every tree she passed expecting to see a body swinging there.

She didn't have any rope but perhaps she could tie the sheets together and string herself up to one of the beams and then jump off the edge of the bed. The idea struck her as ludicrous and a hysterical giggle rose to her lips. What purpose would it serve if she did take her own life, she reasoned.

She didn't want to die!

Resolutely she straightened her shoulders. Why should she give Brynmor the gratification of knowing he'd upset her so much. He'd only gloat with satisfaction and subject his next victim to even greater obscenities. The episode was over and she'd make sure it never happened again.

Once she found David all this would seem like a nightmare, nothing more.

Instead of trying to hang herself it might make more sense if she knotted the sheets together so that she could climb out of the window and make her escape. That way she could put Machen Mawr and the whole incident behind her and never see Brynmor again.

Or would that also afford him pleasure, inflate his feeling of power, make him even more sadistic, she wondered.

Her anger against Brynmor over what she had suffered at his hands made her all the more determined not to be intimidated by him.

If only she could reach David.

Perhaps what she ought to do was ask Olwen Price or Morgan Edwards to help her to find David.

She imagined herself walking up to the front door of his home and asking for him by name. The idea sent shivers of excitement through her.

She paced the room, considering all aspects of such a plan. Gradually her enthusiasm waned. What would happen if she went to David's home and discovered he wasn't there. Or, worse still, that he was planning to marry Penelope Vaughan, or had already made her his bride.

Angrily she pushed such thoughts away. How could she doubt David's love for her? They had lain together, united not just by sweet loving words but by the power of his body over hers.

But so had Brynmor lain with her, she shivered.

As the memory of how Brynmor's body had dominated hers, the way in which he had forced her to partake in obscene acts, came flooding back, she pulled frantically on the bell cord.

Glynis arrived, her hair straggling from under her cap, her sacking apron askew, eyes wide, her mouth agape.

'Is something wrong, Miss Kate?' she panted. 'I was cleaning out the grates.' She held out her hands which were black with coal dust.

'I need hot water, several big jugs full, so that I can take a bath.'

'You mean right now . . . before I lay Master's breakfast?' Glynis gasped, her eyes widening still more.

'Yes! Right away. Hurry!'

While she waited for the water to be brought upstairs, Kate paced the room. She felt sick. Her senses were swimming, her stomach heaving. She fought back the nausea, shuddering at the bitterness of the bile that rose repeatedly into her throat.

How could Brynmor have treated her so despicably, she fumed. Uncle Charlie's lasciviousness melted into mere aberration in comparison. She felt unclean. She needed to scrub away every trace of Brynmor's touch from her body before she could look people in the eye again.

Would she ever be able to face David knowing her body had been so sullied? How would he react? Would he take her in his arms and comfort her with gentle words or would he consider her defiled, she wondered.

She held her head in her hands. How could she have such doubts! David loved her. He would teach Brynmor Edwards a lesson he would never forget, she thought savagely.

As soon as Glynis arrived with the first jug of water, Kate dragged out the zinc hip bath from the cupboard and placed it in the centre of the room.

After the final jugful was poured in, Kate locked her bedroom door, stripped off every stitch of clothing and submerged her bruised body. The comforting warmth was soothing. When the water began to cool, she sat up and scrubbed herself vigorously until her skin tingled.

As she dried herself briskly and began to dress, her confidence returned. She chose a dress of blue and white gingham with a broad, white collar hoping her demure, pristine appearance would keep her shameful secret hidden from everyone else in the house.

She studied her reflection in the dressing-table mirror, running a forefinger over her brow, anxiously scrutinizing her face for any change in her looks as a result of the ordeal she had endured. There was none. Her blue eyes were sparkling clear, her skin as smooth and soft as it had always been. Not a single tell-tale wrinkle marred her cheeks.

She brushed out her hair, tying back the dark curls into a coil behind her ears. Only the pallor of her cheeks conveyed the slightest hint that anything was amiss.

Morgan Edwards was already in the hall pulling on his outdoor clothes when Kate went downstairs.

'Good morning.' His greeting was brief but cordial.

When Mathew told her that Brynmor had gone to Newport and probably wouldn't be back until the next day, her spirits soared. A day's breathing space and she would be over the trauma, no one need know her secret.

She had counted without Olwen Price.

'You're not intending to have a bath every morning, I

trust,' Olwen Price asked sharply, intercepting Kate as she was on her way upstairs after dinner to tuck Mathew in bed.

'Young Glynis is rushed off her feet as it is first thing in the morning trying to clean out the grates, light the fires and lay the breakfast all before half past seven,' Mrs Price persisted.

'I'm sorry if it inconvenienced you,' Kate said with a light shrug.

'It did that all right. It put everything back for the rest of the day,' Olwen retorted, smoothing down the front of her crisply starched white apron.

'I won't do it again,' Kate said quietly, biting her lip and turning away.

'Well, I'm glad that's settled.' Olwen Price patted her bun of grey hair in a satisfied manner. 'Nothing like speaking out and coming to the point, I always say. Much better to set things right than bottle them up and brood about them. Once a thing is out in the open it doesn't seem half the problem it was. Perhaps you'd better tell me what else is biting you,' she added, huffily.

'Biting me?'

'You've not been near the kitchen all day. I thought we were supposed to be friends!' She laid a hand on Kate's arm. 'I'm just going to take a nightcap. Why don't you join me?'

Kate hesitated, torn between guarding her secret and the solace she knew she would find in pouring out her story into the older woman's sympathetic ear.

'I must see to Mathew,' she murmured evasively, continuing on up the stairs.

'There's no hurry. You know where to find me. Glynis has already gone up to bed so we won't be disturbed,' Olwen Price added meaningfully.

Kate took her time in settling Mathew. He seemed quiet and withdrawn, not disposed to chatter to her about the day's events as he sometimes did.

120

'What's wrong, Mathew? Are you worried about something?'

His lips tightened and he pulled away when she tried to stroke his hair.

'Do you want me to leave your candle?' she asked as she tucked in his blankets.

When he didn't reply she bent and kissed him on the brow. 'Good night then, Mathew. Don't forget, if you have a nightmare, come along to my room.'

As she reached the doorway she heard his muffled sob and went back to his bedside.

'I came in last night,' he whimpered. 'Brynmor was there with you. . . .'

Her shocked gasp made him sob louder. She dropped on her knees, cradling him in her arms, her face hot with shame as she wondered what he had seen or heard. Rocking him to and fro she comforted both him and herself, reassuring him that he could come to her at any time.

She sat by his bed, holding his hand until his steady breathing confirmed that he was asleep, silently praying that in his innocence he had been unaware of what had been going on. Her legs were trembling when she finally crept from the room.

Halfway to her own room she remembered Olwen Price's invitation.

She needed something to calm her and a nightcap might be the very thing, she decided as she made her way down the back stairs.

'So you've condescended to come after all,' Olwen Price sniffed as she unlocked the corner cupboard in her room and reached for the whisky bottle.

'It took time to settle Mathew.'

'Given you up I had.' She peered more closely at Kate as she passed her drink to her. 'What's happened now? You've not looked yourself all day but at the moment you look all in.'

'Just tired.'

'Finding young Mathew a bit of a handful?'

'No, of course not. Mathew is a delight.' Kate took a long drink from her glass, gasping as the fire of the whisky caught the back of her throat.

'Take it slowly,' Olwen Price warned.

'I'll be all right in a minute.'

'Take your time. When you're ready, I'm listening,' murmured Olwen Price, her bright beady eyes narrowing speculatively.

'I don't know where to start.'

'At the beginning might be best.'

'I'm not even sure if I should be telling you,' Kate sighed. She twisted her handkerchief, rolling and unrolling the hem between thumb and forefinger, straightening the tiny square of lace-edged linen out on her lap and studying it as if expecting to find the answer written there.

'Here, let me fill up your glass again. Nothing like a drink to help loosen your tongue.'

Once Kate started the words flowed. Her feelings of hatred towards Brynmor, her disgust and revulsion over his obnoxious behaviour, and her fear in case he ever molested her like that again, were unleashed.

It was as if every emotion she had ever felt poured out, draining her until she could feel nothing except a great void inside her mind.

It was a confessional purging that left her exhausted but purified.

The relief of sharing her turmoil, together with a second glass of whisky, made her feel lightheaded.

'I think we'd better have a cup of strong tea after all that,' Olwen Price commented. 'I've never heard of such goings-on in my life! Not that I don't believe every word you've told me,' she added quickly. 'There have been plenty of wild tales about Brynmor and his carryings on, as I've already told you, but this . . . this is almost beyond belief.'

'You mustn't breathe a word. . . .'

'Master must be told. He's the one to deal with it and put a stop to such practices once and for all.'

'No, no! I told you in confidence. You gave me your promise.' Kate's voice rose hysterically as deep gulping sobs shook her body.

'There, there. I won't breathe a word to a living soul unless you say so.'

'You promise?'

'I still think Master should be told but if that's not the way you want things, then I won't try to force you.'

'No, no one must know. If this got around, just think how upset Mathew would be if he heard it being discussed.'

'Master could deal with Brynmor and hush it all up without anyone else being any the wiser.'

'No, you promised!' White-faced, Kate grabbed Olwen's arm.

'It's your decision.'

'Not a word to a living soul.'

'That's all very well but if you say nothing, that little toad, Brynmor, will think he's got away with such behaviour! And who knows what devilry he will get up to next time?'

'You mean I should think of others beside myself?'

'Indeed I do! Supposing he was to attack young Glynis!'

'He would have to go through your bedroom to get to her,' Kate reminded her.

'I wouldn't put it past him having his way with her some place other than the bedroom; animal, that he is. You think about it, Kate.'

15

Brynmor's persistent attentions haunted Kate.

She knew she ought to take Mrs Price's advice and tell Morgan Edwards but she couldn't bring herself to talk to him about such calamitous happenings.

She felt soiled. To have to reveal what was taking place and the strain she was under to a third person, and a man at that, would bring an even deeper shame. The very fact that she had let it go on for almost a month might make him think she condoned what was happening. He might even wonder if she had encouraged Brynmor! But it had to stop. She would go insane if it didn't.

She dreaded going to bed at night.

After the first time she had locked her bedroom door. She would never forget lying there as Brynmor rattled the door knob, calling her name in a hoarse whisper. She had trembled with fear when he put his shoulder to the door and tried to force the lock.

The following night when she went up to her room she found the key had vanished. She searched the floor and the landing outside, annoyed by her own carelessness that she'd left it in the door.

Later, when Brynmor had crept into her bed, he had shown her the key, laughing at her dismay. Then, as a form of punishment, he had used it to do unspeakable things to her.

How could she tell that to Morgan Edwards?

Brynmor was sick in his mind, there was no doubt about that. Mrs Price confirmed it. But would she speak out when it might cost her not only her job but her home as well?

Since he had taken to visiting her at night, Brynmor

had become more and more erratic in his behaviour. One minute he was moody and introspective, the next he would be making wild jests, teasing Mathew or boasting of his latest achievements.

Often he left the house before anyone was up in the morning and didn't return home until dinner was almost finished.

'Brynmor's work is his life,' Morgan Edwards would state proudly when explaining his elder son's absence or excusing his lateness in coming home. 'When he's involved in some new process everything else goes from his mind. He forgets the time of day, the time of year even.'

Kate wished he'd become so involved in some new product or invention that it would take his interest away from her.

Whenever he was in the house there was no escaping from his insolent stare. He seemed to be in every room she entered.

Desperate to be on her own, she left the house, taking the road that led to Nantyglo. She'd noticed, when driving out in the trap with Mathew, that before reaching the town there was a steep, narrow road, little more than a track, that seemed to wind upwards to the open hillside behind the rows of houses.

She climbed for almost twenty minutes, until she reached the crest of the ridge and could see right across to the other side of the valley.

Breathless, she looked for a sheltered spot where she could rest.

As she contemplated the arid view, she felt homesick. She thought with longing of the golden ripeness of the Wiltshire countryside in autumn, the fragrance of fruit-laden orchards, great purple clumps of Michaelmas daisies in the cottage gardens and walls covered by the glowing flame of Virginia creeper. So much colour. Here, everything was stunted and drab, shrouded in a brown haze from the ironworks or black dust from the coalmines.

Even the air had an acrid, sulphurous smell and the coarse tufted grass spiked through her dress.

Once I find David and can be with him, these grim, unfriendly surroundings will be forgotten, she told herself. She let her thoughts drift, remembering the magical moments at Bramwood Hall when she had been in David's arms and his lips had been on hers.

Even those sweet memories were besmirched. Brynmor's savage attacks dominated her thoughts and filled her with a sense of dread. She had to do something to stop him abusing her, she resolved. And as always when she began pinpointing in her mind how it had all started, her thoughts went back to the morning when she had overslept.

If only Morgan Edwards hadn't left the house early that morning, if only he hadn't asked Brynmor to take Mathew to school. If only Mrs Price had sent Glynis up to waken her. If only Brynmor hadn't come looking for Mathew.

So many 'If onlys'!

She still couldn't understand why Brynmor had decided to come to her bedroom to look for Mathew.

She shivered at the recollection. She had seen lust in a man's face before, but never accompanied by such an evil glint as there had been in Brynmor's eyes.

She bitterly regretted not having told Morgan Edwards right away about what had happened. She'd held back because of Brynmor's warning that Mathew would be severely punished because he'd been found in her bed. For that to happen just as Mathew was getting over his mother's death, and taking an interest in his school work, seemed so unfair. Kate couldn't bear to say or do anything that might undo all that, not now that he was so much more lively and sure of himself.

Seeing Mathew as happy and carefree as any normal boy of his age had lifted Morgan Edwards' spirits. In the few weeks she had been at Machen Mawr the grim lines that had been etched around his mouth and eyes

126

had faded. He no longer watched every move Mathew made, as if on tenterhooks in case something triggered off an asthma attack.

To undermine all this would have been unforgivable. Yet the cost to her own health and peace of mind, if she didn't complain about Brynmor, seemed a tremendous price to pay.

Her temples pounded.

She covered her eyes with her hands, wondering if she was letting her imagination magnify the night-time horrors she'd endured.

'No!' She sat bolt upright, shouting her denial aloud.

Her voice echoed down the valley before being thrown back in a mocking distortion.

The thought of Brynmor continuing to come to her room every night was abhorrent, something she could endure no longer. She shuddered, her skin crawling, at the memory of his hands on her body.

'No, no, no!' she muttered, clenching and unclenching her hands. Brynmor must be stopped. She refused to be trapped into giving in to his demands.

Her mind made up, she resolved to tell Morgan Edwards that very night. She would wait until Mathew was in bed so that there was no possibility of him overhearing the revolting story she had to relate.

She was sure that Morgan Edwards valued her presence and appreciated what she had done for Mathew. He would know how to deal with the situation. He would put a stop to Brynmor's nightly visits. Everything would return to normal.

And if he wouldn't believe her, what was she to do then? she wondered. He might even tell her to go, to leave Machen Mawr. A chill chased down her back. Well, better that than to be subjected to perpetual abuse and misery, she decided.

If she was dismissed then she'd waste no more time but go straight to David's home. He would take care of her.

A deep sigh escaped her as she remembered his tenderness and the sweetness of the love that had flowered between them. The few times when David had held her in his arms, whispering endearments, now seemed a lifetime away.

A lump came into her throat as the memories were unleashed. The hard knot inside her began to dissolve. She owed it to David as well as herself to put a stop to what was going on.

Kate took special care dressing for dinner that evening. She chose the most simple of the dresses Helen had given her, a grey silk one with a demure white lace collar.

She combed her hair into a soft coil in the nape of her neck, so that its shining blackness contrasted starkly against the creamy whiteness of her skin. As she tamed the unruly curls that framed her face, she leaned nearer to the mirror and frowned as she saw the dark shadows beneath her eyes, evidence of the harrowing, sleepless nights of recent weeks.

Brynmor was already seated when she arrived in the dining room. As she took her place at the table he gave her such a sharp, penetrating stare that she found herself flushing uncomfortably. It was as if he read her mind and knew what she intended to do.

She tried to ignore him, addressing her remarks either to Morgan Edwards or Mathew, but she felt so self-conscious that she found it difficult to eat.

After Glynis had cleared away the dessert dishes, Kate made her excuses, leaving the two men to enjoy their port while she saw Mathew to bed.

As she rose from her chair, a feeling of nausea swept over her. She clutched at the table. The room swam. A rushing in her ears and an overpowering giddiness assailed her. She heard herself cry out and then knew no more until she found herself lying on a sofa with Mrs Price rubbing her hands and Morgan Edwards trying to force brandy between her lips.

She made an effort to sit up but reeled back as a myriad spots swam before her eyes. From afar off she heard Morgan Edwards telling Brynmor to send Dai Jenkins for the doctor, or ride out himself if it was quicker.

She struggled desperately to tell them not to bother but the words never came, only waves of grey mist that no matter how hard she tried she couldn't push away.

When she finally managed to shake off the terrible feeling of dizziness, and take a few sips of water, she tried to stammer out an apology for all the fuss she was causing.

Morgan Edwards shushed her to silence. Patting her shoulder, he ordered her to lie still until the doctor arrived.

Dr Davies, a thin, grey-haired man with a sharp voice, had an irritating way of clearing his throat after everything he said. He waved Morgan and Brynmor from the room, took Kate's temperature and pulse, snapped out a few pertinent questions and turned away.

'What is wrong with me . . . why did I faint? I've never done anything like that before in my life!'

Dr Davies didn't answer. He cleared his throat noisily, closed his black bag with a decisive snap, picked up his tall silk hat and abruptly left the room.

Kate could hear him in the hall conversing with Morgan Edwards. Bewildered by his attitude and anxious to know what they were saying, she stumbled to her feet, holding on to the back of the nearest chair for support as she stood upright.

Before she reached the door, Morgan Edwards returned.

'What did he say was wrong with me?' Her voice faltered, as his dark eyes pinned her, staring so relentlessly that she shivered, cold fear gripping her.

'You don't know?'

She shook her head, puzzled by the tightness of his mouth, the contemptuous tone of his voice.

'He said he suspected you were pregnant!'

Her mouth gaped. A faint sheen of perspiration glistened on her upper lip. Her eyes clouded, like milk-blue marbles. For a moment she felt so giddy that she thought she was going to faint again.

'Can you explain your condition?'

She flinched, a sudden rush of colour staining her cheeks. She wondered what he knew.

'Have you anything to say?' His face remained passive, only the slight twitching of a facial muscle belying his impatience.

'I intended speaking to you this evening about what has been happening,' she said in a low voice. 'I hardly know how to begin. . . .'

'Concerning Brynmor coming to your room at night?'

'You know,' she gasped, 'yet you've done nothing about it!'

She couldn't believe she had endured the long weeks of torment in silence when all the time Morgan Edwards knew what was happening.

'Why didn't you order him to stop!' she challenged, her voice shrill with anger.

'You hadn't complained,' he commented drily.

'Only because I was afraid to do so!' She shuddered convulsively.

'Why?'

'Brynmor said you would whip Mathew if I said anything to you and I couldn't bear the thought of that happening.' Her breath caught audibly in her throat.

'Whip Mathew! Why should I do that?' he asked frowning.

'Brynmor said you would. . . .'

'Perhaps you had better start at the beginning,' he snapped curtly. He indicated a chair and then sat facing her.

Hesitantly at first, then with a growing determination that he should know everything, Kate told her story.

A peculiar stiffness seemed to freeze Morgan Edwards' features as he listened to her revelations. He allowed no glimmer of sympathy or condemnation to show on his face. When she had finished he rose from his chair and walked over to a side table that held a whisky decanter and glasses. He stood for a moment with the decanter in his hand, as if digesting what she had just told him. Then he poured out two drinks and handed one to her.

'So what are you planning to do now?' he asked in a clipped voice.

'I don't know!' She took a sip of her drink, choking as the fiery liquid seared the back of her throat. Unsteadily, she rested the glass on the arm of her chair. 'I had intended telling you tonight about what was happening and insisting you should stop Brynmor coming to my room!'

'Are you fond of Mathew?' he asked abruptly.

'Oh, yes!' Kate's face softened. 'It will be a terrible wrench to leave him.'

He gave her an appraising stare, then rose and began to pace the room. He paused and refilled his glass, studying the amber liquid abstractedly.

'I want you to know that I am extremely satisfied by the way you have taken over the running of things here. There has been a marked improvement in Mathew since you arrived.'

He took a drink from his glass, swilling the liquid around in his mouth, savouring it before swallowing it, watching her reaction from under lowered lids.

'Brynmor is in the first flush of youth, so we can dismiss what has happened as a passing experience,' he said, breaking the uneasy silence.

'You mean . . .'

'We'll say no more about it. I will deal with him. He won't trouble you again.'

'That may be so but . . .'

'I haven't finished yet,' Morgan Edwards interrupted. 'This child you are expecting will need a home . . . you would find it difficult to find another position in your condition.'

He looked at her questioningly.

As she saw the sensual gleam directed towards her, Kate realized the role he was expecting her to play. She felt outraged, filled with a dark anger.

To do what Morgan Edwards was suggesting would simply be exchanging one illicit affair for another! When she'd become a Nanny she'd seen it as an opportunity to better herself and escape from the rut of being a skivvy. Now she seemed to be in danger of slipping into an even worse furrow.

Inwardly she railed against the invidious situation she found herself in, but common sense warned her that it would be foolish to walk out of Machen Mawr.

She had very little money left, and even if she found David, the chances of him still being free to marry her diminished with each passing day.

It was no good sighing for the moon. She must forget her dreams and be practical.

Refusing to wilt under Morgan Edwards' direct stare she held her head high, biting the inside of her cheeks to stop herself speaking until she had worked out what to say.

She studied Morgan Edwards from under lowered lashes, knowing he was impatient for her answer yet determined not to be intimidated.

'You are right. If I am expecting a child then it will need a home,' she agreed, struggling to keep her voice steady.

'Then it's settled.'

'You mean I can stay on here?'

'Mrs Price will have to be told about the baby, but there is no need to mention our arrangement,' he warned.

'So everything will be just the same as before.'

'Well . . . almost!' he agreed with a smirk.

'Not quite!' She drew in a deep breath, determined that if his desires were to be met then she would demand that he pay the ultimate price.

'What do you mean?'

'My child will also need a father.'

Morgan Edwards frowned as if baffled by her words. She sensed the struggle going on in his mind. The lascivious smile had left his face, but knowing how much he was lusting for her she never doubted what his answer would be.

16

Brynmor Edwards looked bewildered.

'You are handing over the Pontypool Works to me as a wedding settlement?'

'That's what I said.'

'I don't understand! I haven't made any marriage plans!'

Morgan Edwards leaned back in his high-backed leather armchair, rubbing a hand over his chin as he studied his elder son, wondering if he should have administered the reprimand first and told him the good news afterwards.

If he'd done that, there would have been a lengthy harangue as Brynmor protested his innocence and it would have seemed as if he was handing over the Pontypool Works as some sort of peace-offering. And that certainly wasn't his intention!

'Sit down, Brynmor. There's a great deal I have to say to you.'

'I hope you are not going to tell me that you have fixed up some sort of marriage agreement on my behalf,' Brynmor blustered as he lowered himself into a chair on the other side of his desk and scowled at his father.

'Would it matter if I had?'

'That would depend on the woman involved,' Brynmor prevaricated, crossing one leg over the other and studying the toe of his highly polished boot.

'You have someone in mind?' Morgan's dark eyes narrowed.

'Of course not!'

'You're quite sure?'

'I haven't time for squiring girls. Nor much opportunity

to meet them socially since we never entertain,' he added defensively.

'I thought there was one already under this roof who'd taken your fancy.' Morgan's tone was deceptively quiet. As his gaze locked with Brynmor's he saw the dull flush creep up over his son's collar and for him it was proof enough that all Kate had told him was true.

'Don't trouble to lie,' Morgan said quickly as Brynmor drew in a sharp breath and was about to launch on some garbled tale in order to avoid admitting his involvement.

Brynmor slumped back in his chair, deflated. He scowled back at his father from under beetling brows, and wondered just how much he knew. And who had told him. Surely not Kate. She was much too concerned about the consequences if she did.

His threats about what would happen if his father ever found out that she had taken Mathew into her bed obviously still terrified her. And for good measure he constantly reminded her that if she ever breathed a word about what was going on between them he would swear she had enticed him into her bed and she'd be thrown out of Machen Mawr.

Her distress had surprised him. It made subduing her even more exciting. He never tired of thinking up new and ever more devious ways of subjecting her to his will.

No matter what he did or demanded of her, Kate Stacey accepted it stoically. He sometimes wondered just how far he had to go to break her nerve, to reduce her to tears and have her begging for mercy.

Far from discouraging his attentions, it stimulated him when she lay there, eyes closed, gritting her teeth, her mouth grim with distaste. It spurred him to a sexual frenzy. With his bizarre knowledge of sensual games and perversions, one of these nights he must surely touch some wellspring within her and make her respond to him. His mind filled with so many erotic images that he found it difficult to concentrate on what his father was saying.

'Perhaps I should remind you of what happened in the

135

dining room. Aren't you interested in why Kate Stacey fainted . . . or perhaps you already know the reason!'

Brynmor stared in alarm. He ran the tip of his tongue over his dry lips. He had sent Dai Jenkins for the doctor and, sensing trouble, taken himself off to Pontypool. Now it all seemed to jell. She was pregnant! That was why she had fainted!

His brain floundered. Had she named him as being responsible? He might be an astute businessman but on this occasion he hadn't planned his next move. He knew his father was waiting for him to say something. Should he admit it or deny it, he wondered.

A cold sweat dampened his palms and brow. Hell's teeth! This was a fine mess. Lie and be found out and he'd earn his father's scorn and contempt. Admit he'd fathered a child on Kate Stacey and he might lose out on his father's offer to make over the Pontypool Works as a wedding settlement.

As a wedding settlement!

His jaw dropped. He stared at his father. Had he heard right? His hand strayed to his stiff white collar, easing it so that he could breathe. He'd never been in a quandary like this before. He had no idea how to act.

Strange heats burst inside him, as he watched his father fill a pipe, tamping the golden strands of tobacco into the bowl with calm deliberation.

'Have you been listening to kitchen gossip, Papa?' he grinned, attempting to treat the matter in a jocular way.

'About what?'

'Kate Stacey . . . why she fainted.'

'I asked for an explanation, naturally.'

'And did she give one?'

'Is it true?'

Brynmor wilted under his father's direct stare. He shrugged, knowing it was useless to deny what had been going on, determined to deal severely with Kate for landing him in this wretched predicament.

136

'What you were saying about the Pontypool Works . . .' he blustered, trying to bluff it out. His voice faltered as his nerve failed. How could he hope for such a prize now. He tried to control his rage. To think he had been on the point of owning his own works. The red began to creep up above his collar again as he fought back a sour taste in his throat.

'I said I would sign them over to you.'

'You still mean to do that!' Brynmor exclaimed incredulously.

'As a marriage settlement.'

'Marriage settlement!' Brynmor shook visibly.

'Are you saying that if I marry Kate Stacey you'll give me the Pontypool Works . . .?'

'I mean it will be yours as long as you never lay a finger on her ever again,' declared Morgan Edwards in icy tones. 'Is that perfectly clear?'

'No . . . it's not. I don't understand.'

Perplexed, Brynmor wondered which of them was going mad. His father talked about a marriage settlement yet when he agreed to marry Kate Stacey his father looked as though he was about to explode with anger.

The haze of confusion deepened as Morgan Edwards barked, 'I'm the one who's marrying her, you young fool. Paying for *your* mistake. Acknowledging the child you've fathered. I'm giving you the Pontypool Works as part of your inheritance. Find your own establishment, there's no longer any room for both of us under the same roof.'

'*You* are marrying Kate Stacey! Great heavens, why?' Brynmor asked in shocked tones. 'Mama's been dead not a year!'

'You should have thought of that when you started playing around, boyo. Fine education you might have had but your brains are still between your legs,' Morgan added coarsely.

'And you want me to leave Machen Mawr?'

'That's right. Buy yourself a house in Pontypool. I'll advance you the money, or you can go into lodgings there.

Do what you damn well like but not under my roof,' he barked. 'Is that understood?'

'How soon?' Brynmor's voice was strained, his throat tight and hot.

'It can't be too soon for my liking. Kate won't feel safe until you've gone.'

'She's the one who told you?'

'I already suspected what was going on.'

'But you said nothing!'

'If you were randy, and she was willing, then what was there to say. . . .'

'So why make an issue of it now?' Brynmor interrupted petulantly.

'I've learned the truth about you, boyo. Disgusted I am!'

'What do you mean?'

'Lust is one thing, but your behaviour is unnatural.'

'What . . . what has she been telling you?'

'I suppose you picked those tricks up when you were down in London.'

Brynmor pushed back his chair and stood up. He felt as though he was in some tortuous maze. For once he was afraid to argue in case he brought further incriminations upon himself. He had been found out. He was being offered an easy solution and he was sharp enough to realize that the best thing he could do was to accept it.

'I'm going up to bed,' he mumbled, walking towards the door.

'Just make sure it is your own bed you climb into,' his father warned.

'Goodnight, Papa.'

'I'll tell Mrs Price to give you an early call in the morning. We'll be leaving for Cardiff first thing.'

'What for?'

'There's a lot of papers to be signed. We'll probably be there for a couple of days.'

'You mean to do with the Pontypool Works?'

'That and the forthcoming marriage. My marriage, that is.' His father smiled grimly. 'There's more than just your inheritance to sort out. Everything else must be settled legally.'

Brynmor couldn't sleep. His mind was a whirlpool of jumbled thoughts and revenge was uppermost. For one wild moment he was tempted to creep along to Kate's room. She ought to be punished. Vengeful yearnings sent a fire spreading through his loins. He wanted to make her cringe like a fear-frozen rabbit. He wanted to see those vivid blue eyes darken with despair as he defiled her. Remembering the sweetness of her mouth, the full ripeness of her milk-white body, he ached.

The realization that his father would be the one enjoying her favours tortured him still further. Vivid images of them lying together teased his mind. Would his father be dominant and demanding, he wondered, or would he be a gentle, considerate lover?

The thought that perhaps Kate would respond to his father's touch wrapped cold tentacles round his heart. An orgasmic shivering consumed him. Whenever he had possessed her body, her icy compliance had always cheated him of full satisfaction.

If only he could break down her reserves . . . just once!

The temptation to visit her room one last time took possession of him. He tossed and turned, unable to ease his overpowering need. Throwing back the bedclothes, he rose and dressed rapidly, anxious to be out of the house. He couldn't stay away from her, not while she was under the same roof. His father had been right on that score, he thought bitterly.

Moonlight bleached the gaunt hillsides. A dull glow from Morgan Edwards' blast furnaces at Nantyglo bloodied the velvet canopy of sky. An autumn wind showed its teeth.

Brynmor paused in the gravel driveway, studying the square-built structure of Machen Mawr. A glimmer of light showed at the window of his father's study but the rest of the house was in darkness. In a few days' time it would no longer be his home. He wasn't ready to make such a break. He wasn't sure he wanted the sole responsibility of the Pontypool Works.

The knowledge that his father was behind him in everything he did, a pillar of strength if things should go wrong, had given him the confidence to be bold. Knowing his father would cushion any mistakes he made had allowed him to be reckless and to take chances that more cautious men envied.

Already he was beginning to feel vulnerable because that protection had been withdrawn.

Was it really for his benefit that his father was marrying Kate Stacey and making himself responsible for the coming child?

Even as the doubt bubbled up in his mind it was overtaken by resentment and a sense of personal violation. How dare his father snatch his new-found pleasure away from him.

Comparing Kate's voluptuous curves with the svelte, muscular bodies he had known in the past tantalized his senses.

If only she'd responded to him, showed some feeling, it might have cured him of his perversions. Even anger would have been preferable to dumb submission.

He thought of her lying in his father's bed, her black hair fanned out over her white shoulders, covering her pink-tipped, rounded breasts and wondered what her response would be. Their coupling would be pallid . . . but perhaps that was what she wanted after what he had subjected her to, he thought snidely. If his father thought for one moment that he was getting a wanton woman he was in for a disappointment. For all her ripe look, Kate Stacey had turned out to be a prude.

Burning with anger, Brynmor made his way to the stables. Sleep was impossible. Perhaps if he saddled up and rode out he might rid himself of the black devils on his back.

He'd need a clear head when he met the lawyers in Cardiff. If his father was planning to set his affairs in order it might affect his own inheritance.

He had never considered the matter before but Morgan Edwards was a man of considerable property and wealth. He was not in the first flush of youth and he would be under considerable physical strain keeping a young bride happy, Brynmor thought cynically.

Doubtless his father would make sure that Mathew was well provided for in the event of anything happening to him, but what were his plans for the rest of his personal fortune?

The future of Machen Mawr, the ironworks and the coal mines suddenly seemed highly important.

As the elder son surely I deserve more than just the Pontypool Works, Brynmor thought angrily as he let himself into the stables. He viciously slapped the rump of his stallion. The horse kicked out, his hoof striking the side of his loosebox. The noise reverberated, startling the other horses and causing uproar.

'Who's down there?'

The voice took Brynmor by surprise. He had forgotten that Twm Jenkins slept over the stables.

'It's all right. There's no need for you to get out of your bed,' he growled.

His words came too late. Twm had already shinned down the ladder.

He stood there facing Brynmor, a tall, strapping lad of fifteen with curly dark hair and flashing dark eyes. He was bare-chested, his breeches pulled on in such haste as he'd sprung from his bed that they were still undone.

Brynmor's eyes narrowed, startled by the fresh young maleness. As Twm advanced to take the stallion's head and calm him, he touched the boy's arm, letting his fingers slide slowly upwards. He felt the muscles tense as the youth held his breath. Their eyes locked. As a look of understanding passed between them, the boy relaxed, slowly exhaled and then turned away.

'Shall I saddle him up for you, Master Brynmor?'

The question hung in the air. Even the stallion's ears pricked, waiting for Brynmor's answer.

'If it's company you are looking for, then I've ale up in my room and you're very welcome to share it,' Twm Jenkins invited.

Brynmor hesitated.

He found the bed-warm youth's offer enticing. He knew he was on dangerous ground. There were hardly the same risks as he had taken with Kate Stacey but his father would be less lenient if he learned of a second misdemeanour taking place under his own roof.

It might be his father's home but soon it would no longer be his, Brynmor reminded himself, so why not enjoy what was on offer. The added danger brought exquisite excitement.

Hungrily, he eyed the lean, taut young body standing in front of him, then nodded curtly.

The boy's mobile mouth widened into a welcoming smile. Without a word he turned and led the way back up the ladder to the loft above.

Heart beating, pulses racing, Brynmor followed.

The sickly sweet smell of hay and straw, mingled with that of leather and horses, filled his nostrils, bringing back vivid memories of young ostlers he had known and enjoyed in the coaching houses when he had been in London.

17

'Mistress of Machen Mawr!'

Kate held her chin a fraction higher as she heard the surprise in Olwen Price's voice.

'Well!' the older woman let out a long breath, shaking her grey head from side to side in disbelief. 'Mistress, is it!' She paused, the teapot poised over Kate's cup. 'I suppose that means we won't be having any more of these little get-togethers.'

'Don't be ridiculous!' Kate felt her cheeks burn. 'Why shouldn't I join you for an afternoon cup of tea. We enjoy each other's company and our bit of gossip, now, don't we,' she added cajolingly.

'It's been fine while you're Kate Stacey and working as a Nanny,' Mrs Price agreed, stirring sugar into her own cup, 'but once you are the Mistress . . . when you become Mrs Morgan Edwards . . . well, that puts a very different complexion on things, now doesn't it!'

'I don't see that it makes any difference.'

'It will hardly be right for us to drink tea and confide in each other when I'm just a servant and you are Mistress here.'

'Oh, come on, Olwen! Stop putting on airs and graces,' Kate laughed awkwardly.

'Things won't be the same.'

'Why should anything have to change?'

'Like I said, you'll be Mistress and me your servant.'

'I thought you'd be pleased by the news.'

'Shocked more than anything else!' blustered Mrs Price.

'Oh, really, Olwen!'

'I never for one moment thought that you and Master had any feelings for each other.' She pursed her lips disapprovingly. 'And now you tell me you're getting wed to him!'

She stared at Kate belligerently, wondering if her judgement had been wrong and she had been taken in after all. Her very first thoughts when Kate had arrived out of the blue came rushing back.

She had thought then that any girl travelling around the countryside on her own after dark, knocking on the door of a complete stranger and being prepared to stay the night without even making sure there was another woman under the same roof, must be something of a young hussy.

Yet, when Kate had turned out to be quietly spoken and helpful, and so good and kind to Mathew, she'd changed her mind and given her the benefit of the doubt. Until now she had not had any reason to think that her revised judgement had been wrong.

Even when Kate had taken over the day-to-day running of Machen Mawr, Olwen Price had never for one moment suspected any ulterior motive. Now, less than two months under their roof and she was to be the new Mistress.

It took your breath away, Mrs Price thought mutinously.

Somehow she'd never thought of Morgan Edwards taking another wife. Not after being married to her Myfanwy.

He was still in his prime, of course, not yet fifty, and a pretty young woman like Kate Stacey would stir any man's blood, she supposed.

She studied Kate covertly from over the rim of her teacup. There was no denying she was well favoured. Her wide-set eyes glowed like bright blue gems. The glistening black curls framing her cheeks made her skin look like pink-tinted rose petals. And she had a generous mouth, with even white teeth and a ready smile.

144

Despite the dark shadows beneath her eyes, she'd filled out since coming to Machen Mawr, Mrs Price reflected. It suited her. There was a new roundness to her figure and . . . Mrs Price stopped sharply. Her dark eyes glittered with speculation.

'Was there anything else you had to tell me, Kate?' she asked, holding her breath, dumbfounded by the sudden presentiment that crossed her mind.

'I don't think so,' Kate murmured evasively.

'After what happened last night I thought there might be some other news?'

'You mean when I fainted?'

'Kate . . . you're not . . .' Her gaze focused on Kate's waistline, then slowly she looked up into Kate's eyes, a look of disbelief in her own.

'Pregnant, you mean,' Kate's voice was casual.

'Oh, my heavens! I . . . I don't know what to say. I feel flummoxed, I really do!' Mrs Price exclaimed, fanning her face with her apron.

'You must have already had your suspicions since you asked if there was any news.'

'I did wonder what the doctor had said . . .'

'Well, now you know and I can see you are as surprised as I am.' Tears filled Kate's eyes and she brushed them away quickly.

'*Duw Anwyl*! What a state of affairs!'

The rising shrillness of Olwen Price's voice jarred on Kate's ears. Did she have to make such a scene about it, she thought irritably.

Olwen's look of distress did worry her, though, and left her feeling she hadn't handled the situation at all well. She wondered what story Morgan Edwards expected her to tell.

All they'd agreed was that she would explain what was happening to Mathew.

'You'll make the necessary arrangements for our wedding?' she'd asked.

'I'll attend to the legal side.'

145

'And the reception afterwards?'

He'd frowned. She suspected he would have liked to ignore such formalities but she didn't intend for it to be a hole-in-the-corner affair that would lead to gossip and speculation.

'You can organize that with Mrs Price. Nothing too grand,' he'd cautioned.

'Of course not.'

'It wouldn't be right under the circumstances.'

She hadn't seen him since. He'd absented himself from the house, taking Brynmor with him.

'They've gone to Cardiff on business,' Olwen told her. 'Master said he would be away for several days.'

Kate wasn't sure whether it was to give her time to get used to the idea that she was to be his wife, or to give him the chance to deal with Brynmor.

That predicament, at least, was behind her.

Now, looking at Olwen Price's stricken face she wondered how many more problems she was going to have to shoulder.

Glynis had to be told, though she didn't for one moment expect her to show any concern. She'd probably giggle and then forget all about it five minutes later. No doubt there would be plenty of gossip behind her back amongst the others who worked at Machen Mawr, but it would pass.

The only one Kate felt really concerned about was Mathew. She had no way of knowing how he would react. The closeness they had enjoyed during her early days at Machen Mawr had been ruined by Brynmor the morning he had discovered Mathew in her bed. Since then there had been almost a barrier between them, as if Mathew was fearful of being hurt again.

It was ironic, she thought, that Brynmor had been able to blackmail her because she'd acted like a mother towards Mathew and now she was going to be his stepmother.

Which also meant she would be Brynmor's stepmother!

Bile rose in her throat, she felt grave-cold at the thought, filled with a disquieting presentiment of trouble ahead. If only she could turn back the clock, erase the past months and be back at Bramwood Hall, seeing David most weekends.

A shiver ran through her. Was she being too hasty in marrying Morgan Edwards? Was she making a terrible mistake?

It was a question that had tormented her ever since she had fainted.

The shock of discovering Dr Davies had told Morgan Edwards she was pregnant had clouded her judgement. Like Morgan Edwards and Olwen Price, she assumed it was Brynmor's child she was expecting. But was it? On reflection, it was much more likely to be David's.

Marriage to Morgan Edwards would be a mockery. She couldn't go through with it. She must find David. Once he knew about the baby . . . Cold fear gripped her heart. If he didn't acknowledge the child was his, or if he was already married to Penelope Vaughan, what then? Morgan Edwards would certainly throw her out if he heard about David Owen and suspected the truth.

Her mind darkened. It was David she wanted.

Yet, under the circumstances, it made sense to become mistress of Machen Mawr and accept Morgan Edwards' attentions than to be faced with a life of poverty, she thought, looking round the warm, comfortable kitchen.

She should be filled with relief that she had been able to solve her problem so adroitly. Instead, the hopelessness of the situation filled her with a deep sense of sadness.

What sort of future could she expect, bonded to a man she didn't really know, having been abused by his son, and carrying another man's child?

She stood up, straight and proud, her chin high as she carried her empty cup over to the sink. The die was cast, there was no turning back, so she must make the best of it.

'I'll see to that!'

Angrily, Kate swung round, two bright spots of colour staining her high cheekbones, her blue eyes glittering, her lips compressed in a tight line.

'If you're going to be the Mistress here then you'd best leave washing the pots to the servants,' Olwen Price told her in a grieved voice.

'If that's the attitude you're going to take, Olwen, then I assume our friendship is over,' declared Kate, her voice rising with indignation.

'And what is that supposed to mean?'

'You know well enough what I mean, but just to make sure I'll spell it out for you,' Kate told her tartly. 'You have the choice: either consider me your friend, like you've done ever since I've been here, or else I warn you, Olwen, I'll show no leniency.'

'You mean you'll behave like a Mistress generally does towards a servant.'

'That's right. And remember,' Kate gave a tight smile, 'I know all the little secrets of what goes on down here.'

'I don't know what you mean!'

'If you value your comfortable way of life you'd better make the right decision,' warned Kate.

'You're the one who's going to be Mistress.'

'Well? Do we stay friends?'

Hands on her hips, Kate faced Olwen Price. She knew she was playing a dangerous game but in the time she had been at Machen Mawr she had grown fond of Olwen Price. The older woman had a warm heart and had proved to be a good friend. Marriage to Morgan Edwards was uncharted seas, she wanted to be sure she had a shoulder to cry on.

Before Mrs Price could answer, a strangled cry from the passageway took them by surprise. Kate reached the kitchen door first, in time to see Mathew scuttling away.

Forgetting their differences, both women stared at each other questioningly, wondering how long he had been there.

148

'You'd best go and see to him,' Mrs Price admonished. 'No knowing what he has heard. The shock might bring on one of his attacks.'

Kate found Mathew huddled on his bed, his breathing, ragged with sobs, dragging harshly from his heaving chest.

She spoke his name softly but he wouldn't even uncover his face, so she sat down on the side of the bed and stroked his hair, hoping to calm him. When she could stand it no longer she gathered him into her arms but he fought her off, kicking and struggling, like a mad thing.

'All right, all right, stop getting yourself into such a state,' she told him firmly.

'Leave me alone!'

'I don't know what you overheard downstairs but I'll tell you the truth, if you'll listen.'

'Go away!'

His scream was so hysterical that for a moment she felt panic rising inside her. If he carried on like this he would have a full-scale asthma attack and she was not at all sure how to cope on her own.

'Listen to me.' She tried to keep her voice firm and steady even though her own heart was thundering. 'I was going to tell you all about it the moment you got home. I hoped you'd think it was good news that I was going to be your Mama.'

'I hate you!'

'I thought you were fond of me, Mathew, and that we were good friends.'

'Go away!'

'It will be even better now,' Kate persisted. 'We will be a real family. You and me, and your Papa and . . . and . . . the new baby. A brother or sister, Mathew, just think of that!'

She could hear the hysterical note in her own voice and willed herself to stay calm. She wanted him to accept the situation. She knew she could never take his mother's place, but neither did she want Mathew to resent her.

149

Tentatively she stretched out her hand and placed it on his shoulder. This time he didn't shrug it away. He held his breath and lay perfectly still as though etched in stone.

Her momentary relief changed to panic as he choked and fought to breathe again. His eyes, wide with fear and desperation, locked with hers. His mouth distorted into a grimace of agony as he gulped for air. The strangled rasping in his throat frightened her.

'I'll send Dai Jenkins to fetch Dr Davies?'

Olwen Price had followed her up to the bedroom and was standing by the door, her round face concerned.

Kate nodded gratefully.

While she waited for the doctor's arrival, Kate tried desperately to persuade Mathew to relax. As soon as he was a little calmer, she helped him into a sitting position, propping him up with pillows.

When Olwen Price came back upstairs to see if there was anything more she could do, Kate asked her to open the window and let in some fresh air. With Olwen's assistance, she wrapped Mathew in a blanket and they lifted him on to a chair.

'Try and keep your back straight, Mathew,' urged Kate.

Whimpering with distress, he tried to sit upright.

'Now, lean forward and let your arms rest on your knees. Come on,' she exhorted gently, 'it will help you to breathe more easily.'

Persuading him to inhale deeply, instead of in shallow gasps, so that air filled his lungs, took patience and perseverance.

Her own brow was damp with perspiration by the time the doctor arrived, her problems forgotten as she concentrated on Mathew's breathing.

Dr Davies summed up the situation in one swift glance.

'Bring a glass of water, Mrs Price,' he ordered.

'This will put you right, Mathew,' he promised as he mixed up a whitish powder.

'Is there anything else I can do?' asked Kate.

'No. You've handled things well,' he told her.

An hour later Mathew was breathing calmly. Exhausted by his ordeal, he let Kate undress him and put him to bed.

'What brought on the attack this time?' Dr Davies asked abruptly as they left the room together.

'He overheard me telling Mrs Price about the baby and the new arrangements here.'

'I'm surprised that should upset the boy.'

'He also heard me say that I was marrying his father.'

'Marrying Morgan Edwards! I see!' He pursed his lips. 'It would have been better if you had taken Mathew into your confidence instead of him overhearing gossip,' he censured.

'I had every intention of doing so,' Kate snapped.

'But you didn't!' He coughed irritably.

'I never got the chance. I didn't even know he was in the house.'

'Humph! I would have thought it was his father's place to explain matters to him.' He cleared his throat again. 'Where is Morgan Edwards?'

'Mr Edwards and Brynmor have gone to Cardiff on business. They'll be away for two or three days.'

'So you sent for me to be on the safe side, eh?'

'It seemed to be the right thing to do,' Kate told him, shrugging her shoulders lightly.

'Should we send for Master to come home, Doctor?' Mrs Price asked, emerging from the kitchen and looking at him anxiously.

'No need. Mathew will sleep now until morning.'

'I've never seen him so bad before,' stated Mrs Price. 'Choking he was. Miss Stacey sat him up and told him how to breathe.'

'Yes. Highly commendable. It must be a relief to you to know that Miss Stacey is to become one of the family.'

'A bit of a shock, doctor.'

151

'Yes, I suppose so. Now, if you will hand me my hat I will be on my way.'

'Thank goodness that's over!' Olwen Price let out a long sigh of relief as Dr Davies left. 'I'd better get back to the kitchen and cook your dinner. I wonder if Glynis has laid the dining table yet.'

'She probably hasn't,' agreed Kate. 'Since Mathew won't be coming down tonight it hardly seems necessary. I'll eat with you in the kitchen.'

'Well . . .' Mrs Price looked indignant. She was about to protest when she caught the look on Kate's face and shrugged helplessly. 'If you're sure that's what you wish . . .'

'I do! Friends should stick together when there's a crisis,' Kate told her meaningfully. 'We'll eat right away.'

'It will take me an hour at least to cook . . .'

'In that case we'll just have some bread and cheese and an apple,' Kate ordered.

'I can do better than that,' Olwen Price protested, her professional pride roused.

Half an hour later they were sitting down to a cheese omelette, followed by cold apple pie and fresh cream.

'It's not the sort of meal you should be having,' Mrs Price said worriedly. 'Is there anything else you would like to finish off?'

'While Glynis clears the table and washes the dishes, I think we should both adjourn to your Parlour and enjoy a cup of tea . . . or perhaps something a little stronger,' Kate told her.

At first, Olwen Price was reluctant to talk about the changes that would take place at Machen Mawr once Kate and Morgan were married. After the second nip of whisky she became more garrulous. By the time they both retired to bed their friendship was on an even firmer foundation than before.

18

Within days, news of Morgan Edwards' forthcoming wedding had spread throughout Ebbw Vale and the Top Towns. Tradesmen calling at the kitchen door of Machen Mawr discreetly pumped Mrs Price, eager for details.

'They like a bit of gossip, don't they,' she remarked caustically to Glynis.

'Lovely, I think it is,' sighed Glynis, dreamily. In her eyes Kate had become more like the girl on the chocolate box with each passing day.

'Don't stand there day-dreaming, get on with your work.'

'Just fancy, she'll be Mistress of Machen Mawr!' Glynis murmured.

Mrs Price's double chin juddered as her mouth tightened disapprovingly. Overnight, her world had been knocked sideways. She didn't know which had disturbed her most, finding out that Kate was pregnant or learning that Morgan Edwards intended marrying her.

It wasn't as if he was all that taken with Kate, or she with him. They spoke civilly to each other but she'd never seen him so much as peck her cheek, let alone take her in his arms.

She felt uncomfortable at the thought of Kate sleeping in the great oak four-poster Myfanwy had shared with Morgan Edwards. It didn't seem right.

'Something fishy about it, if you asks me,' sniffed Dai Jenkins' wife, Blodwyn, wide-eyed with astonishment when she first heard the news.

'Just what do you mean by that?' asked Olwen Price sharply.

'I'd bet my best Sunday bonnet that neither Kate

Stacey nor Master care one jot for each other, so why is he marrying her?'

'I thought you'd know the answer to that,' rejoined Olwen Price sarcastically. It wasn't like her to gossip, but events had taken her off balance and undermined her natural reserve.

'She's so much younger than him, barely older than Brynmor . . .'

'*Duw Anwyl*! Is it possible?' gasped Olwen. She sat down heavily in the straightback wooden armchair, fanning her face with her apron.

'What do you mean?'

'Nothing . . . nothing at all.' Olwen Price shook her head, refusing to say anything, her thoughts so confused that she wondered if she was imagining things.

After Blodwyn Jenkins left, though, she began putting two and two together, remembering what Kate had told her about Brynmor's nocturnal visits.

The more she remembered the more confused she became.

It was one thing to think of Brynmor as a man because he was running his own business, but in years he was a mere youth.

Thoughtfully, she chewed on the inside of her cheek as she tried to marshal her thoughts. Surely, under the sort of outrageous circumstances Kate had described, it was hardly likely to be Brynmor's child.

Thoroughly upset, Olwen Price went through into her own parlour, unlocked the cupboard and took out the bottle of whisky she'd secreted there. Although it was early in the day, she felt she needed a tot to settle her nerves.

The more she thought about it the more involved it all seemed and the more confused she became. It couldn't be the Master's child that Kate was expecting, she now reasoned, so it had to be Brynmor's . . . or was it?

Kate could perhaps have already been pregnant when she arrived at Machen Mawr. Perhaps she had encouraged Brynmor to visit her room so that she could accuse him of being the father.

Was that why she hadn't complained to Morgan Edwards right away about what was going on? Or had he taken his place in her bed after he'd dealt with Brynmor?

Once she and Glynis were asleep on the top floor, then anything at all could have gone on, Olwen Price told herself as she put her empty glass down on the table. Both Master's room and Brynmor's were right across the passageway from where Kate slept.

'To think when I said I'd thought I'd heard someone moving around in the night she told me young Mathew had been restless,' she muttered out loud. 'Young Mathew indeed!'

Olwen Price was filled with righteous indignation. She'd had the wool pulled over her eyes and she didn't like it. The more she thought about it the more uncertain she became about whose child it might be that Kate was expecting.

If it was Brynmor's child then why was the Master planning to marry Kate, she pondered. What was wrong with letting Brynmor accept the responsibility for his actions? He could well afford to set up his own home.

None of it made sense as far as Mrs Price was concerned and as preparations for the wedding went ahead she became increasingly tetchy.

Kate misinterpreted her mood. She assumed that Olwen was afraid that things at Machen Mawr would be different so she went out of her way to constantly reassure her that everything would remain exactly as before.

'Nothing is going to be any different for you after the wedding, Olwen.'

'That remains to be seen.'

'It won't . . . I promise you.'

'I'm not so sure. You're fond of changing things to suit yourself.'

'Everything is just as I want it . . . and will stay that way. Even to our cups of tea and chats together.'

155

The feeling of constraint remained.

Olwen was suspicious of every movement Kate made. She listened avidly to every snippet of gossip that came her way, not only from Blodwyn Jenkins but from the delivery men and even old Sarah who came in to help out.

'So you're getting married in a registry office,' she sniffed when Kate told her what was being arranged.

'That's right.'

'I would have thought Morgan Edwards would have wanted it to be done properly. I suppose, though, his conscience wouldn't let him be married in church before God.'

'Everything will be quite legal.'

'Underhand way of doing things if you ask me.'

'We wanted it to be a very quiet affair. Just the immediate family . . . and you, of course, Olwen.'

'Very different from when he married my Miss Myfanwy,' Olwen Price sighed. 'A proper wedding that was. Old Rhys Carew put on one of the finest spreads ever seen in the Valleys! Barrels of beer for the workers and tables out in the streets laden with food for their families.'

'I'm sure people loved it.'

'They did, I can tell you. They talked of nothing else for weeks.'

'Then they will be able to say that this is the quietest wedding they've ever known. That is if they trouble to mention it at all.'

'Oh, they'll mention it! Tongues are wagging nineteen to the dozen already.'

'Yes? What are they saying?'

'Most of them are wondering why a pretty young girl like you should want to marry a crabbed, middle-aged man.'

Knowing Olwen didn't condone what was happening, Kate refused to discuss it.

In the days leading up to the wedding, the tension worsened. Kate sensed Olwen Price watching her every movement. She even suspected her of listening at doors.

Morgan Edwards, too, seemed to be nervous and edgy.

Often he stared at her in an inscrutable manner, sending a shiver of apprehension through her, reminding her that she knew next to nothing about him and that he might be even more demanding and perverted than Brynmor.

If only things could remain as they are now, she thought wistfully. Morgan had obviously taken Brynmor to task about what had happened and Brynmor hadn't spoken a word to her since. He was seldom in the house and never joined them for dinner. She learned from Mathew that he was planning to go and live in Pontypool and she hoped it was true.

Several evenings when she had gone in to draw Mathew's curtains she had seen Brynmor walking across the yard to the stables.

The nearer the day came for the wedding, the more distracted Morgan Edwards seemed to be. He was short-tempered with Mathew and barely civil to her. She wondered if he was having second thoughts about going through with the arrangement.

Her mind was set at rest on that score when she overheard Blodwyn Jenkins and Olwen Price talking and learned the real reason for his preoccupation.

'My Dai says they're bringing in the Redcoats from Brecon Barracks.'

'*Duw anwyl*! No wonder the Master is so distracted.'

'With so much on his mind he should leave marriage for a while.'

'In her condition it's not possible!'

'To my mind there'll be a revolution before there's a wedding,' Olwen Price prophesied.

'You could be right. Plenty of secret meetings at all the pubs, my Dai says.'

'Blaenafon has always had more than its share of mountain fighters . . .'

'But the discontent has spread.'

'It's these Chartists that are to blame.'

'Brynmor told my young Twm that there are even men at his japanning works joining the agitators. Says it's their duty even though the wages he pays them are more than fair.'

'Jack Frost is the one stirring things up in Pontypool, you mark my words,' Olwen opined.

'My Dai says they're coming from all over the place to hold secret meetings,' agreed Blodwyn morosely. 'Not just from Nantyglo and Brynmawr, but from Beaufort and Blaina.'

'They're coming from even farther afield than that!' agreed Olwen.

'Brandishing their Benefit Club banners like an army raising its colours, Dai says.'

'All of Wales it seems is caught up in this Chartist movement. They are after more than just fair wages.'

'Is that the reason why this wedding is such a hole-in-a-corner one, then?' prompted Blodwyn slyly.

'What do you mean?'

'I thought Master might be afraid to put on a show in case he gets lynched by his workers.'

'Your head's as empty as your larder, Blodwyn Jenkins!' Olwen told her angrily.

'I don't know so much. Look what happened over at Fforbrecon colliery . . .'

Kate's heart raced at the mention of Fforbrecon. She strained to hear more of what the two women were saying but suddenly they lowered their voices. Seconds later she heard a man's voice raised in anger and knew that Dai Jenkins had come into the kitchen looking for his wife and the gossiping was over.

She was worried and disturbed by all she had heard. In the few weeks she had been in Ebbw Vale she had seen for herself the awful conditions the people lived and worked under. As she drove through Blaina or Nantyglo in the trap with Mathew, ragged, barefooted children ran alongside them, their dark Celtic eyes mutely begging.

She was always glad to get clear of the towns, the sulphurous, odorous air was so stifling and the sound of hammers clanging, engines rumbling and snorting and the deafening noise from the blast furnaces defied description.

As they drove past the furnaces, she was horrified by the sight of men, stripped to the waist, dripping with sweat in the unbearable heat, their bodies stained by splashes from the ore they were handling, and tainted by the smoke and fumes that hung like a pall over them.

Everywhere there were signs of deprivation. The squalid homes had faded, peeling paintwork. Broken windows were stuffed with rags to keep out the treacherous winds that crept round the mountains, whipping up dust from the coalmines and slag tips and forcing them into every nook and cranny. Even the tiny babies, wrapped in shawls, bundled so close to their mother or an older sister that the outline was of one grotesquely shaped body, had faces streaked with grime.

The whole place was a breeding ground for revolt.

It was ironic, but as the wife of one of the leading ironmasters of Nantyglo she would become one of the Gentry. She'd be one of the tight-fisted owners who imposed such unbearable conditions on their workers, paying them in shillings while they reaped pounds, condemning them to live in filth and degradation while they had riches and comfort.

On which side of the fence did she really belong, she wondered. David, too, was Gentry and one of the hated owners. Like her he believed everyone should have some schooling. Perhaps if things had been different they could have opened a school together, worked side by side to teach these poor children to read and write instead of being forced to work in such harrowing conditions.

Hearing Blodwyn Jenkins mention trouble at Fforbrecon colliery had revived her doubts about marrying Morgan Edwards. If only she had heard from Helen.

159

There was so little time left now that the wedding date had been set. Everything was fixed. Unless she ran away there was no escaping her Fate. Yet, if she married Morgan Edwards and afterwards David came looking for her, still wanting to marry her, what then?

Her mind darted like mayflies in spring. She couldn't settle on one single thought for more than a second before another claimed her attention. She wondered what Blodwyn Jenkins had meant about trouble at Fforbrecon colliery. If the problems had been greater than David had expected it might account for there having been no news from him.

If the uprising was supported by Chartists then the men would hardly settle things at one meeting. It might take weeks, or even months, before agreement was reached.

David had said it was necessary for him to take up his responsibilities because his father's health was failing. If his father had become worse, then David may have been forced to stay with him.

Supposing his father died . . . David would be free to marry her!

Again, so many 'ifs' and 'supposes' that she felt dizzy.

She went into the library in search of writing paper, determined to send a letter to Helen and discover the truth.

To her consternation Morgan was in there, sitting at the desk perusing some documents. Taken by surprise, she found herself explaining her intent.

'I'm writing to tell Lady Helen about our forthcoming marriage,' she told him, colouring furiously.

'I suppose it is more courteous if she hears it direct from you than by some devious means,' he grunted. 'Be quick then, I'm just leaving for Newport and I'll despatch it from there.'

After she had handed over the letter to Morgan Edwards, Kate wondered if perhaps she'd acted foolishly. If he decided to scan the letter before mailing it, how would she explain that it was a request for news of

David and that she had not mentioned one word about their forthcoming wedding?

She watched him covertly for the next few days but he seemed so engrossed in his own troubles that in the end she dismissed the matter from her mind.

When, almost a week later, Mrs Price brought a sealed package to the dinner table and spoke in a low whisper to Morgan Edwards before handing it over, it never entered her head that it might have been intended for her.

Clocksprings of veins bulged at his temples as he studied it. He let out a roar that rocked the silver on the sideboard, then brought his fist down on the table so hard that it sent the glassware and cutlery jingling. Kate instinctively stretched out and took Mathew's hand, squeezing it reassuringly.

'Take your hands off him you . . . you whore!'

Mathew's face went ashen and his breathing became ragged as he stared wide-eyed at his father.

'It's all right Mathew, don't get upset,' cautioned Kate as she released his hand.

'Oh yes, everything is all right for you, Miss Stacey,' Morgan Edwards ground out between clenched teeth. He stared at her balefully, open animosity in his dark eyes.

As he waved the letter in the air she recognized the Sherwood crest and knew it must be from Helen. Cold fear gripped her heart. She tried to speak but the words died on her lips.

'You must think me a naive fool to have believed your story! Raped by Brynmor!' His lips curled in a sneer as he flung the letter down on the table.

As she reached to pick it up he grabbed her wrist, twisting it savagely between his hard, bony fingers. 'Get out! Out of my sight and out of my house,' he hissed.

She flinched away from his purple-faced fury. Stumbling to her feet she grabbed the letter, then backed away from the table.

'Harlot! Jezebel! Whore!'

He hurled insults after her as she stumbled up the stairs. Her heart was thundering by the time she reached her bedroom. She scanned the letter but the words blurred before her eyes as she read what Helen had written.

'There has been no news from David since he left Bramwood Hall. My father's health is still precarious so I imagine he has found settling in at Llwynowen very onerous. I understand there have been serious troubles at Fforbrecon, so I am sure he has probably not had a moment to attend to his own affairs.

You are ever in my thoughts, dear Kate, just as I am sure you are in David's. I still think of you fondly . . . as a sister, and I trust David will soon be in a position to redeem all the promises he made to you.

Beth and Mary are both well but miss you sadly. They send their warmest greetings.

Like them, I look forward to the day when we will all be reunited as one happy family.'

Kate read the missive over and over, gaining courage from its warmth. Knowing where she could reach David changed everything. Nothing else mattered.

19

As he sat in the hansom that was taking him from Llwynowen to Fforbrecon Colliery, David felt resentful that once again his father was treating him in the same high-handed manner as when he had packed him off to boarding school.

He had known for quite a while that his father was impatient for him to return home and take an interest in business affairs. He had put off such involvement for as long as possible because he enjoyed the cloistered life at Oxford.

Mingling with young men of his own age who shared his love of words appealed to his academic nature. He found blending serious studies with leisure very fulfilling. To wander along the river banks or row on the Thames, to take part in debates, or attend literary soirées, all gave him a sense of well-being and contentment.

He lacked his father's business acumen.

The world of coal and iron, where the furnace was master and men scrabbled for black gold in the bowels of the earth did not appeal to him. He felt averse to being part of an industry where men were treated more harshly than animals, lived in squalor, became maimed and disabled and regarded death as a happy release, the graveyard as heaven.

Knowing his father would never agree to him leading an academic life he had toyed with the idea of putting up for Parliament, but found it impossible to agree with the policies of either the Whigs or Tories.

The Law offered interesting possibilities and over dinner on his first night at home he had tried to persuade his father to support him while he undertook further studies and acquired the necessary legal qualifications.

Tudor ap Owen's snort of derision left him in no doubt that the idea did not find favour.

'You have had all the education I intend to pay out for,' his father told him curtly. 'You're twenty-three! It's high time you gave up philandering and earned a living.'

Over the next few days the argument waged fiercely whenever they were together. An additional irritation was that Penelope Vaughan had learned of his home-coming. Rarely a day passed without her calling at Llywnowen on some pretext or the other. Often it was to invite him to attend some social function where he knew his presence at her side gave rise to knowing smiles and speculation.

David felt trapped. Several times he was sorely temp-ted to walk out of Llwynowen and return to Bramwood Hall.

As if suspecting this, Tudor ap Owen repeatedly stressed the fact that he was growing old and his health was deteriorating, and constantly reminded David of the inheritance that would eventually be his if he was prepared to play his part.

It was a form of blackmail David found hard to ignore. All his life he had been feather-bedded by his father, given a generous allowance and indulged in every possible way.

It had shaped his character.

He had none of the hard-headed drive that was expected of him, that was the hallmark of a businessman. He preferred studying the Classics to poring over a Balance Sheet, reading poetry rather than a Profit and Loss Account.

'I have no interest whatsoever in commerce, Father,' he protested as they sat sipping their port at the end of dinner, a few weeks after he had returned home.

'I'm counting on you to take control, David.'

164

'I know that, Father. That's why I think some legal training would be beneficial.'

'It's too late to think of that now.'

'Just a year . . . maybe two. I needn't complete the entire course.'

'Quite unnecessary! I can teach you as much as you need to know.'

'Things are changing, Father. I want to keep abreast of all the new laws they're bringing in.'

'And so you shall. Tomorrow you can accompany me to Fforbrecon and find out for yourself how things are run.'

'I'm not interested in mining. I would far rather teach others . . .'

'Then teach the men to work, to accept their rightful place in the scheme of things,' barked Tudor ap Owen, his eyes glittering fiercely. 'That's why I sent for you. There's trouble brewing. Agitators have infiltrated both the iron works and the pits fomenting discontent with their talk of Rights for the Workers.'

'They are only asking for fair treatment because they are being exploited . . .'

'Exploited! Utter rubbish!' Tudor ap Owen slammed his fist down on the table. 'They should think themselves lucky that they are in full employment, have a roof over their heads and food in their bellies. Give in to their demands for shorter hours and higher pay and we'd all end up in the bankruptcy courts. And where would the workers be then, eh?'

Their discourse was interrupted by a manservant bringing in a letter. Frowning, Tudor ap Owen opened it.

'The messenger is waiting for a reply, Sir.'

Tudor ap Owen's pointed beard quivered, his breathing became laboured as he scanned the missive. He mopped his brow with a large white handkerchief.

'Are you all right, Father?'

'My pills . . . I need my pills.' He clutched at his chest, groaning with distress.

165

'Where are they?' David glanced up at the manservant questioningly.

'Here . . . here,' gasped his father, fumbling at his waistcoat pocket.

It was several minutes before the pills had the desired effect. David waited anxiously until his father's breathing returned to normal and his hands stopped shaking.

Tudor ap Owen took a sip of wine, waving his hand irritably as David leaned towards him. 'You will have to deputize for me tomorrow at a meeting of the Colliery Owners,' he panted.

'That's impossible! I know nothing of what is going on,' exclaimed David, taken aback.

'Fforbrecon must be represented and I'm not well enough to attend myself,' Tudor ap Owen said tetchily.

'You would do better to send your Agent.'

'No! The meeting has been called by the Owners, they'd not wish to have lackeys present.'

'But under the circumstances . . .'

'I've decided. You will take my place.'

'It's senseless for me to be plunged in so deeply right away,' protested David.

'It's high time you accepted your responsibilities.'

'Very well. But not like this.'

'This is an emergency. There's been a cave-in at Fforbrecon, which is why the meeting is being held.'

'I'm not qualified to sort out something like that!'

'Just attend the meeting. Listen to what is being said and offer your opinion.'

'No one would listen to me!'

'Stay on afterwards. Inspect the mine, talk to the men, make sure our Agent has been doing his job properly.'

'But that may take days . . . or even weeks!' protested David.

'There's a Company house close by. Stay there. Don't come back here until everything is running smoothly. Do you understand?'

'If you say so, Father,' David acceded reluctantly. 'Have you any idea just what the trouble is and why this meeting is being called?'

'Something to do with pay and conditions for the men involved in the accident according to this.' He waved the letter agitatedly. 'I'm sure you can handle it.'

'You're wrong, Father. I have no idea what should be done or what sort of settlement is expected.'

'Then it will be an opportunity to put your learning and skill with words to some real use,' his father snapped.

Now, David thought uneasily, as they drew up outside Fforbrecon colliery, he was about to find out whether he did have such capabilities.

'Mr Owen, sir?' A youngish man approached, touching his cap.

David nodded.

'If you'll come with me, sir, I'll show you the way.'

They walked in silence. It had been raining and as David looked around him he thought he had never seen a more desolate and grim scene in his life. The sky was still leaden as though to match the earth beneath. The land on either side of the steep, rough road comprised more stone and slate than soil. The vegetation was sparse and what there was of it was covered with a black film of coal dust. To the left, there were barren slag heaps and beyond them, stark against the skyline, was the winding gear of the pithead.

As they climbed on up the road, David could see the village of Fforbrecon lying to their right, in the valley below them. It appeared to be little more than a few rows of Company houses, blackened by coal dust and built in terraced tiers into the mountainside. One big fall of rock from those craggy sides and they'd tumble like ninepins, David thought with a shudder. After the lush pastures of southern England, the place seemed brooding and hostile.

167

, 'Not a very pretty place, is it, sir?' the man commented with a crafty, sidelong glance.

David ignored the implication in the man's words but his feeling of unease increased with every step he took.

There was veiled hostility on the faces of the few men they passed on the road. They stared resentfully, their faces black with coal dust, dark eyes glinting beneath greasy cloth caps.

He was glad when their walk ended.

'This way, they're waiting for you, sir,' his guide told him as they reached a long, low building. He knocked on the door and then stood aside to allow David to enter.

The room was clearly the office of a senior pit official. About a dozen portly, well-dressed men were sitting there on an assortment of chairs. His entrance momentarily silenced the discussion that had been under way.

All eyes were on him as he entered.

An elderly man, with white mutton-chop sideburns, who appeared to be chairing the meeting, rose to his feet and proffered his hand in a perfunctory manner.

'I'm surprised your father saw fit to send you along on a matter of such importance,' he frowned. 'My name's Pennington . . .' He proceeded to introduce David to the other men. One or two rose and shook hands, the others gave a curt nod, indicating their impatience at his lateness and annoyance that the discussion had been interrupted.

Pennington pointed to a vacant chair and as David sat down he explained quickly: 'There's been a cave-in. Seven men trapped in one of the galleries. It seems certain that they are dead. We are here to decide whether to clear the gallery or close it down and leave the bodies there.'

'There is nothing to decide, we already know that seam was becoming unproductive,' growled a hard-faced man directly opposite.

'It was due to be shut down. The only sensible course is to seal it off. Getting the bodies out will cost too much both in time and lost production,' added another.

There was a murmur of agreement from some of the others but many remained silent.

'If we agree to that it will cause trouble,' warned a thick-set, corpulent man sitting next to David. 'The families won't like it if the men can't have Christian burials so we may end up having to retrieve the bodies anyway.'

David remained silent. He didn't feel qualified to voice an opinion. It horrified him that the meeting was more concerned with the cost involved than the fate of the victims.

'The best thing we can do now,' Pennington said, 'is to make the miners themselves see the sense of this decision.'

He paused, looking hard at each of them.

'We'll tell them that it will take at least two weeks to recover the bodies,' he went on, a cold smile playing on his thin lips. 'Two weeks without any wages . . . they'll soon see which side their bread is buttered.'

'How can you be sure that none of the seven men is still alive?' asked David.

No one answered.

Raising his hand, Pennington summoned Roddi Llewellyn, the manager of the pit, who had been waiting patiently at the back of the room, to come forward.

He was a wiry-looking man in his late forties. His bowed shoulders told their own story of the years he had spent underground. His sharp, dark eyes were set deep in his sallow face and his scant black hair was greying at the temples.

He listened impassively as Pennington told him that the decision was unaminous and that the chamber would be sealed off.

'The men have been waiting for the past four hours to hear what you intend to do and this will mean trouble,' he said uneasily.

Pennington raised an eyebrow. 'It is your job to ensure that the men do not give trouble,' he snapped. 'You are employed as manager to carry out orders, not question them. You should know how to handle the men. Am I not right in saying that it's not all that long, Llewellyn, since you were one of them . . . working at the coal face?'

Pennington's words brought an angry stain of colour to the manager's sallow face and David saw the man's fists clench. For a moment it looked as though he was going to defy Pennington. David let out a small sigh of relief when Llewellyn strode towards the door saying, 'I'll tell the men you are ready to speak to them.'

Once Llewellyn left the room the tension eased. Mining was a high-risk occupation and the owners were all anxious to see that the money they had invested brought in the maximum return. There was no room for sentiment. The men who had died would easily be replaced.

David walked across to the window and stared out. The yard which had been almost deserted when he arrived was now surging with people. Short stocky men with blue-scarred faces, badges of their trade. They were shabbily dressed and in an odd assortment of jackets and trousers, patched and grimy with coal dust. Most of them wore mufflers around their necks and cloth caps on their heads.

There were women among them, their voluminous dark skirts covered by snowy white aprons. Some of them carried babies, almost completely hidden in the shawls wrapped round both baby and mother to form a carrying cradle.

As Llewellyn walked across the yard and spoke to them, David sensed their growing hostility.

'Is there a rostrum out there for us?' Pennington asked when Llewellyn returned and told him that the men were ready to listen.

'Not a proper platform, there's a cart . . . it's the best I can do.'

'Right. Move it into position. See that the men stand well clear of it, we don't want to have to push our way through a mob,' Pennington snapped.

David followed the other owners as they clambered up a step-ladder on to the makeshift podium. As Llewellyn joined them, the murmurings from the crowd grew louder.

To David's ears it sounded ominous. He looked at Pennington and marvelled at the man's calm as he stood there, a disdainful look on his face, staring down at the crowd as if he were looking at cattle in an auctioneer's pen. He didn't seem to notice that they'd advanced nearer and nearer to the cart until they were almost touching it, or the angry, surly look on their faces.

'Men!' he held up a hand for silence. 'We are grieved by the tragedy here at Fforbrecon since it affects us all. We shall do what we can to relieve the distress of the bereaved but, in the interests of the living, we have taken the decision to seal off the gallery where the accident occurred.'

He waited as an angry murmur swept through the crowd.

'I am sure you all realize that it would take you two weeks or more to clear the collapsed gallery.' He paused dramatically. 'Two weeks of unpaid hard work since your earnings are based on the number of trucks of coal at the pithead weighbridge. If we allowed you to clear the gallery there would be no coal coming to the surface,' he paused again, 'and no money for any of you!

'So, in your interests,' he went on, stressing each syllable, 'we have decided to leave the bodies where they are and to seal off the section in order that the rest of you may continue to earn your livelihood . . .'

Pennington got no further. The crowd seethed. Angry shouts filled the air. Threatening fists were raised. A large piece of coal came hurtling towards the cart, followed by a barrage of shale and stones.

The affray was violent. A lump of coal struck David on the side of the head at the same moment as the cart was overturned. For a moment he lay on the ground dazed. As he struggled to his feet a hand grabbed his arm trying to pull him down. In self-defence he fought back. Blood oozed from his forehead, running down his face, obscuring his vision.

Summoning all his strength, David lashed out. Bodies locked; he and his assailant crashed to the ground, the other man's head taking the full force as it crunched against a boulder. They both lay there unconscious, trampled on by the scuffling crowd.

'Christ!' Llewellyn stared in disbelief as he separated David from the mangled body entwined beneath him. 'The buggers have killed each other . . . and this one's the Owner's son!'

20

Kate felt bewildered as she packed her possessions into the same sturdy canvas bag and tin trunk she had brought with her from Bramwood Hall. Helen's letter had not only changed the pattern of her life but renewed her hope of finding David.

She counted her money carefully. Four gold sovereigns and three shillings in silver was all that remained of the money Sir George Sherwood had given her. She had received no wages while at Machen Mawr and it was impossible now to ask Morgan Edwards for any money.

She wrapped each of the gold coins in separate handkerchiefs so that they wouldn't jingle against one another and then secreted them in a linen pocket which she tied around her waist next to her skin. Two of the shillings she wrapped together and put in her skirt pocket. The remaining shilling, to buy food and a bed for the night, she dropped into her reticule.

As she pulled her cape around her shoulders ready to leave there was a tap on the bedroom door. She held her breath, afraid it might be Morgan Edwards.

'Kate! Are you in there? Open the door, it's me . . . Olwen.'

The voice was breathless as if Olwen Price had run all the way up from the kitchen. When Kate opened the door, she rushed inside, puffing noisily, her apple cheeks brilliant from her exertion.

'Oh, there's glad I am that I managed to catch you,' she gasped as she collapsed on to the side of the bed, fanning herself with her apron. 'Master's just told me he's turned you out! Are you leaving right away . . . on a night like this?'

'Raining, is it?'

'Cats and dogs! Never heard the like in my life!'

'I must leave.'

'Why? What brought this on? Was it to do with that letter I brought in?'

'Yes.'

'Oh, dear! I should have waited until you'd finished dinner, then he need never have known anything about it.'

'No good thinking of that now, Olwen.'

'Eager I was to get it to you. Thought I was doing you a good turn, see. There's foolish I was. I'll never forgive myself. If I'd left it until later then . . .'

'Stop getting yourself into a state,' sighed Kate. 'You weren't to know he'd take it from you, or the way he'd react when he read it.'

'What was in it then?' Olwen Price's eyes were dark with curiosity. 'Looked like a woman's handwriting to me, so what did he get so worked up about?'

'It was from Lady Helen Sherwood.'

'From Miss Helen! Well, there's nice now!' She frowned. 'So why was Master put out over that?'

'She mentioned David in the letter and . . .'

Kate's voice broke. The tears she had been holding back ever since the scene in the dining room gushed down her cheeks.

'There, there, my lovely, don't take on so,' Olwen Price comforted, reaching out and taking Kate's hand.

'Oh, Olwen, just everything seems to go wrong for me,' Kate sobbed, sinking down on to the edge of the bed.

'Has David Owen got something to do with this baby you're expecting?' asked Olwen Price bluntly.

Kate looked at her startled.

'Well, I'm not blind,' the older woman told her, patting her hand understandingly.

'What do you mean?'

'The moment I heard Master was going to marry you I thought that's a funny kettle of fish. I knew it couldn't be his, he's not the kind of man to go lifting the skirts of someone he employs.'

'Really, Olwen . . .'

'After what you'd told me about young Brynmor's carryings-on then naturally I thought it must be his and that Master was marrying you in order to give the child a name, Brynmor not being man enough yet to take on a wife and family.'

'You seem to have worked everything out,' Kate said drily.

'Not quite!' She shook her grey head. 'That's what we were all supposed to think, but you haven't been here long enough! When that letter arrived Master must have realized that for himself.'

Kate made no answer.

'Is that why he's sending you packing?'

Drying her eyes and squaring her shoulders, Kate stood up, straightening her crumpled dress.

'I'd better be on my way,' she said stiffly. 'If Morgan Edwards found me still here it might mean trouble for you, Olwen.'

'Where will you go?'

'To David's home at Llwynowen . . . or to Fforbrecon colliery.'

'Talk sense, girl! They're both on the other side of the Blorenge mountain. You can't walk that far tonight.'

'Once I get as far as Blaina I might get a lift.'

'At night!'

'If I don't, then I'll have to walk,' Kate said, her mouth set in a grim, determined line.

'Think of the risk, *cariad*. Wait until first light and then set out.'

'Morgan Edwards might check to see if I'm still here.'

'You can sleep in Glynis's bed and she can share with me just for the one night. No one can find you there since they'd have to walk through my bedroom, and that's more than either Master or Brynmor would dare do, I can tell you.'

'It's kind of you, Olwen, but it's too much of a risk.'

'Well, if you're determined to go I'll give you the name of someone in Nantyglo who will help you.'

'Give me a bed for the night, do you mean?'

'And take care of your problem if you want her to,' Olwen Price added with a meaningful look.

'What's her name?'

'Mollie Parry. She lives in Coalbrookvale Terrace.'

'How do I find that?'

'It's only a stone's throw from Crawshay Bailey's Roundhouses. Once you pass them it's the road on your left.'

'Mollie Parry, Coalbrookvale Terrace,' repeated Kate.

'That's right. Number Seven. She'll take you in. Her husband, Ianto Parry, caught the iron some four years back when he was working on the blast furnaces. The Owners told her she could stay on in the Company house if she was willing to look after some homeless youngsters. Young boys who work as trammers in the pits or fillers at the furnace top. You tell her I sent you and she'll make you welcome.'

'Thanks, Olwen.' Kate bent and kissed her plump cheek.

'Will you come back again . . . someday?' asked Olwen, her voice choked with emotion.

'Of course I will.' Kate picked up her canvas bag in one hand, her trunk in the other, then hesitated as she saw the disbelief in Olwen's eyes. 'I tell you what, Olwen, I'll leave my trunk with you until then for safe keeping,' she offered.

It was pitch dark and rain was falling when Kate finally left Morgan Edwards' house.

Shivering in the chill night air, she made a dash across the courtyard to the shelter of the stable block. As she stood there looking back at the lighted windows of Machen Mawr, she wondered if she should change

176

her mind and accept Olwen Price's invitation to stay the night.

She drew back into the shadows as footsteps crunched on the gravel and she saw Brynmor coming towards the stables. For one terrifying moment she wondered if he had heard her leave the house and was looking for her. He passed so close to her that she could have touched him.

She held her breath as he started to climb the loft ladder, calling out softly to Twm Jenkins.

She could hear the low murmur of their voices above her head and wondered how long Brynmor would be. It was impossible now for her to leave without them hearing her. Shivering, she crept deeper into the straw and covered herself with one of the thick horse blankets.

As warmth permeated through her limbs, lulling her senses, Kate was afraid of drifting off to sleep. She tried to fight it, knowing how important it was for her to keep alert until Brynmor came down from the loft, but her lids drooped, her head lolled, her senses drifted.

When Kate opened her eyes again, the first shafts of morning light were poking grey fingers through the slits in the door. She strained to listen but no sound came from the loft. Cautiously she stood up, brushing the straw from her dress and cape. Picking up her bag she made her way quietly towards the door. When she lifted the heavy wooden bar that secured it the noise seemed as loud as thunder to her ears.

In her haste to be clear of Machen Mawr she made no attempt to close it after her.

The luminous dawn light was already dappling the sky, making her visible to anyone who might chance to look out of the windows.

As she trudged towards Nantyglo the sky was a dull red beckoning beacon. To her dismay, what had taken ten minutes in the horse and trap when she had been with Mathew took her half an hour on foot. Every few minutes she stopped to change her heavy bag from one hand to the other and massage her frozen fingers.

The rain from the night before had eased to a mere drizzle but a thin, biting wind swept down off the bare grey sides of Coity mountain. Kate breathed a sigh of relief as the two Roundhouses loomed against the skyline, knowing that she had not much further to go.

With their thick, impenetrable walls and cast-iron window casements they looked like medieval battlements. Olwen had told her they had been built by the Baileys as places of retreat if ever the workers attacked. She looked for the magnificent mansion, Ty Mawr, where the Baileys lived, but it was hidden from view by an impressive avenue of trees.

Coalbrookvale Terrace was coming alive as she reached it. Mollie Parry's house overflowed with boys of all ages and sizes. They scuttled like rabbits, shouting and squealing, as they washed under the outside pump, then darted back into the overcrowded living room to make ready to begin their working day.

Kate hesitated in the doorway, marvelling at the way Mollie Parry kept order. She was a short, plump woman in her late thirties, and wore her dark hair twisted into a bun and fastened on top of her head. She was dressed in a black skirt that reached to her boots and a dark red blouse with the sleeves rolled up to the elbows. It seemed to Kate she must have eyes in the back of her head. She never once turned round from where she stood frying bacon in a pan over the open coal fire, yet the boys' pushing and shoving stopped abruptly as she yelled to the offenders by name.

The silence that descended as the children caught sight of Kate was so intense that it did claim Mollie Parry's attention.

'*Duw anwyl*, there's a fright you gave me,' she frowned, staring ferociously at Kate.

'Are you Mollie Parry?' asked Kate.

'What do you want?' she asked suspiciously, her small mouth tightening.

'Olwen Price sent me.'

'D'you mean the housekeeper from Machen Mawr?'

'That's right.'

'I can't stop to talk to you now,' scowled Mollie. 'I must get this lot on their way or they'll be late and the site foreman will stripe them.' She began shouting orders to the children who now ignored Kate and made short work of the food she placed on the scrubbed wooden table.

'Sit down and have this while I see to the boyos and then we can talk.' Abruptly Mollie Parry thrust a slice of bread topped with bacon into Kate's hand.

'Thank you!' Hungrily Kate bit into the succulent wedge. Grease trickled from the corner of her mouth, she caught it with a forefinger, then licked her finger appreciatively.

'Drink this while it's hot.' Mollie Parry poured out a cup of strong tea from the big pot keeping warm on the hob, and handed it to Kate.

Fifteen minutes later and the house in Coalbrookvale Terrace was as quiet as the grave.

The children, many of them barefoot, their thin bodies barely covered by their ragged clothes, had set off for pit or foundry in batches of two or three. Each of them was clutching their 'bite', a slice of bread and dripping wrapped up in a piece of cloth which had to last them until they got home again at night.

'Now then, what's all this about?' Mollie Parry asked as she wiped the sweat from her face with a corner of her apron. She poured herself a cup of freshly made tea and refilled Kate's cup. 'I haven't seen Olwen Price for the past year or even longer. Not ill, is she?'

'No, no! Nothing like that.'

'So it's you that needs the help, is it?' She cast a quick eye over Kate's figure. 'In the family way, not married and so you want to get rid of it. Not that it shows as yet,' she added, sipping her tea.

'It's not like that at all.' Angrily Kate put her cup down on the table and pushed it away, upset by Mollie's remarks.

179

'So, why has Olwen Price sent you then?' Mollie asked in a puzzled voice.

'She said you would let me have a bed for a couple of nights. I'm trying to find someone . . .'

'A man?'

'Well . . . yes.'

'The father, I suppose! Don't tell me! Once he knew you were in the family way he vanished from . . .'

'No!' Kate's voice rose indignantly as she cut Mollie Parry short. 'It's not like that at all.'

'You mean he doesn't know you're looking for him.'

'No . . . of course not!'

'Then why d'you want to stay here?'

'To give me time to decide what to do for the best.'

'Been sporting with one of the Gentry, eh? Lifted your skirts at the Picnic outing to Abergavenny, did you!' She laughed raucously.

'No, no! Nothing at all like that. I've never been to Abergavenny, and I'm not expecting a baby,' exclaimed Kate in shocked tones. I'm trying to find someone from Fforbrecon colliery,' she explained.

'Fforbrecon! That's miles away.'

'I was told it was near Blaenafon.'

'Well, that's the other side of the Blorenge. It's a tidy walk, and no mistake. A couple of miles from here to Brynmawr and then another five miles at least to Blaenafon.'

'Perhaps I can manage to get a lift?'

'Perhaps and perhaps not,' Mollie pursed her lips. 'There's been a lot of trouble at Fforbrecon in the past weeks.'

'What sort of trouble?'

'They had a cave-in. Underground explosion that brought down the roof. The men working the seam were trapped.'

'Did . . . did they get them all out?'

'No. They decided not to bother, they sealed up the tunnel.'

180

'With the men inside!' gasped Kate.

'Said it was too difficult to do anything else.'

'How could they be sure that all the men were dead?'

'There was a meeting and the Owners agreed it was the best thing to do.'

'It couldn't be! Didn't the men's families protest?'

'No point. It would take two weeks to dig through so they'd be dead by then, anyway.'

'What about the bodies . . . for burial?'

'Well, they were buried already, weren't they?' muttered Mollie. 'When you're dead you're dead and I don't suppose it much matters what happens to your body after that.'

'It still seems terrible,' shivered Kate.

'The Owners said they could dig them out if they wanted . . . but it would mean no wages for two weeks. They get paid according to how much coal they dig, see.'

'And that decided it!'

'Not without a scuffle. Rumour has it that two men died. One of them was Gentry.'

'Really! Who . . . who was it?'

'I'm not one to listen to gossip. There's always trouble at one mine or the other. I have enough to worry about with the children they ask me to look after.'

'The boys you've just sent off to work?'

'Them and the other sort they send me.' She reached under the table, and dragged out a boy of about eight years old.

'Poor child, what happened?' Kate gasped in horror when she saw that his right leg ended just above the knee.

'He had his legs run over by a truck. Usually they've been crushed by one of the trams,' said Mollie, sitting the child on her lap and unwinding the bandages.

'How dreadful!' whispered Kate, her stomach heaving at the sight of the raw, seared flesh.

'If they manage to get over this sort of accident,' went on Mollie, 'then like as not they'll catch cholera or typhoid.'

181

'That's heartbreaking!'

'I've put fifteen of them into the ground already this year and now with winter ahead, probably as many again will die of the cold. Most of them are orphans so perhaps it's for the best,' she added, shrugging her shoulders. 'If you were from around these parts you'd not be showing such surprise.'

'No, I'm not from Ebbw Vale,' agreed Kate. 'And from what I've seen the people here are far worse off than where I come from.' Her face grew dreamy as her thoughts drifted back to Bramwood Hall. Even working at The Manor as a skivvy had been like paradise compared to the life these children led.

The memories stirred her to action. The thought of staying in the sour-smelling confines of Mollie Parry's home was repugnant.

'I'll be on my way. Thank you for the food and for letting me rest a while.'

'I thought you said you wanted a bed and help?' declared Mollie, openly affronted by Kate's sudden haste to leave.

'I did but I've changed my mind,' Kate told her, picking up her canvas bag and making for the door.

'If you're determined to go then take this with you, *cariad*.' Mollie thrust a hunk of bread and cheese into Kate's hand. 'Don't be afraid to come back if things don't work out,' she added, patting Kate's shoulder.

21

The air was as sharp as a knife edge as Kate left Coalbrookvale Terrace. October squalls filled the sky, clouds racing and chasing along the mountain ridge from one end of Coity to the other.

She breathed deeply to try and rid her nostrils of the stench of Mollie Parry's home. She had no clear idea of where she was going. All she wanted at that moment was to distance herself from the crowd of small, ragged children setting out for their long day of toil and the memory of the maimed child crouching under the table.

She felt utterly confused about her destination. She'd intended following the road to Brynmawr and from there heading for Blaenafon. Now, after what Mollie had said, she wanted to get to Fforbrecon as quickly as possible. Instead of continuing along the main road she decided to take a short cut over Coity Mountain.

Following the sheeptracks she climbed higher and higher up the scraggy side. The short, sparse grass was coarse and slippery, the stony track so narrow that at times she found it difficult to keep her foothold because of the weight of her canvas bag.

The blustery October winds made her eyes water. They tore at her dress and whipped the ends of her cloak around her legs or across her face. Her hair had long since blown free and hung to her shoulders in a tangle of dark curls.

It was midday when she crested Coity. She could see Blorenge in the distance and from where she stood it seemed to be as bleak as the mountain she'd just climbed.

The lower slopes of both mountains were polluted by

slag heaps and glowing cinder mounds with their spirals of grey smoke.

In the valley between, tall chimneys sent sulphurous smoke billowing into the air. She could look down on the red glow of blast furnaces and hear the resounding blows of the giant steam hammers ringing out as rhythmic as giant heartbeats.

As she made her way down the other side of Coity, storm clouds began to gather until she could no longer tell where the sky and earth divided. Afraid she would lose her way completely, Kate headed towards Blaenafon, guided by the glowing inferno of blast furnaces surrounding the town.

The rain came suddenly. Huge spots warned of the deluge to come. She looked around desperately for shelter. The few scraggy bushes were far down the hillside, but just as the storm broke she spotted a fissure between two folds of mountain ridge and ran towards it.

What had appeared to be merely a crevasse turned out to be an opening to a cave large enough to provide adequate shelter.

As the hail lashed and the sky grew even darker, Kate edged her way in deeper.

Her exclamation of astonishment as it widened out, echoed in the eerie gloom, making her wish she had a candle or lantern to light her way. Feeling her way along the rough, damp walls she found that it was not just a single cave but a honeycomb of small chambers.

Half an hour later, when Kate made her way back to the main opening, it was still raining heavily. Water poured down the hillside as if some enormous lake had overflowed. There was no break in the slate grey sky that rumbled overhead. Shivering, she moved back into the shelter. Her eyes were now accustomed to the gloom and she was able to see clearly into the numerous minor caverns leading off the central area.

She explored them all.

In two of them she made a discovery that left her shaking with fear. Hidden under a pile of straw was a heap of guns and, in another, several boxes of ammunition were piled up in one corner.

She returned to the central cave wondering what it all meant and who used the cave as a secret hideout, knowing she'd be in danger if she was discovered there.

She huddled into one corner and tried to calm herself by thinking of Bramwood Hall, of Helen and of David. When that failed she went once again to the entrance to see if the storm had abated and if she could be on her way. The rain was beating down even more fiercely and the greyness overhead made it as dark as night.

She felt anxious. She'd planned on reaching Blaenafon before nightfall but it now looked as though she might be forced to shelter there until morning. Cold and hungry, she ate the bread and cheese Mollie Parry had given her.

When she'd finished the last morsel, she tried singing and reciting poems that she knew by heart. She recalled how David had enjoyed hearing those by William Barnes and found that speaking them out loud seemed to bring him nearer.

As darkness fell and the rain still beat and blustered outside, Kate prepared to stay the night. She chose the smallest of the empty caverns. The blue cashmere shawl that had been her mother's was in her bag so she wrapped it round her head and shoulders, then fastened her cloak over the top of it and lay down with her head on her bag to sleep.

Kate was wakened from a deep sleep by the sound of men's voices and the clump of hobnail boots. Light from flickering lanterns sent grotesque shadows dancing on the wall.

For a moment she couldn't remember where she was. She felt stiff and sore from lying on the hard ground. It was as if she was living through a frightening nightmare. Then it all came rushing back. Remembering the guns and ammunition, she crouched tight into a corner, as

185

close against the wall as possible, hoping no one would come in or, if they did, that they wouldn't notice her.

She strained her ears to hear what was going on. From the mingling of voices there seemed to be quite a number of men gathered there.

At first she couldn't make out what they were talking about, but when she heard the name Owen repeated several times she listened more intently. Frissons of fear ran down her spine as she realized they were planning an uprising. She heard other names mentioned: John Frost, Zephaniah Williams, Jones the Watchmaker, men Olwen Price had claimed were agitators.

She held her breath as they unveiled their plans.

The men they'd mentioned would be leading groups from Blaenafon, Coalbrookvale, Brynmawr and Blaina and other places she had never heard of before. There they would all meet up in Pontypool and take the Risca Road on to Newport.

'We need to find out how the authorities will defend the town.'

'Mayor Phillips will have the constabulary as well as the military.'

'We should easily outnumber them. The constabulary only amount to a few hundred men.'

'And we will have thousands . . .'

'The military will be well armed . . .'

'And properly trained . . .'

'But there's no more than about fifty of them . . .'

'The 45th Regiment are billeted at the Workhouse on Stow Hill . . .'

'There's only seventy of them and they will have to keep some of them there to guard . . .'

'But the ones in action will have been trained in the use of guns . . .'

'But we'll outnumber them. And we've pikes and . . .'

Kate felt numb with terror. The guns and ammunition she had seen stock-piled were to be used by the men taking part in the uprising! If they found her hiding they'd think she had been sent by the Redcoats or Gentry to spy on them and there was no knowing what they would do to her.

They might even kill her!

She wondered if she told them that she was looking for a friend called Owen they would be lenient with her.

It gave her hope. After all, she reasoned, there must be some God-fearing men amongst them who wouldn't want the blood of an innocent girl on their hands.

They sounded so incensed as they continued to plan and argue amongst themselves that even that faint ray of hope began to fade.

Crouched in the darkness, Kate grew stiff with the cold. The men had moved into the caves where the guns and ammunition were stored and she could hear them sharing them out amongst themselves. She could still see the glimmer of light from their lanterns and was afraid to move in case they heard her, though she began to wonder if discovery would be any more of a risk than the one she was already taking in wandering alone in such alien countryside.

She wasn't even sure which path led to Blaenafon. It was hours since she had eaten the bread and cheese Mollie Parry had given her and even longer since she'd had anything to drink. If the weather worsened then she'd be completely cut off. She could die before anyone found her.

Tears began to roll down her cheeks. She brushed them away and began silently reciting William Barnes' poems again, letting the West Country dialect sing inside her head, conjuring up visions of her grandmother's cottage and the countryside she'd known as a child.

The sound of the men leaving brought her back to the present. The lanterns had been extinguished and everywhere was in complete darkness. As the sound of the men's hobnail boots receded, Kate crept from her hiding place.

The reek of tobacco smoke was the only trace that anyone had visited the silent, deserted caves.

Through the narrow aperture she saw the rain had stopped. A thin crescent moon was riding high, dipping and dodging between the clouds. One minute it was lighting the mountainside with thin, cold brilliance, the next plunging it back into darkness.

Moving out into the open, Kate thought she could make out one or two shadowy movements far down the mountainside, but then the moon was hidden as a fresh bank of cloud soared up over Coity. When the cloud had passed the landscape was bare and grey in the moonlight with no sign of human life except for the dull red glow far below in the valley from the forges and blast furnaces.

She had no idea what time it was but surmised that the men who'd come to the cave had either just finished a shift and now gone their separate ways home, or had been on their way to work.

She collected her canvas bag. The moment she moved from the shelter of the cave she was buffeted by the wind and the occasional spiteful spit of rain. As well as the dull roar of the iron works there was a new sound that she didn't recognize.

Shivering, she drew back into the shelter of the cave as she realized water was rushing past her as brooks in flood roared down the mountainside.

She decided to stay where she was until it was daylight. In the spasmodic darkness she could easily fall into one of the brooks and drown, or slip and be trapped if there were any other crevices or caves.

At first light she set off. The rutted path was treacherously slippery. Mile after mile she trudged, stopping only to change her bag from one hand to the other.

When she finally reached the roadway her relief was so great that she collapsed in a heap beside a low wall. Resting her back against the damp uneven stones, she took stock of her surroundings. There was something vaguely familiar about the place and she groaned aloud when she caught sight of the round towers that had been built by the Baileys. Her meanderings had brought her back to the same point in Nantyglo that she'd left the previous day.

Tears threatened but she blinked them away, refusing to accept defeat. She felt too weary to continue any further and longed to sleep. The choice seemed to be under a hedge by the side of the road or back to Coalbrookvale Terrace. The thought of Mollie Parry's house filled to overflowing with small boys was far from enticing but at least she would be dry and warm there.

Mollie stared as if she was seeing a ghost when she opened the door to Kate's persistent rapping.

'What's happened, *cariad,*' she gasped, stretching out a hand and seizing Kate's arm to make sure she was real.

'I got lost on the mountain. I must have walked in a circle and I found myself back here again.'

'You've been walking all this time!'

'I sheltered from the rain in a cave on the mountainside and I must have dropped off to sleep,' Kate told her quickly, deciding it would be better not to mention the men or the cache of arms hidden there.

'Come on in by the fire and warm yourself. I'll brew some tea. Are you hungry?'

'Ravenous! All I've had to eat since I left here is the bread and cheese you gave me.'

'*Duw anwyl!* Get this down you.' She thrust a bowl of steaming soup into Kate's hand. 'Drop of cawl left over. I was going to have it myself while the boys are still asleep.'

'I can't take it if its yours,' Kate protested.

'Rubbish! Have you seen the size of me! Always eating, I am. Breakfast before the boys get up and another when they've all left. Same thing in the evening. If there's anything left over I put it to one side and enjoy it once they're all asleep. Eating and drinking is my comfort now my Ianto's gone,' she sighed.

The heat from the fire combined with the comforting warmth of the food made Kate so sleepy that she found it difficult to keep her eyes open.

'Bed for you, my girl,' Mollie told her. 'You can use mine, it's still warm.'

'I can't turn you out of your bed,' protested Kate.

'You won't be turning me out because I wasn't in it,' cackled Mollie.

'Go on, get your head down. In a few minutes I'll be rousing the boys for work and then all hell will be let loose. Be like bedlam in here. Pull your shawl up over your ears, then you won't hear the racket they make. Off with you now.'

The moment Kate's head touched the pillow she was asleep. She knew nothing until late in the afternoon when she woke feeling wonderfully refreshed. She lay for a few minutes gathering her thoughts, trying to plan what to do next, until savoury cooking smells made lying in bed impossible.

22

Refusing Mollie's invitation to stay on for another day, Kate set out again for Blaenafon at first light the next morning.

'No clever short cuts over Coity this time then, *cariad*,' warned Mollie.

'No,' Kate promised, 'I'll keep to the main road all the way and perhaps I'll be lucky enough to get a lift.'

'Now just you mind who you're riding with,' cautioned Mollie, standing in the doorway, arms akimbo, laughing raucously.

The rain of the previous day had stopped but the sky was still grey and overcast. Puddles shivered in the wind and there was the bite of winter in the air.

To Kate's surprise, the road was as crowded as a fair day. When she had driven down in the trap, mid-morning or early afternoon, with Mathew at her side, they had never seen more than a dozen people between Blaina and Nantyglo.

Now, men in moleskin trousers, mufflers round their scrawny necks and greasy caps protecting their heads from the cold, were walking in droves towards the pit face or the ironworks.

Dark-eyed women with shawls over their heads and shoulders, children hanging on to their voluminous black skirts, pushed and jostled her as they hurried on their way, babbling in Welsh; words she was unable to understand.

It was so alien that it sent waves of fear through her.

As a hand reached out and grabbed her canvas bag Kate screamed, thinking she was being robbed.

'There's heavy that looks for a slip of a thing like you,' a deep sing-song voice murmured at her side.

A man in his twenties, coal-grimed cap set at a jaunty angle over his black hair, regarded her with amusement.

She relaxed her grip. He didn't look the sort to run off with it.

'Making for Blaina?' he asked.

'No!' She shook her head. 'I . . . I'm going to Blaenafon.'

'Blaenafon!' He let out a low whistle. 'Tidy way off, you know.' He jerked his head towards the grey barren mass of land to their right. 'Over the other side of Coity Mountain.'

'I know. I'm hoping I might get a lift when I get to Brynmawr.'

'You'll be lucky!'

'I'll keep hoping.'

'You'll never make it walking, not with this,' he added swinging the canvas bag.

'I will if people carry it for me,' laughed Kate.

'Best thing, my lovely, is to go to The Top, then take the road to the right when you get to Brynmawr. That way you might get a lift from one of the carriers going to Blaenafon.'

'Thanks, I'll do that.'

'You going into service there?'

'No. I . . . I'm trying to find someone at Fforbrecon colliery.'

'Fforbrecon! They've had trouble there . . .' he paused, giving her a sideways glance as if to determine whether it was safe to say any more.

'I was told there'd been a cave-in.'

'Followed by an uprising of some sort.'

'Because of the men trapped underground?'

'That's only part of it.'

'To do with the Chartists' movement?'

'There's discontent throughout the Valleys,' he said bitterly.

192

'Protesting about their working conditions, you mean.'

'And their Rights as citizens. Everywhere there's men mustering. Jack Frost, who used to be Mayor of Newport, is behind them. Powerful speeches he makes, *cariad*! You should hear the fine words he uses to get the men to rise up against the ironmasters and coal barons.'

'A revolution,' shuddered Kate, thinking of the men who had gathered on Coity. 'It's like the Tolpuddle Martyrs all over again.'

'Who are they?'

'Some farm workers in Dorset who demanded better wages and working conditions. The ring-leaders were transported to Van Diemen's Land.'

'Probably the same thing will happen to the Chartists,' the man muttered angrily. 'There'll be Redcoats from Brecon in Nantyglo and Blaina before it all ends,' he added bitterly. 'And there'll be bloodshed. . . .'

He stopped abruptly as a shrill siren rent the air. 'I turn off here for the pit,' he said, thrusting her canvas bag back into her hand.

As she tried to thank him she found herself jostled to one side as men, women and children responded in a mad frenzy to the siren's summons.

'Good luck to you,' he shouted. 'Perhaps we'll meet again, both marching towards Newport! My name's Idris Lewis.'

'I'll look out for you,' she called after him.

'I'll be the one carrying the Blaina Benefit Banner!' he shouted over his shoulder before he was swallowed up in the crowd.

Kate stood stock-still as people surged around her. Some rushed to where colliery wheels ground and jarred as cages packed tight with human cargo were lowered into the blackness. The rest scurried towards the ironworks where great chimneys belched acrid smoke and giant furnaces glowed like a devil's kitchen. Within minutes the road was empty as if they'd all been swallowed up in the pall of sulphurous smoke that swirled in yellow clouds.

Now it was as if the only people left in the world were crippled old men, a handful of women with young babies tucked inside a carrying shawl, and barefoot toddlers playing in the mud and filth outside their houses.

Compared to these people she was wealthy, Kate thought, as she trudged past them. Furtively, she slid a hand under her cloak to reassure herself that the pocket containing her money was still tied securely round her waist beneath her petticoats.

The smell of freshly baked bread wafting out on to the chill air reminded her that Olwen Price would be serving breakfast about now at Machen Mawr. She thought longingly of hot creamy porridge followed by succulent bacon, devilled kidneys and fried eggs. And there would be hot, sweet tea, and freshly made rolls, with plenty of butter and honey to spread on them.

The hairs on the nape of her neck rose as she heard a cart drawing up alongside her and a lilting voice calling out, asking if she wanted a lift.

'Are you going to Brynmawr?' she asked nervously, looking up into the bearded face.

'Is that where you're making for, my lovely?'

'I want to get to Blaenafon eventually.'

'Blaenafon, is it! Now there's a long journey! Were you thinking of walking all the way?' The man's laugh was deep and reassuring.

'Not really.'

'Come on, hop up.' He reached down and took her canvas bag from her. 'I'm going to The Top and like as not I can find someone to give you a ride the rest of the way.'

In spite of his assurance that if she stayed with him until they reached Beaufort at the head of the Valleys he could be sure of getting her a lift all the way to Blaenafon, Kate insisted on being put down in Brynmawr.

'Bleak old place, if you ask me,' he scowled. 'Cold as charity. Highest hill town in Wales, you know.'

In that he was right. The road had risen ever since they'd left Nantyglo and when she climbed down from the cart in Brynmawr she found the wind had become sharper and colder.

Walking was far from pleasant. She had to stop constantly to change her bag from one hand to the other and rub her numbed fingers. Her shoulders and back ached, her feet were tender where her boots pinched, and she was ravenously hungry.

Pausing to rest, she tried to work out some plan of action. The mountains flanking the scrub moorland beside the road were like impenetrable walls. Even the foraging sheep that dotted their sides looked scrawny and seemed to shiver as gusts of wind parted the fleece on their backs.

Could she be certain of finding David at Llwynowen, she wondered, or would it be more sensible to go straight to Fforbrecon colliery? Since she wasn't sure where either of them were she decided the time to make up her mind was when she got to Blaenafon.

It was almost dark by the time she reached the outskirts of the town. In the far distance, beneath a dull red glowing sky, she saw the towering chimneys of the ironworks.

As she neared the gothic church in the centre of the town, people emerged out of the gloom, coming down the hill towards her like an army of ants as they made their way home.

Men, women and youngsters, work-weary and hungry, they moved in a ragged wall of humanity, pushing and jostling her out of their way. As they reached Stack Square they seemed to divide up into two columns. The men towards the pubs and ale-houses, women and children homewards.

Kate leaned against the enormous great stack that gave the square its name and wondered if she could rent a bed for the night. She took out the two shillings from her reticule and clutched them in her hand, uncertain which door to knock on.

As she hesitated, someone tripped over her canvas bag which she'd rested for a minute on the ground, and began to curse in Welsh. Kate screamed and struck his hand away as he reached out and grabbed her.

'What's going on, boyo?' a voice rasped.

'Mind your own business, mun.'

'Thought I heard a woman scream . . .'

'With excitement, mun! Proper little darling! Her and me's got business, see!' Kate's assailant joked as he grasped Kate's wrist and twisted it cruelly.

Pain shot up her arm, numbing her fingers so that the coins she held in her fist rolled on to the ground.

A crowd had gathered and there was a scuffle to pick them up.

'They're mine!' She held out her hand for them to be returned.

A heavily built man with a check muffler wrapped round his neck spun one of the coins in the air, shouting to his mates to join him for a beer.

'That's my money you're spending,' protested Kate.

'Come with us and have a drink then,' he bellowed.

The ale-house was packed with men who'd just finished work. They greeted her arrival with ribald remarks.

Grabbing hold of the man who had her money by his coat sleeve, Kate demanded food as well as ale.

'Here you are, my beauty!' He shoved a beef butty and a pot of ale into her hands. Kate took them and made her way to a far corner of the room where she could sit down and enjoy them. The beef was salty and tough, the bread coarse-grained and thickly cut but she was so hungry she devoured them rapidly.

At the same time she kept a wary eye on the men crowded around the bar. They were watching her and making remarks in a mixture of Welsh and English which she didn't understand. Instinctively, she knew they boded no good and she was afraid of what might happen next.

She breathed a sigh of relief when the man who had taken her money, ignoring her completely, left in a babble of farewells from his cronies.

Relaxed by the warmth of the room and the food, she felt too weary to move on. Drowsily she listened to the banter around her, only half aware that one by one the rest of the men were leaving.

'Right then, Missy, time for you to settle up.'

The landlord came from behind the bar and stood, legs straddled, looking down at her. 'Three shillings, if you please.'

'Three shillings!' Kate stared at him wide eyed, then struggled to her feet. 'What are you talking about? All I had was a butty and a tankard of ale.'

'And what about all the ale your friends drank, then?'

'Friends?' She frowned. 'I don't know a single soul in this town.'

'What about the crowd you came in with, then! Ifor Addams said you were standing them all a drink so I gave it to them.'

'Then you had better ask him for the money,' Kate retorted spiritedly. Anger fired her cheeks. 'That man stole money from me as it is.'

'So you can't pay?'

'Not can't pay, but won't pay,' she told him heatedly.

Dai Roberts glared at the defiant figure in front of him. He had been landlord at The Bull long enough to know that this girl was a cut above the Molls and Polls who came in to pick up a man and fleece him on a paynight. Her clothes were of good quality cloth. Her boots were muddied but she looked clean and well fed, her cheeks plump, her black curls glossy.

Even so, he told himself firmly, he couldn't afford to give drink away. Three shillings she owed him and one way or another he was determined it should be paid.

'The law is it, then?' he threatened.

'What do you mean?'

'Them as doesn't pay gets clapped into gaol . . . or sent to the House of Correction,' he told her grimly.

He saw the colour drain from her face, her blue eyes darken and her teeth bite down on her lower lip to stop it trembling.

'You have the choice.'

Her mind sifted the options. She had heard terrible accounts about the treatment meted out in a House of Correction and she had no intention of ending up there.

In the pocket concealed under her petticoats was her hoard of sovereigns. If she produced one of those, having led him to believe she was unable to pay, he'd probably take her for a thief. Furthermore, there was the added problem of reaching them. She could hardly remove her top skirt while he was standing there.

'Are you going to pay or would you rather work instead?'

'Work?' She felt a glimmer of hope, she needed a bed for the night. 'Doing what?' she asked suspiciously.

'Cleaning, serving the customers, doing a bit of cooking. Helping out generally, like. I could do with a woman about the place, see.'

'As long as I get a bed and a room to myself?' she said firmly.

'Of course you will! *Duw anwyl*, what do you take me for?'

'I just want to be sure. I've been taken in once since I've arrived in Blaenafon so I want to be certain it doesn't happen again.'

'You're not from around here, are you?' His needle-sharp eyes raked over her.

'No! I'm from . . . from the south.'

'You don't talk like someone from Newport or Cardiff.'

'I come from much further south than that . . . from Wiltshire.'

'So what are you doing in these parts?' he asked suspiciously.

'I'm looking for someone.'

Their eyes locked, each wondering if they could trust the other. The Bull was the meeting place for Frost's supporters and from her appearance and the soft way she had of talking, she could be Gentry. She didn't look like she might be a spy but then neither was she like any of the women who came into The Bull. They were either shabby-shawled wives, ragged working women or garishly dressed tarts with painted mouths.

'I'm looking for someone who . . . who works at Fforbrecon colliery.'

Dai Roberts eyes narrowed. There had been trouble at Fforbrecon. First the cave-in and then a riot of some sort. It had been hushed up but he'd heard rumours that one of the coalmasters had been badly hurt. He'd only heard rumblings since none of the men wanted to talk about it. A strike had been threatened, but after the accident the men had dropped their action and the arbitrators who'd been called in had gone away.

Dai Roberts studied Kate's appearance again. From the look of her she could well have been sent by one of the Gentry to find out the names of men involved.

'Why come here to Blaenafon if it's Fforbrecon you want?' he asked suspiciously.

'I've walked from Nantyglo and I was told this was the best road to take.'

Dai Roberts rubbed his chin thoughtfully. She sounded genuine enough and he liked the look of her. Once the weariness was gone from her face she would be quite pretty and an attraction behind the bar. The men liked to have a woman handing out their ale.

'Make your mind up, *cariad*,' he told her as he began swabbing down with an old rag. 'It's generous I'm being offering to let you work off your debt rather than be sent to the House of Correction.'

'How much are you going to pay me?'

'Sixpence a day and your food. One week and the debt will be cleared.'

'All right,' she agreed, squaring her slim shoulders and lifting her chin proudly.

'Get started then. Collect the pots and wash them. When you've finished that I'll show you where you can sleep. Tomorrow morning, six sharp, I'll tell you the rest of your duties.'

23

Kate found the work at The Bull harder than anything she'd ever done in her life.

Her day started at six o'clock each morning scrubbing the slopped ale, dollops of spittle and the coagulation of coal dust and iron stains off the bar floor. That done, Dai Roberts expected her to clean the rest of the house and do the washing as well as serve the customers.

Too stingy to pay out for help after his mother had died two years earlier, Dai Roberts had muddled along, running The Bull single-handed. As she cleaned and scrubbed, Kate vowed that she should have walked out at the end of her first day rather than face such accumulated grime.

She regarded it as a respite when he sent her shopping, even though women grabbed their children by the hand, pulling them close for safety because she was a stranger and looked Irish.

And the Irish themselves, knowing that for all her colouring she was not one of them, openly resented her. Most of them were crowded into leaking shacks or sleeping in bricked-up arches with only cinders on the floor and straw for a bed and envied her living in comfort at The Bull.

As she walked through the town they delighted in throwing their slops into the roadway ahead of her so that she was forced to slow her pace, lift her skirts and pick a path through their refuse.

'It's that curly black hair of yours and those bright eyes,' Dai Roberts told her when she complained. 'Droves of young Irish girls we get over here, see. Don't worry, my flower, folks will soon accept you.'

And he was right. Within a couple of days, knowing she worked at The Bull, people nodded and smiled. In the shops, the women would stand back to let her be served first. As her order for mutton, sugar, cheese and bacon was weighed up she was conscious of them enviously eyeing her fine dress and blue bonnet with its fly-away streamers the colour of her eyes.

Kate longed to win their confidence. She wanted to question them about the man she was seeking, but she knew better than to rush things.

Having made her purchases she would wander away from the High Street and Broad Street, through the narrow, overcrowded areas of Stack Square and Engine Row where the small terraced houses were packed to overflowing with as many as fifteen people under the same roof. Even those dwellings, however, seemed luxurious when she compared them to the walled-up arches near the ironworks where immigrants, vagrants and orphaned children were herded together like animals in a pen.

As she breathed in the sulphurous air, or saw the sky redden with fire from the forges, heard the deep pulsating hammers and the rattle of loaded trams bound for Llanfoist Wharf, Kate grew impatient with her self-imposed caution.

A reluctance to put her relationship with David to the test kept her there. She was within a few miles of his home and yet she couldn't bring herself to visit Llwynowen. She longed desperately to see him, hear his voice, be in his arms, feel his lips on hers, yet she hesitated to make the move.

The malodorous chimneys, fire-belching furnaces, iron puddling and vats of molten ore dominated the scene. The surrounding countryside was scarred by coal mines and cinder tips, the grass scorched, the bushes stunted. Coity Mountain stretched out like some great grey whale, the ridge of its back resting against the skyline, an impenetrable wall that blotted out the sun and imprisoned the people living in Blaenafon.

It was all so different from the lush green fields and gentle rolling downs of Wiltshire that sometimes she found it difficult to believe she was in the same world. There, the hedgerows had been a continuous delight; a celebration of colour.

Snowdrops in January, followed by glittering yellow celandines, soft pale primroses, violets, wide-eyed daisies, bluebells, wild roses; a profusion of colour all through the year. Even this late in the year, she reflected, there would be hawthorn and holly berries, food for the birds and a delight for the eye.

There had been poverty but even that had been made bearable by the harvest of berries and nuts in the hedgerows, and apples and pears overhanging from the orchards. Most cottagers had a patch of garden for potatoes and vegetables. Many owned a cow or pig and a clutch of hens so they had a supply of milk and eggs.

The whole of Blaenafon seemed to be in a ferment of discontent. The uprising at Fforbrecon, she learnt, had been the result of the Owners' callous attitude to the cave-in and refusal to extricate the bodies. But it was all part of a much greater unrest linked with workers in North Wales, the industrial North and the Midlands. Union agitators were persuading the workers that only by rising up in a body would they achieve better conditions and shorter working hours.

A Charter of Rights had been drawn up by the leaders of the movement and the terms laid down in it were the subject of lengthy arguments and heated discussions.

The Bull was one of the principal meeting places for Chartist supporters. They would come in straight from their shift, their eyes glazed with tiredness: the colliers still grimed with coal dust, as noisy as pit ponies in their hobnail boots; men from the ironworks, the skin on their hands and faces tattooed brown with pigment, their ragged clothes stained ochre-yellow with dust, giving off a rank, sour smell that made Kate's stomach heave.

They would huddle in groups planning the forthcoming uprising with passion and excitement. The rise and fall of their voices reminded Kate of the men who had gathered in the cave on Coity Mountain where she'd taken shelter.

Moving amongst them as she collected up empty tankards, Kate listened. A word here, a phrase there, she stored them as avidly as a squirrel does autumn nuts. Later, in her attic bedroom, unable to sleep because of the vivid glow from the blast furnaces that gilded the walls and ceiling, she would ponder on what she'd heard. The words built up a picture, pieces falling in place as neat as any patchwork quilt.

Kate's heart went out to those who slaved underground in the blackness of the coalmines or worked in the stinking heat of the ironworks. She sensed that their heartfelt cry for better conditions and proper representation was not one of greed but borne of the need for survival for themselves and their families.

The demands she'd heard repeated over and over again seemed reasonable enough to her. She summarized them in her mind:

Votes for all men over the age of 21.

Elections to Parliament every year.

The abolition of property ownership as a qualification to becoming a Member of Parliament.

Members of Parliament to be paid for their attendance in London so that even working men could afford to stand as representatives.

Three hundred constituencies of equal number of electors.

A secret ballot so that workers could not be pressurized as to how they must vote.

The names of the Chartist leaders, Jack Frost, a draper in Newport, who had at one time been its Mayor, William Jones from Pontypool and Zephaniah Edwards from Nantyglo, were spoken in whispers. Repeatedly she heard the name Owen mentioned and longed to ask questions, yet knew that once she did every man amongst them would clam up. Dark-eyed Celtic men, suspicious and furtive, they often lapsed into their native tongue if they thought she was listening.

'Just wait until we attack London, mun. Then we'll bloody show 'em!'

'Plenty of support, see. I heard we'd collected over a million signatures.'

'D'ye know, if those sheets of names were joined together they'd be three miles long!'

'Signatures are no good, boyo, it's an attack we need.'

'Any day now!'

'Just as soon as we receive word from the men in Birmingham.'

'What about the cotton workers from Lancashire?'

'And men from the woollen mills in Yorkshire?'

'Just hold on . . . they're all with us.'

Although she listened and remembered, it was always the mention of the name Owen that made her ears prick up. Her heart would thunder with excitement, then dip down into her button-boots as soon as she realized the Owen they were talking about couldn't possibly be David.

There were so many men called Owen that her mind was in a welter of confusion.

For some it was a first name, like Owen Roberts, one of the Puddlers at Pwll-dhu, or Owen Hughes who lived in Stack Row. Then there was Owen the Bread in Market Street and Eli Owen, a sidesman at Horeb Chapel, who had lost his left leg when molten iron ore had splashed it so badly that it had to be amputated.

Every day, or so it seemed to Kate, she heard of a new Owen and none of them was the man she longed to find.

Towards the end of the week, Kate began asking the men who drank in The Bull for directions to Fforbrecon colliery.

'What do you want to go there for, *cariad*?'

'The far side of Blorenge.'

'Not the sort of place for you to be visiting on your own, my lovely.'

'You'd be safe enough if you'd let me take you,' they joked.

'All right then, which of you is it to be?'

Ifor Hughes, one of the engineers from Garnddyrys, was eager to accompany her but he withdrew his offer after a tongue-lashing from some of the other men.

'Best not, *cariad*,' he told her, laying a heavy hand on her arm.

'And why not?'

'There's been a lot of trouble over there recently, see!'

'I know. I thought that was why I needed an escort,' teased Kate.

'The Scotch Cattle might set on us if they find us poking our noses in where we shouldn't and then where'd we be?' he prevaricated.

'In real trouble, I can tell you!' another man warned.

'Why are you in such a hurry to leave here, anyway?'

'I've got to find someone at Fforbrecon,' Kate told them stubbornly, all laughter gone from her voice.

As she lay in her hard narrow bed that night, watching the red glow on the ceiling and listening to the thundering pulse of the ironworks, Kate made up her mind. She'd go there alone. Why should she fear the Scotch Cattle? They might look fearful dressed up in skins, their faces blackened and horns strapped on their heads, but it was hardly likely that they would apprehend a woman or try and take her to the military.

She'd been assured that Fforbrecon was on the other side of the Blorenge so if she followed the sheeptracks along the lower slopes she should reach there in due course. She'd leave her canvas bag behind at The Bull. If David wasn't at Fforbrecon then she'd come back and collect it. If she did find him, then Dai Roberts could give her things away to whoever he pleased since she wouldn't need them. David would buy her as many new gowns as she wanted.

'You owe for breakages,' Dai Roberts glowered when Kate reminded him that she had completed her week and that now her debt was cleared she was moving on.

'One glass and a chipped cup!' she said scornfully.

'Stay on another week and I'll pay you another three shillings,' he promised.

'Is that all!'

'Better than nothing when you're penniless.'

With order restored in his living quarters, hot food prepared for him daily and another pair of hands doing the bulk of the work in the bar, Dai Roberts felt himself to be in clover and knew he would be a fool to let her leave.

'Make it four shillings.'

Knowing the men clustered round the bar were listening, he agreed. He would have liked her to stay for good. She was a hard worker and the men had accepted her. It was as if she had always been about the place. She had a ready smile and was good to look at. He'd noticed that since she'd been there many of the men who dropped in on their way home returned again later in the evening. Whether for the pleasure of drinking in her company, or to discuss the Chartist issues, he wasn't sure but it pleased him because his takings were up.

Her presence seemed to have a calming influence on the men. Uncertain of her political loyalties they kept their heated discussions in check.

Not that she seemed in the least interested in them or their gossip. In her plain blue gown, her black curls pulled back into the nape of her neck, she looked more like a nun than a barmaid. From the way she rebuffed any who tried to take liberties, she might well have been one.

'Why move on when you've nowhere to go? You can have the bedroom next to mine,' he offered. 'Much warmer than up in that attic.'

'There's handy now! You could be real cosy, my lovely,' added one of the men with a meaningful wink.

'It's kind of you but no thank you,' Kate told him. She flushed delicately. 'I must go to Fforbrecon, I have to find someone.'

'This man you're looking for . . . is he your husband?'

Kate smiled non-committally. She didn't wish to confide in Dai Roberts or anyone else, but she was willing to listen if any of them had more to say.

'You know there's been trouble over there,' Dai Roberts said guardedly, his dark eyes watching her.

'Only to be expected the way they treat their workers,' argued one of the men.

'They even use young children in the coal pits at Fforbrecon,' added another.

'They use them here at the iron works, as well,' Kate flashed angrily. 'Last night a lad came with a scarred face and one hand so badly burned he couldn't use it.'

'Walli Howell's boy, you mean.'

'Terrible accident that!'

'Hardly call him a child, though. Going on twelve, he is. Old enough to watch out when they're ladling hot ore and make sure he is standing clear.'

'Daydreaming he must've been and missed the shout.'

'Silly young bugger!'

'No one to blame except himself, really.'

'At Fforbrecon, it's said they use little ones of only four or five to open the safety doors.'

'Poor little mites!'

'Down there, all on their own in the blackness, with rats running over them.'

'Twelve-hour shifts, mind you!'

'More often than not they're that tired and hungry that they drop off to sleep.'

'And that's when they fall on to the track and get run over by the coal trucks.'

'If they're lucky they die.'

'If they don't they end up begging.'

'Too crippled to ever work again, see!'

'And that's not the worst part,' Dai Roberts said, clearing his throat. 'Some of the galleries are so low and narrow that a grown man can't even crawl through them, so the wicked buggers use the smallest children to haul the trucks!'

'Strap a harness on them, see, same as on a pit pony!'

'Two or three tons of coal in some of those trucks that they have to pull.'

'With their blackened faces and hands and their half-naked bodies, covered with grazes and sweat, they're barely human.'

'The chains rub 'em so raw that they can't stand or sit after a few days. Bleeding they are!'

'A lot of them collapse under the strain,' sighed Dai Roberts as he pulled himself some ale.

'Or from hunger,' added another as he pushed his tankard across the counter for a refill.

'It's a happy release for them when they die.'

'Hard on their families, mind.'

'A few pennies a week less towards paying the rent, see!'

'Stop!' Kate's hands went up to cover her ears, to shut out the cruelty the men were describing so graphically. She couldn't believe David would allow such exploitation. He was far too kind and gentle. He couldn't even bear to see a horse ill treated. If he knew such atrocities were going on at Fforbrecon he would stamp them out.

Was this what had given rise to the trouble that everyone hinted at but seemed unwilling to talk about? she wondered uneasily.

24

Kate's arrival had made life more pleasant for Dai Roberts, yet, for all that, he felt uneasy. He had been landlord of The Bull long enough to sense when trouble was brewing and was aware of the unrest amongst his customers.

Although he sympathized with the Chartist aims he kept his opinions to himself. He'd had experience of the conditions the men worked under and was aware of the depths of degradation to which many of them and their families had sunk. His own wife was dead and he had no children, yet he still felt concern for youngsters who were put to work underground as soon as they could walk and talk.

The Bull, like so many other ale-houses in Ebbw Vale, was owned by one of the ironmasters. Although Dai Roberts was left to run things in his own way he was as much a slave of Crawshay Bailey as any man who drank there.

The beer was bought by men who worked for Crawshay Bailey with wages he'd paid them and the profits went back into his coffers. To make doubly sure of this, the men's wages were paid out in The Bull and Dai Roberts had instructions that if the Agent was late to give the men credit until he arrived.

The price of the four or five pints of beer that went down each man's throat while they waited was deducted from their wages, together with any other credit they may have chalked up since the previous payday. Often the men were too drunk to count if the money eventually handed over to them was correct or not.

Crawshay Bailey also owned most of the Tommy

shops in Blaina, Nantyglo, Brynmawr and Blaenafon. The prices of the goods in them were a third or more higher than in the nearby towns. The women had little option but to use them since the only way to get paid in full was by accepting the specially minted brass coins.

Those who demanded the silver coin of the realm, so that they could spend them in the open market in Pontypool, Abergavenny or Newport, had a levy deducted.

Dai Roberts hated the system. Many times since his wife had died he'd thought of leaving The Bull and seeking some other kind of employment. Then, he would remind himself how much better off he was than puddlers, coal trimmers, or limestone carriers, and hesitate about making any change.

Running an ale-house was child's play compared to working twelve to fourteen hours in the heat of the blast furnaces, or deep underground in the dark confines of the pits.

He'd known men have their hand, wrist and forearm burnt to the bone, one enormous red weal where the molten flash of ore had splashed. He'd seen men with legs rigid and swollen, the skin heaped in a high, puckered ridge where molten iron had settled, making the blood boil. He'd watched men having slugs of lead removed from arms, legs and even their faces.

A knife would be levered in beneath the rigid lump, prising the metal upwards until it came clear, dropping with a resounding thud on to the floor. The long, jagged gash that remained was too painful to clean so it was left to bleed or fester. A gaping wound that, when it eventually healed, would leave an unsightly scar.

He'd seen puddlers with their faces blistered, going blind, their red eyes constantly watering. Others, with their hands bandaged against the cruel heat, knowing that within a few years all their joints would dry out and then their legs would grow heavy, their walk painfully slow.

Blaenafon was the refuse dump of the Bailey Empire. Men, maimed and deformed by accidents, short of a leg or an arm, crouched on their hunkers at street corners or hobbled along on crutches. Others staggered uncontrollably, afflicted by nystagmus caused by working for long periods in the flickering light of candles or oil lamps. There was no cure for the giddiness and blackouts they suffered.

Kate's arrival had resurrected all his doubts and misgivings. She was so young, so pretty with her pink and cream cheeks, her big blue eyes and glistening black curls. She was like a breath of the countryside he'd known as a boy, when he'd lived in a farm cottage in Govilon.

Then, one Fair day in Abergavenny he'd met Marie. He'd crossed over Blorenge the next weekend to court her. She'd won his heart and fired his ambition with her stories of the big money to be made working in iron.

His youthful mind had been inflamed, his heart pounding in time to the giant thud of the drop hammers. He'd not noticed that children in Blaenafon looked old at ten, or the men whose eyes had been put out by a blast-kiss, or whose empty sleeves were tied with string. He'd been too excited by the sight of the entire mountain becoming one single fire as flames from the maze of furnaces blended into the darkening sky. The thundering, whining background had been music in his ears.

Marie had been dark-haired and dark-eyed, brawny from working underground pulling a coal tram since she was eight. She'd been ripe for love. Besotted by what Marie offered he had taken a job underground, exchanged farm for pit, not realizing the terrible mistake he was making.

Slowly his senses returned and the sights around him sickened him. Marie laughed when he protested about children as young as six and seven being forced to work underground, in charge of the ventilation doors. Or about girls, as well as boys of ten or younger, being harnessed like animals so that they could haul the loaded coal trams through cuttings too narrow for them to even stand upright.

Then came the day when he couldn't stand working underground, in the claustrophobic darkness, another minute.

'What will you do?' sulked Marie. 'My wages won't pay the rent.'

'We'll manage.'

'There's something else you'd best know before you quit. I didn't intend telling you yet.' Her dark eyes softened and she pressed herself close against him, her arms around his neck, pulling his ear down to her mouth as she whispered her secret.

For a moment he couldn't believe what she was saying.

'Are you sure about this, *cariad*?'

'Of course. A woman knows, doesn't she,' she replied coyly.

He held her close, knowing he wasn't ready for such responsibility. He was barely twenty. They'd no real home, just a curtained-off half of a room in Shepherd Square which they rented for two and sixpence a week from Marie's sister, Jenni. There was barely room for their narrow bed and the hooks they hung their clothes on, so how would they ever cope, he wondered.

'I can go on working. Our Jenni will look after the baby,' Marie told him as if reading his thoughts.

'No!' His pride was shattered. He'd seen a woman give birth underground and his stomach had churned at the sight. Those working alongside her had taken no notice as she screamed and groaned, her feet drumming against the roof of the gallery. Not until the moment of birth had they stopped to help her. Minutes later, because they were on piece work, they were back filling and hauling the trams. The woman had wrapped her newborn in a shawl and placed it on a ledge until the shift ended.

He was determined that Marie should never have to suffer such indignity. Back home at Govilon, even the cattle his father looked after were given better treatment.

Next day, to prove to himself and Marie that he could earn enough money to support both her and the baby, he'd changed jobs and become a puddler at the ironworks.

Two weeks later an accident left him disillusioned and horribly maimed. A vat of molten iron tipped, striking his middle. The pain, before he'd passed out, had been indescribable.

He regained consciousness in time to hear the doctor explaining in a grim voice to Marie that he would never father another child.

After his accident he pleaded with Marie to return to Govilon with him. Ebbw Vale had lost its enchantment. He longed to be back where the air was clear, where the sun wasn't obscured by a yellow sulphurous smog. The glowing furnaces had become the pit of hell, the pounding drop hammers a death knell in his ears.

Marie refused to leave her family.

'So where do we live? You can't go on working much longer,' he protested, eyeing her swollen body.

'There's plenty of time yet.'

'I'll not have you giving birth underground. We can't go on sharing half a room with your sister either once the baby's born, so what else is there for us?'

Tight-lipped, Marie refused to comment.

In desperation, cap in hand, Dai went to Crawshay Bailey's home, to Ty Mawr itself. He was turned away and told to see the Agent. Knowing how pointless this would be, Dai waited day after day, haunting the gateway, hoping that sooner or later he'd be lucky enough to catch the ironmaster. When he managed to intercept Crawshay Bailey's carriage he clung on to it, oblivious to the coachman's whip as it lashed his shoulders and drew blood from his cheek.

Crawshay Bailey, resplendent in morning coat and top hat, heard him out in silence.

Three days later, when he was told by the Agent that he could run one of their ale-houses, Dai couldn't believe his good fortune.

He felt sure that moving into The Bull with Marie would solve all his problems. The hours were long but the work was easy. He hated the system under which the ale-house was run and despised himself for being a Master's man, but it was a safe haven and he determined to pocket his pride and his principles until their child was born.

After that he'd do his best to persuade Marie to move back to Govilon with him. He could see it all in his mind's eye. Their cottage with his son growing up and playing in the fields alongside, fishing the stream, gathering wild flowers, helping him in the garden.

But it was not to be.

Maria came to term early and lost the baby. Dai blamed it on the fact that she'd still been working underground, harnessed to a coal tram, and that had induced the early labour.

Knowing there could never be another child, he'd said no more about moving back to Govilon. He understood that Marie needed her family around her.

By the time he was twenty-five, Dai Roberts was set and stolid in his ways, a physically maimed man, bearded and grim-faced. Sharp-eyed too, he ran a well-ordered ale-house, but confided in no one.

Marie, soured after her miscarriage, became fat and blowsy. She drank heavily, taking nips from the spirit bottles when his back was turned and topping them up with water when he started marking the bottles.

Her liver began to fail. By the time she was thirty, her skin was as yellow as the sulphurous pall that hung over the valley, her once bright eyes bleary and unfocused. Her legs became so swollen that she could barely stand on them.

Marie took to spending most of her time sitting at one end of the bar, nodding and smiling at the men as they came in, her speech too slurred and her senses too fuddled for proper conversation.

She'd just turned forty when she died.

Dai Roberts didn't mourn. He regarded it as a happy release for both of them.

At last free to return to Govilon he found the desire had gone. Instead, he brought his widowed mother to live with him at The Bull. She cooked and cleaned but kept in the background, refusing to help out in the bar.

Dai accepted this stoically and hardly noticed that as the months passed she became more frail and did less and less about the house. Then came the morning when, finding his breakfast wasn't ready, he went to her room and found he couldn't waken her.

Once again he thought of starting afresh but he'd been at The Bull for so long that he couldn't imagine any other kind of life. He knew every man that came in and, as time passed, their sons as well. He was well respected and had earned their trust. They knew he never cheated them no matter how drunk they might be and that he kept a wary eye on the Agent on payday to see they received what was due to them.

Eyebrows were raised when Kate arrived on the scene.

Dai Roberts had never shown any interest in women. Some of the older men who remembered the accident at the ironworks muttered darkly as to the reasons. They said that was what accounted for the way his wife, Marie, had turned from a bright, sparkling-eyed young woman into a gross, overweight slut.

At first many had thought Kate was just another of the Irish women, shipped in like cattle by the Masters as cheap labour. After a couple of days they'd revised their opinion.

'Quite the lady!' they grinned as their eyes followed her straight back and lithe movements. They admired the dark glossy curls, they tried to catch the vivid blue eyes and many of the younger ones schemed and dreamed about taking her up Coity.

Kate smiled disarmingly but said little as she moved amongst them. She served their beer, provided bread and cheese, meat, or a bowl of hot cawl when it was

216

ordered, but turned a deaf ear to their suggestive quips and invitations. She felt safe, confident that Dai Roberts would not allow any of them to molest her.

He found her presence soothing. She was pleasing to look at and he liked her low soft voice with its West Country burr, so different from the sing-song lilt of the women of Blaenafon.

Alone in his bed at night he found himself wondering about her background. She'd told him so little. He knew she was looking for a man called Owen and he surmised she must be pregnant and this man was the father. He didn't share her optimism about finding him. There were so many men named Owen.

It wasn't until she told him she intended moving on at the end of the week that the idea had come to him. He'd been astounded by his own temerity and had persuaded her to stay on for another week to give him time to consider his idea in more detail.

The more he thought about it the sounder it seemed to be. It would provide him with a companion and a willing worker. It would give Kate a roof over her head when her baby was born and a home to bring it up in.

He was so excited at the prospect that he wanted to grab her by the arm and watch her blue eyes shine with relief as he unveiled his plans. He'd marry her, so that things would be legal between them, provided she was prepared to accept that he would be husband in name only.

The thought that she might provide the son he'd always longed for inflamed him. The fact that it was from another man's seed was of no consequence. The child would be brought up as his, known throughout Blaenafon as Dai Roberts' boy. He'd name him Rhys after his own father. Rhys Roberts! It had a fine ring to it.

He tugged at his beard anxiously as he planned his approach to Kate. He'd need to be careful. She was proud, that one, and independent.

Still, he liked a girl with spirit.

25

Half-way through her second week at The Bull, Kate became aware of growing restlessness amongst the men and it worried her. A wrong word, or a jogged elbow would start a fracas. Fists flailed; heads were cracked open with tankards; chair legs, or even iron bars were swung in anger.

Dai Roberts blamed it on the fact that the men had just been paid six weeks money so they were all drinking more ale than they could handle.

She had seen her Uncle Charlie in his cups and knew how men's tempers could flare up, making them say and do things which they regretted once they had sobered up again. But Charlie's lapses were nothing like the anger that erupted amongst the men of Blaenafon.

From mumblings Kate overheard she knew the constant propaganda, urging them to support the Chartists and fight for better working conditions, was having an effect. When their tempers were roused all their misfortunes bubbled to the surface, making them as fiery as the conditions most of them worked under. It was as if their very souls were blackened by the fumes and degradation they suffered day in, day out.

The more aware they became of how they were being exploited, the greater their anger and frustration. She kept asking herself what the outcome would be if they clashed with the bosses while they were feeling so incensed. Was this what had happened at Fforbrecon, after the cave-in, she wondered.

Kate still couldn't understand why David had never written to Helen. Remembering his sweet promises, their golden moments together, she couldn't believe he had put all thoughts of her from his mind so easily. He had always been so punctilious and considerate and would know she'd be anxious for news.

She sighed as she sat back on her heels to rinse out the floorcloth in the pail of soapy water at her side, marvelling at the strange quirks of Fate. If Helen's letter hadn't fallen into Morgan Edwards' hands she would have been Mistress of Machen Mawr by now. It seemed hard to imagine living in comfort, never wanting for anything; pampered, waited on by servants, and sheltered from the harsh realities of the life she now saw all around her.

Living in luxury provided by the sweat and toil of small children, she reminded herself, and the idea was so repugnant that she felt a rush of relief that things had turned out as they had done.

It would have been such a terrible mistake to have married Morgan Edwards anyway. She shuddered at the thought, closing her eyes to shut out the memories. It seemed unbelievable that she had even contemplated such a step. Looking back she knew it had been fear. When Dr Davies had implied that she was pregnant, all she could think of was what would happen to her and her baby.

She shuddered again as she wrung out her cloth and swabbed at the floor. It would have been a terrible mistake. Not only would it have put an end to her hopes of ever being reunited with David but it would have sentenced her to a lifetime of unhappiness. A living lie since her heart belonged to David. She felt guilty about forsaking Mathew but she was sure Olwen Price would do all in her power to comfort him.

'Day-dreaming about that fellow of yours again?' Dai Roberts probed. He drew himself a tankard of ale and leaned against the bar to watch her work.

'Can't you keep off the floor until it's dry,' grumbled Kate, scrubbing round his feet.

'I reckon he's one of the Gentry!' Dai Roberts mused,

shuffling out of her way.

'What if he is?' Kate wrung out her cloth and mopped up the soapsuds.

'Wasting your time going looking for him if that's the case, believe me.' He spat morosely on to the floor.

'I've just cleaned that!'

'They're no different than a working man when it comes to rolling a wench in the hay,' he pronounced, taking a long swig of ale and running his tongue over his lips to remove the froth.

Kate concentrated on her cleaning, wishing he would go away.

'Mind you, most of the boyos round here cough up and pay for their pleasures, not leave the girl to fend for herself.'

'I don't know what you mean.'

'*Daro*! They tie the knot which is more than can be said for most of the toffs.'

'Really!' Her cheeks burning, Kate turned away, her head high, refusing to confide in him.

She knew Dai Roberts was right. Dallying with a maidservant was considered fair game by most of the Gentry. And if a baby resulted then at best they'd marry the girl off to one of their labourers, at worst send her packing to the nearest poorhouse.

David hadn't been like that. He hadn't just been amusing himself. He'd told her how much he loved her.

Has he also told Penelope Vaughan that he loves her, asked a voice inside Kate's head. Did his silence mean he'd dismissed his flirtation at Bramwood Hall from his thoughts? Was he so busy planning the wedding his father had set his heart on that he hadn't had time to write to Helen, Kate wondered miserably.

'If you're set on going to Fforbrecon then talk to Llew Lloyd,' Dai Roberts prompted. 'He knows every move made at Fforbrecon . . . and the name of every man or boss who has ever worked there.'

'You mean he works there?' she asked hopefully.

'No, but his brother was foreman there until the cave-in. Poor dab! Terrible end!' He shook his head morosely and refilled his tankard.

'What happened?'

'After the explosion the owners refused to let anyone go near, see,' Dai Roberts went on. 'They wouldn't even make sure if the men trapped were dead or not. They waited two days for news.'

'That's terrible!' gasped Kate.

'Bitter about it is Llew. Mind you, he has cause to be since he now has his brother's widow and four kids to look after.'

'Which one is Llew Lloyd?'

'Big chap with greying hair and a curly beard. Shoulders on him like a bull. He's in here most nights.'

'I'll talk to him but it won't make me change my mind about leaving here,' Kate told him determinedly. 'So you'd better have my money ready at the end of the week.'

As she busied herself in the kitchen, Kate thought about what Dai Roberts had said. She had often listened to Llew Lloyd talking to his cronies. He was a spirited agitator, always urging the other men to join the Chartists. He was the one, she recalled, who had been talking about an uprising bigger than anything ever seen before. Men from Benefit Lodges in Blaenafon, Blaina and Nantyglo would all be taking part. They'd muster at Pontypool and there they'd be joined by men from Unions the length and breadth of Wales.

From what she'd overheard all they seemed to be waiting for was a signal from the leaders.

So much intrigue and espionage, so much at stake for so many men. It was hardly likely that he'd have time to talk to her about David Owen, let alone go with her to Fforbrecon.

Not unless. . . .

She remembered how much David had hated mining and his reluctance to have anything to do with it. After all

221

she'd seen and heard she could understand his feelings. If the cave-in had been the reason his father had sent for him, she tried to reason what she would do if she was in his shoes.

She was sure David would have tried to do something to help the men, even if it had meant opposing his father. A frisson of excitement ran through her. Could he have joined the Chartists? She'd heard the name Owen mentioned often enough.

A plan began to form in Kate's head. Preposterous though it was, she brooded on it, mulling it over until she could think of nothing else. She wasn't sure if her nerve would hold, or if she could carry it out without giving herself away, but she felt it was worth a try.

That night when Llew Lloyd came into The Bull she put herself to the test.

'You've been sent to help us?'

The doubt in Llew Lloyd's voice sent a frisson of fear through Kate but she steeled herself to meet the sharp dark eyes.

'Who sent you?'

'A man called Owen. I'm to meet him again in Newport.'

He stared searchingly, the grim lines of disbelief around his mouth slowly relaxing.

'Free with your information, aren't you,' he snapped. 'How do you know you can trust me?'

'He described you well. I've been watching you for over a week to make sure I had the right man.'

'So why've you not spoken out before?' asked Llew Lloyd, running a hand through his grey hair until it stood on end, giving him a wild look.

'I had to be sure, you know that! A word in the wrong ear and where would we all end up?'

'Is this where he said you'd find me?'

'Either here or a cave, half-way up Coity.'

'He gave you directions to the cave?' Llew Lloyd's eyes narrowed.

'I was only to go there if I couldn't contact you any other way,' she told him in a low voice.

'You're not from these parts?'

'I've come from Wiltshire,' she sighed softly.

'What are you doing here then?'

'You've heard of the Tolpuddle Martyrs? My uncle was one of them . . .'

She left the sentence unfinished, letting him think whatever he wanted and felt a glow of satisfaction when he nodded understandingly.

'Is that proof enough for you?'

'A tea party compared with what we are planning,' he told her scathingly.

' 'Tweren't to them,' she flared. 'Six of them were sentenced to seven years' transportation.'

'Including your uncle?'

'No. Uncle Charlie was too wily,' she boasted. 'Vowed he'd get even with them one day, though,' she added, her eyes shining. He was suddenly a hero, a champion of ideals instead of being an evil, licentious man she'd once feared and then despised.

'Poor man, he was never the same afterwards,' she embroidered. 'The shock of it all killed his old mother. She trembled every time there was a knock on the door in case they'd come to take him away.'

'And what part did you play in all this?'

'I was little more than a child, barely fourteen!'

'So why do you want to be involved now?'

'I . . . I loved my granny dearly and it broke my heart to see her shaking with fright and wasting away from fear. I made my mind up there and then to do what I could to put food in the bellies of the starving and roofs over their heads. And I'm as determined now as I was then,' she added so fervently that she convinced herself of her sincerity.

'Fine talk, but how can you help?' Llew Lloyd stared at her questioningly as if reluctant to accept her involvement.

'I'll do whatever you ask of me,' she told him eagerly.

'There'll be no women on the march. Only men who can fight,' sneered Lloyd.

'You'll need someone to prepare food. . . .'

'They'll bring their own bite. We'll refresh ourselves at the ale-houses along the way.'

'I can help in a hundred and one ways,' persisted Kate.

'Can you leave here without him knowing?' he jerked his head towards Dai Roberts.

'Whenever you need me. This place has served my purpose; it has led me to you.'

Llew Lloyd took a long swig of his ale, watching her shrewdly from over the rim of his tankard, then rubbed the back of his hand over his mouth.

'Have you spoken to Owen since you've been in Blaenafon?'

'And put both our heads into a noose?' she retorted scathingly.

'I take it that means you haven't.' He stroked his beard thoughtfully.

'It was late July when I last saw him,' admitted Kate.

'And you haven't spoken to him since?'

'I didn't expect to. I'd been given my orders . . .'

'There's danger in it,' he warned, cutting her short.

Their eyes locked. Each summing up the other. Kate bit her lips nervously, her blue eyes pleading, afraid he was going to refuse her offer.

'When we decide to move, a cart will be following the marchers to Newport.'

'Can I ride in it?' she interrupted eagerly, smiling with relief when he nodded in agreement.

'Now get about your business,' growled Llew Lloyd, frowning. 'Serve the ale and keep your mouth tight closed. Say nothing to Dai Roberts, mind, he's in the employ of Crawshay Bailey.'

'Promise you won't go without me.'

'I'll give you the signal when we are ready to leave.'

Kate was conscious that his dark eyes followed her speculatively as she moved amongst the men and she felt overwhelmed by her own daring.

She knew Dai Roberts had seen her talking to Llew Lloyd but she parried his questions. The Chartists might use The Bull as their meeting place but, as Llew Lloyd had pointed out, the landlord might well be an ear for Crawshay Bailey.

Two days later, as she placed a tankard of ale in front of him, Llew Lloyd murmured softly so that only she could hear, 'Be round the back at midnight on Saturday.'

'I'll be there!'

'Not a word to Dai Roberts or anyone else, understand?'

Kate thought the evening would never end. She served the customers mechanically, her mind ablaze with excitement, a jumble of what she had to do in readiness.

That night, when she went up to her attic bedroom, she packed everything into her canvas bag except the clothes she would be wearing and the money she'd secreted in the pocket tied round her waist. She'd come back when it was all over and collect her bag and the wages Dai Roberts owed her.

She had no idea how long she'd be gone, or what sort of conditions they would encounter so she'd chosen her warmest clothes, and her cashmere shawl as well as her cloak. The weather had turned colder. High winds were scouring the mountainside, coating houses and people alike with brown ash from the ironworks.

The nearer the time came for their departure, the more churned up inside Kate felt. Llew Lloyd had not been near The Bull since he'd passed her the message, but Dai Roberts seemed to sense that something was being planned. Several times he'd tried to pump her for information, but her wits were sharper than his and she parried his questions with good humour, refusing to betray the trust placed in her.

By Saturday her nerves were on edge. She kept to

her usual routine, cleaning the bar as soon as she came downstairs, then cooking Dai Roberts a breakfast of bacon and eggs.

The grey November day dragged by. The taproom was crowded, the men noisy and argumentative. As she wiped down the tables and washed the tankards at the end of the evening her hands were shaking.

'I'm away to bed,' she told Dai Roberts as she rinsed out the cloths and spread them over the barrels.

'Why do you insist on sleeping up in that draughty old attic,' he jibed. 'What's the matter with you, girl? Why don't you move down to the room next to mine?'

'I like it up there.'

'You'd find it more pleasant to be looking out on to the street instead of the backside of Coity. And much warmer now winter's in the air.'

'I'll think about it,' she told him placatingly, anxious to get away.

'You do that. And think about staying on here for good. I'm willing to marry you and give your child a name,' he offered.

Kate felt the colour drain from her face. She stared at Dai Roberts wide-eyed, her hand over her mouth to hide her trembling lips. Whatever had made him say that, she thought aghast.

'Think about it, *cariad*,' he told her, clutching at her arm. 'I'll give you a name and a good home.'

She shook his hand away, panic-stricken at what his offer implied.

'We don't have to stay here,' he added quickly. 'We could live in Govilon, the place where I grew up.' His eyes grew hazy. 'You'd like it there. A cottage with fields and trees all round it,' he promised as she made for the stairs.

26

The anger of the Fforbrecon miners died almost as suddenly as it had flared.

Roddi Llewellyn's exclamation of alarm brought the scuffling and fighting to an abrupt halt. Mouths agape, they stared in horror at the two entwined, mangled bodies lying beside the upturned cart where minutes before the fighting had been at its worst.

'Poor dabs, they both look dead.'

'*Duw anwyl*! That one's head's cracked open like an egg!'

'The one on top looks like a bloody Owner!'

'Bugger would be on top. Die the same way as they live.'

'He mightn't be dead. Could be he's just out cold.'

Having expressed their unease the men shuffled back. In groups of four or five, they muttered amongst themselves, shrugging their shoulders, turning up their collars against the keen wind as they moved away, unwilling to be involved.

'We'd best see what we can do for them.' Llewellyn grabbed the arm of the man nearest him.

'Not me!' Griff Rogers shook himself free. 'My Da's lying in the bottom of that pit and no one wants to do sod all for him.'

'You there, Garth Samuels, tell Prys Howell I want him. And you, Tomos Smart, fetch the doctor,' Llewellyn ordered.

'Bugger off.'

'Fetch 'em yourself.'

'I don't give a damn which of you goes for Howell and the doctor as long as someone does,' snapped Llewellyn as he dropped on his hunkers beside the two inert bodies.

'Here's Howell now,' a voice called out.

'There's bad they look,' Prys Howell grunted as he reached Llewellyn's side.

'There'll be the devil to pay for this day's work,' Llewellyn told him gloomily.

'What d'you suppose we should do?'

'God knows!' Llewellyn stood up, running a hand through his scant hair.

'We can't just leave them lying here.'

'I tried to tell the Owners that the men wouldn't stand for that gallery being sealed off,' muttered Llewellyn, 'but you can't talk to that bloody Pennington.'

'Never mind about that now,' interrupted Howell, 'what are we going to do with these two? Have their families been told what's happened?'

'No,' grimaced Llewellyn. 'One of them is Owen Jones.'

'Owen Jones! It can't be.' Prys Howell bent forward and gingerly pushed the mass of blood-soaked hair clear of the man's face. 'His shift was trapped by the cave-in. He'd changed over with his brother Ieuan.'

'*Duw*! Why was that?'

'Ieuan's wife dropped their seventh the night before so he'd stayed home to give a hand, then he did Owen's shift in return, like.'

'So it's Ieuan who's down there. *Duw anwyl*! What will happen to his family now?'

'God knows. Perhaps Owen Jones will take on his brother's lot . . . that's if he pulls through.'

'Owen's a man who likes his freedom and that sounds like a life sentence to me,' muttered Prys Howell.

'Anyway, Ieuan's wife'll have enough on her plate with a new babba. She won't want to be bothered with a sick man. Be a long time before he's fit again, I reckon,' Llewellyn said gloomily.

'Who's the other one, then?'

'Not sure. From the way he's dressed he could be one

228

of the Owners.'

'God almighty! Don't say that, mun. They'll crucify us.'

'They're going to seal off that gallery, you know. Leave all the bodies down there,' Llewellyn muttered. His dark eyes glittered with suppressed anger.

'Nothing we can do about that at the moment,' Prys Howell told him, 'Anyway, it won't help matters to leave this poor dab lying here to die, now will it?' He dropped on one knee and, opening David's jacket and shirt, slipped a hand inside.

'Is he gone?'

'No, he's still alive. Come on, give me a hand to move him.'

'You look after him if you want to,' muttered Llewellyn shaking his head. 'Me, I'm sick of the whole bloody pack of them.'

'Don't talk daft, mun. You're the manager here, not me!'

'If he dies then good riddance to him. It'll be one less Owner we have to fight,' retorted Llewellyn dourly.

Howell looked hopefully at the men still clustered within earshot, trying to decide if any of them might be willing to help. As if guessing his intention they began to edge away.

A group of women, his wife amongst them, who'd come to see what all the commotion was about, stood their ground. Arms folded, they waited and watched.

'Megan, girl,' he called. 'Come over here a minute.'

'What for?' Her neat figure stiffened.

'I need a hand. There's been a couple of fellows hurt.'

'You'd better send for a doctor then, *cariad*.'

'It may be an hour or more before he gets here. Come and see what you can do for them.'

There was a murmur of dissent from the other women as Megan moved to do her husband's bidding, but no one tried to stop her.

'Looks terrible!' she gasped. On her knees she

229

smoothed back the blood-matted hair from the men's pulped faces. Untying David's white stock she removed it and folded it into a pad to staunch the flow of blood from a deep cut on his temple.

'This one's Owen Jones, isn't it?' she asked, looking up at her husband, her brown eyes anxious. 'He's had a terrible crack on his head, enough to turn him dippy.'

'They're both in a bad way, girl.'

'You say someone's gone for the doctor?'

'Yes, a while back. There's no knowing how long he'll be, mind.'

'Proper state they're both in,' tutted Megan. 'We'd better get them inside then and clean them up.'

'Don't talk so daft, woman! The others would never stand for it if we tried to move them.'

'They won't lift a finger to try and stop us,' Megan said confidently. 'The fight's gone out of them.'

Howell looked at his wife in silence, wondering if she was right. Small and scrubbed, with her dark hair pulled back into a tight bun, Megan possessed wisdom that often surprised him even after ten years of marriage.

'We'll have to see what Roddi Llewellyn says. He might let us move Owen Jones but I don't know about the other chap.'

'Why is that then?' queried Megan.

'Llewellyn's so bloody mad with the Owners that he can't see sense at the moment.'

'You mean this other fellow is one of the Owners?' Megan murmured as she reapplied the blood-soaked makeshift pad.

'That's what Llewellyn said.'

'Has he thought of the consequences if he leaves the poor dab here on the ground? He'll catch pneumonia for a start in this weather.'

'One less Owner to fight is what he says.'

'They'll crucify the lot of us if they find out that one of their lot's been hurt,' pointed out Megan.

'It's happened so it's too late to do anything about that

now,' grumbled Prys Howell. 'I'm beginning to wish I'd done the same as the others and just walked away.'

'Perhaps we should try and find out who this other man is, then we could send him home and let his family nurse him,' mused Megan.

'That's one way out.'

'But is it the right one, I wonder?' she frowned.

'Probably not. They'll still want revenge because he's been hurt.'

'So what are we to do?'

'Nothing at all, as I see it.'

'We could nurse him back to health . . .' She looked down at David's inert body thoughtfully. 'He's quite young, he might be so grateful that he'd be reasonable about what's happened.'

'I doubt it! Owners are never reasonable, Llewellyn will tell you that,' scowled her husband.

'Well, instead of just standing around doing nothing, why don't you ask Roddi Llewellyn what he thinks?' remonstrated Megan.

'Waste of time. You try talking to him. He might take some notice of a woman but I know he won't listen to me.'

Megan was silent for a moment, her lips pursed as if deep in thought. Then she walked over to where Llewellyn was arguing with a group of miners. Howell waited. He saw Llewellyn shake his head angrily. Minutes passed, then, as Megan persisted, Llewellyn shrugged his shoulders as though capitulating.

'What's he say, then?' demanded Prys Howell impatiently.

'We can move them.'

'Where?'

'I told him I'd take them both back to our house.'

'You did what!' exploded her husband angrily.

'What else can we do with them . . . Leave them lying here on the ground?' she questioned, her eyes flashing angrily.

'You're daft, that's what you are. *Daro*! It's just asking for trouble, Megan.'

'You were the one who called me over and said you wanted help,' she reminded him tartly.

'I know that but I didn't mean for you to take them home.'

'No one else will.'

'But if one of 'em is an Owner . . .'

'We don't know that for certain. He might only be a clerk working for one of the Owners. That might be the reason no one's missed him yet, or bothered to come looking for him.'

She turned away as a group of men approached carrying an assortment of planks of wood.

'Where d'ye want these, missus?'

'Right here. We're going to use them as stretchers so that we can move these men.'

'Waste of time moving this one, missus. He looks dead already.'

'Hang on a minute, it's Owen Jones!' exclaimed one of the others.

'His head's all bashed in! What bugger did that?'

'He was fighting with the other chap,' Prys Howell told them. 'Looks as though they knocked each other out cold and then they've been trampled on in the general scuffle. Pretty bad they are.'

'Who's the other one then? Not one of our boyos.'

'No one seems to know. He might have come with the Owners.'

'Dressed like a bloody toff an' all. Must be one of the Gentry.'

'Bleeds and bruises like the rest of us.'

'*Daro*! And it's red not blue.'

'That'll do,' scolded Megan primly as they laughed uproariously at the crude joke.

'Can we go now, missus?'

'Not until you've given a hand with these two,' she told them sharply.

Under Megan's directions they lifted the two inert bodies on to the makeshift stretchers.

'You'd better use your belts and mufflers to strap them in place so that they don't fall off when you're carrying them,' Megan warned.

'We'll take Owen Jones but not the other chap,' growled one of the men.

'Yes, you will,' insisted Megan. 'You'll carry both of them to my house. I'll go on ahead and make some beds ready for them,' Megan said, ignoring their grumbles.

'Remember to tell Roddi Llewellyn where to send the doctor,' she called back to her husband as she hitched up her ankle-length black skirt and began to run down the rough track.

Roddi Llewellyn glowered when Prys Howell told him what was happening.

'*Duw anwyl*! You're bloody mad. You'll get us all in trouble,' he stormed, his sallow face flushed with anger.

'Couldn't leave them lying where they were. Anyway, you were the one who gave my wife permission to move them.'

'Nagged into doing so would be nearer the mark.'

'Send the doctor over to my place then, will you?'

'Wait a minute.' As Prys Howell started to walk away Llewellyn called him back.

'What is it now? My Megan will be needing a hand with those two.'

'A word.' Llewellyn took his arm and propelled him out of earshot of the other men. 'Do you and your missus know what you're doing . . . have you thought this thing through?'

'What d'ye mean?'

'If Owen Jones dies, that other bugger'll be a murderer. They were fighting, remember!'

'Hardly murder, mun. Just an accident. Owen Jones probably struck his head when he fell.'

'And why did he fall?'

'Well . . . as you said . . . they were fighting.'

'More likely Owen Jones was attacked from behind.'

'We don't know that. The worst of their injuries are probably from being kicked and trampled on by the men when they were fighting.'

'Before they fell to the ground, Owen Jones was attacked from behind by the other fellow. Plenty of the men saw it happen,' Llewellyn's dark eyes glittered.

'In that case then, someone must know who he is.'

'I've already told you, mun! He's one of the bloody Owners' lot.'

'You're sure about that?' Prys Howell felt uneasy.

'Facts speak for themselves.' Llewellyn's face was impassive. 'I saw him at the meeting and watched him climb up on to the cart with the rest of them.'

'*Duw anwyl*! What's to be done then?' Prys Howell's mouth dropped open in bewilderment. He broke into a cold sweat and wished he'd never got embroiled. If he hadn't called Megan over and she hadn't taken it upon herself to care for the two men none of this would have mattered as far as he was concerned.

'It's complicated.' Llewellyn pushed his cap to the back of his head and scratched his head. 'I know what I'd do.'

'Go on then, tell me.'

'I'd keep that Owner bloke well away from Owen Jones and let him think he'd killed 'im.'

'What good will that do?'

'Give us power over him, see!'

'I don't follow you . . .'

'If we protect this fellow from the law we'll be able to ask whatever terms we like from the Owners. By the time they find out Owen Jones is still alive it'll be too late, they'll have given in to our demands.'

'What if Owen dies?'

'As long as we've completed our negotiations it won't matter.'

'It's blackmail, and either way, once we're rumbled they'll make things bad for us.'

'They'll make it hot for us if we admit one of their lot has been injured.'

'They must already know that . . . I can't understand why they've not come looking for him.'

'Because they're afraid,' snapped Llewellyn. 'They'll lie low and say nothing as long as we do the same.'

'But why?' frowned Prys Howell.

'Why? Think, mun, think! They're up against enough trouble as it is. Every mine worker in Ebbw Vale and throughout Wales and England would join the Chartists if they knew a miner had been attacked and killed by one of the Owners. And that's just what we're going to let them believe has happened.'

27

The rain which had threatened on and off all day came down in a blinding deluge as several thousand men, led by John Frost, assembled in the centre of Pontypool late on Sunday night.

Ever since early morning they had been gathering at mustering points throughout Ebbw Vale. Men who for years had listened passively to impassioned speeches were at last ready to act.

Kate had been astonished when she had made her way to Stack Square just after midnight, looking for Llew Lloyd, to find a crowd of some fifty or more people already there. Within half an hour the numbers had swelled to several hundred. A motley crowd of all ages, shapes and sizes. Men and young lads straight from their shifts, begrimed with coal dust, stained by iron, and smelling of sweat. Ready and eager to fight for their rights, and to overthrow the tyranny of the coalmasters and ironmasters.

They had an assortment of weapons. Those with guns and muskets were testing them out and the noise and smell of gunpowder incited the others. Impatient to be on their way, they shook off restraining hands, turning deaf ears to the entreaties of their womenfolk who were begging them to stay at home.

From the talk going on around her, Kate learned that in Dukestown, Brynmawr, Beaufort, Nantyglo and Blaina they were gathering in their hundreds, waiting for the signal from Zephaniah Williams to begin their march to Pontypool.

'Over the other side of the valley, in Tredegar and Sirhowy, it's the same story,' one woman told her.

'They've turned the Red Lion at Colliers Row, and the Colliers Arms in Park Row, into pike factories.'

'The men from there are being led by Williams Evans, John Morgan and Thomas Morgan,' said another.

'Meeting up with John Frost at Blackwood, or so I've heard.'

Tongues wagged. Everyone was eager to impart their own snippet of information.

'Rees Meredith and Dai the Tinker are leading a contingent a hundred strong from Twyn Y Star.'

'And they're joining up with men from Benjamin Richards' Star Inn lodge at Sirhowy Bridge.'

'By the time they all meet up at the Welsh Oak at Risca, there'll be at least two thousand of them.'

'And when they've joined with Frost's forces, it'll bring their number up to over four thousand!'

The sound of hobnail boots rang on the cobbled streets as the men of Blaenafon set off. Proudly they held aloft banners showing which Benefit Club or Union they represented.

Full of grim determination, they ignored the rain that steadily streaked their faces and soaked their clothing and the gusts of wind that threatened to rip their banners into shreds. And they turned deaf ears to the pleas from mothers and wives, many with small children clutching at their skirts.

Boys too young and men too old or too disabled to join the march cheered the marchers on their way, inflamed and excited by the stream of light from their waving torches.

Kate clambered up into the large horse-drawn cart that brought up the rearguard. Its high sides were emblazoned with banners giving it a bright, festive air as though it was a haywain on a summer outing.

Hidden beneath the rough board seat she shared with Shonti Jenkins were documents and papers relating to the Chartist Cause, as well as ammunition for some of the guns and muskets. A canopy had been hastily erected over the top of the cart and gave a modicum of protection from the rain.

Old Shonti was in his seventies but still indefatigable and full of fire. He sang lustily as they set off. Kate hung on grimly to the edge of her seat, afraid of losing her balance as the cart splashed through deep puddles and bumped over potholes.

The keen wind cut across her face and made her eyes water. She pulled her heavy cloak closer and found herself wondering what her grandmother would have thought about her taking part in such a wildcat expedition.

She wished now that she had plucked up courage and gone to Llwynowen. It was inconceivable to think that David, one of the Gentry, would be in any way involved with the Chartists . . . except to oppose them. It had been foolish to give way to intuition.

He might be kindly and understanding but his family wealth came from the black nuggets that were hewn from the earth. They had paid for him to attend University, kept him in fine clothes and provided him with money to spend at will.

She sighed, knowing she had let herself be carried away by her longing to find David. More than anything in the world she wanted to feel his arms around her, hear his deep voice gently reassuring her that he would take care of her.

It had been sheer folly to come on this march. If any of the men realized her true intent was to track down one of the hated coalmasters, expecting him to marry her, there was no knowing how they would react towards her. She'd heard some of the younger men boasting about what they would do once they met up with the Redcoats and it had frightened her.

'*Daro!* We're winners before we start. We outnumber the military by ten to one,' they gloated.

'If you believe that, mun, you're a fool.'

'Most of the military are on our side anyway and will

only be putting up a token resistance.'

'What about the others?'

'Soon deal with them, boyo. Why d'ye think I've brought a pick with me!'

'String 'em up and let 'em swing, I say.'

'Shoot the buggers, then you know they're dead.'

Listening to them, Kate grew increasingly apprehensive. She hoped fervently that since Shonti Jenkins would be the very last to arrive at Newport, any fighting would be over before she got there. It was all very well for these hot-blooded men to relish a set-to, and see it in terms of glory, but all she wanted was to find David.

She eased herself into a more comfortable position on the swaying cart, refusing to give up hope, still clinging to her conviction that this foray would lead her to David.

She wished that she could question some of the men who were on the march. For the most part, though, they were concerned only with their own forthcoming exploits, seeing themselves as valiant defenders of liberty and fair play.

They talked in fiery terms about their ideals, the solidarity of their Union or Benefit Club, and how they intended to fight. Or they grumbled about their working conditions, the long hours, the gruelling conditions, the heat, the dust, the unfair treatment meted out by the Managers and Owners.

While she sympathized with their problems, deep in her heart Kate despised them. They allowed their wives to work down the mines, harnessed like animals to the trams at the coal face. And even while they bemoaned their poverty, and the fact that their children were starving, they flocked to the ale-house straight from work.

They complained about the scandalous wages paid to them and their families, yet many of them spent more on beer in one night than their children earned in a week. Surely they could see that if they drank less, their children need not work, she thought angrily. This was the state of affairs they should have been trying to put right rather

239

than being concerned about the right to vote, or to sit in Parliament.

Already the march seemed to be out of control. The singing and shouting swelled to a crescendo as the men trudged down the narrow valley. They made so much noise that she was sure the military in Newport could already hear them.

And all the time the procession grew larger and larger. Like some horrendous wild animal on the prowl, the column snaked through the darkness, ignoring rain and wind.

'There's three separate columns marching towards Newport,' Shonti told her. 'Jones the Watchmaker, the man who addressed us as we set out, is leading ours.'

'John Frost's leading one, isn't he?'

'He is. And Zephaniah Williams is leading the other.'

'Are we planning to stay at Pontypool overnight, Shonti?' she asked after they had swayed and jolted for what seemed hours.

'Remains to be seen. Doubt it though.' He drew hard on his pipe. 'Press on to Risca or to Cefn, I shouldn't wonder.'

'Where is Cefn?'

'Half-way between Risca and Newport.'

'Do we join up with the other columns there?'

'That's right. Then we descend in a body on Newport either Monday or Tuesday.'

'Do you know how they're planning to attack?'

'Capture the town, of course, and stop the mailcoach to Cardiff from getting through.'

'What's the point of that?' frowned Kate.

'When the mail coach fails to arrive, every town and city, from Cardiff to London, will be alerted. By that time,' he enthused, 'we'll control Newport. That will be the signal for two million other workers throughout England to rise up in rebellion as well. *Diarch!* A great day that will be in our fight for freedom.'

'The military will never let us get as far as Newport.'

240

'*Daro*! They'd have a job to stop us!'

'Surely if we rest over at Risca they will either attack during the night or be waiting to waylay us when we resume our march in the morning.'

'There's rubbish you talk, girl,' scoffed Shonti irritably. 'Easy to see why no women have come on this march if they think like you. Foolish it was to let you do so, if you ask me.'

Kate bit back her angry retort. Since she might have to share the cart with Shonti for several days there was no point in getting on bad terms with him. He was an old man and a querulous one and, to her mind, if anyone would have been better left at home it was him.

'To hear you going on you'd think there were no brains behind the movement,' he snorted. 'Leaders like Zephaniah Williams have been planning this rising for as long as I can remember. Long before you came to these parts, I can tell you.' He refilled his clay pipe, shielding it from the wind with one hand as he lit up.

'Has anyone ever told you about the time Henry Vincent met up with Crawshay Bailey in Brynmawr?' he asked in more conciliatory tones once his pipe was going well.

'Back in the early part of the year, around April, it happened,' he went on without waiting for a reply. 'This chap Henry Vincent, wonderful speaker he is. Charismatic! Goes all over the place. He's opened up more Chartist lodges than any other man in Wales.'

'Go on.'

'The night I'm telling you about he'd just finished making a speech at the King Crispin pub in Boundary Street and was on his way to the Royal Oak. As he walked along the tramroad between them, Vincent met up with Crawshay Bailey.' Shonti paused, took his pipe from his mouth and stared hard at Kate. 'D'ye know who he is?'

'The most powerful of all the local ironmasters?'

Shonti nodded. 'Well, they exchanged words that were

far from friendly. Crawshay Bailey told Vincent that he deserved to be thrown into the works pond. A couple of weeks later, Crawshay Bailey refused to employ any men he suspected of being Chartists and he declared the Royal Oak at Coalbrookvale out of bounds to all who worked for him. Not satisfied with that, a month later Henry Vincent, along with some others, was arrested.'

'What happened to him?'

'He was taken off to Monmouth Goal and imprisoned there.'

'So what did his supporters do?'

'Do! I'll tell what they did. On Whit Monday thirty thousand people rallied at Blackwood to set up a petition for Henry Vincent's release.'

'And was he set free?'

'Not on your life, *cariad*. Devils are those ironmasters. There was another rally at Coalbrookdale a couple of months later. Over ten thousand attended that. They signed a petition that was taken up to London, to Parliament itself.'

'And was he set free then?'

'What do you expect? It was rejected, of course. Over a million signatures!'

'And they've done nothing more about it?'

'*Duw anwyl!* Do you take us for fools? Of course there's been action since then.' Shonti sucked fiercely on his pipe. 'Where were you, my flower, that you didn't hear about what happened in August? People said it was the largest gathering ever known. Over forty thousand people met at Star Field in Dukestown!'

'To sign more useless petitions?' she asked derisively.

'To agree that the Chartist Convention should be reconvened. Hardly a night went by after that without gatherings somewhere out on the mountains. So much fiery, spirited talk!' he sighed.

Kate's thoughts went back to the night she had been stranded on Coity, and a shudder went through her as she remembered the men who had met in the cave there.

'That's when they decided that if they were ever going to defeat the gentry they'd need to arm themselves. Clever, they were. Evan Edwards, the clockmaker in Tredegar, and James Godwin who's a mason at Brynmawr turned out bullets like hot cakes. Puddlers and colliers made muskets, men working at the forges or smithies made pikes for themselves and their friends. At the Victoria Works in Ebbw Vale, John Wiles made over fifty, or so they say. They hid them carefully. . . .'

Shonti's voice droned on and on and despite being stiff and cold from the driving rain, Kate dozed as they travelled through the night, waking only when they halted to fortify themselves with ale and the resulting roistering made sleep impossible.

Landlords were brought from their beds by the clamour and demands of the marchers. Those who supported the Chartists opened up willingly. Anti-Chartists were pushed to one side and their pubs raided.

At half-past six on Monday morning, drenched by rain and shivering with cold, they reached the Welsh Oak at Risca and joined up with Frost's forces.

The clamour as the men greeted old friends and comrades was ear-shattering. Every ale-house in Risca was drunk dry, the shops raided for food.

When the order came for them to form up in ranks the noise was deafening as men argued and jostled for strategic positions.

Six abreast with a gun at the end of each line they waited for the signal to begin the final part of their march.

A loud cheer went up as John Frost gave the order. A motley band of men, five thousand strong, armed with pikes, guns, coal picks and sticks, they set off for Newport.

28

The Chartists arrived in Newport just before nine in the morning.

There was an uneasy calm over the town. Normally on a Monday morning the place would have been alive with activity but throughout the weekend rumour had been rife and as a result there was a general air of unrest.

Wealthier townsmen had taken the precaution of packing their families off to the safety of the countryside. Shops remained closed. Anxious townsfolk, peering from behind their shutters during the early hours of the morning, had seen special constables bringing in a trickle of prisoners and taking them into the Westgate Hotel.

At half-past eight that morning they had also witnessed Lieutenant Gray of the 45th Regiment, accompanied by Sergeant Daley, march twenty-eight young privates into the Square. They had wheeled right and filed into the Westgate Hotel.

Just after nine o'clock, the tense silence was broken by shouting and cheering and the sound of men marching down Stow Hill towards the Square. Six abreast they came, the men at both ends of each row carrying firearms. They marched like an army, oblivious to the fact that their rain-drenched clothing clung like a second skin.

At their head was John Frost, once Mayor of Newport and a magistrate, now the Chartist Leader. He strode out boldly, his red cravat a flag of defiance.

Shonti Jenkins followed the marchers down Stow Hill and into Westgate Square. He halted his cart across the road from the Westgate Hotel and tied the horse to the wrought-iron railings that flanked the porticoed front. He filled his clay pipe and waited patiently for his next orders.

Stiff and sore from the long ride, Kate climbed down, steadying herself against the side of the cart as she stepped into the rutted roadway. The rain had stopped and a thin, watery November sun winked from between the cloud banks. She pulled her cloak closer, shivering and wondering apprehensively what would happen next.

Local people watched from the safety of their windows. A frightened-looking woman and small girl scurried across the square towards the house where the cart stood. The woman stared hostilely at Kate as she shepherded the child inside and slammed shut the heavy oak door.

More Chartist supporters continued to arrive in the already crowded Square, jostling those on the periphery as they tried to form up in line.

All eyes were fixed on the entrance to the Westgate Hotel knowing that the Mayor, Thomas Phillips, had set up his headquarters there.

Word spread that he'd summoned every one of the town's five hundred special constables to the support of the local regular police force. It was also rumoured that he had demanded the assistance of more special constables from throughout the county and was awaiting their arrival before making a move.

The square was crowded almost to suffocation. Kate had never seen so many people. Their own contingent had joined the orderly ranks of Chartist supporters already drawn up facing the Westgate Hotel.

Other marchers were still pouring down Stow Hill, crowding into the square until it was packed solid with men of all ages, from brawny colliers to red-eyed puddlers, educated engineers to unschooled lads, standing shoulder to shoulder with tradesmen.

There was no sign of any of the Chartist prisoners reported to be inside the Westgate Hotel, or of the sixty special constables that were supposed to be guarding them, or the infantrymen from the 45th Regiment, under the command of Lieutenant Gray.

Kate climbed back into the cart to get away from the mêlée. From where she sat the crowd appeared as a colourful patchwork. The coal-grimed drabness of those who had joined the march straight from their shifts made a sombre background to those men who had dressed up in their brightest gear with caps and bowler hats set at a jaunty angle, as though they were setting out for a day at the Fair or the hiring market.

The scuffling of feet, and the deep-toned medley of voices that rose and fell, filled the air as the men waited.

Although spirits were lighter now the rain had ceased, most of them were still cold, wet and tired from their long trudge through the savage, storm-swept night. Their one common bond was their burning sense of injustice and their determination to see that the People's Charter was made law.

A black dog roamed, nostrils flaring as it sniffed the unfamiliar scents. A young boy, without hat or jacket, his shirt-tails flapping, ran into the square after him. The animal sought refuge underneath the cart, cowering there, snarling with fright.

'What's his name?' asked Kate, jumping down from the cart to try and help entice the dog out into the open.

'Gelert,' the boy called, then began to sob noisily.

'Shush! You'll never get him to come out if you make that noise.'

Calming the boy, Kate encouraged him to call the dog by name. When the animal finally responded, Kate grabbed it by the scruff of the neck and dragged it out.

The boy's mother, clutching a green cloak around her shoulders, her auburn hair streaming in the wind, came running across the Square. With a hurried word of thanks to Kate she escorted both child and dog back home, scolding them both as she went.

A special constable appeared in the doorway of the Westgate Hotel, a burly figure, arms akimbo, face set.

246

A murmured chant that became a chorus rose on the morning air.

'Give us up the prisoners. Give us up the prisoners.'

Bracing his shoulders to prove his authority, the special constable shouted back. 'No, *never!*'

Incensed, a small group broke rank and rushed forward. There was the sound of a gun going off. Pandemonium broke out.

Chartists stormed the doorway. A few of them managed to get inside. Kate recognized some of the regulars from The Bull amongst them. The broad shoulders of John the Roller from Nantyglo, the white shock of hair of Abraham Thomas, a collier from Coalbrookvale, Paddy Donovan, an Irish labourer.

She held her breath as she saw young Ianto Davies from Brynmawr pushing his way forward with the verve and agility of youth, and guessed from his eagerness that his father, David Davies, must already be inside.

A movement at one of the side windows, as one of the shutters was pulled back, caught Kate's attention. She screamed out a warning as the soldiers concealed there began to fire.

In helpless horror, she watched them file past the window in rapid succession, firing in sequence at the crowd. They didn't even stop to take aim, simply fired straight into the mass of men outside.

The Chartists were packed into the square so tightly that there was no chance for them to retreat or take cover.

When the soldiers trained their muskets on to those who had managed to penetrate inside the doorway, Kate clapped her hands over her ears to shut out the screams as men were mown down in the passageway. There was a crashing of windows, as men still in the square tried to reach those inside and those inside tried to make their escape. The groans of the dying clamoured for attention as the 45th Regiment filled the air with lead and smoke.

The battle lasted a mere twenty-five minutes.

247

Before ten o'clock the fighting was over. The passages were ankle-deep in gore. Men who'd planned the uprising with such dedication and fervour for so many months scattered. Men who'd led the march, steadfastly declaring how invulnerable they were, left their followers bewildered. The weapons that had been secretly amassed over the previous months lay abandoned, littering the square.

Under the portico of the Mayor's house, one of the Chartists lay dying, pleading for help. Pushing aside Shonti Jenkins' restraining hand, Kate made her way to the man's side. As she bent down to comfort the groaning, blood-stained figure, the butt end of a rifle caught her sharply across the shoulders as a soldier pushed her to one side.

'Let me help him . . . please!'

'Clear off.'

'But he's dying. . . .'

Despite her pleas, the soldier chased her away.

'I'll shoot if you try to come back,' he warned.

Helpless, she withdrew.

An hour and a half passed before the injured man finally stopped crying for help and breathed his last.

In that time, Kate counted ten other bodies being dragged away to the hotel stables. Voices on all sides cried out piteously for help.

She had no idea how many had been shot down in the hotel passageway. Hundreds seemed to have been wounded in the massacre. They pushed past her, blood soaking their sleeves, jackets and trousers. Men with bloodshot eyes, parts of their faces blown away, being supported by their comrades, dragged half unconscious from Westgate Square to a place of safety.

Now that the danger of battle was over, local people began to appear. Mayor Thomas Phillips, a tall, slim figure in his white breeches, short black jacket with shining brass buttons and a red cloak lined with white silk, came out on to the steps of the Westgate Hotel.

Flanked by officers of the 45th Regiment, he stood there proudly, arrogant in the knowledge of their victory.

Mayor Phillips had received a wound in his right hip and a bullet in his left arm. When he was confident that he had the crowd's attention, he threw back his red cloak so that all could see that his arm was supported by a leather strap slung around his neck.

Kate felt dismayed by the turn of events. The faces of the men nearest her bore the marks of shock and defeat. Bemused, she watched as they began making their way up Stow Hill, heading back to their homes in the Valleys.

She looked round in vain for the Chartist leaders but John Frost, Zephaniah Williams and Henry Vincent were nowhere to be seen.

All around her the defeated Chartists were leaving, anxious to be on their way back to the Valleys. Soldiers and special constables chased after them, arresting them and dragging them off into town. Once or twice she thought she saw a face she recognized but when she drew closer she was always disappointed.

Disillusioned, she made her way to the corner of the square where Shonti Jenkins had hitched the cart.

It wasn't there.

She thought for a moment that she must have made a mistake. It looked to be the right place. The house had wrought-iron railings and a portico and faced the Westgate Hotel.

She stared round her in bewilderment. As she did so she saw someone staring down at her from one of the windows and recognized her as the woman who earlier that morning, just before the fighting had started, had crossed the square with a young girl and gone inside.

Kate found it hard to believe that Shonti Jenkins had driven off and left her stranded. She elbowed her way through the surging throng, intent on walking right round the square in case he had driven to some other spot and was helping move some of the injured.

The hopelessness of her situation washed over her.

Defeated and exhausted, Kate sank down on a door-step, buried her face in her hands and wept.

When a hand descended on her shoulder, Kate shrank back in terror thinking she was being arrested. Instead, she found herself looking into a pair of green eyes that dominated a small heart-shaped face, framed by auburn hair, partly concealed under the hood of a green cloak. Instantly, she recognized the mother of the child who owned the black dog, Gelert.

'Come on, quickly now!'

Kate felt the woman's hand under her elbow, forcing her to her feet, half dragging her towards an open doorway a few yards away where the small boy was peering out anxiously.

'Inside with you, Dafydd,' the woman scolded. She glanced nervously over her shoulder before slamming the door shut and guiding Kate into a comfortably furnished room.

'Sit there and warm yourself, you look half-frozen,' she said, indicating a comfortable armchair drawn up in front of a glowing fire.

The blood sang in Kate's ears as she sank back in it. She knew the woman was still speaking but the pounding inside her head obliterated what was being said. She shook her head from side to side, trying to clear the mist from in front of her eyes. She felt hot, choking. Then blackness descended.

When she came to she was lying on a couch and someone was bathing her brow with a cool cloth. She struggled to sit up but a firm hand pressed her gently back against the cushions.

'Wait. Lie still and I'll fetch you a drink.'

Still feeling light-headed, Kate closed her eyes. Her limbs felt as if they were floating. Then an arm was slid under her shoulders, raising her up and supporting her. A glass was held to her lips.

The liquid felt cool and smooth as she sipped it, then set her mouth on fire, burning her throat as she swallowed. She gulped for air, choking until tears sprang to her eyes.

The mist cleared as if a curtain had been drawn aside and she felt the strength returning to her arms and legs. When she tried to speak she was shushed to silence and the glass was held once more to her lips.

This time she sipped more cautiously.

'Feeling better?'

'Yes! I'm fine now. You've been very kind.'

'So were you earlier today,' smiled the woman. 'I hate to think what would have happened to Dafydd if he had still been out there when the soldiers started firing. Terrible it's been and there could be more trouble to come.'

'I think it is over now, leastways the fighting is,' Kate sighed. 'Most of the Chartists have made off for home.'

'Not many of them will reach there. The soldiers and constables are out after them. The magistrates won't rest until the leaders have been caught.'

'What will happen to them?'

'They'll charge them with High Treason and sentence them to be hanged and quartered!'

'That's terrible!'

'Indeed, yes. Any others they manage to capture will probably be transported. Well, imprisoned at least.' Her green eyes narrowed. 'I shouldn't be talking like this to you really. I don't even know your name. . . .'

'Kate Stacey.'

'My name is Morag Lewis. When my husband heard early this morning that the Chartists had set off from the Valleys, he made me promise to stay indoors. He vowed there'd be trouble once they reached Newport.' Her green eyes widened. 'I never even knew the dog was out until Dafydd saw him from the window. Before I could stop him he was out of the door after him. I can't bear to think what Iestyn would have said if anything had happened to Dafydd. It was good of you to help the boy.'

251

'I've been a children's Nanny, so I suppose I acted instinctively,' Kate smiled. Her glance rested on Dafydd who lay on the hearthrug, playing with the black dog that had caused all the upset.

'It was still kind,' Morag insisted. 'I've been watching you from the window ever since. I saw the cart drive away and I wondered why you weren't on it. Fancy them going without you!'

'Yes, it means I'm stranded,' Kate agreed ruefully.

'Whatever will you do?'

'I don't really know . . . I'd better start walking.'

'There's some hot broth on the hob, have a bowlful of that first,' Morag said quickly. 'I bet you've not had anything to eat all day.'

'Not since we set out from Blaenafon,' smiled Kate.

'Ahh! So you are from up the Valleys,' Morag exclaimed triumphantly. 'Though your voice is different, softer, like.'

'I'm not Welsh. I believe in what they are trying to achieve, though. Is your husband a Chartist supporter?'

'Not openly!' Morag placed a finger against her lips. 'Iestyn works for John Partridge, the printer who's a friend of John Frost. He knows all that is going on because they usually print the broadsheets. Iestyn took me once to hear Henry Vincent speak. Handsome he was. And so eloquent! He roused his audience to fever pitch. First time I ever heard any man say that women, as well as men, should have the vote. Fine voice he had. He ended the meeting by breaking into song and there wasn't a dry eye in the place.'

'The only Chartist Leader I've seen is Zephaniah Williams, landlord of the Royal Oak, in Blaina,' Kate told her.

'I can never tell the difference between him and William Jones. They're about the same age, both dark-haired and they dress alike. John Frost, of course, had a drapery business in the High Street, here in Newport. In fact, about four years ago he was Mayor of Newport!' She

252

gave a deep sigh. 'I don't know what Wales is coming to, all this bickering and fighting. If they'd just share money out a bit more fairly, so that everyone had enough for food and to provide a roof over their heads, the men would be contented. Well, that's what my Iestyn says and he understands these things.'

'I'm sure he's right.'

'Why don't you stay and meet Iestyn,' invited Morag, her face lighting up. 'He is bound to know someone willing to give you a lift back to Blaenafon.'

29

It was evening before Iestyn Lewis arrived home from work. By then Morag had grown anxious, unable to understand why he was so late, worried in case it had anything to do with the events of the morning.

She gave Dafydd his supper and undressed him ready for bed, but he had pleaded to be allowed to stay up until his father arrived home.

His constant chattering and questions seemed to distress Morag so Kate took the boy on to her lap and kept him amused by telling him stories about when she had lived with her grandmother in a cottage in Wiltshire. The black dog, Gelert, lay at her feet, his muzzle resting on his two paws as if he, too, was listening.

She and Morag had talked non-stop all the afternoon, exchanging views and confidences until Kate felt she knew Morag as well as if they were sisters. And yet, for all their deepening friendship, she'd not spoken about David.

Now, as she sat in front of the blazing coal fire nursing Dafydd, Kate wondered why she had held back. They were much the same age and shared the same views on so many things, so surely Morag would understand her predicament.

Deep down, she envied Morag her comfortable home, lovely little boy and a husband she obviously cared for deeply.

Unlike her, Morag had done everything according to tradition. Her parents had approved of Iestyn when he came courting. She'd been married in Chapel with her family and friends in attendance. There'd been a grand celebration party afterwards and she'd been showered with gifts when she moved into her new home with Iestyn.

Dafydd had been born just over a year later and once again all her family and friends had celebrated and brought her presents.

The more they'd talked, however, the more Kate realized that although Morag was married, with a home and child of her own, she had very little experience of what went on in the outside world. Most of her knowledge had been imparted by Iestyn and Kate suspected that many of the opinions Morag expressed were also Iestyn's.

Even this Kate found touching, remembering how close she'd felt to David when they had recited the poems of William Barnes together. It was as if exchanging opinions and sharing the same memories melded them so much closer than mere physical contact ever could.

As they waited for Iestyn to come home, Kate sensed that Morag was becoming more and more anxious and whether it was because he was late, or because she was there, Kate was not sure.

Their meal was cooked and waiting: a casserole of lamb stew, thick with vegetables and dumplings keeping hot in the brick oven alongside the fire. And the apple pie that was to follow was in there as well.

The table, covered with a white linen cloth, had cutlery laid out for each of them. Morag had placed a platter of crusty bread and a dish of creamy yellow butter in the centre, alongside the salt cellar.

Morag had spent a long time tidying herself in readiness for Iestyn's homecoming, brushing her auburn hair until it shone, then coiling it high on the crown of her head and securing it there with tiny velvet bows. She had also donned a white lace collar, fastening it at the neck of her dark green gown with a small gold brooch.

Gelert sensed Iestyn's arrival before any of them. Raising his nose from his paws he let out a sharp bark, followed by an eager whine as he bounded towards the door, tail wagging in anticipation.

Dafydd shot off Kate's lap to race after him. Morag, too, hurried to the door and Kate sensed the warmth of their greeting from the tone of their voices, even though she couldn't hear what they were saying. They came into the room all talking together. Iestyn, a tall dark man of about thirty, dressed in a dark blue frock coat, black fitted trousers and a large-brimmed top hat, swept Dafydd up into his arms, patted the dog's head as it jumped up excitedly, and then pulled Morag close and kissed her tenderly.

Only then did he notice Kate.

He stood there, an imposing figure with curly hair, handsome features and a lean jawline. His keen dark eyes locked with Kate's as Morag introduced her. He listened in silence as Morag explained that Kate had come into Newport with the Chartist supporters from Blaenafon and then been left stranded when the cart had gone off without her.

'I think we should take Dafydd upstairs to bed before he either falls asleep or gets over-excited,' Iestyn said cautiously, his mobile mouth becoming a tight line.

Kate felt a tenseness in the atmosphere as they left her on her own and for a moment was tempted to leave before they came back downstairs again.

Morag had been so kind that she didn't want to upset such a united family, and it was obvious that Iestyn was less than happy about her being there. She looked around helplessly, listening to the murmur of their voices in the room above her, wondering where Morag had hung her cloak.

Before she could make her escape, Morag came back downstairs. There was an air of happiness about her that showed in her step and in her bearing. She had obviously dispelled Iestyn's concern about their visitor and she was once again queen of her domain.

'Come, sit up at the table, Kate,' she invited. 'We can talk while we eat,' she added as she lifted the lid from the tureen of bubbling stew, filling the room with a delicious, savoury smell. 'Iestyn is just tucking Dafydd in bed. He'll take the armchair and I'll sit opposite you.'

'Everyone in Newport has been talking about the terrible happenings at Westgate Square but I never once heard it mentioned that there were any women marchers,' Iestyn commented when they were all served and he had said grace.

'I wasn't exactly marching,' Kate told him. 'I rode on the cart that followed the marchers.'

Iestyn stared at her in silence, his dark eyes piercing.

'They . . . they thought I could help if any of them were wounded.'

'So, what happened? There were certainly plenty of them injured,' he remarked in a dangerously soft voice.

'There wasn't much I could do,' Kate bit her lip, shaking her head sadly. 'I tried to warn them when the military started to fire but it all happened so fast. The soldiers didn't even take aim! They just fired at random into the crowd . . .' she broke off, shuddering at the memory.

'There were a great number injured!' Iestyn persisted. 'More than twenty killed and over fifty badly hurt. Shot in the back some of them . . .'

'I saw Kate try to help one man who'd been shot,' interrupted Morag. 'I was watching from the window. He was lying in the Square but when Kate went to him, one of the soldiers pushed her away with the butt of his gun.'

'They left him there on the ground, lying in mud and filth, crying out in agony,' Kate said angrily. 'It was terrible to hear him and not be able to help.'

'It's been a dreadful defeat for the Chartists,' Iestyn sighed. 'I tried to come home earlier in the day to make sure Morag and Dafydd were safe, but the roads were so jammed that it was impossible. Men were streaming out of town, trying to get back to the Valleys. Impossible. And then there were the wounded to attend . . .'

'You mean you took some of them in . . .' Morag stopped, putting her hand over her mouth as Iestyn frowned at her. Then she shook her head and smiled at him. 'Kate and I have talked most of the day, she thinks like us on these matters. It's safe to speak openly in front of her.'

'I hope you're right, my love,' sighed Iestyn. 'With all that has happened today one cannot be too careful.'

'I do understand,' Kate told him quietly. 'Morag is right, though. I did try to help the wounded. One man who was badly injured, his head pouring blood, was crying out for water, but they wouldn't let anyone go near him. The soldiers threatened to shoot me unless I moved back and it would have been pointless to argue with them.'

'No, you did right.' His eyes narrowed speculatively. 'You can still help with the injured though.'

Kate looked at him uncertainly.

'Unless we find someone to tend their wounds many of them will die,' he said impatiently.

'So you do know where some of them are being sheltered,' Morag exclaimed breathlessly.

Iestyn nodded, his glance darting from Kate's face to Morag's and back again.

'But where, Iestyn? How many are there? Are you going to bring them here, we have enough room to take one or two . . .'

'No, no! That would be both foolish and dangerous,' he frowned. 'The details have already been taken care of, that was why I was late home,' he added, his hand reaching out to cover Morag's in a reassuring way.

'We must go to them!' Morag pushed back her chair. Her green eyes were shining and there was a fanatical eagerness in her voice. 'I want to help!' she declared.

'No!' Iestyn's hand rested on her shoulder, pushing her firmly back on to her seat. 'It's not safe for you to become involved. Your place is here . . . looking after Dafydd.'

'But . . .'

'Morag, please!' Though his voice was harsh, his dark eyes were pleading.

Morag's mouth tightened and her green eyes grew moist but when she spoke, her voice was warm and acquiescent.

Kate felt deeply stirred by the understanding between

them. Their closeness was touching. Though each was strong-willed and decisive they were prepared to give way and compromise in order to please the other.

When Iestyn looked questioningly at her, Kate turned away. She had regretted joining the marchers almost from the moment she'd set out. As they'd jolted through the cold, wet night, she'd had plenty of time to realize that such a wild-goose chase was unlikely to help her find David.

The fighting had terrified her. The noise, the smell of gunpowder, the agonized screams of the injured and the pleas and groans of the dying had left her thoroughly shocked. Only Morag's kindness had brought her out of that nightmare and back into the normal world. Now, all she wanted to do was find David.

She'd planned it all in her mind as she'd sat in front of the fire nursing Dafydd. Everything had seemed so clear, so straightforward. She knew she'd been foolish not to go directly to Llwynowen when she had first arrived in Wales. Now she intended to waste no more time. She wouldn't go back to Blaenafon, not yet at any rate. She'd go straight to Llwynowen. If David wasn't there then she would speak to his father and insist on being told where she could find him. If she said she knew Helen, then surely he'd tell her what she wanted to know.

If she let herself be distracted from her purpose by Iestyn's request it could be too late. David may have already tried to reach her at Machen Mawr and, finding she'd left there, may have decided he would never see her again.

As a result he might already have gone ahead and married Penelope Vaughan!

She didn't want to contemplate that. David was the only man she would ever love. If she lost him then all her hopes for the future, all her dreams of happiness, were shattered.

There would be no alternative but to return to The Bull!

The thought of marrying Dai Roberts sent shivers of distaste through her, but she supposed she should be grateful for the offer. As long as he kept to his promise that she need be his wife in name only, then at least she'd have a roof over her head.

'Well, Kate. What about it?' repeated Iestyn, the challenge in his voice bringing her back to the present. 'You say you came with the marchers so that you could nurse any men who might be injured. Well, I know where there are twelve of them who right now are desperately needing help.'

'Say no! Decline. Tell him you have other plans,' a voice inside her head prompted.

She desperately wanted to refuse. Her throat felt dry, her lips moved but no sound came, the right words eluded her.

She looked round the warm, comfortable room, remembering how Morag had taken her in, and made her part of the family, even though she was a complete stranger.

Now she was being asked to do something in return, so how could she demur.

'Yes, I'll help.'

Even as she spoke her heart felt heavy, knowing that with every passing day her chances of finding David lessened, or even if she did find him it might already be too late.

Was Fate once again taking a hand? she wondered.

Was she sighing for the moon? Had she as little chance of David marrying her as she had had of being a teacher?

Perhaps her grandmother had been right to believe the vicar when he said everyone had their rightful place in the scheme of things. When she'd left The Manor she was so confident that she had managed to better herself, yet she'd been impeded by countless events she'd not foreseen.

Ever since she'd tried to find David there had been so many obstacles in her way that it was as if she had no will of her own any more.

She sighed resignedly. Another day, another week, could it really matter?

30

The low-ceilinged attic over the print works, where Iestyn Lewis took Kate later that night, resembled a hospital.

Twelve seriously injured men lay on improvised beds. Their torn clothing was caked with mud, the stench of blood filled the air. Some were delirious, others only semi-conscious, the remainder trying desperately to suppress their groans and cope manfully with their pain.

Half a dozen pairs of willing hands were already helping when she had arrived with Iestyn. Men who fully supported the Chartist cause even though they had not played an active part in the uprising earlier that day. They'd rallied round, and were helping to feed the men, tending their wounds, and making them as comfortable as possible.

They accepted her presence without question.

'Fortunate indeed!' exclaimed Dr Elwyn Pugh when Iestyn explained who Kate was and how she came to be there. 'She can tend to these men while the rest of us go about our daily business in the normal way.'

'That way no one will suspect what is going on,' enthused Samuel Etheridge.

He'd been on tenterhooks ever since agreeing with his colleague John Partridge that the wounded could be hidden in the attic over his printing works in the High Street.

'I'll be holding surgery and making my daily rounds the same as usual, so that as many people as possible see me out and about,' confirmed Dr Pugh, 'and I suggest the rest of you conduct yourselves in the same way.'

'Behave as normal, remember,' urged Etheridge.

'Take an interest in what's being said, though, and what is happening, that way we can keep abreast of events,' added another voice.

'And the dead? What has happened to them?' Iestyn asked anxiously.

'They've been taken care of,' Dr Pugh assured him. 'All twenty bodies are safe and they'll be buried in St Woolos' churchyard.'

'We can do no more for them.'

'God rest their souls.'

'These men here are our concern now,' affirmed Dr Pugh.

'How are we going to feed them?' asked Iestyn.

'I'm prepared to provide what meats I can, but they'll need other food,' commented Will Preese, the butcher from Commercial Street, wiping the back of his hand across his sweating brow.

'We'll need clean linen for bandages, too,' Eynon Roberts murmured, his long, thin face haggard with strain.

'You're right there, mun. Still bleeding like pigs, some of them!'

'I'll bring along more medication and bandages, all in good time,' promised Dr Pugh.

'Here,' he handed over a bottle of laudanum and a flask of whisky to Kate. 'The laudanum is in very short supply so use it sparingly.'

'Is that all we have to keep them quiet?' Samuel Etheridge muttered nervously as the men's groans and cries sounded all around them.

'There's no need to be so concerned,' the doctor told him. 'Their cries are hardly likely to be heard above the rattle and clatter your printing presses make.'

They muttered and argued amongst themselves for a further ten minutes or so, then one by one they left, slipping out discreetly after checking there was no one in the street outside who might recognize them.

They were eager and willing to help but concerned for their own safety and that of their families. They were all men of standing in Newport, running independent small businesses, with plenty to lose if anyone suspected them of helping the Chartists.

'Are you sure you'll be all right, Kate?' Iestyn asked, his dark eyes anxious. 'Heaven knows when you last slept.'

'Don't worry,' Kate assured him, 'I'm fine.'

'We'll have to wait until dark tomorrow before it is safe for any of us to come back.'

'I can take care of things here until then.'

'Keep away from the windows and don't let anyone in,' he warned, patting her shoulder encouragingly.

A high wind was clearing the clouds from the sky as Kate closed the heavy back door of the printing works behind Iestyn, barricading it as she'd been told to do. Her limbs ached with tiredness as she climbed back up to the attic.

She walked slowly between the beds, checking that each man was as comfortable as possible, giving sips of watered-down whisky to those who were conscious in the hope it would help them sleep, or at least ease their pain. The laudanum she put to one side for emergency use only.

There was not even a chair in the room so she sat down on a pile of straw, leaning her back against the wall. She struggled desperately to fight off the fatigue that paralysed her limbs and made her eyelids heavy. She knew she was slowly sliding and slipping, until she was stretched full length on the floor, but was powerless to stop herself. The last thing she remembered was that she mustn't fall asleep in case any of the men needed her.

It was many hours later when Kate woke to a chorus of groans. November rain was battering the tiny window through which she could see storm clouds lumbering across the sky. The room was rank with the smell of blood, urine, excrement and vomit, making her stomach churn.

She scrambled up, shaking the straw from her gown, pushing her hair back from her forehead and running her fingers through the tangle of her black curls. Her skin felt tight, as if it was stuck to the bones of her face. She longed to dip her hands into a bowl of water and splash it over her skin, but there was no water left and the only damp cloth in the place was stained with blood.

Kate picked her way between the beds, wiping sweat from a brow here, vomit from lips there, straightening the meagre covers, trying to lessen each man's discomfort.

Her ministrations were met with sighs and moans. Many clutched at her dress, pleading with her to ease their pain.

She had no idea what time it was but since the presses in the workshop below were rumbling and clattering, she assumed it must be at least morning. It would be hours before anyone would arrive with fresh supplies for the men.

The time passed with the slowness of eternity. The effect of the whisky and water had long since faded and most of the men were now in dire distress. Hunger and thirst added to their agony and she felt helpless, knowing there was nothing she could do to ease their predicament.

Those well enough to understand the situation tried to console the more seriously injured, talking to them, endeavouring to keep them from crying out for fear their voices might be heard above the clamour of the printing shop.

Those sufficiently clear in the head to recall all that had happened and where they were, talked bitterly about their defeat, and the way they'd been taken by surprise outside the Westgate Hotel.

They felt let down.

They'd not expected to be fired on, having been assured that the military from Brecon Barracks were on their side.

264

Some blamed the Redcoats, calling them traitors. Others upbraided John Frost, Zephaniah Williams and the rest of the leaders for being so gullible as to trust those in a service governed by the Gentry.

'And where are our leaders now?' was the question on most of the men's lips.

Kate had no idea. She could only beg them to be patient.

'When Iestyn Lewis or one of the others returns, then doubtless they'll bring us the very latest news,' she told them.

'What if they don't return?' Twm Oliver, a puddler from Blaina, demanded. A bullet had entered the flesh of his right shoulder, shredding the muscle, leaving his entire side paralysed. He lay huddled in an ungainly heap in his own filth, refusing to let Kate tend him.

'They will be back, of course they will,' Kate assured him.

'But when, my lovely? When?'

'They'll bring food and drink and some more bandages. Dr Pugh will be coming, too, with more whisky and laudanum.'

'They'll be risking their necks,' pointed out Jed Jones, who had already lost one arm in a pit accident before the uprising and now had part of his right leg shot away. 'There's foolish they'd be to do that for such a bunch of old crocks!'

'*Diawlch!* They can't just leave us here to die! Blind I am, see,' sobbed Walli Penrhyn. 'And all for nothing.'

Walli was sixteen. His elder brother Daryth had talked him into joining the Chartists. When they'd set out on Sunday night they'd let Walli march at the head of the column. It had made him feel he was a man at last.

'They let him carry the Blaina Benefit Club Banner because he was the youngest one on the march,' the man lying next to him told Kate as she dripped the last dregs

265

from the laudanum bottle between Walli's lips to quieten him.

Her heart ached as she looked at Walli. The blast of shot had not only blinded him but had shattered the top half of his face.

'All for nothing!' Walli Penrhyn's strangled cry echoed her own feelings.

Why had she got involved with the Chartists, she asked herself, as she fought her own growing hunger, as impatient as the injured men for Iestyn Lewis and his friends to return. No one had persuaded her, she reminded herself. She had come of her own volition, her head filled with nonsense that it would lead her to David.

She sighed at her own foolishness.

True, she sympathized with the Chartist cause, and believed they should have the rights they sought, but it wasn't her fight, after all.

It wouldn't give women the right to vote, she thought angrily. And she couldn't claim that she was doing it for David. He already possessed all the rights the Chartists were trying to claim. He and his family owned land and property so he already had a vote and was qualified to become a Member of Parliament should he so wish.

She sank down on to a pile of straw as waves of nausea swept over her. She felt too weary to move. She tried to push away the doubts that crowded her mind like threatening ghouls. Time, like her money, was running out. Her life since she'd left Bramwood Hall had been a series of mistakes. She had experienced one disaster after another. She felt vulnerable, fearful of what the future held in store. She might even have to end up accepting Dai Roberts' proposal.

If only she'd gone direct to Llwynowen when she'd arrived in Wales, she thought with a surge of regret. Her spirits had been high then and she could have faced David's father resolutely. Now, with all that had happened, she felt drained, her will weakened, her powers of reasoning, and her ability to fight her corner, undermined.

Until she had come to Ebbw Vale she'd no idea how wretched life for the poor could be. Or their unending fight against poverty.

She shuddered as she recalled the squalor and hardship she had witnessed in the past two months. Women who looked like old crones before they were thirty, struggling to cook and clean and bring up a family in one room. Men maimed and blinded, children mutilated by iron splashes or pit accidents. Women and children chained like horses, crawling on all fours through rubble and filth, hauling trucks through underground tunnels.

And if she didn't find David she might well find herself condemned to such a living nightmare.

'No! Never!'

Shouting the words out loud she scrabbled to her feet and stood clutching her arms around herself to stop the nervous shaking that assailed her body.

She began to pace the room, tears streaming unchecked down her cheeks as she looked at the unshaven faces of the injured, wondering what torment their wives and children were going through because these men had not returned.

It was the horror of it all that was affecting her, nothing more, she told herself. She need never sink to working down a pit, or scrabbling on a coal face. Dai Roberts had already offered her a home.

The thought of what else he'd told her made her stomach churn. Her nostrils flared, she could almost smell the searing flesh as the hot iron splashed, covering him from waist to thigh in white-hot liquid metal that reddened, then hardened to a deep purple like a grotesque bruise.

She could sense his stunned shock, feel the agony as the hardened metal squeezed down on to his guts, crushing the life force from him. And the fresh agony as they cut through his clothing and prised away the solid metal mass that claimed as its own the flesh from his thighs and his very manhood.

Yes, she thought wryly, Dai Roberts had been quick to offer her a home, even though he had no use of her as a wife, because he thought she could provide him with a son; a child that would be regarded as his. Would he still feel the same when she told him he was mistaken and that all he would be getting was someone to cook, clean and serve ale to his customers? she wondered.

Rather than put it to the test she'd make one last effort to find David and, if that failed, then she would return to Wiltshire.

Maybe she could persuade Helen to recommend her for a post of companion, or better still as a Nanny. In time she'd forget her dreams about David. And one day, she'd fulfil her other ambition. She'd seek out William Barnes and see if he would still help her to become a teacher.

By the time the rumbling and rattling of the printing presses faded to silence, signalling the end of the working day, she'd planned a new life.

Her spirits rose.

Soon Iestyn or his friends would return bringing food, drink and clean bandages.

She walked backwards and forwards between the inert bodies, straightening their makeshift beds, wiping perspiration from their brows, doing what she could to alleviate the men's suffering.

As soon as she'd dressed their wounds and eased their agony with whisky or laudanum, so that they were all as comfortable as possible, she would leave, she promised herself.

No matter what Iestyn or Dr Pugh said, her mind was made up. The long hours of semi-isolation had helped her to think, and shown her that she must be forceful and resolute. She must not allow others to dissuade her from her purpose as she'd done in the past.

31

The sky had become a dark blanket spangled with stars before Iestyn, Dr Elwyn Pugh and John Partridge returned.

Kate looked in dismay at the meagre quantity of food they brought with them. Two small loaves of bread, a hunk of cheese, some beer and bottles of cold tea. She could have eaten the whole lot herself she was so ravenously hungry. How on earth could they expect her to divide up so little between twelve men?

Dr Pugh handed over a flask of whisky. 'Use it sparingly,' he cautioned, 'the same as you would if it were medicine.'

'You said you'd bring laudanum as well,' Kate reminded him, her voice sharp with disappointment as she remembered the promises she'd made to several of the men who were almost delirious with pain. 'And I need more bandages and clean water for drinking and to bathe their wounds . . .'

'I will bring some laudanum as soon as possible. In the meantime you must manage as best you can,' he told her brusquely.

'Morag's sent along this linen sheet for you to tear up into strips to use as bandages,' said Iestyn placatingly.

It took her only a few minutes to share out the food and drink between the men and even less time for them to consume it. She had kept up their spirits with promises of hot cawl and dumplings and now she felt she'd betrayed them.

'Here, Kate, this is for you. Morag sent it special, like!' whispered Iestyn, drawing her to one side and pulling a cooked chicken leg from his jacket pocket. 'Eat it! Morag says you must keep your strength up if you are to help these poor devils.'

'I'm planning on leaving here tonight,' warned Kate as she tore ravenously at the bone.

'That's impossible!'

'I must go,' she insisted stubbornly, remembering her resolve to be firm, not to let people dissuade her from her plans.

'It would be suicide,' he exclaimed, his eyes darkening with concern. 'There are Redcoats everywhere!'

'Like tigers after their supper, they are,' added John Partridge. 'It's taken us until now to dodge them ourselves.'

'My mind is made up!'

'All in good time, girl! Samuel Etheridge is just as anxious to have you out of his attic as you are to leave, but he doesn't want to put his neck in a noose any more than you do,' John Partridge told her sternly.

'Listen to what we are planning,' urged Iestyn.

'Tomorrow night, or the one after, just as soon as it is dark, we'll come and move those men who are fit enough to travel.'

'We'll take them to their families, or to friends who can look after them until they're fully recovered.'

'So why can't I leave as well?' Kate protested, struggling to keep her voice steady.

'I'm surprised you should ask,' Dr Pugh said gruffly. 'If you go, who will nurse the ones too sick to be moved?'

'You mean you expect me to stay here until all of them are better?' Kate flared. She looked quickly from Iestyn to Dr Pugh and back again, unable to believe her ears.

'Just a matter of a few days, my lovely,' soothed John Partridge. 'We'll bring you more food and some nice warm blankets. You'll be that comfortable . . .'

'We need you here, Kate. We could do with a dozen more like you,' interrupted the doctor. 'There were twenty men killed and some fifty injured in the carnage.'

270

'One poor fellow from Sirhowy who'd been shot through the back managed to get almost to his own door, but they caught up with him,' added Iestyn.

'Another, who'd been shot in the leg, was hustled off to the workhouse to have his leg amputated and he was taken prisoner before the surgeon had cleaned his knives,' Dr Pugh told her grimly. 'Without your help, Kate, we'd never be able to look after the men we've got hidden here,' he added.

'A couple more days, that's all we ask, girl,' pleaded John Partridge.

'They arrested John Frost last night,' Iestyn told her. 'Hiding he was, right here in Newport, in the house of one of his friends.'

'There's rumour, too, that William Jones has been caught,' butted in Dr Pugh. 'They say he was found at the Navigation Inn at Crumlin and that he put up the devil of a struggle.'

'I refuse to do it!' Kate said sharply.

'In that case you had better go now, right away!' John Partridge snapped, pointing to the door.

'Stop, Kate! Listen to me.' As she snatched up her cloak and wrapped it round her, Iestyn grabbed her arm. 'You must stay here, it's not safe on the streets! There are Redcoats on every corner and special constables posted all over the place. It would be suicide for you to go out there. They'd pick you up before you'd gone a hundred yards.'

'He's right. They're searching high and low,' agreed Dr Pugh. 'They're determined to find anyone who has helped the Chartists. You won't stand a chance if you leave here now.'

'It's the truth,' affirmed John Partridge. 'The soldiers will have seen you in Westgate Square and they'll take you prisoner as soon as look at you, even though you're a woman. Be a feather in their cap, see!'

Hungry, weary and frightened, Kate finally agreed to stay. She only hoped they would remember their promises to bring more food and whatever else they could manage so that conditions would be more bearable.

She knew she was no match for these determined men.

It had been so easy to make elaborate plans and convince herself that she would carry them out. Now, faced with reality, she felt lost and unsure of herself. She'd still do it though, she promised herself. She'd go to Llwynowen the moment it was safe to do so.

Ten days passed before the last of the twelve men was well enough to be moved out of the attic over the printing shop. Ten days during which Kate was virtually a prisoner, sharing the same discomforts as the men, and their fears.

As she looked round the deserted, blood-stained room, she felt a sense of dismay. The longing to get right away that had tormented her during the first few days of her incarceration had gradually given way to resignation.

Completely cut off from the outside world, time had hung heavily. Because of the overcast November skies, it had been dark in the attic by mid-afternoon, the gloom dispelled only by a single candle.

Unless the printing machines were rumbling and rattling they had been afraid to move about in case someone in the shop below heard them. Talking in low voices had been their only diversion. Their disillusionment because the uprising had failed, and their fears that even yet they might be caught, dominated the conversation.

Kate had constantly urged them to talk about other things, hoping to take their minds off the impending sense of doom. She asked about their homes and families, persuaded them to talk about their wives and children, brothers and sisters until she knew everything there was to know about each and every one of them.

Now it was all over and she could leave, free from all commitment, Kate felt as if she'd been abandoned. Nursing the injured men, tending to their every need, she had become attached to them.

272

She'd had plenty of time also to think about her own dilemma. She kept asking herself if all along she had been blinding herself to the truth, and indulging in romantic fantasies. Had she wrongly interpreted David's words, reading far more into their exchanges than he had ever intended she should?

She was still reluctant to admit that David might have dallied with her for his own amusement. His intoxicating kisses and sweet words of love when they'd strolled through the lanes, or met in the summer house at Bramwood Hall, had surely meant something.

In the long hours of isolation, Kate held imaginary conversations with her dead grandmother, drawing on the old lady's store of wisdom as she had done so often in the past when she had gone to her with problems.

When she had been growing up, her grandmother had warned her to guard against becoming a plaything for one of the Gentry, and had told her what happened to young girls who succumbed to such temptation.

'Sometimes, they'm married off to an ageing cowherd, or shepherd, whose own wife's died in childbirth and left 'im with a growing family to look after. In return for a name for the child and a roof over her head, the girl'll be little more than a slave. She'll be at the beck and call of the man's older children, and expected to cook and clean for them all as well as being a willing bedmate for 'im.'

'What about the others . . . the ones who are not married off?'

'They turn to their families for help. If they refuse to give 'em shelter the only other option's the poorhouse. That means drudgery from dawn to dusk, rags to wear, and straw to sleep on. The food's poor and there's precious little of it.'

Her incarceration in the attic above Samuel Etheridge's printing shop had given Kate a taste of such hardships and she knew it was a fate to be avoided at all costs.

Most days she had experienced pangs of hunger, accompanied by harsh burning sensations that sent bile as bitter as gall flooding into her mouth. And there had been a dry constriction in her throat that made her long for a draught of cold water. At times, swallowing became almost impossible. Her tongue seemed twice its normal size, her lips so parched that they became dried up and cracked.

She wondered if her appearance was as calamitous.

When it became dark outside a ghostly, distorted image was reflected back at her from the small window. It was so unflattering that in the end she tried not to look.

To add to her discomfort, because she was not able to wash she felt sullied. Morag had sent her a clean shift and a petticoat to replace the one she'd torn into strips to bind up the men's injuries the first night she had been there. She had donned them while the men slept, using her cloak to screen her nakedness in case any of them were awake.

Two days later, Twm Jenkins had moved too vigorously and his wound had opened up and haemorrhaged, so she had been forced to use Morag's petticoat to stem the flow of blood.

Now that she could leave and put it all behind her, a sense of reluctance kept her rooted there. As long as she lived she would remember these nightmarish ten days of confinement and the groans and suffering of the injured men. The smell of blood and excrement, that had constantly assailed her nostrils in the airless room, would remain with her forever.

It was amazing that there had been no infection since there had been no water to bathe their wounds and barely enough clean rags to cover them.

Despite their deprivations, all of the men had survived. They had also retained their grim determination to go on supporting the Chartist Movement. Their spirits were high.

She couldn't understand why she was the one so afraid to return to the everyday world. As she vacillated between what her heart desired and what her head told her was the right thing to do, she knew her grandmother would have scorned such shilly-shallying!

As footsteps sounded on the rickety staircase, Kate pulled herself together. It would be Samuel Etheridge come to take possession of his attic and he would not expect to find her still there.

'Kate!' The sound of Iestyn's anxious voice shattered the silence. 'Thank goodness I've caught you, I was afraid you might have left.'

'Is something wrong?'

'No, of course not. Morag wants you to spend a little time with us before you set off back up the Valley.'

'Oh, Iestyn, I would like nothing better,' she exclaimed, overcome by joy that she could delay any decision for just a little longer. 'Is it safe? For you, I mean.'

'It's your safety we are concerned about, Kate,' he told her gently. 'They've arrested all the leaders but they are still on the lookout for stragglers. They found Dai Pritchard hiding in a chest at the King Crispin and they took Zephaniah Williams off a merchant ship that was docked in Cardiff. He was just about to set sail for Portugal.'

'What will happen to them?'

'They're being kept in Monmouth goal. They'll go on trial and doubtless they'll be convicted of High Treason.'

'And condemned to death?'

She thought of the three men he had mentioned. Zephaniah Williams who had kept the Royal Oak Inn at Coalbrookvale and who had led the contingent from Blaenafon. A dark-haired man with his hair brushed forward, a retroussé nose and a full face with heavy eyebrows. His wife, Joan, and his two children would be waiting anxiously for his return. She wondered what would happen to them if he was condemned to death.

She thought sadly of the families of those men who had lain dead outside the Westgate Hotel and whose bodies had been interred at St Woolos under cover of darkness a few nights later.

Abraham Thomas had been one of them. She remembered how his wife had pleaded with him not to join Zephaniah's contingent. Wrapping their youngest child in a shawl she'd braved the torrential rain to run after the marching column, begging him to come back home with her.

He had resolutely refused.

Less than fifteen hours later he'd been dead. Trampled on by the fleeing Chartists, his body kicked to one side by the pursuing Redcoats.

Her own problems seemed trivial compared with theirs.

'You will come?' Iestyn's plea brought her back to the present. Tempted by the thought of a warm fire, hot food, an opportunity to wash, and the chance to see Morag again, she accepted eagerly.

32

Morag's green eyes sparkled with pleasure as she greeted Kate. Her enthusiasm as they hugged and kissed overwhelmed Kate and left her speechless. Dafydd, too, seemed pleased to see her, jumping up and down excitedly and telling her of things he had been doing since she went away. Even Gelert wagged his black stubby tail in welcome.

Iestyn had taken such a devious route from the print shop, avoiding the main streets, and entering their house in Westgate Square from the rear of the property, that Kate had grown uneasy.

Remembering his warning immediately after the uprising that the Redcoats were still seeking those sympathetic to the Chartist cause, she had wondered if he was taking a risk in inviting her to their home. Once or twice she had been on the point of asking him, but each time he had diverted the conversation to other topics.

Now all that was forgotten in the warmth of their welcome. Toasting her toes in front of the glowing fire, sipping the first hot drink she had tasted for ten days, she felt wonderfully content. It was as if she was awakening from a harrowing nightmare to find everything normal again.

The moment Kate finished her tea, Morag asked Iestyn and Dafydd to take Gelert for a walk. As soon as the door closed behind them, Morag brought in a hip bath and placed it in front of the fire.

'Come on now, you should enjoy this. It will be a treat after so long without the chance to wash properly,' she smiled as she poured in hot water from the cauldron and saucepans she had been heating up in readiness.

'I'll take your clothes and see if they're fit to be washed. For now, you can wear some of mine,' she added, placing a pile on one of the chairs.

'I'll be in the scullery, shout if you want anything. Take as long as you like. There will be a hot meal waiting by the time you've finished,' and she left Kate to enjoy the luxury of wallowing in hot water up to her neck.

As she washed her hair and soaped every inch of her body, Kate felt a sense of well-being permeate her limbs. She lay back, closing her eyes, enjoying the languorous warmth of the water and the heat from the fire. The fragrance of the herbal oils Morag had added to the bath obliterated the malodorous smells that had filled her nostrils for days past.

As the water began to cool, she stirred from her dream-like state and stepped out, wrapping herself in one of the white towels Morag had placed within reach.

By the time Iestyn and Dafydd returned she had dried her hair and was dressed in clean, borrowed clothes.

The days with the Lewises sped by, days of utter relaxation and enchantment. They were such a close-knit family, so full of love and concern for one another, it was a joy to be with them.

Morag and Iestyn were both gentle but firm with Dafydd and he responded like a flower opening in the sun. His eagerness to please them was delightful. The sadness in his dark eyes when he was rebuked for wrong-doing touched Kate's heart.

Kate found Morag a wonderful confidante. Her eyes would widen and she would draw her breath in sharply as Kate related the more poignant details. She was so sympathetic and understanding that Kate had no hesitation in telling her all about David and their love for each other.

'And after he left Bramwood Hall you missed him so much you came to Wales looking for him?' breathed Morag, her eyes shining softly.

278

Kate nodded, biting her lip for fear of saying too much. She didn't want to ruin the romantic illusion by mentioning any of the sordid happenings at Machen Mawr, or that she had been on the point of marrying Morgan Edwards.

The more she remembered that incident the more ashamed she felt that she should even have contemplated marrying him. She blamed it on her inexperience and her fear of being homeless if she didn't find David. She even felt grateful that things had turned out the way they had done and that she had been saved from making such a colossal mistake.

'So how long have you been in South Wales?' frowned Morag.

'Several months. I've been looking for Fforbrecon and Llywnowen. I worked whenever I could,' she said vaguely. 'For a few days I stayed in Coalbrookvale Terrace in Nantyglo but things there were so terrible I moved on again as quickly as possible.'

'Why was that?'

Morag listened wide-eyed with disbelief as Kate related the harrowing details of the life endured by the orphan children at Mollie Parry's house in Coalbrookvale Terrace.

'Wouldn't it be wonderful to do something for the poor little dabs,' she sighed, wiping away her tears.

'They should be at school, learning to read and write,' sighed Kate. 'Now that really is something I would feel was worth fighting for. More important than the right to vote, even.'

She went on to tell Morag about the heavy drinking that went on in the pubs and ale-houses, and how the Agents cheated the men of their money on pay days. She told her about life at The Bull, although she said nothing about Dai Roberts' offer of marriage.

By distancing herself from it, that, like everything else that had happened since she'd left Bramwood Hall, took on an air of unreality.

Morag had been moved by her revelations and was full of sympathy and understanding.

'You must promise me you'll go to Llwynowen, Kate, and find David,' urged Morag, her green eyes intense, her face eager. 'I'm sure he still loves you. His silence is because of the pressure of responsibility, nothing more,' she said earnestly. Her green eyes sparkled as she added, 'I'd like it all to be resolved, and for you to be as happy as I am.'

'I can think of nothing I'd like better,' agreed Kate. 'My stay in your home has been one of the happiest times of my life.'

'Then promise me you will go to Llwynowen soon and that you will let me know what happens,' begged Morag.

They talked at length about how this should be accomplished, Kate drawing strength from her friend's enthusiasm and good advice.

'Say nothing to Iestyn about all this,' warned Morag. 'He might not view the matter in quite the same light as me.'

Kate agreed readily. The ambience between the three of them was so precious that she was unwilling to risk incurring his displeasure.

Whenever Iestyn was present, she would talk instead about her hopes of one day becoming a teacher and tell him how her schoolmaster, William Barnes, had encouraged her in this.

The discussion would become intense and centre on the need for the children in Ebbw Vale and the surrounding valleys to attend school.

'I'm sure if the Chartists ever gain power this will become possible,' Iestyn affirmed.

Kate was so happy in her new environment that she would have been content to stay there indefinitely. The only irritation, which deepened with each passing day, was that both Morag and Iestyn insisted she must remain indoors. She would have liked to have accompanied

280

Morag when she went out shopping but whenever she suggested it Morag begged her to stay home and look after Dafydd. Even when she wanted to attend the Ebenezer chapel with them Iestyn refused to let her.

'So far, no one knows you are staying here and I feel it is better that things remain that way,' he murmured.

'I don't understand. . . .'

'We'll talk about it another time.' His warning glance indicated that Dafydd was listening with bright-eyed keenness.

Later that evening, after Dafydd had been tucked up in his feather-mattressed bed, and the three of them were sitting in front of a blazing fire, Iestyn said he had a proposition to put to her.

Kate felt apprehensive.

'Are you in any haste to return to Blaenafon?' Iestyn asked. He leaned forward, picked up the iron poker and concentrated on stirring the fire.

'I have a job at The Bull to go back to and my few belongings are still there,' Kate said cautiously.

'You've been away for over three weeks, surely the landlord will have replaced you by now?'

'I doubt it. He managed on his own for several years before I arrived on the scene.'

Her thoughts focused on Dai Roberts, remembering his proposal, and a shudder ran through her. Having witnessed the pleasure that could be derived from a marriage that was compatible, and based on love, it was impossible to contemplate settling for anything less.

'Why do you ask?'

'Dr Pugh would like you to stay a while longer.'

Kate looked at him quizzically, wondering what he had in mind. Were they going to agree to her idea of starting a school? She darted a glance towards Morag but she was staring into the fire, her curtain of red hair screening her face so that Kate had no idea what thoughts were going through her mind.

'He needs someone to nurse a man who has been

injured.'

'I see. Is it one of the Chartists?' she asked, disappointment in her voice.

'We don't know,' Iestyn said hesitantly. His alert eyes held hers as if he was trying to decide how much to reveal.

'This man wasn't in the Newport uprising,' he confided, 'but in some previous fracas. He's been unconscious ever since!'

'And you need someone to look after him, feed him and tend to his wounds.'

'That's it. I've not seen him but I've been told his injuries are extensive. Elwyn Pugh thinks you have a healing touch and thinks you could help save this man's life. What do you say?'

'I think you should do it, Kate,' Morag said earnestly, looking directly at her.

'I need to go to Blaenafon to collect my belongings. I left all my clothes. . . .' her voice trailed off as Iestyn shook his head.

'It wouldn't be safe, Kate. The Redcoats are still on the lookout for anyone who was involved in the uprising. If they caught you, then you'd have to stand trial at Monmouth along with the others already in custody.'

'But I had nothing to do with the uprising!' Kate cried.

'You'd find it hard to convince them. You were in Westgate Square at the height of the disturbance,' Iestyn reminded her.

'And if they discover that ever since then you've been looking after men who were injured when the military fired, you'll certainly be guilty in their eyes,' Morag pointed out.

'Then should I be here?' Kate exclaimed aghast. 'If I was found under your roof surely you could both be in trouble.'

'We are well aware of that risk,' Iestyn admitted.

'I had no idea I was putting you in such grave danger,'

Kate muttered contritely. 'You said nothing. . . .'

'We didn't want to worry you,' Morag told her. 'We're grateful for the way you helped nurse the injured men and felt you needed time to recover from such an ordeal.'

'That's why we've insisted on carrying on as normal, with Morag doing the shopping, and going on our own to Ebenezer,' explained Iestyn.

'It seems to have been very successful,' smiled Morag, 'no one has said a word.'

'We were concerned in case Dafydd mentioned to anyone that you were staying here but he has been obedient and kept our secret.'

'I must leave at once,' gasped Kate. 'I had no idea. . . .'

'There's no need for unseemly alarm,' parried Iestyn. 'If you agree to Dr Pugh's request then I will take you along to his house tonight after dark.'

'You can trust Elwyn Pugh implicitly, Kate,' Morag assured her, reaching out and squeezing her hand as Kate looked hesitant.

'He will take you to the secret hideout where this man is,' continued Iestyn. 'You'll be safe there, and we'll have no further worries.'

The implications of the terrible danger in which she had placed her friends overwhelmed Kate. She had never thought for one moment that the Redcoats were still interested in her movements. Now, remembering the many occasions when Morag had persuaded her to stay home with Dafydd, making excuses that it was too cold or too wet for him to go out, she realized what a simpleton she'd been. At the time she'd even felt resentful, yet the truth was they'd been trying to protect her.

'Do it, Kate,' begged Morag. 'Another few weeks and all the fuss and bother should have died down and it will be quite safe for you to go on your way.'

'Yes, of course,' agreed Kate.

Suddenly all her plans had no meaning. If it wasn't safe for her to walk freely in Newport, then how could she make her way to Llwynowen to look for David?

'Good! Go with Morag and sort out some clothes and anything else you may need,' urged Iestyn.

'It's kind of you to lend me your things,' Kate said gratefully as Morag plied her with skirts and dresses, urging her to take the pick of her wardrobe.

'You are more than welcome to anything that takes your fancy.'

'If this poor man is in a coma then I don't suppose it matters very much what I wear,' Kate said ruefully as she selected a skirt and several blouses.

'If you feel smart it will help keep your spirits up,' smiled Morag, as she insisted on Kate taking another dress.

'A second change of underwear would suit me better,' grinned Kate.

'Now, is there anything else I can do for you?' asked Morag when the skirt and blouses were packed into a bundle. 'Would you like us to try and get a message to The Bull at Blaenafon?'

'No. I don't think so.' Kate shook her head. 'I mightn't even go back there . . . at least not right away. Getting to Llwynowen is far more important.'

'I know!' Morag drew Kate into her arms, hugging her impetuously. 'Be patient! It would be silly to risk going there just yet. Once the trial at Monmouth is over, and the Leaders have been sentenced, those in authority will feel that justice has been done and then they'll lose interest.'

'But that may not be for months! I can't wait that long.'

'Try not to worry. I shall pray for you night and morning so have faith, *cariad*. Something tells me that you are doing the right thing and that everything will work out as you want it in the end.'

33

It was with great reluctance that Kate prepared to leave the Lewises' house in Westgate Square.

It was not just the warmth and comfort, the prettily furnished bedroom or the good food, but also the atmosphere of happiness and contentment that permeated their home that had impressed her.

She and Morag had enjoyed each other's company and both women wept as they said farewell.

'I'll always be your friend, and you'll always be welcome here, do remember that,' Morag told her, pushing back her cloud of red hair and wiping the tears from her green eyes with the back of her hand.

'I'll be back to see you, I promise,' Kate assured her. 'I'll have to return all the clothes you've loaned me,' she added with a conspiratorial smile.

Iestyn accompanied Kate to Dr Pugh's surgery. He led the way down a narrow path at the side of the tall, red brick house, to a side door that bore the doctor's brass plate.

Without knocking he took her into a small waiting room and then through another door that led into the doctor's consulting room.

Kate looked around her with interest. The room was large and sparsley furnished. A cluttered desk, a high-backed leather chair, a shelf containing pickled embryos and other specimens in wide-necked glass bottles, a high brown leather couch, a weighing machine and a table on which were a variety of instruments laid out with great precision on a starched white cloth.

Dr Pugh joined them almost at once. He greeted Kate affably.

'I'm pleased you've agreed to help,' he said gruffly as he began to fill a large, black leather bag with an assortment of medicines, ointments and bandages. 'We'll waste no more time. Are you ready?'

'It's time for me to say goodbye,' murmured Iestyn. He took both Kate's hands in his own, his smile warm as he wished her well.

'We must be leaving,' Dr Pugh said impatiently, pulling a heavy woollen cape around his shoulders. 'The trap is already harnessed and waiting for us by the stables. Slip out the way you came, Iestyn, and make sure no one sees you.'

'Good luck, Kate.' Iestyn suddenly pulled her towards him, hugging her fiercely, kissing her cheek. Then, releasing her abruptly, he was gone.

Leaving Kate no time for reflection, Dr Pugh picked up his bag, indicating for her to follow him through a door on the other side of the room. It led into a tiled passageway. On the right was a large kitchen with a flagstone floor. A small oil lamp, placed in the centre of the scrubbed pine table that ran down the middle of the room, cast grotesque shadows on the walls but did little to relieve the gloom.

Clutching her bundle of clothes, Kate followed the doctor, edging her way between the table and the ceiling-high dresser that stood against one wall.

'Hurry!'

The cobbled yard was slippery underfoot, and she had difficulty in keeping up with him as he strode towards the stables.

Within minutes they were bowling along at a spanking rate. Dr Pugh handled the reins competently, with the assurance of a man who knew exactly where his destination lay. Once they were clear of the town he slowed his pace and turned to see if she was all right.

'People always imagine it must be a case of life or death when I turn out at night so they expect me to drive like fury,' he said with a sharp laugh. 'If I drove in a leisurely manner they might become curious.'

'Have we far to go?'

'Quite a long way. There is a woollen rug on the seat beside you. Wrap it round your feet and legs if you feel cold.'

'Can you tell me something about this patient and what I am expected to do?' asked Kate nervously.

'Much the same as what you have been doing for the past two weeks,' he told her tersely.

'Iestyn said he didn't think this man was anything to do with the Chartists.'

Dr Pugh remained silent for so long that Kate began to wonder if he had heard her question, or whether he was deliberately ignoring it. When he did speak it was with obvious reluctance.

'Iestyn hasn't told you all the facts because he didn't know them.'

'Oh!' Kate felt a wave of apprehension.

'This man is in a coma. He needs as much care as a baby.'

'Poor man!'

'You will not only have to feed him and keep him clean but tend his wounds and administer medication.'

'I'll do all I can for him,' she promised. 'I have no nursing experience though. . . .'

'You seemed to manage well enough back in Newport,' Dr Pugh exclaimed drily.

'I did my best,' Kate admitted, her cheeks burning.

'That's all I'm asking you to do now.'

What had she let herself in for this time, she wondered, as they drove through the dark night. She wished she had stuck to her original plan to go direct to Llwynowen. She was much too easily persuaded by other people to do what they wanted, she thought dolefully.

'We'll be stopping in about half an hour at a tavern. The landlord's name is Huw Jenner, he'll be coming the rest of the way with us,' announced Dr Pugh, breaking the silence that had become as solid as a wall between them.

287

'There's just one other point which perhaps I should make clear,' Dr Pugh cleared his throat uncomfortably. 'We've no idea who this man is or anything at all about him.'

'I thought you were only interested in helping Chartist supporters?' frowned Kate.

'Neither politics nor religion comes into it when someone needs medical help,' snapped Dr Pugh, in a reprimanding tone.

'No, of course not,' Kate said hastily. 'What I really meant . . .' her voice trailed off uncertainly. She shot a sideways glance at her companion and saw that his mouth was set in a tight line.

'What sort of injuries does he have?' she asked in an attempt to dispel the uneasy atmosphere between them.

'Broken bones and multiple head and face injuries.'

'How terrible!'

'The bones will knit together, given time. It's the head wounds that trouble me,' confided Dr Pugh. 'He has been in a coma now for such a long period that there is always the danger that when he does regain consciousness he may have become mentally deranged.'

'You mean . . . you mean he'll be mad?' gasped Kate in a horrified whisper.

'That,' he sighed scornfully, 'is the non-medical term for it. Mind you,' he added hastily, 'exactly what form it will take remains to be seen.'

'What do you mean?' Kate frowned.

'At best, he could be simple . . . the mind of a child. Unable to comprehend things on an adult level.'

'And at worst?' Her eyes darkened apprehensively.

'At worst . . .' the doctor hesitated. 'At the very worst he could be aggressive or even violent.'

'And between those two extremes?'

'A great number of possibilities. It could be that his memory will be impaired, or that he will be slow to comprehend things. He might suffer from headaches,

288

or bouts of depression. His vision or hearing might be affected, he might have a reaction to noise. He could suffer from some form of phobia. It might be a morbid fear or aversion, an intense dislike of somebody, or an irrational anxiety related to the experience that caused his injuries.'

'Is there no way of knowing in advance which of these it's likely to be?'

'Hatred, horror, overwhelming anxiety are the most likely symptoms we can expect,' mused Dr Pugh.

'How old is he?' asked Kate.

'Oh, he's a youngish man, somewhere in his twenties. He looks as though he was physically fit before the accident. This is a great advantage, of course. With careful nursing he should certainly return to full health.'

'But with his mind impaired!'

'Well, that remains to be seen. I thought it wise to warn you what to expect,' he told her gruffly as he reined in the horse.

As they came to a stop outside a tavern a young boy appeared out of the darkness so promptly that it was obvious he had been waiting for them. Without saying a word he took the horse's head.

Kate was so stiff from the cold that as she made to step down from the trap she would have fallen had not Dr Pugh taken a firm grip on her arm.

He escorted her into the tavern and they went through to a small parlour at the back of the taproom. Although it was well after midnight, there was a fire blazing in the hearth.

As Kate bent down to warm her chilled hands the sudden heat made her feel giddy. Her senses reeling, she sat down on the nearest chair, passing a hand over her eyes.

'A drink and something hot to eat; we are both frozen after our journey,' Dr Pugh declared authoritatively as a rotund, grey-haired man appeared in the doorway, rubbing his hands together and looking inquisitively at Kate as he enthusiastically greeted the doctor.

'Hot toddy? A bowl of chicken soup thickened with vegetables?'

'That sounds fine. Quick as you can then, the young lady is feeling faint with the cold.'

'Right away, Dr Pugh. Make yourselves comfortable.' As he spoke, the man picked up a log and thrust it into the heart of the blazing coals, sending up a shower of golden sparks.

'Take off your cloak, Kate,' advised Dr Pugh, removing his own cape and laying it across the back of a chair.

'Is the sick man here?'

'No, but it will be an hour or so before we're ready to continue our journey so you may as well be comfortable. We've hidden him some distance away. Rather an isolated spot, I'm afraid. Will you be able to stand loneliness?'

'I managed in Newport.'

'That was rather different. The men you were nursing were all conscious and able to talk. You were part of a group. Here you will be completely on your own, with a man who is in a coma and desperately ill.' He stared at her. 'You're quite sure you will be able to cope?'

'I think so,' she told him quietly. 'There is one thing I don't understand, though.'

'Well, speak out then,' Dr Pugh said impatiently.

'This man . . . why are you so concerned about him?'

Dr Pugh scowled but remained silent.

'How did he get injured?' Kate persisted.

'I've already told you! He's a fellow human being and I am a doctor,' Dr Pugh growled.

'I know that but why hasn't he been brought here to the Inn and nursed openly. Why can't the local doctor attend him?'

'You ask too many questions,' Dr Pugh blustered.

'If you want me to nurse him then I think you should give me some answers,' Kate told him boldly.

290

The arrival of their food brought the conversation to a temporary halt. The soup was thick and hot and they both ate hungrily. When her appetite was sated, Kate returned to her probing.

'I still want to know who this man is I'm going to nurse and why he's being hidden away.'

Dr Pugh mopped up the last of his soup with a piece of bread, masticated it slowly, then pushed his empty bowl to one side. Picking up his glass of hot toddy he took a long, slow swig. Cradling the glass between both hands he looked across at Kate as he chewed thoughtfully on his lower lip.

'Please!' she entreated.

'Very well. I'll tell you what I know. I don't think this man has anything to do with the Chartists, but I can't be sure.' He held up his hand as she was about to speak, 'I do know that he received his injuries during a fracas at one of the coal mines not far from here. There'd been a cave-in and a dispute arose when they tried to sort matters out. A fight broke out between management and workers.'

'Go on!' breathed Kate as Dr Pugh paused to take another swig from his glass.

'That's all there is to tell you. As I said, fighting broke out. Sticks, stones and lumps of coal were hurled around and when it was all over this man was left lying on the ground badly injured.'

'If he was a local man, isn't it strange that no one has come looking for him?' asked Kate, frowning.

'Maybe they have and not found him.'

Kate shook her head disbelievingly.

'His family may have been told he was dead,' suggested Dr Pugh.

'Even so, they'd want his body for burial!'

'If he was a known rebel they may have decided it was wiser to keep quiet in case they brought retribution on their own heads,' he told her sagely.

'Surely not!'

'There has been so much unrest of late that people are no longer certain who is their friend and who's their enemy. Families are divided. Men who have worked side by side for many years no longer trust each other. Poverty stalks the land and with it fear and suspicion.'

'How long ago did all this happen?' asked Kate, trying to quell the alarm bells sounding in her mind.

'The cave-in was shortly before the Newport uprising, I think.' Dr Pugh sighed heavily. 'So much unrest it's difficult to keep track of everything.'

'And you think this injured man could be a stranger to the area.'

'It's possible. He might be one of the arbitrators who came up from Cardiff or London to try and help settle the dispute.'

'You haven't told me his name.'

'I think I've said enough.' Abruptly Dr Pugh stood up. 'Stay here. I'll go and see if Huw Jenner is ready and we can be on our way.'

Kate's mind buzzed. The possibility that the injured man might be David filled her with excitement, brought a light to her eyes and a flush to her cheeks.

She knew it was foolish to hope, let alone voice aloud her innermost thoughts. It was like sighing for the moon.

Yet she couldn't completely disregard her intuition.

34

They set out on foot, Kate carrying her bundle of clothes, Dr Elwyn Pugh his black bag of medicines and Huw Jenner a small sack of provisions.

Frost glistened on the bushes with a ghostly whiteness as the moon flitted between scurrying clouds. Twigs snapped and crackled underfoot as they left the roadway and made their way uphill towards a ruined tower that pointed a stark warning finger into the night sky. Kate shivered. The coldness of the night air froze her cheeks and seared her throat as she panted for breath, trying to keep up with the two men as they strode out along the steep, rutted path.

They skirted a mass of buildings, gabled ruins, that looked as if they had once, together with the distant tower, formed part of a castle. Great piles of grey stone radiated an eerie translucent gleam and cast grotesque, dark shadows on to the frozen ground.

The unnatural stillness filled Kate with unease. She jumped and let out a small cry as an owl screeched and, with a sudden rush of wind and wild flapping of wings, swooped low over their heads before disappearing into the darkness.

'Not scared are you, Miss?' guffawed Huw Jenner. 'Some say that owls are the spirits of the departed and their hooting signals death . . .'

'That will do! A load of Old Wives' Tales and I'm sure Miss Stacey doesn't believe a word of it,' interrupted Elwyn Pugh sharply. 'Anyway,' he added in more conciliatory tones, 'most people believe it's a warning that snow is on the way and judging by the nip in the air tonight I think that's more than likely.'

'I prefer my own version since it frightens folks off,' stated Huw Jenner. 'Some even claim to have seen the Red Dogs of Morfa running up here at night and everyone knows they are a warning from the underworld.'

'I suppose you are justified in encouraging such superstitions if it helps to keep people away,' Dr Pugh agreed grudgingly. 'If they believe such nonsense then should they see a light flickering they're more likely to run a mile than come and investigate it.'

'There's any number of manifestations people claim to have seen here after dark. A very superstitious lot, are miners.'

By now the ruins were just a blur in the background. In front of them the tower dominated the skyline. Dr Pugh held out a hand to steady Kate as they clambered through the curtain wall, and over piles of rubble, to reach a narrow entrance.

From the shape of its arched top, she assumed it had once been an impressive doorway. Steep stone steps spiralled into a narrow passageway that ended in a vast room with a stone-flagged floor and high ceiling.

In the dim light of the candle-lantern hanging from a beam she could see that there was a stone fireplace, with a sloping hood of ashlar, built across the angle of one corner. And along the wall to the right, beneath a vaulted window, a stone seat was set into the embrasure. The window had been blocked in and only a narrow, arrow-slit aperture allowed air into the room.

As her eyes grew accustomed to the gloom, Kate saw there was a rough table holding some dishes and cooking pans and, drawn up near the fire, a high-backed wooden chair with carved arms.

On the far side of the fire was a bed, but it was difficult to tell if anyone was lying in it or not.

'Here's your patient, then,' Dr Pugh announced. 'I did warn you he was in pretty bad shape,' he added as he walked towards the bed.

Tingling with excitement, Kate joined him.

Her optimism that it might be David turned to dismay. She drew in her breath sharply, clamping her teeth over her lower lip to keep it from trembling. It was impossible to discern the man's features, because his head and face were completely swathed in bandages. Slits had been left over his nose and mouth to allow him to breathe. He looked more like a corpse than a living person. His right arm was set in splints which were held in place with a sling that went round his neck and was then bound around his chest.

She watched in silence as Dr Pugh slid his fingers round the man's wrist, feeling for his pulse. He seemed to have difficulty in finding it and for one awful moment Kate was sure they'd arrived too late.

Her spirits had been buoyed up by the notion that it might be David. Now that feeling was ebbing fast.

She watched bemused as Huw Jenner cleared the ashes from the stone fireplace and coaxed the dying embers back to a lively blaze with dry twigs.

'You've no need to worry about the smoke,' he explained, as he skilfully banked up the fire with nuggets of coal. 'This room is within the tower and by the time the smoke reaches the outside it's a mere wisp and barely noticeable.'

'Very few people ever come up here but it might be wise for you to keep out of sight during the daytime, Kate,' advised Dr Pugh. 'If you need a breath of air then go out at dusk or dawn.'

'And remember to let your cloak flap in the breeze, then if anyone should chance to see you they'll take you for a ghost and run off screaming,' joked Huw Jenner. 'There's some terrible tales told about the hauntings up here. . . .'

'That will do!' Dr Pugh scowled. 'We'll be on our way now, Kate. Is there anything more you need to know?'

'There's a dozen tallow candles as well as plenty of coal and logs for the fire so pile on all you need to keep warm,' urged Huw Jenner solicitously.

'I've left enough medicine to last for two days. There's broth and gruel for your patient as well as plenty of food for you until our next visit.'

'Thank you. I'm sure I shall manage fine.'

'Don't expect to see any change. Drip the broth and medicine into his mouth a little at a time so that they trickle down his throat. If you try to hurry the process he may choke. Now you do understand?'

'Yes,' Kate assured him. 'I'll take good care of him.'

'And have you everything you require yourself or is there anything you wish me to bring on my next visit?'

Kate looked round the bleak, windowless room and shivered. Two days would seem like eternity with no one to talk to and so little to occupy her time.

'Could you bring me something to read?' she asked shyly.

'You mean a bible?'

'No!' Her eyes widened and a smile lifted the corners of her mouth. 'I would much rather have a book of poetry. Something by William Barnes, if that's possible,' she added hopefully.

'Poetry!' His eyebrows shot up in astonishment. 'You read such stuff!'

'I was taught to read and write by William Barnes,' she added simply.

'Well, I've never heard of the fellow but I'll see what I can do. I'll bring you something,' he promised.

'How about the *Mabinogion* that Lady Charlotte Guest has just translated into English,' prompted Huw Jenner.

'What is that?'

'Stories based on Welsh folk-lore,' he explained. 'Years she's spent collecting these tales. Wonderful they are! They were first recorded in the *White Book of Rhydderch* and the *Red Book of Hergest* in the Middle Ages. Ever since then they've been handed down, by word of mouth, from father to son, mother to daughter.'

'We'll see, we'll see,' Dr Pugh stated in clipped tones, snapping his medical bag shut to signal his anxiety to be on his way.

Kate walked to the outer door with them and stood there shivering until their footsteps had faded away before she slid the wooden latch into position.

Picking up the candle-lantern which Huw Jenner had left burning on the table she carried it across to the bed and stood gazing uncertainly at the man lying there.

Although his hair and features were completely hidden she felt there was something familiar about the set of the man's shoulders and the shape of his body beneath the covers. Once again, she felt hope rising within her like a surging tide.

Setting down the lantern on the floor, she reached out to draw back the bedclothes. Her fingers were shaking and she was trembling from head to foot but the man remained impassive, his chest barely rising his breathing was so shallow.

She stood there, biting her lower lip, afraid to make the next move, knowing that it would confirm whether her intuition was playing her false or not. Would it be better not to know? she wondered. Would she be prepared to nurse a stranger? If it wasn't David, could she give him the care and attention he needed, or would she feel resentful and disillusioned?

She gathered her courage, her mind made up. She must know the truth. With bated breath she drew back the covers to expose the man's shoulders and chest.

For a moment she felt unable to move, then with trembling fingers she began unbuttoning his nightshirt. Her heart racing, her breath catching in a choked sob, she opened back the striped flannel to look for the dull-red, egg-shaped birthmark she knew to be on David's chest.

Kate stopped, sinking to her knees beside the bed, numb with shock when she found the man's body was bandaged from waist to armpits.

Tears streamed from her eyes. Waves of despair washed over her.

The flickering candle marked the passing of time. When it had burnt so low that it was guttering, she roused herself, knowing that unless she replaced it the room would be in darkness.

Her mind was a jumble of plans and schemes as she heated up broth in a small pan over the open coals. With infinite patience she fed her patient, desperately anxious that he should have all the nourishment possible, yet fearful that he might choke.

Afterwards, she steeled herself to check for the one blemish that would prove his identity. Each time she tried, she could not bring herself to unwind the barrier of bandages.

Frustrated, she administered the medicine Dr Pugh had left, and then wrapped herself in a blanket and slept.

The whole of the next day the man remained completely impassive and her own mood floundered from elation to morbid fears about his condition and her concern as to whether he was David. The loneliness became so oppressive that she felt she was suffocating. In a state bordering on panic she unbarred the door, desperate for fresh air.

Outside, everything was shrouded in fog, a ghostly cloak of grey that swirled round her, encompassing her in dankness.

The following day, the weather was no better. Nothing stirred. The grey silence closed in all around her. She began to worry. Her own food supplies were dwindling and there was very little medicine left.

She had no way of telling the time, except by the number of candles she burned. She longed for something to read; anything to occupy her mind. Countless times she had cleaned and tidied the room, made up the fire and attended to the man's needs. She had bathed his feet and hands with warm water to make him more comfortable. She talked to him constantly, reciting all the poetry she knew, until her throat ached and the words became a blurred jumble, but he gave no sign of life other than a shallow, rhythmic breathing.

She dozed, waking with a start as a coal fell from the fire, or a candle guttered. When next she ventured to look out the fog had cleared, the moon shone like a beacon high in the sky and her feeling of optimism returned.

She had just used up the last of the medicine when she heard hammering on the door.

Dr Elwyn Pugh swept into the room bringing the icy coldness of the night with him. Huw Jenner followed, laden with provisions. While he unpacked these and replenished the stock of coal and wood, Dr Pugh examined the recumbent figure.

'There's been no change?'

'None at all,' Kate admitted reluctantly.

'You've fed him regularly?'

'Yes, and dosed him with medicine as you instructed.'

'We've brought enough for four days this time.'

'After that if there is no improvement we shall have to think about handing him over to the authorities,' Huw Jenner stated.

'But you can't do that!'

'We can't keep up this charade for ever,' he answered bluntly. 'The weather is deteriorating. Once the snow comes it will be impossible to get up here at all.'

'Anyway, our footsteps would be visible and our secret become common knowledge,' pointed out Elwyn Pugh.

'Mr Jenner said no one ever comes up here because people think the place is haunted,' she reminded him swiftly.

'If they saw two pairs of footprints leading up from the roadway they'd investigate quick enough,' he told her drily.

'It may not snow.'

'I'm afraid it will. It always snows by Christmas or early January.'

'It may not do so this year, you can't be sure!' Kate argued stubbornly.

'We'll have to see,' Dr Pugh murmured evasively. 'If he remains in a coma much longer there will be no question of him making a complete recovery, anyway.'

Fear tightened Kate's throat. If it was David then she ought to give him the chance of returning to his family, but she couldn't bring herself to speak out.

Left on her own again she paced the room, trying desperately to think of some way out of the dilemma. She felt guilty about saying nothing but if it was David and they took him away she might never see him again.

She sat brooding for a long time, until the fire dwindled so low that she had to go in search of the kindling Huw Jenner kept stored in the next room.

She gathered up a handful of the small dry twigs and roughly screwed-up balls of paper she found there and carried them back to the main room.

As she waited for the fire to blaze so that she could bank it up with coal, Kate straightened out some of the pieces of paper. Hungry for the printed word, she pored over them, curious to read what was written. They were old broadsheets announcing the time and place of public meetings to be held by the Chartists.

Everything else was forgotten as she read them. Notices to the Tradesmen of Newport and to the working men of Monmouthshire from John Frost, and to the Men and Women of Newport from Henry Vincent.

Some sheets were so torn or crumpled that it was impossible to tell what they were about, others stirred her greatly.

'In the present excited and alarming state of the country,' she read, 'when no man can say what a day can bring forth, it will be enough to tell the men of the Hills, that Wales expects every man to do his duty, and may God bless their righteous cause.

'My advice to you is be cool but firm. It is the object of your enemies to drive us to some outburst in order to destroy us. This is the state on which our country is now placed. The people ask for bread and the answer is the bludgeon or sword. Let not the desire of the enemy be gratified.'

Where did David fit into all this, she puzzled as she read the words over and over again.

If it was David in the bed, she reasoned, then he was being cared for by a doctor who sympathized with the Chartists. Yet he was one of the Owners, one of the oppressive men in authority that these broadsheets decried.

She stood looking down at the inert shape in the bed for several minutes, wrestling with her conscience, silently begging for forgiveness if what she was about to do went wrong. She knew that Dr Pugh would be horrified when he discovered the action she had taken but that no longer seemed to matter, not as long as she obtained the answers she needed.

35

Taking infinite care, Kate began to peel away the bandages that swathed the man's head.

His hair had been shaved close to the scalp and the first glimpse of the livid flesh beneath the strips of bloodied linen made her shiver. Taking a deep breath to overcome her revulsion she braced herself to go on with her grim task.

At first she was filled with hope. Any moment now, just as soon as his features were exposed, she would know the identity of the man she had been nursing.

Horror struck her like a padded fist as she paused to survey her handiwork. She felt stunned. What had she done? The man's face was badly scarred but the features were quite distinguishable and it was certainly not David.

She felt a deep sense of despair. Ever since she had been there she had been telling herself it was David, even though deep in her heart she knew it was only remotely possible. This man might be the same age but he was shorter, more wiry and muscled, a different build altogether.

She stood staring down at him, her hands hanging limply at her sides.

Now that her hopes were completely shattered, all that was left was a cold hollow inside her. She wished she'd never uncovered his face, then she could have gone on deluding herself. It was easier than knowing she was looking after a stranger.

Her eyes filled with tears as she compared the scarred features with those which had haunted her dreams ever since she'd left Bramwood Hall. There was absolutely no comparison! The shape of the face even was different.

This man had never had a 'square chin, a strong straight nose or aristocratic features. His head was round and bullet-shaped, his face small and lean with a squat nose and close-set eyes.

Kate regarded him dispassionately, thinking how much he must have suffered, wondering how he came to be so badly injured.

She picked up the discarded bandages, wondering if she should try to wrap his face up again. Then she pulled back sharply. Her gasp of shock filled the room. Had she imagined it or had the man's eyelids moved?

Now that his wounds were exposed to the air, the rhythm of his breathing seemed to have changed. She was sure it had deepened and quickened.

Fearful lest the pain she must be causing him might be more than his heart could stand, she felt for his pulse and was alarmed by the way it raced beneath her fingers. It had been foolhardy to give way to her selfish impulse, she thought guiltily. She had no medical knowledge and if her meddling proved detrimental to his recovery, how would she explain her actions. Dr Pugh was bound to find out since she couldn't replace the bandages with his professional skill.

She held her breath. She had not imagined it, his eyelids had moved. The lids flickered again and very slowly opened, flinching as if even the soft glow of candlelight dazzled them.

Shielding the flame so that his face was almost in darkness, she bent closer.

'Can you hear me?'

His eyelids slowly lifted, but the dark brown eyes beneath seemed glazed and vacuous. When she spoke again they focused on her face, picking up the reflection of the candle in their depths.

The apathetic vagueness disappeared.

'Who are you?' The hoarse whisper from his cracked and swollen lips exhausted him. He drifted back into the twilight world he had occupied for so long.

She dropped on her knees beside the bed, patiently waiting for him to open his eyes again.

After a while, she moved away and went to heat up some broth. The minute quantities she had been feeding him over the past days had been barely enough to sustain him. Now, if he remained conscious he might be able to cooperate, and then she could increase the amount.

She would try and prop him up, then there would be less fear of him choking. Once he was getting proper nourishment, he would make a much quicker recovery.

The next time he opened his eyes, she rolled up her cloak and the blanket she used at night and slipped them under his shoulders, supporting him so that she could spoon-feed him without the liquid trickling down his chin. He ate hungrily, seeming to gain fresh strength with each mouthful.

When the bowl was empty his swollen lips widened into a crooked smile.

'Are you an angel?' he croaked, as gently she eased him back flat on the bed. Then his eyes closed and his breathing became the deep, steady rhythm of natural sleep.

After covering him over, she reheated the remainder of the soup for herself and sat in the chair alongside his bed to eat it.

As she contemplated all that had happened, her own eyelids grew heavy as sleep claimed her.

When she awoke, Kate's first conscious thoughts were of her patient. Apprehensively, she walked over to check on him and breathed a sigh of relief when she saw that he was awake, his dark eyes studying her. It was a tense, watchful look with no trace of vagueness.

His shaven scalp, his puffed-up, red-rimmed eyes and swollen lips, showed the extent of his injuries but the livid purple bruises that covered the rest of his face seemed less inflamed than when she had first removed the bandages.

'Am I still alive . . . or is this a dream?' he murmured hoarsely. 'My mind's a blank. I can't remember anything.'

'No, you're not dreaming!' she murmured, fighting to keep her voice steady.

'So who are you?'

'Kate . . . Kate Stacey. Can you remember your name? Or what happened?'

She waited hopefully but he shook his head.

'Can you remember what happened . . . how you came to be in such a terrible state?'

He looked at her bewildered, then closed his eyes.

'Never mind, it will all come back to you in time,' she murmured soothingly, taking his uninjured hand between her own.

'But who are you?'

'I told you. Kate . . . Kate Stacey.'

'I don't know you. Where am I?' The puzzled look clouded his eyes again as he stared uncomprehendingly at the bare walls. 'Am I in gaol?'

'No! Of course not. Don't worry. You're quite safe.'

She tended him carefully, reassuring him when he became fretful because he could remember nothing from his past.

Her task was made easier because now that he was conscious he was able to cooperate. Raising him into an upright position, so that she could feed him, became routine and made the process so much quicker and much less messy. He still had considerable difficulty in swallowing but he responded valiantly to her encouragement.

He tired very quickly and was highly sensitive to pain. In an attempt to make him more comfortable she agreed to his request to bathe the wounds that covered his body.

When she began to strip away his soiled garments the suppurating sores made her heave. He cried out in agony as she soaked away the cloth that adhered to the raw flesh and deftly cleaned away the vile green pus below.

Several times she was on the point of giving up, knowing from his contorted face the agony she was inflicting on him, wondering if the ultimate relief justified the present pain.

'*Daro*! Get on with it, can't you,' he gasped each time she paused and looked at him questioningly.

Every groan and twinge set her nerves tingling, the sight of the horrific scabs and sores churned her stomach.

By the time she was finished her hands were shaking and she felt weak with fatigue. Quickly she cleared away the debris, burning the soiled pieces of rag on the fire.

When she turned round, he was supine, his eyes closed, breathing shallowly, his face drained of colour.

Desperately she tried to revive him, propping him up and holding a cup of diluted whisky to his lips. Gradually his breathing grew stronger, the colour returned to his lips but it was a long time before he was sufficiently recovered to talk to her. When he did he seemed bewildered.

'Why can't you tell me where we are?' he asked peevishly, as he looked round at the bare stone walls of the austere room in bewilderment.

'Because I don't know. We're in a ruined tower. After you were injured you were hidden here so that you'd be safe . . .' her voice trailed off as she saw how baffled he looked.

'But why are you here?' He turned his head from side to side restlessly.

'Dr Elwyn Pugh from Newport asked me to nurse you. It's such a complicated story,' she prevaricated, unsure how much she ought to tell him. 'Perhaps I should wait until you are stronger.'

'Please,' he gasped. 'I want to know now. Tell me about yourself and how you come to be here. It might help me to remember what happened.'

He seemed baffled when she told him about the Chartists' uprising in Newport and the tragedy that had resulted.

'And when the men I nursed were better, Dr Pugh thought it might not be safe for me to return to Blaenafon right away so he suggested I should come and look after you,' she explained.

There was a long silence. The man turned his head from side to side as if trying to clear his way through a fog of memories.

'I don't remember any uprising . . .' his voice trailed off. 'It wasn't there . . . I would have remembered if there had been guns and soldiers.'

'Don't worry about it now. You will remember in time,' she assured him.

He slept a great deal. Each time he woke she fed him. At first he could manage only spoonfuls of broth but gradually his appetite returned and he was able to eat the same food as she prepared for herself. She rationed it out carefully, hoping desperately that Dr Pugh would arrive before her supplies were exhausted.

By the end of the next day he was stronger and much more alert.

'I think I remember what happened,' he told her. 'It's all coming back . . . unless it's a dream,' he frowned worriedly.

'Just tell me what you remember.'

'I was working at Fforbrecon colliery . . .'

'Fforbrecon! You were a miner at Fforbrecon?'

Kate's excitement disconcerted him. He looked puzzled, the apathetic vagueness returning to his face.

'Yes . . . I'm sure I was . . .' He frowned heavily.

'Does the name Owen mean anything to you?'

Her question hung in the air. She waited anxiously for his reply, her eyes fixed on his face, waiting for his reaction. Her heart pumped wildly when she saw his eyes light up. This was it! Her intuition had been right. This man would lead her to David.

'Owen. Owen,' she repeated excitedly. 'David Owen.'

The glimmer of interest that had brightened his eyes faded. He shook his head in bewilderment.

'You remember someone called Owen,' she prompted.

'Owen . . . Owen . . . Owen Jones,' he muttered in a confused manner.

307

Her soaring hopes collapsed. It was bitterly disappointing but something she should have foreseen. The name Owen was widely used in Wales, as a forename as well as a surname.

'Are you called Owen Jones?' she asked quietly.

'That's right. Owen Jones from Fforbrecon.'

'Have you not heard of David Owen?'

He shook his head.

'The Owner of Fforbrecon colliery.'

'You're wrong there, *cariad*.' His face brightened. 'The Owner is Tudor ap Owen from Llwynowen over towards Govilon. Very important he is too. Damned hard Master,' he added wryly.

'David is his son,' explained Kate. 'Have you never heard of him . . . or seen him?'

'I never knew he had a son.'

'You worked at Fforbrecon colliery, though? Did you never see him there. In the last few months, I mean.'

'No, but then he'd not be working in the mine, would he!'

'I knew him when I lived in Wiltshire,' Kate said wistfully. 'He came back here to help his father. In time he was to take over the colliery.'

'I should have been the one trapped down there,' Owen Jones exclaimed in a distraught voice, ignoring what Kate was saying. 'If I hadn't changed shifts with our Ieuan I would have been underground when the cave-in happened!'

He was silent for a long time, staring into space as if reliving those moments over again.

'He was killed and I'm still alive,' he exclaimed in a shocked whisper.

'Was that when you were injured?' asked Kate, gently trying to draw him back to the present.

'No, no. I wasn't hurt. I just told you, I'd changed shifts with my brother, see. I wasn't even there when it happened.'

'So how did you get hurt?' prompted Kate.

'It was days afterwards. There was some sort of a meeting. We stood around for hours waiting to know what they were going to do. Things became heated. Roddi Llewllyn, the pit manager, told us the Owners had decided not to get the bodies out . . . *Daro!* Terrible thing to hear, that was. My brother Ieuan was down there. Changed shifts we had. . . .'

He paused, and the vacant look came back into his eyes as if he'd travelled back in time and was reliving it all.

Kate gave him a sip of water and waited patiently for him to go on.

'We were all outside in the yard, see. They were standing on some sort of makeshift platform. There were raised voices . . . arguments . . . a lot of shouting and threats.'

'Who were these men?' she asked tentatively.

'The bosses. The men who own the coal mines. When there's trouble at a pit they gather in a body to give one another support.'

'And was the Owner of Fforbrecon Colliery there?'

'Probably not. He's an old man now, mind. Usually sends his Agent to do his dirty work for him,' he added bitterly.

'So tell me what happened.'

'The platform the Owners were standing on tipped over, throwing them on to the ground. A free-for-all broke out. Men were grappling with each other, sticks, stones and lumps of coal were being hurled around. I remember being in the thick of it all and then . . . nothing.' He looked at Kate blankly. 'Just nothing. I don't remember any more. I don't know how I came to be injured!'

'Dr Pugh thinks that the blow to your head would have knocked you unconscious and that your broken arm and other injuries may all have happened afterwards,' she told him.

'I don't know!' His face puckered, a blank look came into his eyes. The lids drooped as though he wanted to

309

shut out the memories hovering at the edge of recall.

Kate left him to rest.

Eager as she was for more details, and to ply him with questions, she felt that what mattered most was that he should make a full recovery. She was worried in case forcing him to remember what had happened was taxing his strength.

He was not easily pacified. His thoughts rambled. Repeatedly he asked where they were and how he had come to be there.

'Dr Pugh will be able to answer all those questions when he gets here,' Kate assured him.

'But when will that be?'

She turned away, not wanting him to see the fear in her eyes and realize how anxious she was because the doctor was overdue. They had very little food left and all the medical supplies were exhausted. Soon they would be without candles.

She tried to distract them both by reading to him from the crumpled pamphlets she had found and telling him what she knew of the Chartist uprising.

He would listen for a while then grow restless, so she would talk to him about how different life was in Blaenafon to where she had lived in Wiltshire. Or she would recite the poems by William Barnes that she knew by heart, trying almost anything to hold his interest and keep him awake because it stopped her worrying about why Dr Pugh had not come and kept her from asking questions about David that she knew he couldn't answer.

36

Dr Elwyn Pugh was in a quandary. Having finally decided that it was impossible to continue tending the man concealed at Tretower he had no idea how to put an end to the situation.

People were becoming curious about his thrice-weekly turnouts around midnight. The occasional emergency was acceptable but such consistent journeyings were hard to justify. Several of his patients had already commented and tried to question him and he had no doubt that tongues were wagging behind his back.

Since the Chartist uprising in Westgate Square everyone in Newport had become suspicious of his neighbour and it seemed to Dr Pugh that not even his professional calling exonerated him completely.

He had always been regarded as a pillar of society and now, in his declining years, he had no wish to change that status. Furthermore, he found the need for secrecy and the long, tiring drive at the end of a busy day played havoc with his constitution.

It had been traumatic times but now that all the Chartist ring-leaders had been arrested, life was slowly returning to normal in Newport and he didn't want to cause any scandal.

Fourteen men in all were now in Monmouth gaol. They would appear before the Special Assizes at the end of December charged with High Treason and doubtless they would be sentenced to death or deported to Van Diemen's Land.

Many more faced lesser charges.

So far, his own name had not been adversely associated with the uprising and Elwyn Pugh didn't want to chance his luck. He felt he'd taken enough risks, having found himself in the invidious position of tending to the injured from both sides.

'I'm getting old, and that's a fact,' he muttered aloud as he packed his black leather bag. 'I prefer to be abed by midnight, not traipsing round the countryside. And what happens if I'm stopped by the military and they start to question me?'

What to do now with Owen Jones was the problem. He couldn't hand his patient over to the authorities. There would be far too many questions asked. The man seemed to cling on grimly to life. With careful nursing he might last for weeks, or even months, without ever regaining consciousness.

And there was Kate Stacey to consider. If only she had never become involved, sighed Dr Pugh. It had seemed a good idea at the time, a way of keeping her out of sight of the military. Yet if the man had been left unattended he would have sunk deeper into the coma he was already in. He would have felt no pain, known nothing about what was happening.

He thought back to that eventful Monday morning. At the height of the skirmish, he'd been summoned to attend the Mayor, Thomas Phillips, who'd been wounded in both the hip and arm as he valiantly stood his ground at the Westgate Hotel.

It was no wonder that he had been regarded as the hero of the hour by the citizens of Newport, mused Elwyn Pugh.

Such was the way of things, he ruminated. He could remember when Thomas Phillips had first come to Newport, a cinder-tip labourer from the Ebbw Vale Ironworks. Within a very short time though he had put his humble beginnings behind him and become a scholar.

He'd married well. His wife Anne, one of the Gentry, had come from Crickhowel. She was a descendent of the famed Sir David Gam, who became a hero at the battle of Agincourt for saving the life of King Henry V.

Now it was the turn of Thomas Phillips to be a hero. And as he had stood outside the Westgate Hotel, his cloak flung back to show his injured arm supported by a sling, the people of Newport had duly accorded him that honour.

His own friendship with the Mayor had served him well, though, Elwyn Pugh reflected. When he'd called at Thomas Phillips' home a week later, to check his progress, he'd been alerted to the fact that the military were looking for Kate.

'Did you see a young woman in the Square at the height of the troubles?' Mayor Phillips asked.

'A woman, you say?' His eyes narrowed and he snapped his teeth together sharply.

'She had dark hair curling round her face and over her shoulders. She was trying to comfort some of the dying men. One of the soldiers who went over to see what she was doing butted her out of the away with his gun.'

Elwyn Pugh made no reply but concentrated on dressing the Mayor's wounds.

'Are you sure that she never came to you for help?' persisted Thomas Phillips. 'Not a face I've seen in the town before.'

'Probably a wife or sweetheart who'd come down from the Valleys with her man,' answered Elwyn Pugh evasively.

'To fight? A woman!'

'They can resent injustice just as deeply as men and feel the need to change the conditions they have to live under,' the doctor replied drily.

'We must find her. She must be brought to trial with the others,' avowed the Mayor.

Knowing the power Thomas Phillips had and the fact that he could use both the military and the constabulary to do his bidding, Elwyn Pugh fretted over Kate's safety.

'We must do something to protect her,' he told Iestyn. 'She worked valiantly nursing the injured men we had in our care.'

313

They'd talked at length before agreeing that it would be best for her to remain at Iestyn's house for a week or two.

And that would have been the end of the matter, reflected Elwyn Pugh, had not Rhys Pendric, the doctor at Abergavenny, been taken suddenly ill and begged him to look after a man he and Huw Jenner were hiding at Tretower.

Hugh Jenner had shrugged non-commitally when Dr Pugh had told him it was much too far for him to visit more than once or twice a week.

'I know of someone who might be willing to stay there and nurse the man,' the doctor had added.

'Those arrangements are up to you and Dr Pendric. All I ever agreed to do was supply food and fuel,' Huw Jenner grumbled.

And now he was anxious to be relieved of even that responsibility.

'Troubled I am, Doctor,' he protested. 'People are becoming suspicious. All this coming and going late at night. They've only to mention it to the constabulary and then they'll be keeping watch on me. It's too much! I can't stand the worry of it all any longer, see!'

'What can we do?' frowned Elwyn Pugh, snapping his teeth together irritably.

'I was going to ask you the same question, it being your responsibility like,' answered Huw Jenner slyly.

'If only we knew who this man was, then perhaps we could persuade his family to look after him.'

'No! *Duw anwyl*! If that had been feasible we wouldn't be hiding him out here now, would we?'

'How did he get here in the first place? Surely you know that much.'

'*Daro*! Of course I do, but I was told not to say anything.'

'Is he a Chartist?'

'No! He's not one of them.'

'How can you be sure?'

314

'Dr Pendric brought him here after the dispute at Fforbrecon colliery. This man had been injured, left for dead, like.'

'Then he must be a local man! Can't we find out his name?'

'Not quite that simple, see,' Huw Jenner muttered, rubbing his hand over his chin in a worried manner. 'Dr Pendric said this chap had been involved in a fight with one of the Owners. Everyone thought they'd killed each other.'

'And what about the other man?'

'Can't say.' Huw Jenner fidgeted uneasily. 'All I know is that the dispute was called off, the men went back to work and the whole thing was hushed up.'

'Has no one come looking for this chap?'

'Not a soul. A bachelor he was, see. They'd just add his name to the list of those trapped by the cave-in.'

'So if he dies?'

'Bury him and that's the end of it,' shrugged Huw Jenner.

It certainly seemed a simple solution, thought Dr Pugh, and for a fleeting moment wished he had never taken the Hippocratic oath and sworn to save lives.

December snow gave him an excuse to delay his visit. He half hoped there would be a further fall, enough to make the roads impassable and the journey impossible. Without fresh supplies of medicine it was unlikely the man would recover.

But there was still Kate Stacey to be considered, he reminded himself.

She was young and robust though and would survive a few days without food. She'd be upset if the man died but she'd soon put it all behind her.

For his own sake, as well that of the Lewises, he would have to make sure that all interest in her whereabouts had died down before he sent her on her way. It would be calamitous if she was arrested on suspicion of taking part in the uprising and sent for trial.

Perhaps she could go back to the Lewises for a while, he mused. They seemed fond of her, Morag was always asking after her.

Huw Jenner would be no problem. He wouldn't question where she'd gone.

As he trotted through the night, Elwyn Pugh began making new plans. He decided to tell Kate that because of the weather and the risk of them being snowed in, the man was being moved and he was taking her back to Newport to stay with the Lewises. She would be so delighted at the thought of seeing Morag again that she wouldn't question his decision, he assured himself. After all, what did an unknown man matter to her!

The plan seemed perfect. And once they were all sure that Mayor Phillips and the military had lost interest in Kate's whereabouts she could go on her way. He sighed. She was an attractive young woman with a manner as pleasing as her looks. It was regrettable that Mayor Phillips had noticed her, otherwise he might have considered offering her employment.

Meg Roberts, his housekeeper, was old and had grown crabby. Kate Stacey would have brought a freshness to his home that was sadly lacking, he decided. Twenty years of being a widower had not completely blinded him to the comforts a comely woman could provide.

His thin mouth twisted into a grim smile as he thought what people would say. Or Meg Roberts for that matter. She'd hardly welcome the girl with open arms, he thought wryly.

Unless . . . He pushed the thought away as though it was a red-hot cinder. At his age, close on sixty! He must be going out of his mind.

Yet the idea warmed and comforted him as he made his way towards Tretower. Perhaps after Kate Stacey had stayed a while with Morag and Iestyn Lewis he could give it more thought, he decided.

He shook the reins, urging the horse on, anxious to reach his destination and put the first part of his plan

316

into effect. He'd stop at the tavern and tell Huw Jenner there was no need for him to accompany him. They'd not be needing any further supplies of food and fuel.

Having carefully rehearsed what he was going to say to Kate about why he was moving the man she was nursing and why he was taking her back to Newport, it came as a shock to Elwyn Pugh when he arrived at Tretower to see the dramatic change in their patient.

Kate, her face wreathed in smiles, was eager to tell him all that had happened and everything Owen Jones had told her about his accident.

Elwyn Pugh listened in silence, knowing that it had scuppered all his plans.

37

Tudor ap Owen was not a man to be easily dissuaded from his ambitions. He was proud of his noble ancestry and ruled what he considered to be his kingdom with a fierce possessiveness.

His determination that his son should marry Penelope Vaughan was not a passing whim but a carefully formulated plan, one that he had envisaged from their very birth.

There had been Vaughans in the area since the Middle Ages. Penelope's ancestry could be traced back to Sir Roger Vaughan the Younger who had resided at Tretower Court, in the fifteenth century. One of his descendants, William Vaughan, had served as High Sheriff in 1591, followed by his son Charles who held the same rank between 1621 and 1625.

Sadly, there were no longer Vaughans at Tretower Court.

What had once been a fortified manor house was now a farm. Tretower Castle that had stood close by was reduced almost to rubble. Only a single tower remained, rising starkly above the ruined twelfth-century hall and solar.

Tudor ap Owen held such past glories in high esteem and was determined that one day he would own both Castle and Court and restore them to their former illustriousness, a perfect setting for the future ap Owen dynasty.

If David and Penelope didn't marry, then, of course, such a vision no longer held any meaning.

Selecting the right partner was all-important. No one knew the value of selective breeding better than Tudor ap Owen. He had proved it with cattle, earning a far-reaching reputation with his pedigree herd. That was why he was so determined that David should marry Penelope Vaughan.

The crux of the matter, as far as he was concerned, was the continuation of the ap Owen line. Penelope Vaughan had the right background and splendid child-bearing hips. Her no-nonsense outlook would keep David's feet on the ground.

It would recompense for his own laxity in the way he had brought the boy up, Tudor ap Owen thought grimly. Elaine dying when David was little more than a child had been a sore trial.

He had at least been fortunate in being able to marry Helen off as well as he had done. George Sherwood might be many years her senior, and a pompous ass to boot, but he was wealthy and had a title. She seemed to have settled to her new life well enough even though she had produced only two meek and mild milksop girls.

The news brought to him by George Sherwood that David was enamoured of a young woman whom Helen had engaged as a Nanny for their daughters had irritated him. The sooner such an indiscretion was nipped in the bud the better.

It was a trifling matter, of course, since David was now old enough to marry and settle down, and dallying with servant girls was a recognized prerogative of the Gentry, Tudor ap Owen reflected.

David was his great hope. He'd father sons who would bear the ap Owen name and follow in the family tradition of mining and farming. Penelope Vaughan was as fit and healthy as any prize animal in his herd. She could handle a horse as well as any man and she would certainly make sure their offspring were raised with a firm hand.

Penelope was no beauty, he had to admit that. If he hadn't been so determined that she was to be his daughter-in-law he would have described her features as showy. Her flaming red hair gave her an aggressive look, her green eyes were bold and as direct as a man's. Her mouth was much too straight for a woman and her chin as firm and square as her father's.

She took after her father in other ways, too, Tudor ap Owen reflected. Tomos Vaughan was an arrogant man, a harsh employer who demanded loyalty as well as hard work and was loathe to pay a penny more than he had to for the privilege.

His ironworks were the most profitable in Ebbw Vale partly because he employed a higher percentage of women and children than any other Owner.

He kept a register of every man, woman and child who worked for him. Married men were obligated to inform his Agent whenever there was an addition to the family. He insisted that this information was necessary so that they could be properly housed. It also made sure that every child was gainfully employed the moment it was old enough to work.

Unlike some of his fellow Owners in Blaenafon, Tomos Vaughan did not approve of families living under the viaduct arches. Instead, he housed them in the rows of terraced houses he had built in the shadow of the ironworks. Packed in along the foot of the Blorenge mountain they looked as though they were huddling together for shelter, but each one had a kitchen and living-room downstairs and two bedrooms up over.

The women's pleasure in such adequate accommodation was marred by Tomos Vaughan's unexpected visits. He would walk straight into any one of the terraced cottages, at any time of the day, without warning. It had earned him the nickname of Vaughan the Nose.

'Not even allowed to live as you wish within your own four walls,' the women grumbled.

They bitterly resented such intrusion, especially those who broke the strict tenancy laws imposed by Tomos Vaughan and took in a lodger. They did it to eke out their meagre earnings, even though it led to over-crowding and their children having to sleep as many as four to a bed.

320

'It's the only way to find enough money to pay the exorbitant rent he charges us,' they argued when they were found out.

'Tell them it's time to send another child to work,' he would instruct the Agent. And the youngest, just four or five years old, who until then had spent his time happily playing, would be dragged bleary-eyed and snuffling to earn his fourpence a day minding a truck or opening vent doors.

'Wicked, so it is, that a child not much more than a babbi should have to work in such conditions,' the women grumbled. Yet none dared to defy Tomos Vaughan, knowing that if they did they might find themselves homeless and their entire family out of work.

Penelope was her father's daughter. Her harshness with both the domestics and the stableboys was widely feared.

From what he knew of his son's character, Tudor ap Owen reflected, Penelope would be the ruling force in their household after they were married.

David was certainly a gentleman and although he admired his son's fine manners and polished way of speaking, Tudor ap Owen secretly wondered whether perhaps the boy suffered from too much learning. Here he was, almost twenty-three years of age, and had never done a day's work in his life. In fact, he was more interested in reading poetry, or becoming a teacher, than in earning money.

The time had come to change all that, he decided and, anxious to have a marriage contract drawn up between the two families, he invited Tomos Vaughan to dine with him at Llwynowen as soon as he'd despatched David to Fforbrecon.

The two men were past-masters at bargaining. Both knew what the other wanted and they played their cards carefully. Tudor ap Owen's invitation was acknowledged but Tomos Vaughan regretted that he was not free to dine for several weeks and suggested a date in early December.

Tudor ap Owen fretted about the delay. By then winter snow might make the roads impassable, or he himself might not be well enough.

His fears proved unfounded, however, and when he at last greeted his guest, Tudor ap Owen felt that the culmination of all his plans was in sight.

They enjoyed their meal in perfect harmony.

Tudor ap Owen had selected the finest wines from his cellar and instructed his cook to prepare dishes he knew his guest favoured.

The table groaned under the magnificent spread.

Barley broth was followed by trout freshly caught from the stream that flowed through his land. A succulent roast of lamb, venison pie and boiled capon were accompanied by roast potatoes, baked parsnips and boiled carrots. To follow there were tarts made from gooseberries and plums that had been preserved in wine, and the fresh clotted cream served with them was from his own dairy. On the cheese-board that ended the meal was a selection of crumbly Caerphilly and biting blue Stilton.

When the port had been passed between them for the third time, Tudor ap Owen suggested they should retire to the drawing room and enjoy a pipe and a fine brandy that he'd been saving for the occasion.

Mellowed, but still aware that so far they had not touched on the reason for their meeting, Tudor ap Owen made the opening gambit by explaining why David was not dining with them.

'I've sent him to Fforbrecon,' he explained. 'There were a great many things to be sorted out following the cave-in.'

'I heard you lost a number of men in that explosion.'

'Yes! It was necessary to seal off the gallery afterwards.'

'The men agreed?'

'Not at first. That's why I sent David along there.

Eloquent, the boy is. Had them back to work the next day.'

'And he's still there?'

'I told him to stay on for a few weeks until he knew how things are run.'

'There's rumours that they're making demands for shorter hours and more money at Fforbrecon,' Tomos Vaughan pressed.

'More money and less hours! The entire mining enterprise will collapse around our ears if owners give in to such foolish demands,' snapped Tudor ap Owen, taking a mouthful of brandy and swilling it round his mouth before swallowing.

'There's unrest in all the coal and iron mines throughout Ebbw Vale,' sighed Tomos Vaughan, slowly exhaling a cloud of smoke. 'Things have reached a point where plain, blunt talking has no effect.'

'The men are possessed of the devil, or so it seems!'

'And now they're demanding to be paid in silver! They complain because the money we've had specially minted for their use can only be exchanged in company shops.'

'Shops run for their benefit!' exploded Tudor ap Owen, angrily. 'The whole situation is getting out of hand.'

'To my mind, it's these agitators from London who are to blame. They're inciting the workers into rebellion by telling them that they are being exploited.'

'I put a stop to such nonsense at Fforbrecon by forbidding Chartist supporters to hold meetings on any of my premises,' stated Tudor ap Owen. 'I've stopped them from congregating in any of the pits or at any of the ale-houses I own in Blaina, Nantyglo or Blaenafon.'

'It hasn't stopped them from meeting out in the open.'

'What do you mean?'

'A cave on Blorenge, a sheltered niche on Coity, even down on the canal bank they gather in their half-dozens,' Tomos Vaughan told him.

'The Chartists are the worst sort of agitator,' grumbled Tudor ap Owen.

'They want the workers to fight not just for more wages, or improved working conditions, but for the right of all men over the age of twenty-one to be able to vote in a secret ballot.'

'They'd even have working men sitting in Parliament if they had their way,' Tudor ap Owen said grimly, thumping the arm of his chair to emphasize his point.

'I blame it on this newfangled notion of universal schooling. Labouring men don't need to waste their time learning to read and write. Working skills are all they need to know.'

'Yes,' Tomos agreed grimly, 'children should be sent to work, not to schools.'

'The sooner they come to grips with the reality of life the better workmen they turn out to be.'

'Every one of my foremen started work when they were five or six and look at them today,' Tomos Vaughan stated.

'Sound men of good judgement.'

'Their energies have been channelled into earning their living.'

'No time for idling their days away or poaching and getting into trouble.'

'You're right,' said Tomos Vaughan heatedly. 'These young agitators are products of the newfangled ideas about education. Letting them attend school until they are ten or twelve simply fills their minds with all kinds of nonsense.'

'It hasn't taught them economics though,' Tudor ap Owen declared angrily. 'How can the Owners hope to give their shareholders a fair return on their investments if the turnover is frittered away on higher wages?'

'Very few complained about their lot until these Chartists' meetings started,' agreed Tomos as he refilled his pipe from the aromatic-smelling jar on the table beside him. He studied the long golden strands thoughtfully. 'Discontent started in Yorkshire with the handloom weavers.'

'Then it spread to Somerset, then to the stocking makers in Leicestershire and the nail makers in the Black Country,' put in Tudor.

'Now, the "People's Charter" has become the battle cry of the discontented.'

'It was one of the reasons I had to send David to Fforbrecon,' Tudor ap Owen confided. 'My patience is exhausted with their nonsense.'

'I don't suffer fools gladly, either.'

'If I had to deal with them, then like as not I would lose my temper and sack the lot of them, every man, woman and child.'

'It would be ruination to your business if you did,' Tomos warned.

'They'd come crawling back in next to no time. I could afford to wait longer than any of them,' scoffed Tudor ap Owen. 'Men are no different to animals; hungry bellies would soon bring them to heel.'

He paused to refill their glasses with brandy.

'On my doctor's advice, I decided the time had come to sit back and let David handle the situation.'

'Why not! He's had the finest education money could buy. He will have been taught the art of skilful debate at University, so he'll know precisely how to talk to these dissidents,' reflected Tomos.

'If he can confound them with fine speeches they might accept defeat more quietly. No sense in sending my blood pressure soaring.'

'Quite right. Give yourself a heart attack and the scoundrels would regard that as a victory for their cause.'

'So, I thought I'd let the boy have his head. I decided to put the matter entirely in his hands and I told him to stay on at the Company house at Fforbrecon for a while, and find out at first hand how the work force is organized. It will show him where his responsibilities lie.'

As he tipped back the last drop of brandy in his goblet, Tomos's eyes narrowed. He knew they had at last reached the real reason behind their meeting.

It was several hours later before every detail had been thrashed out to their mutual satisfaction. Both men drove hard bargains. There was so much at stake.

'Can that be the time?' frowned Tudor ap Owen, his tone querulous as he peered across at the grandfather clock in the corner of the room. With much fumbling, he drew out his gold hunter and checked the hour again. 'Almost two in the morning!'

'I trust my coachman's not frozen to death!' grunted Tomos as he pulled himself out of the deep armchair, staggering slightly, and stretching out a hand to hold on to the mantelshelf to steady himself.

'Sitting in front of the kitchen fire drunk more likely,' growled his host as he tugged on the bell pull, summoning a manservant to see his guest on his way.

Tired but content, Tudor ap Owen remained in front of the dying fire long after Tomos Vaughan's carriage had crunched its way down the gravel drive. It had been a rewarding evening. Tomorrow he would speak to his solicitor and have the necessary documents drawn up ready for signing, and then a wedding date could be fixed.

38

Dr Elwyn Pugh was both surprised and relieved to find that his colleague, Dr Rhys Pendric, was already at the Howells' house when he drove up with Kate and Owen Jones.

He had sent Huw Jenner into Abergavenny to alert Pendric that the man they had been sheltering at Tretower had regained consciousness and knew who he was and also had a fair idea of how he had come to be injured.

'Now be sure and tell Dr Pendric that I am moving this man out of the tower right away,' Elwyn Pugh repeated.

'Tomorrow would be soon enough, I would've thought,' argued Jenner. 'Not good for a man who's been at death's door to have to face the night air.'

'And it's not good for him to stay where he is without food or fuel,' retorted Elwyn Pugh.

'I don't mind providing both seeing as it will be for the last time,' protested Huw Jenner. 'I'd prefer that to riding all the way to Abergavenny at this time of night. It might snow at any minute and . . .'

'Precisely. Another reason for moving Owen Jones back to the Howells' place in Fforbrecon right away.'

'I'll take your message, doctor, if you insist, but I can't promise that Dr Pendric will ride over to Fforbrecon to meet you. He's a sick man, too, see. That's why he asked you to help look after this man in the first place, remember.'

'He'll come providing you give him my message correctly,' retorted Elwyn Pugh with more conviction than he felt.

The temperature had dropped several degrees since he had set out from Newport and, as Huw Jenner had prophesied, flakes of snow were beginning to fall. Apart from the fact that he had brought no supplies whatsoever with him, there was the added hazard that in another twenty-four hours, if the weather worsened, it might be impossible to even reach the tower.

'Do you need a hand to get him into your trap before I leave?' volunteered Jenner.

Elwyn Pugh hesitated, then reluctantly accepted the offer. As far as he knew, Owen Jones hadn't yet stood up on his feet so he would certainly need all the assistance possible to get him along the passageway and hoist him up into the cart. He wasn't sure that he and Kate could manage on their own.

'Shouldn't we wait a few more days, until Owen Jones is stronger,' protested Kate when the doctor told her what was happening.

'No! There've been developments . . . it is better this way.'

He didn't trouble to explain but he knew from the flicker of fear in her blue eyes that she thought it was her safety he was concerned about. He'd let her go on thinking that, then she'd comply more readily.

'You can be on your way to Abergavenny with Dr Pendric now,' he told Huw Jenner as soon as they'd settled Owen Jones on the cart and covered him over with blankets. 'I'll hope to see you both in Fforbrecon within an hour or so.'

'You may see the doctor there but you'll not see me again,' Jenner told him sharply. 'When I've alerted the doctor I'm back home to my bed. *Daro*! More than my life's worth to get mixed up in this lot.'

'That's between you and Dr Pendric,' Elwyn Pugh told him curtly. 'Just one thing more. Remove any evidence that this place has been in use. Clean out the fireplace, remove the chair, make sure nothing is left behind, not a trace that anyone has been living here.'

'Yes, yes. I'll see to it all tomorrow,' Huw Jenner told him impatiently.

328

The ride to Fforbrecon was slow and tedious. Owen Jones groaned at every bump in the rutted road. In spite of being cocooned in blankets he shivered violently and the cold night air made it increasingly painful for him to breathe.

'Have you nothing you could give him to ease his distress?' begged Kate.

'We've not far to go now.'

'Are we taking him to your house at Newport?'

'Heavens no! We're only going a few miles down the road. Just as far as Fforbrecon,' he added quietly.

'You mean we're taking Owen Jones back to his own home?'

Her eyes glinted blue in the whiteness of her face and he heard the tremor in her voice and wondered why she seemed so startled by his statement. Before he could question her, Owen Jones claimed her attention and the moment was lost.

After that they had travelled in silence, each occupied by their own thoughts, until they stopped outside the Howells' terraced house.

Prys and Megan came out to meet them. They asked no questions. Quickly, silently, they bundled Owen Jones out of the cart and into their living-room. They were relieved to find that Dr Pendric had indeed already arrived. Prys settled him into an armchair drawn up by the fire then stood back to allow Dr Pendric to examine him.

Megan fussed round Elwyn Pugh and Kate.

'I don't know who you are, *cariad*, but I can see you're frozen to the bone,' she crooned as she helped Kate off with her cloak. 'Drink this, my lovely, you'll soon be warm,' she promised, handing Kate a mug of tea.

'And you, Dr Pugh. Would you like a spot of something stronger in yours?' she asked with a conspiratorial smile. 'Normally we wouldn't have anything of this sort in the house but Dr Pendric brought some whisky with him. For medicinal purposes, you understand.'

'Most welcome.' Elwyn Pugh held out his cup and Megan poured a liberal tot into his tea. 'I think Kate might benefit from a drop as well.'

'Of course, if she can take it. Me, I can't stand the stuff.'

'What about Owen, doctor? Is he allowed any?'

'Well diluted it will do him good,' Dr Pendric assured her. 'Steady his nerves as well as warm him up.'

'I'll soon have some hot cawl for you all,' promised Megan, placing a large iron saucepan over the glowing centre of the fire. She lifted the lid and a delicious savoury aroma filled the air as she peered inside and stirred the contents.

'There's no hurry,' Elwyn Pugh told her. 'We have to decide what our next course of action is to be, that's why I asked Dr Pendric to meet us here.'

'Food first, mun,' insisted Prys. 'Starving I am,' he laughed. 'It's well past our normal time for eating, see.'

'If that's settled then I'll lay the table,' stated Megan.

Refusing Kate's offer of help, she bustled to and fro, spreading a starched white cloth over the red chenille cover on the table in the centre of the room.

'I don't know how we're all going to sit down. Be a tight squeeze,' apologized Prys as he moved the chairs around.

'Owen must stay in the armchair by the fire,' ordered Dr Pendric. 'Megan or Kate can feed him later.'

'Right you are. Now the rest of you, come along. I shan't call you again,' scolded Megan.

'There's no need to call me. The smell of your cawl floating up the stairs was signal enough, Megan. I'm absolutely famished and . . .'

Kate's gasp of astonishment was echoed by the man who had entered the room. For a moment they both remained frozen to the spot. Kate's heart seemed to miss a beat, then her pulses raced as she stared at the wraith-like figure in the doorway. Was it David or was it an apparition, she asked herself. He was so thin. Even his face had changed. The wide mouth, the fine aristocratic nose were unmistakable, but a recently healed scar extended from one side of his forehead right down the side of his cheek.

As their eyes locked, she felt relief and happiness and her joy increased as she sensed he felt the same.

Oblivious of the curious stares, Kate flung herself into the welcoming arms stretched out towards her.

For several moments she was unable to speak. Tears streamed down her cheeks. Then she pulled back and stared in disbelief.

'David . . . is it really you? I've dreamed of seeing you again so many times that it's hard to believe you're real.'

'Oh, Kate!' He pulled her back into his arms, pressing her to his chest, burying his face in her tousled curls.

'You're so thin, so gaunt,' she whispered. 'For a moment I hardly knew you. I thought I must be having one of my hallucinations . . . seeing you even though you weren't there, like I did at Newport.'

'Newport?' He looked puzzled. 'What were you doing in Newport? What made you leave Bramwood Hall?'

'Oh, David, so much has happened since then. . . .' her voice quavered with pent-up emotion.

'Hush. You're safe now,' he consoled her gently.

'But what has happened to you, David?' Her fingers trailed over the livid mark that scarred his face.

'Is anyone going to eat this cawl if I dish it out?' interrupted Megan. 'A minute ago you were all dying of hunger!'

'We still are, Megan. We've both had a tremendous shock, though,' explained David contritely.

'Well, a good hot meal is an excellent cure for shock,' Elwyn Pugh told him. 'Time enough for all the talking and explanations when we've eaten our fill.'

They talked until late into the night. There were so many stories to be told and plans to be made for the future.

David's relief when he found he was not a murderer, mingled with his delight in having Kate by his side, made him the happiest man in the room. During his incarceration his memories of Bramwood Hall and Kate had filled his thoughts and he had determined that no matter what happened he could never marry Penelope Vaughan.

Owen Jones, though still weak, was anxious to be reunited with his dead brother's wife and children.

'I owe it to our Ieuan to look after them,' he said earnestly. 'After all, if I hadn't changed shifts with him then I would be dead now anyway!'

'Not much you can do for them, boyo, not for a while at any rate, not the way you are,' commented Prys Howell.

'Don't worry, Owen,' David said quickly. 'I'll see you have a job above ground . . . and wages that will make it possible for you to support them.'

'*Daro*! Almost worth fighting you for, mun,' grinned Owen. 'Mind, I'm not at all sure that I could ever again go back underground. Like a nightmare to me now, see. All that blackness and fetid air. . . .' he shuddered.

'Stay here with the Howells for a few more days and get your strength back and then Prys or Megan will let your family know you are still alive,' Dr Pendric told him.

'Break it to them gentle, like, you mean. Just in case they think I'm a ghost.'

'Well, mun, it's bound to be a bit of a shock, after all this time!' exclaimed Prys Howell.

'They mightn't want me back. Might resent the fact that I'm still alive and our Ieuan is dead,' Owen Jones muttered gloomily.

'There's silly you are. They'll welcome you with open arms, boyo,' Megan told him firmly.

'Right. That is settled then,' Rhys Pendric pronounced crisply. 'Owen Jones to stay here for two or three days and then return to his family.'

'Won't people think it strange that we've not said he was here all this time?' challenged Megan.

'They probably know you've had a sick man here in the house,' Dr Pugh observed.

'No one has mentioned it, or asked any questions.'

'What about Roddi Llewellyn and the men who carried these two back here after the accident?' asked Rhys Pendric.

'Not a murmur from any of them,' Prys Howell affirmed.

'None of them want to be mixed up in it, see,' Megan said briskly. 'They've known something was going on, though. What with the doctor calling two or three times a week and so on.'

'Roddi Llewellyn washed his hands of the whole affair. He said there'd been enough trouble and as long as the men were willing to return to work, and the Owners to say nothing, then the dust should be left to settle.'

'Well, there you are, this incident will probably end just as quietly,' prophesied Rhys Pendric, a smile of satisfaction on his rotund features.

'I hope so. The strain has been chronic,' grumbled Prys Howell. 'Every knock on the door I was afraid it was someone to say Owen had died and they'd come to arrest David for his murder, or me and Megan for harbouring him.'

'Right, you've no more worries now and since there's nothing more I can do, I think it's time I returned to my own sick bed,' announced Dr Pendric.

'Just a minute! What about me?' questioned David.

'You're certainly exonerated from any suspicions of murder now, so I suppose you're free to return to your home the same as Owen Jones intends to do,' Rhys Pendric told him.

'And Kate?' put in Dr Pugh swiftly. 'Are the military still interested in her whereabouts?'

'I have no idea. The Chartists are not my concern. You are more likely to know the gossip in that connection than I am,' Pendric said tetchily.

'All I know is that the trial of those taken after Westgate Square is to be at Monmouth early in the New Year.'

333

'January 16th is the exact date,' confirmed Prys Howell.

'Until then they probably will be on the lookout for anyone who was in any way involved in the uprising,' admitted Dr Pendric.

'Then I think it might be best, Kate, if you came back to Newport and stayed with Iestyn and Morag Lewis,' Elwyn Pugh told her.

'No! Kate is coming back to Llwynowen with me,' David announced, putting his arm around her shoulder protectively.

'Oh, David!' Her sharp intake of breath was one of mingled excitement and enthusiasm.

Her obvious pleasure silenced the others. She brushed back her dark hair with a trembling hand and her long-lashed blue eyes were bright with joy as she gazed at him.

'You'll need time to prepare your father . . . to acquaint him with the reason for your absence. . . .'

'Has he been searching for me?' He studied their faces, a sardonic smile twisting his mouth as one by one they shook their heads or shrugged negatively.

'His instructions were for me to settle the dispute and then stay on at Fforbrecon until things there were running smoothly. My initiation into being an Owner,' he added grimly.

'*Duw anwyl!*' breathed Owen Jones. 'He's as great a tyrant at home as he is a boss.' He suddenly looked shame-faced. 'I shouldn't have said that,' he laughed awkwardly. 'Letting my tongue get me into trouble again, see.'

'What you said is perfectly true,' David assured him.

'Then prepare the way, handle him diplomatically,' warned Dr Pugh. 'Wouldn't do to cross him, now would it.'

David made no reply but braced his shoulders. His chin jutted and there was a gleam of determination in his brown eyes.

'If you're ready then, Kate.' Elwyn Pugh pushed back his chair and stood up.

'She's coming back to Llwynowen with me . . . right now!' David said firmly. 'I know it would be taking you out of your way, Dr Pugh, but if you could give us a lift there in your trap I would be greatly indebted.'

'At this hour! In your condition,' interposed Rhys Pendric heatedly. 'You're still a sick man, David Owen! Going out on a freezing cold night might bring on pneumonia!'

'Owen Jones is a sick man, yet you didn't hesitate about bringing him out into the night air,' mocked David.

'Perhaps we should ask Kate what she wants to do,' Megan said gently. 'She could always stay here for a while.'

'I want to be with David,' Kate replied with quiet dignity. 'If he is ready to go back to Llwynowen right away, then I'll go with him.'

39

The sound of a carriage grinding its way over the gravel roused Tudor ap Owen from his reverie. Frowning, he walked over to one of the windows overlooking the front of the house and parted the dark red velvet drapes.

Was Tomos Vaughan returning already to dispute some clause in the contract, he wondered, as he peered out into the night.

His frown deepened when he saw it was not a carriage with the Vaughan coat of arms emblazoned on the side and drawn by two fine greys, but a two-seater trap with a Welsh cob between the shafts.

His curiosity aroused, he decided to investigate what was going on. Before he reached the hallway, the man-servant who had shown Tomos Vaughan to his carriage, and who was still waiting impatiently for his Master to retire so that he could go to bed himself, was already unbarring the front door.

Yawning heavily, Tudor ap Owen watched in disbelief as David, looking gaunt and distressed, was helped inside.

The two people supporting him were strangers to Tudor ap Owen. One was a tall, middle-aged man enveloped in a dark cloak, the collar pulled up around his ears, the other, a young woman, was also muffled up against the cold night air.

'*Duw anwyll*' he muttered as they helped David on to the velvet couch that stood against one wall of the hall. He drew in a sharp breath. 'What has happened, have you met with some sort of accident?' he gasped, suddenly noticing the fiery, purple blemish that scarred David's face.

'Didn't you know your son was injured at Fforbrecon?' asked Elwyn Pugh curtly.

'The only report I received was that the dispute had been settled and that the men were back at work,' blustered Tudor ap Owen, pulling at his white beard. 'There were rumours of some minor incident, but then I hardly expected them to accept that the gallery was being sealed off without some kind of confrontation.'

'And you've not been concerned because he's been absent from home for more than three weeks!'

'Why should I be? It was agreed that he would stay on at Fforbrecon and learn how things were run there. If he was injured then why wasn't he brought home immediately? Someone will pay for this!' threatened Tudor ap Owen angrily.

'The man he'd been fighting with was in a coma!'

Tudor ap Owen frowned uncomprehendingly.

'If the other man had died your son would have been guilty of murder.'

'What a load of nonsense!' scowled Tudor ap Owen. 'And who the devil are you, may I ask?' he challenged.

'Dr Elwyn Pugh from Newport.'

'And this is Kate Stacey, Father, who was Nanny to Helen's two girls. I told you about her before I went to Fforbrecon, if you remember,' interrupted David.

Tudor stared at Kate hostilely. He felt a pounding in his temples and a restriction in his throat. His eyes narrowed as he met the warmth of her brilliant blue gaze. Involuntarily, he found himself comparing her heart-shaped face, framed by its cloud of dark hair, her small straight nose and soft full mouth, with the bold features of Penelope Vaughan, and understood how David had become enamoured of her.

A pretty face is unimportant when it comes to marriage, he reminded himself. Penelope with her breeding and strong character is a far more fitting match.

As if she read his thoughts, and sensed his disapproval, he saw the girl's mouth tighten, her chin rise and jut

337

proudly. The friendly warmth in her eyes was replaced by a cold stare.

'You had the audacity to take this person to Fforbrecon with you!' Tudor ap Owen growled fiercely, his lips curling with distaste.

'No . . . no. Kate wasn't at Fforbrecon. Not until last night when she and Dr Pugh brought Owen Jones back to the Howells' house.'

'Explain yourself!' demanded Tudor ap Owen.

'Perhaps I can acquaint you with what happened better than David can,' intervened Elwyn Pugh. 'Dr Rhys Pendric from Abergavenny who was attending Owen Jones, the man found lying unconscious with your son, was taken ill and asked me to deputize for him. At my request, Miss Stacey agreed to help nurse him . . .'

'How very opportune!' Tudor ap Owen made no attempt to hide his rising wrath. He visibly trembled with anger. After George Sherwood had sacked the girl, as he'd ordered him to do, she must have come looking for David. How she had met up with this doctor fellow he'd no idea, but it was easy to see she'd turned it to her advantage.

'I can assure you that neither Kate Stacey nor I knew the identity of either man,' Dr Pugh continued. 'Not, that is, until I informed Dr Pendric that Owen Jones had regained consciousness. Then he explained about the other man who had been involved and it was decided we would bring Owen Jones back to Fforbrecon, to the house where your son was in hiding. David and Kate met and . . .'

'And I persuaded Dr Pugh to bring us both here immediately,' declared David.

'An amazing story,' murmured Tudor ap Owen. His mind moved rapidly. If their account was true, and it seemed likely that it was, then at all costs he must get rid of the girl as quickly as possible.

'Arriving like this in the middle of the night, without any warning, comes as something of a shock,' he commented, struggling to regain his composure. He snapped a finger at the manservant who was still hovering in the background.

'Rouse cook,' he ordered. 'Tell her to heat some soup and lay out cold meats or whatever else is to hand for these people. Then prepare Master David's room, and put a warming pan in his bed. Make sure someone is on call at all times to see to his needs.'

'That will not be necessary,' intervened Kate quickly. 'I can attend to him.'

'Not in this house, you won't!' Tudor railed, once more on the point of losing his temper. 'Your responsibilities are over. I will see that you are adequately paid for your services and then you can be on your way.'

'Father! To offer Kate money is insulting in the extreme,' gasped David, his face white with anger.

'We have no further need of her ministrations. She can leave with the doctor, and I must insist on rewarding both of them for their work,' Tudor ap Owen insisted stiffly.

'If Kate is sent away then I shall go too,' David told him heatedly, struggling to his feet.

'Don't talk nonsense!' roared Tudor, his white beard quivering with fury. 'This is your home and here you will remain until your wedding.'

'Wedding?' David regarded his father balefully.

'Earlier this evening I agreed the details with Tomos Vaughan and arranged for contracts to be drawn up.'

'No, Father! This is a matter on which I will not take orders from you,' David told him angrily. His face was flushed, his brow beaded with perspiration.

'We'll have an Easter wedding,' stated Tudor ap Owen, imperiously. 'Three months should be ample time to make all the necessary arrangements.'

'Since I've been at University I've grown accustomed to making my own decisions,' seethed David, his face contorted with fury.

'I sent you there to be educated, ready to take my place as head of our family. I hoped you would become as astute

339

as I pride myself in being,' stated his father pedantically. 'Already, you have failed the basic test.'

'I may not be as astute as you, or as conniving, but I have been taught to stand by my principles,' David replied heatedly.

'Then you must know that what I say is right and that you are honour-bound to go through with what has been arranged,' declared Tudor ap Owen triumphantly. 'Your marriage to Penelope Vaughan was agreed when you were both still in your cradles. Our pact stands. Her father expects it . . . and so do I.'

'I've never wished for any sort of alliance with the Vaughan family.' David's eyes blazed, his mouth tightened, the scar on his face flared. 'This marriage is your idea, a scheming move to amalgamate our coal with their iron to give you greater power and wealth.'

'Penelope will make you an excellent wife. Your wedding will bring benefits to all concerned! That is the end of the matter,' decreed Tudor ap Owen authoritatively.

'She may have agreed to this marriage from a sense of duty but in truth she is more interested in her horses than she is in marriage!'

'That's a slanderous statement!' Tudor's face turned an apoplectic puce. 'Your head has been turned either by your accident or by the company you keep.' He pointed an accusing finger at Kate. 'I will not have this woman in my house a moment longer,' he barked, pointing towards the door.

When Kate didn't move, but remained standing beside David, Tudor grabbed at her shoulder as if to remove her physically.

'No, Father! Kate stays here . . . I need her,' David exclaimed, his voice hoarse with strain.

Kate placed a restraining hand on David's arm, aware from the way he was trembling how upset he was. The wounds on his face glowed an angry red as his temper rose.

Gently dislodging her hand, David sat down on the

couch again. His temples were pounding, his throat tight. He knew he should have taken Dr Pugh's advice and waited until he felt stronger before returning to Llwynowen. He felt so incensed by his father's manner towards Kate that his eyes misted with tears and that made him angrier still.

'David has come here straight from a sick bed, and is in no fit state to take part in a heated discussion of this sort,' she protested, fighting to keep her own voice steady.

'Our deliberation concerns a family matter, and I have already indicated I wish you to leave. His prospective bride will be more than capable of taking care of him,' Tudor ap Owen told her icily.

'For the last time, Father, I am not marrying Penelope Vaughan!' David exclaimed. 'We are not suited. We don't love each other!'

'Love! Utter balderdash. What has love got to do with it! You are destined for each other. . . .'

'No, Father. Both you and Tomos Vaughan are quite wrong. To you, this marriage is nothing more than a business merger. When I marry it will be for love.'

'I refuse to listen to such meaningless diatribe,' Tudor ap Owen shouted heatedly. A bulging vein pulsed at his temple. Colour suffused his face and neck then drained away leaving him a ghastly grey. Beads of sweat glistened on his brow. He clutched at his chest, his breath rasping, then he slumped and fell heavily to the ground.

Kate was on her knees at his side in seconds, struggling to loosen his cravat so that he could breathe more easily. Elwyn Pugh, his face grave, felt for Tudor ap Owen's pulse and took immediate steps to revive him. The entire household was roused and David despatched one of the grooms to fetch his father's personal physician.

While they waited for Dr Glanmor Wynne to arrive, Tudor ap Owen, who was unconscious, was carried upstairs to his bed. Dr Pugh and Kate did all they could to make him comfortable.

* * *

When Dr Wynne arrived, Elwyn Pugh suggested that David and Kate should go downstairs and eat the meal that had been prepared for them.

They had only just sat down at the table when a maid came in to tell them that David was needed upstairs.

Kate toyed with the food before her, anxious to know what was happening, desperately trying to resolve what she ought to do for the best. She was exhausted and dispirited. Although she had found David, after all that she had witnessed it was impossible for her to stay on at Llwynowen, yet the thought of returning to The Bull filled her with despair.

As David and the doctors came into the dining room she resolved to ask Dr Pugh if he would let her ride with him back to Newport. Morag had said she would always be welcome at their house, so perhaps she could spend a few days with them until she could make other arrangements.

'We hoped you would be willing to stay here and nurse Tudor ap Owen,' Elwyn Pugh frowned when she made her request.

'Do you think that would be wise?' she questioned. 'He ordered me to leave his house!'

'Dr Pugh speaks very highly of your capabilities,' Glanmor Wynne told her.

'Yes, but after what has happened? It was partly because I was here that . . .'

'You mustn't blame yourself for my father's attack, Kate,' interrupted David. 'I'm the one who upset him by refusing to go along with his devious schemes.'

'Do you want me to stay, David? If you do, then I'll be more than willing.'

'Right, that's settled,' declared Dr Glanmor Wynne, nodding in a satisfied manner. 'I shall look in later today to check the patient's progress,' he stated as he prepared to take his leave.

'Perhaps we'll meet again, Kate.' Dr Pugh held out a hand. 'I will let Morag know where you are.'

'Tell her that one day I'll come to Newport to see her,' smiled Kate. 'And will you tell her I've found David?' she added shyly.

'You are quite sure you want to stay, Kate?' questioned David when they were on their own. 'Dr Pugh mentioned you were anxious to return to Blaenafon.'

'Only because I've left my belongings at The Bull, the place where I was working before I joined the march to Newport.'

'Don't fret about that. I'll send a man over to collect them for you. But why on earth did you join up with the Chartists?'

'I came to Wales to look for you, David, but I was afraid to come to Llwynowen in case I was turned away. Then I had this feeling that the Chartists would lead me to you.'

'I suppose in a way they did bring us together,' he admitted, drawing her into his arms.

Hungrily, his lips covered the curving fullness of her mouth. Memories of their idyllic days at Bramwood Hall, days filled with laughter and sunshine, came flooding back with an almost unbearable sweetness. Their embrace became more ardent. Their longing for each other almost overcame their sensibilities.

Reluctantly, Kate broke free.

Her longing to stay in David's arms was every bit as great as his was to hold her, but the fear that someone might see them in such a compromising situation deterred her.

'We must be prudent. It will only be another weapon against me,' she warned David as she moved out of the circle of his arms. 'If we are patient, we still might win your father round to accepting my presence here.'

'I doubt it!' His voice rose. 'He will probably disinherit me because I've refused to capitulate and marry Penelope Vaughan,' he muttered morosely.

'We will still have each other,' she whispered.

343

'No home, no money . . .' he shook his head. 'That's not the sort of life I could ask you to share with me.' His eyes blazed, his body shook as he became consumed by despair.

'Hush! Calm yourself, David.' She tried to console him with tender kisses, although she was near to tears herself, unable to bear the agonizing doubts that assailed her.

'You are so unworldly, my sweet Kate,' he groaned, freeing himself from her embrace and walking to the window.

She felt helpless as she watched him struggle with his inner torment. Rage and frustration seemed to consume him.

'We would manage, somehow,' she murmured. 'I'm not afraid of hard work.'

'Are you suggesting you would keep me?'

'No, but I have a wonderful idea of how we could both work together,' she exclaimed eagerly. 'Do you remember you once told me that you envied William Barnes who used to be my schoolmaster?'

David stared at her blankly.

'Don't you see, David?' her face glowed with excitement. 'We could follow his example and open our own school. . . .' Her voice died away as she saw the expression in his eyes and sensed that once again she was sighing for the moon.

40

Tudor ap Owen was an irascible patient.

Dr Wynne, worried in case any undue exertion might bring on a relapse, insisted that his patient remained in bed for almost ten days.

'You might be as strong as an ox, but you are human, even if you hate to admit it,' he pronounced when Tudor ap Owen rebelled against such treatment.

'I'll never make any progress shut away up here.'

'If it was mid-summer then perhaps I would permit you to sit outside for a short time each day, but in winter your own bedchamber, where you are away from any draughts, is the best place for you to be.'

'Poppycock! How can I organize things from a sick bed!'

'You seem to be managing well enough,' Glanmor Wynne told him drily. 'You have a first class bailiff to look after your farm, an Overseer and an Agent to take care of your mining interests, so nothing is likely to be overlooked or neglected even if you are confined up here for a month!'

'Even the best of workmen need supervision and there are plenty of other matters that need my attention.'

'Then let David see to them.'

'And who is going to make sure that I am properly looked after if he is away from Llwynowen on business?' Tudor ap Owen scowled.

'The same person who has done it ever since you have been ill. Kate!'

'Bah! A children's Nanny. What does she know of my needs?'

'Plenty, I should imagine! She has been listening to your

constant demands for over a week now. Any other woman would have walked out long before this, or insisted you mended your ways,' observed Glanmor Wynne.

Tudor ap Owen glowered but made no answer. He knew his old friend was right. He was behaving in an unreasonable manner yet never once had Kate shown the least sign of anger or resentment. For the first three days and nights she had sat by his bedside the entire time.

Even after it had been confirmed that his temperature and pulse were back to normal and all he now needed was bedrest, she had still remained on call, sleeping on a makeshift bed in his dressing room.

He had made sure she was there by ringing the handbell on his bedside table, three or four times each night. Without fail she arrived within minutes, candle in hand, anxious to attend his needs.

During the day she was just as attentive, coaxing him to eat and making sure he took his medicine. A dozen times a day she would plump up his pillows or straighten his bed and ensure he was as comfortable as possible. When he became fractious, she read to him and he was pleasantly surprised by her fluency and the expressive tone of her voice.

Several times when it was dusk and he had objected to having the lamps lit, she had recited verses from memory. There had been ones he had enjoyed in his youth, as well as poems that she told him David liked, written by a chap called William Barnes who had been her schoolmaster when she was a child in Wiltshire.

Reluctantly, Tudor ap Owen had to admit he had grown to like Kate Stacey. He no longer regarded her as a mere servant, though exactly what her position was in the household he found it impossible to define. He was ready to concede, to himself only, that she had an inborn grace, as well as a great many other qualities, that Penelope Vaughan lacked.

He was also aware of the tremendous influence she had over David. He realized that she was the one who had motivated David into shouldering the responsibility of both Fforbrecon and the Estate. His efficiency in this direction he found surprising. He had never credited David with such latent talent and he was astute enough to realize that once he picked up the reins again it might undermine David's enthusiasm.

He knew he was straining Kate's patience by playing on his supposed frailty, especially when he acted testily, and grumbled or snapped at her, but some inner malevolence seemed to take possession of him. The more he tried to be reasonable the more cantankerous he seemed to become.

He lay back in his canopied four-poster contemplating the situation, pondering why she did not rebel. She had plenty of spirit and was never afraid to argue with him, yet she continued to accept his uncertain temper with such sweet tolerance that it often made him ashamed of his outbursts.

Realizing that he was not listening, Kate laid the book she had been reading aloud to one side and walked across to the window. She stood there looking out, lost in thought.

In the distance, the stark ridge of the Blorenge Mountain lay wreathed in mist, the bushes in the carefully tended garden immediately below sparkled with hoar frost and the grass looked as though it had been lightly dredged with fine sugar. Christmas was only a short while away and her heart ached to be back in Wiltshire. If only she could turn back the clock to the days of her childhood when Christmas had meant carols and the smell of a plump chicken roasting in the oven and plum pudding with a sprig of holly in it to follow. There had been jollity and feasting at The Manor but she had spent most of Christmas Day up to her elbows in hot greasy water, washing the never-ending stream of dishes that came down from the dining room where the Sherwoods entertained as many as thirty guests in high style. Afterwards, she had been too weary to take part in the jollity below stairs and had crept off to her attic bedroom clutching a mince-pie and had fallen asleep eating it.

As his gaze fixed on her, Tudor noticed there were fine lines of weariness around her vivid blue eyes and a droop to her lips.

She looked both tired and despondent and he pondered on how he could keep her in his employ even though her nursing skills were no longer needed.

She had made it clear that she had seen through his ruse when he refused to leave his bedroom after Dr Wynne had stated he was well on the road to recovery. He wasn't sure that she understood the reason, though.

'A week ago you were complaining because Dr Wynne said you must stay in bed,' chided Kate. 'It's mid-morning now, the drawing room is aired and there's a fire in your study, so why are you refusing to get dressed?'

'Because I'm not ready to do so,' he growled.

'Why aren't you?' she asked. 'Your valet has shaved you and laid out your clothes.'

'I don't feel like getting up.'

'If it's too much trouble to get dressed then sit out in your armchair for a while,' she persisted, fetching his dressing gown and holding it ready for him.

'For heaven's sake, leave me alone, or do something useful.'

'What is it you want done?'

'I want to dictate a letter. Can you write, girl?'

A vivid flush spread from her cheeks to her throat.

'You know I can write . . . and read,' she told him angrily. 'I attended school until I was fourteen and my schoolmaster wanted me to become a teacher,' she added with dignity.

'Good. Then ring for some paper and pens to be brought up from my study and you can act as my amanuensis.'

Morning dictation became a regular occurrence. Her penmanship was impeccable, her spelling perfect, yet his praise was negligible. Instead, he kept her waiting by his bedside while he scrutinized each document.

His eyes narrowed as he finished signing the letters and glanced over at her. She was putting on weight. Her figure was far more shapely than when she had arrived. Over-eating at his expense, he thought irritably.

Unaware that he was watching her or that she was silhouetted against the window, Kate gently massaged the small of her back, trying to ease the dull ache which was growing worse with each passing day. She attributed it to the uncomfortable bed she had been given and wondered how much longer it would be necessary for her to go on sleeping in Tudor ap Owen's dressing room.

If only David would stop prevaricating and tell his father that they intended to marry, then surely she would be given a bedroom of her own and treated more as one of the family.

Tudor's deep growl of anger made her turn.

'Is something wrong?' she asked, solicitously hurrying to his bedside and laying a cool hand on his brow.

'Not with me!' He watched her through half-closed lids, waiting to see her reaction, surprised that she could remain so calm. He studied her figure surreptitiously as she stood close by his side. His pulse raced as he planned what to say next, wondering if she would deny it.

He couldn't understand how he hadn't realized the facts sooner. It was the answer to all that had been puzzling him, the reason why she was so amenable, willing to put up with his capricious moods. She was currying favour, trying to make herself indispensable so that she wouldn't be turned out.

His mind worked feverishly. He would bet any money that was why she had come to Wales looking for David. His temples pounded. This was the outcome of the long holidays David had spent at Bramwood Hall. All his explanations about studying, and how he needed to stay near the University, had been so much poppycock.

With his sister's connivance, he'd been philandering with this girl, Tudor ap Owen thought, enraged. No wonder George Sherwood had advised him to send for David, and had been so ready to turn the girl out.

He choked at the thought, feeling that he had been duped. To have taken her into his own house, let her nurse him, to have felt grateful to her for what she had done for him. To have regarded her as being of a higher status than one of his own servants because she was well mannered and had some schooling. He groaned with mortification at the way he had been deluded.

'Are you sure you are all right, you look very upset.'

The concern in her voice and in her blue eyes sent the blood pounding through his temples. He brushed her hand away from his brow as though her very touch seared his flesh.

'The truth. I want the truth. I will not be hoodwinked a moment longer,' he railed loudly.

She frowned, perplexed, shaking her head so that her abundance of black hair moved like a dark cloud around her shoulders.

'Are you expecting my son's child?'

Colour slowly suffused her face, spreading from her neck to her cheeks, then draining away completely leaving her face ashen. There was a haughty gleam in her blue eyes. Her lips tightened as though in anger but she said nothing and held her head proudly.

He stared nonplussed. He had been prepared for tears, for heated denials, for anger even, but her dignified silence left him discomfited.

'Well? What have you to say?'

He felt a stirring of guilt as he remembered the way he constantly summoned her to his presence, had her running backwards and forwards, up and down stairs. Suddenly he felt an overwhelming need to protect the child she was carrying, knowing it would be the grandson he yearned to have.

'Why have I not been told?'

'There is nothing to tell and if there was it would hardly be any of your business,' she told him quietly, her chin

350

rising in a gesture of defiance as her level gaze held his unwaveringly.

His defences crumbled. She wasn't what he had planned for his only son, but he had to admit she had tremendous courage and was behaving with considerable dignity.

His initial anger that she had made herself agreeable, tried to curry favour with him because she needed shelter and a home for a child, he now dismissed as being unworthy. If he was completely honest he would admit that far from endeavouring to placate him she had remained unassailable. She had tolerated his whims with good humour, she had nursed him with infinite care. What more could he possibly want, he asked himself. What cause had he for being upset in any way? Yet he wasn't content to let her think she'd won so easily.

'If you are hoping David will marry you, just remember that there is a long-standing agreement with Tomos Vaughan for my son to marry his daughter.'

'And you would hold him to an arrangement made before he was old enough to understand what such a commitment entailed?'

'Fine words. They solve nothing. It's a question of honour . . . family honour.'

'You would sacrifice his happiness for family honour!'

The contempt in her voice and the look of derision on her face made him inwardly cringe. He lay back on his pillows, panting for breath, groaning faintly.

Immediately she was by his side, feeling for his pulse, loosening the neck of his nightshirt. The scorn had gone from her voice as she spoke soothingly, entreating him to rest.

He could pretend no longer.

He had tested her and far from finding her wanting he had only proved that David had made a sound choice.

He lay with closed eyes thinking of what life might be like if David were to marry Penelope Vaughan. He recalled the last time he had seen her. A flamboyant figure in her dark red velvet riding habit, the skirt divided like a

351

pair of men's trousers, so that she could ride astride. Her fiery red hair had been topped by a black riding hat. She had been standing with legs astride, tapping the side of her black leather boots with her riding crop, her green eyes gleaming as she recounted the kill she had just witnessed.

He shivered with distaste as he admitted to himself that life would become intolerable, not only for David but for himself as well, if Penelope Vaughan should be installed as Mistress of Llwynowen.

'How long did you say it was before your child is due?'

'I refuse to discuss such matters,' she told him coldly.

Her eyes became impenetrable blue shields and he had the odd feeling that she was laughing at him.

Suddenly his life was full of purpose. A son to follow on after David, someone to work and scheme for and ensure that he, too, became a man of wealth and power.

His initial regret that his coal mines would never be linked to those of Tomos Vaughan's ironworks faded. It was better this way. There would be no compromising, no shared profits. Whatever money Fforbrecon and the Llwynowen estates generated would belong entirely to the ap Owens.

The demand for coal was increasing all the time. Subdue the Chartists and get rid of all the other agitators and there was no telling how vast the ap Owen empire could become eventually.

He would put in hand some of the schemes he had been contemplating to make Fforbrecon the most efficient mine in South Wales.

He grabbed hold of Kate's hand, needing to tell someone of his ideas.

'I'm going to lay a track to link up Fforbrecon with the railway so that the coal trucks can be loaded at the mine and then be taken straight to the ironworks at Blaenafon.'

'And where will you house all the extra workers? Here at Llwynowen or in the railway arches?' she asked ironically.

'I shall build more houses. There's sufficient land at Fforbrecon for another twenty if they are built in two rows, one behind the other up the mountainside,' he told her eagerly.

'Forty more families!'

'That could mean an addition of seventy or more workers if you take into account the children as well.'

'I think you should rest.' Firmly she disengaged his hand. 'Try and sleep for a while.'

'Nonsense! I must get back to work right away. I've wasted valuable time lying here for so long,' he grumbled.

'You are rambling.' Frowning, she placed a cool hand on his brow. 'Perhaps I should send for Dr Wynne!'

'Stop talking rot! I'm as fit as a fiddle.'

'Are you?' She regarded him with raised eyebrows. 'You haven't even spent a full day downstairs yet and now you are talking about returning to work.'

'And I intend to do so right away.'

'I would have thought you would behave more sensibly at your age!'

'My mind is made up.'

'Without any consideration for David,' she said angrily. 'He has worked very hard to keep everything operating smoothly. If you suddenly return to work you will undermine his confidence completely.'

He lay back and closed his eyes. She was right of course. He had automatically taken a back seat when he had put David in charge. He would have to handle things very diplomatically.

A slow smile spread across his face. Now that he was reconciled to the idea of David marrying Kate their wedding could take place with his blessing.

He tugged his white beard thoughtfully. He could send them abroad on an extended honeymoon. His eyes gleamed. While they were away he would once more be in complete charge and able to carry out all his schemes without any interference.

41

David listened to Kate's account of the conversation that had taken place between her and his father with growing trepidation.

Whenever she had tried previously to persuade him to speak to his father about their future together he'd placated her, telling her to be patient for just a little longer.

'I must pick the right moment to tell him. He is bound to be shocked, you know that.'

'But he already knows you have no intention of marrying Penelope Vaughan, so it really shouldn't come as very much of a surprise,' she contended.

'He still harbours dreams of amalgamating our coal-mines with the Vaughans' ironworks, so probably he still hopes to persuade me to change my mind about Penelope.'

'Surely your happiness matters more than any grandiose schemes he may have,' she protested.

'I doubt if he thinks so!'

'But you can't be certain,' she persisted obstinately. 'Surely you could talk things over with him and dispel the awful tension that is hanging over our heads all the time.'

Telling her that she was worrying needlessly had little effect. He wished there was someone she could confide in who would lend an impartial ear, and whose opinion he could trust. She seemed to have an attachment to Morag Lewis but it would be reckless for her to visit Newport in case the constabulary were still looking for anyone who had been involved with the Chartists.

He had been angered by his father's assumption that Kate must be pregnant. At first he thought she must have misunderstood what had been said but when she repeated the conversation word for word he knew there was no mistake.

The fact that his father had voiced such suspicions made him sharply aware that he must define the relationship between himself and Kate. Until this moment it had not seemed necessary. He had accepted her presence without feeling the need for any positive commitment. All his thoughts had been centred on avoiding marriage to Penelope Vaughan and he had not admitted even to himself the possibility of a permanent future with Kate.

Perhaps he needed someone to confide in just as much as Kate did, he thought. He decided to write to Helen and ask her to come and visit.

From the moment he despatched the letter, explaining that their father had had a slight heart attack and that Kate was at Llwynowen nursing him, he felt a tremendous sense of relief.

Kate's reaction when he told her what he'd done was one of uncertainty. She was anxious about how Helen and George would react to her being there and thought he should have waited until Helen arrived before saying anything about her presence at Llwynowen.

David knew she was under considerable stress looking after his father but the sharp disapproval in her voice bewildered him.

'I thought you would be pleased that I had written to tell Helen and invited her to come on a visit. You've always liked each other and she has always shown great kindness towards you.'

Tears dimmed Kate's eyes. Her fears that something would happen to stop David marrying her crowded her mind.

'No, you did what was right,' she said bleakly.

'I know this has all been very difficult for you, Kate,' he murmured, drawing her into his arms and burying his face in her hair. 'You mustn't let anything my father says upset you. Do you understand?'

355

Tenderly he tilted her chin, his eyes studying her face, willing her to have faith in the way he was handling things. As their lips met, the reaction she aroused in him overpowered all other feelings.

'I'd better go up and tell my father I've written to Helen, I suppose,' he sighed as he released her.

Kate watched in silence as he passed a hand through his hair, and straightened his jacket and cravat.

'Are you also going to tell him that I'm not pregnant?'

'Of course! Now don't worry, it's all a misunderstanding that will easily be put right,' he assured her.

'David . . . you do love me?' she challenged, her breath catching in her throat.

'Come here!' He gathered her into his arms again, crushing her to him. 'That's what I'm going up to tell my father, isn't it!'

After he went upstairs, she felt as if she was standing on the edge of an abyss. She stood in the hallway, rooted to the spot, listening to the murmur of their voices from the room above, unable to discern what was being said, but filled with a feeling of dread.

Finding the waiting intolerable, she went into the library. Nervously she pulled book after book from the shelves, glancing through them unseeingly, replacing them, unable to concentrate on either words or illustrations.

Time seemed to stand still. She wondered what the two men were saying to each other. She was sure that Tudor ap Owen still thought of her as a servant and would be aghast at the idea of David marrying her. As the ormolu clock on the marble mantelpiece chimed the hour she went out into the hallway again to listen.

She found the silence was more distressing than raised voices would have been. If they had been arguing then at least she would have known that David was trying to make his father see his point of view.

She moved into the drawing room, pacing backwards and forwards in front of the long window that looked out on to the terrace and garden. The sun had melted the early morning frost and the damp grass sparkled with diamond brightness, but the mountains beyond were grey, deadened and wintry. It was all so harsh and alien, so very different from her native Wiltshire countryside that she wondered if she would ever grow to love it.

'I've talked everything over with my father,' David said, coming into the room and shattering her reverie.

'You've told him you are planning to marry me?'

'Yes. And I've made it quite clear that you aren't pregnant!'

'Oh, David!' Her cheeks flushed with embarrassment.

'I told him I was marrying you because I loved you and for no other reason.'

'Was he terribly upset?' She studied his face anxiously.

'No! Amazingly enough, he gave us his blessing!'

'Oh, David, I am so relieved . . . so happy!'

As he took her in his arms, she felt as if an unbearable burden had been removed from deep within her. Then, as she drew back and looked up into his face, the brief period of exhilaration vanished and a shiver ran through her as she saw the strange, melancholy expression in his eyes.

'Is anything wrong, David? Is there something you haven't told me? You look so distraught.'

'No, no! It is just everything is happening so quickly that I feel as if I am being swept along by a tide. So many commitments,' he added, pressing a hand to his temple.

Kate bit her lip, unsure what to say.

'Father wants our wedding to take place right away, before Christmas, in fact.'

'That's barely two weeks away!'

'Can you manage to be ready in such a short time?'

'I'm ready now,' she told him with a smile.

'I must write again to Helen immediately and tell her the news. They must all be here for the ceremony. Is there anyone you wish to have present?'

'It would be wonderful to be able to ask Dr Elwyn Pugh and . . .' she hesitated, then added firmly, 'and Morag and Iestyn Lewis.'

'That's out of the question! My father would certainly draw the line at the idea of inviting Chartist sympathizers,' David said emphatically.

Her heart thudded uneasily. If she and David were going to make their home at Llwynowen then it was important to establish right from the start that she had the right to lead her own life, and have her own friends. And now, before they were married, was the time to do this, she determined.

David heard her out in silence.

'If I accept my father's generous offer that we make our home here at Llwynowen, then he will expect you to put our family first. As Mistress of Llwynowen, you will hold an important place in the community so your actions, and the company you keep, must be beyond reproach,' he explained.

'But David, surely I can have my own friends!'

'Of course! You'll make a great many once we are married. Ladies who are important in the community will be eager to know you.'

'I'm not marrying you to achieve social status, I just want to keep the friends I have,' Kate flared. 'And I'm not having your father dictating what I can and cannot do. I want the right to lead my own life and when we have a family I want to be able to bring up our children in my own way.'

'And so you shall. Just think, by this time next year you could even be holding our son in your arms,' he whispered huskily.

'Oh, David!' Their lips met in a sweet, lingering kiss that confirmed his love for her and dispelled all the shadows of fear that had haunted her for so long.

'You must be prepared to make some compromises,' he warned gently.

'I'll do my best,' she promised. 'Once we have a baby though I might not have the time for social commitments. Feeding, bathing and walking him in the fresh air will take up most of my day, you know.'

'Nonsense, my love. There will be a wet-nurse and nursemaids to take care of such chores.'

'Wet nurse! You think I would let my child be fed by a stranger!' Her blue eyes were stormy with astonishment.

'Most ladies do, it is the custom,' he observed blandly.

'Amongst the Gentry it may be acceptable,' she told him scornfully, 'but the people I grew up with believe in feeding their own babies.'

'You won't have the time or the energy once you take your place in local society,' he warned.

'David, the idea of handing my baby over to a stranger to be fed is unthinkable. Anyway,' she added sadly, 'I've seen what happens to the child of a wet nurse. The one she has been hired to feed flourishes while her own baby, starved of milk, is weak and puny. Some even die.'

She felt dismayed by David's request. Her joy that Tudor ap Owen had agreed to their marriage had turned to unease. It was almost as if David was confronting her with these problems as some sort of test. There was something in his manner that troubled her. A sadness in his eyes that she couldn't understand.

'Kate, please try and be reasonable. We all have to compromise. I've had to make a number of sacrifices before he would agree to our marriage.'

'What sort of sacrifices?' she asked, startled.

'Ideals . . . dreams,' his scarred face twisted. 'Nothing you need worry about . . .'

'But you must tell me,' she insisted.

'I've had to agree to shoulder my full responsibilities as far as the family business is concerned.'

'Isn't that what you want to do anyway so that you can take over from your father when he is ready to retire?'

'Common sense tells me it's the right thing to do,' sighed David. 'It's not easy to take such a decision, though. It means giving up forever my hopes of either returning to University or teaching. I doubt if I shall ever be a good businessman; I'm not hard-headed and ruthless like my father.'

Her throat constricted as she heard the bitterness in his voice. For a moment she hated Tudor ap Owen.

The memory of the house in Coalbrookvale Terrace, of the huddle of barefoot children, skinny and hollow-eyed, old at ten, as they set off in the bleak November morning, clad only in rags, to spend twelve or fourteen hours below ground, came sharply into focus.

Shivering, frightened four-year-olds, who sat in the darkness, waiting to open the safety doors or made to chip away at the ore with pickaxes they could barely wield. Boys of ten handling molten metal that could spit and sear, burning through to the bone and leaving jagged slugs of metal wedged into swollen flesh. Young girls, their tender bodies harnessed with belt and chains, crawling on all fours along the narrow tunnels, hauling loaded trams: such memories would haunt her for ever.

She recalled the heated discussions with Iestyn and Morag, their determination to stop women and children being exploited as cheap labour, and wondered if her destiny lay in marrying David so that she could help overcome such distress. If she asked him to do so, would David be strong enough to stand up to his father and persuade him to make changes? she wondered.

She was sure that if one Owner led the way, and improved conditions for the workers, then the others would follow. How could God-fearing men, such as they claimed themselves to be, subject other human beings to such degradation? They treated animals with more compassion, she thought bitterly.

She loved David so much, but she felt sickened that the privileges of the new life she was about to enjoy were at the expense of such women and children.

If only David wasn't dependent on his father but had enough money to start a school of his own like the one William Barnes had run, she thought wistfully, but that was sighing for the moon again.

'So if I can put away my books and dreams, can't you make just this one sacrifice?' his voice cut into her thoughts.

Kate refused to discuss the matter any further. She needed time to think. She loved David so deeply that she wondered if perhaps, after all, it would be better if she released him from his promise and went away. That would leave him free to make his escape from Llwynowen and lead the kind of life he dreamed about.

The arrival a few days later of Helen and her family temporarily took her mind off the matter.

Sir George was as brusque and as supercilious as she remembered. Helen looked older, more subdued. Beth and Mary welcomed Kate with kisses and exclamations of delight about the wedding.

Kate was quick to notice that as the two girls told her over and over how much they had missed her, Sir George's scowl deepened and Helen became increasingly flustered.

As she accompanied them up to the rooms that had been prepared for them in the North wing, so that they could remove their cloaks and refresh themselves after their journey, Beth and Mary chattered excitedly about the dresses they would be wearing at her wedding. Listening to their girlish raptures, for a brief moment Kate felt as though they had never been parted.

She had so looked forward to being able to confide in Helen that she was devastated when she realized that her future sister-in-law was a pale shadow of the woman she had parted from a few months earlier. Completely dominated by her husband, Helen seemed to be incapable of voicing any opinion of her own.

She felt dismayed and suddenly fearful that if she conformed to what was expected of her she might eventually become as submissive as Helen.

Living in a grand house, wearing beautiful clothes, eating sumptuous meals, and having servants to wait on her and a carriage to ride out in didn't have to become a balm to one's conscience, she told herself firmly.

Whatever happened, she resolved, she would go on trying to improve conditions for those who were forced to work in the pits, especially the young children.

361

42

Kate dressed with care. Her gown of blue and grey patterned silk, with its full skirt falling from a high waist, was not the latest fashion but she had chosen it because it was one of her favourites. Around her shoulders she wore her blue cashmere shawl, pinned high on one side with her grandmother's cameo brooch.

She brushed out her shoulder-length curls, smoothing them back from her forehead and gathering them in a chignon at the nape of her neck. She studied the effect with satisfaction. She looked pale but composed. It was going to be the biggest confrontation of her life and she knew it might even ruin her chances of marrying the man she loved so dearly. If she was to live at peace with her own conscience, however, it was something she must not shirk. She took a deep breath to steady her nerves before going downstairs.

Everyone else was already in the dining room and she felt as if she was standing outside herself and seeing the entire gathering through a stranger's eyes. She marvelled at how complacent and self-satisfied they all were. None of them seemed aware that their expensive clothes and luxurious surroundings resulted from the sweat of workers who lived in squalid conditions, and suffered grinding poverty.

She took stock of them dispassionately. Tudor ap Owen with his snow-white hair and pointed beard exuded a patriarchal air of authority. He was fully recovered from his illness and it had in no way affected his physical vigour. His hazel eyes were clear, unwavering and probing.

Standing beside him, Sir George Sherwood, with his red face and heavy jowls, looked boorish and overbearing. His light blue eyes were half hidden under hooded lids and his straight, sandy-coloured hair was brushed relentlessly to one side to reveal his high, dominant forehead.

Kate felt a wave of sympathy for Helen. She appeared to be in such awe of him, speaking hesitantly as if afraid she might say something of which he disapproved, and darting anxious glances at him whenever one of the girls spoke. Her round face looked crumpled and she kept chewing nervously on her lower lip. She looked staid and matronly in her dark green dress. Her fair hair, already showing wings of grey at the temples, was drawn back from a central parting into a tight bun that was far from flattering.

Beth had lost her coltish grace and was awkward and self-conscious, flushing uncomfortably when spoken to and appearing to be too tongue-tied to reply.

Mary had changed, also. She had grown plump and was wearing a pink satin dress that was so tight around the waist that it looked as if she was bursting out of it. The ruffled neckline accentuated the roundness of her face, the short, puffed sleeves made her arms look fat.

Kate let her gaze linger on David. His face was still gaunt and his eyes shadowed by what he had endured. For a moment her nerve almost failed her. Dare she speak out in front of his entire family, knowing how much it would distress him, she wondered. Yet she knew it was her last chance to let them all know of her deep-rooted concern and appeal to them to take steps to change the order of things.

And if they refused?

She closed her mind to such an eventuality.

She was sure that in his heart David agreed with her and realized that there would always be unrest at Fforbrecon until working conditions were improved.

Her opportunity to put her theory to the test came at the end of the fish course. As the plates were cleared and the chablis was replaced by claret in readiness for

363

the meat course, George Sherwood began to speak disparagingly about the Chartists. Likening them to the Tolpuddle Martyrs, he advised his father-in-law to lobby for action to be taken when the trial of John Frost and his accomplices took place in Monmouth early in the New Year.

'Everyone of them must be hanged,' he urged. 'Transporting them to Van Dieman's land would be foolhardy since if the blackguards ever return they would only stir up more trouble. Once an agitator, always an agitator.'

'But what makes them agitators in the first place?'

There was an uneasy silence and Kate felt all eyes on her. Sir George's face became as red as the glass of wine he held in his hand. Kate ignored David's warning frown, aware only of Tudor ap Owen's unwavering stare.

'Greed and discontent! They're always trying to ape their betters, never content with their lot,' blustered Sir George.

'And do you know what their lot is?' demanded Kate.

'Know what it is? Of course I do! We are all put on this earth with a specific purpose,' he pronounced sanctimoniously, 'and theirs is to work.'

'And yours to be their master?'

'Someone has to be in authority and extend a guiding hand, so naturally it falls to those of us who are educated to exercise that right.'

'And exploit the workers? Make slaves of them! Force women to give birth below ground amidst the dust and debris of a coal mine! Compel children who are barely weaned to work in the mines and older children to be treated little better than animals . . .'

'Kate! That is enough!'

The fury in David's voice halted her passionate flow. Their gaze held. His, angry and confused, as if ashamed of her outburst. Hers, flushed and determined.

She clutched at the arms of her chair, knowing she was trembling from head to foot. She felt exultant because she had brought the matter out into the open.

'Such an outburst is outrageous, coming as it does from someone who was once in my employ,' Sir George exploded, his eyes bulging with fury.

She had not intended her onslaught as an attack on Sir George since she knew he was not one of the main offenders. His servants worked long hours, and were expected to be at his beck and call at all times, but they were well fed and properly housed.

'It was not directed at you, Sir George,' Kate said quietly.

'So it was meant for me,' growled Tudor ap Owen, testily.

'Father . . . please. Kate spoke hastily . . . without thought. She meant no discourtesy.' David's voice trailed away as his father cut in.

'Discourtesy? No, perhaps not. Accusation, yes! Continue, Kate. Let us hear more of my heinous crimes. You've obviously given a lot of thought to the matter.'

Kate felt the silence that followed his words closing in around her like a trap. Her throat was so dry that she was unable to utter a word. Yet, this was the chance she had been waiting for. If she didn't speak up now then the opportunity would be lost to her forever. Once she was married to David she would be expected to support him no matter what he did. With a shaking hand she reached out for her glass of wine. The rich smooth fire steadied her nerves. It also cleared her throat and clarified her thoughts.

'I am speaking of what I know,' she said firmly, her eyes meeting Tudor ap Owen's inscrutable gaze. 'I have seen little children of four years old who have been maimed for life because they were unable to get out of the way of loaded trucks after they'd opened the safety doors to let them through. Children of the same age, forced to spend as many as twelve hours at a stretch, huddled in a dank, dark tunnel, completely alone, and who were whipped if they fell asleep from exhaustion. Boys of nine and ten who have lost an arm or a leg through spilling molten metal over themselves because they didn't have the strength to lift the ladle properly.'

She paused and took another sip from her glass.

'These children are sent out to work because their parents need the extra pittance they bring home in order to survive! Little girls, of seven or eight, harnessed to a coal truck by chains and forced to crawl on their hands and knees to pull it along. A younger brother or sister helping to push the carts up the inclines to ease the load on the older child's back.

'And should the tram run backwards, it will go over the younger child, maiming it for life!

'The more fortunate ones die,' she added bitterly.

'This is very unsavoury talk, Kate, in front of two young girls,' Helen protested.

'Perhaps they should know where the wealth they enjoy comes from,' Kate retorted.

'Kate, you have said more than enough,' warned David.

'Let her continue.'

'But, Father . . .'

The atmosphere in the room was tense. Kate knew all eyes were on her, each with its own message: David pleading for her to stop, Sir George glaring hostilely, Helen bewildered, the two girls wide-eyed with astonishment, Tudor ap Owen inscrutable.

There was so much she wanted to tell them to put right that she didn't know where to begin.

'They are not even provided with decent homes to live in,' she declared balefully. 'The squalor is unbelievable. Three and four families sharing a two-roomed house that has only one cooking grate and no sanitation. Children sleeping four to a bed, covered over by rags.'

'Perhaps if the men didn't drink their wages away they could afford better living standards,' interrupted Sir George aggressively.

'They drink because they are dehydrated after working a fourteen-hour day down the pits or in the iron furnaces.

They drink to overcome their despair. And they drink because the Owners pay out wages in the ale-houses,' Kate said angrily. 'The Agent always arrives late and since the men are allowed to drink on tick until he gets there, they've not only run up a bill but are so fuddled that they don't notice if he swindles them out of their rightful monies . . .'

'Is this true?' Tudor ap Owen's voice lashed out.

'It's true. And what money the workers eventually carry home is minted in your own coin so it can only be spent in Tommy Shops!' she asserted scathingly. 'Company shops where you charge half as much again as they would have to pay in the shops in Brecon or Abergavenny! Oh yes,' she added bitterly, 'the Owners make sure that every penny they pay out is returned to their own coffers by one means or another.'

'And what do you propose should be done about all this?' questioned Tudor.

His voice was so reasonable and he sounded so genuinely concerned that for a moment Kate forgot he was an Owner. As she met his level gaze it was as if there were just the two of them in the room and he was asking her advice.

She took a deep breath, knowing that this was the moment she had hoped for, the chance to expound her theory on how life could be improved for the families in Ebbw Vale and the Top Towns.

'It can't happen overnight,' she began cautiously, 'but every family should have a house to themselves.'

'Is that all?'

'No, but better living conditions should be top of the list so that family dignity can be restored.

'Higher wages and better working conditions are equally important.

'There must be shorter working hours for the women and no child under twelve should be employed down the pits or in the iron works. Pregnant women should not be expected to work underground and should not have to return to work for at least a month after giving birth.

'Wages should be paid out each week so that families do not run themselves into debt. The shops should become cooperatives and any profits ought to be shared out amongst the workers.'

'Fine talk,' blustered Sir George. 'And where is all the extra money to fund all these high-falutin ideas coming from? If the men work fewer hours there will be no profit in it. And as for children under twelve remaining idle, that will lead to nothing but trouble. What will they do with themselves all day, may I ask?'

'Owners will provide schools and it will be compulsory for the children to attend. They will learn to read and write so that they have a better understanding of what is happening around them.'

'Breed a new race of agitators you mean, don't you!'

'Not at all!' Boldly Kate held his gaze as she voiced her opinion. 'Discontent is spawned by frustration. The Chartists have gained support because they understand the needs of working men and have spoken up on their behalf. Their leaders have risked their lives in order to make the voice of the people heard.'

'I really don't think this is a fitting conversation for two impressionable young girls to listen to,' protested Helen, frantically fanning herself. 'I really think I should take them into the drawing room,' she added, pushing back her chair and making to rise from the table.

'Stay where you are! It won't hurt them to learn something of the harsh realities of life,' dictated Tudor ap Owen.

'It will certainly show them their precious Miss Stacey in a different light,' sneered Sir George. 'Now that you have all listened to her highly radical views, perhaps you understand why it was necessary for me to dismiss her from Bramwood Hall.'

'I knew very little of such matters when I worked for you,' retorted Kate, her eyes blazing. 'It wasn't until I came here to Ebbw Vale that I saw and experienced the things which have shocked me so deeply.'

'Yet you are willing to marry one of the Owners and doubtless you intend to enjoy the luxuries derived from such exploitation,' Sir George gibed.

Kate's eyes sought reassurance from David, aware that she had placed him in an invidious dilemma. If he agreed with her views he would antagonize his father. If he sided with his family then he was openly rejecting what she had just said.

Tudor ap Owen looked quizzically from one to the other of them.

There was a long pause. He waited patiently, his face still inscrutable. It seemed that everyone around the table was holding their breath, waiting for her answer.

'I am marrying David because I love him,' stated Kate. 'I hope that perhaps one day he will come to understand how desperate the situation is and do something to improve conditions for his workers. When he does, then perhaps other Owners will do likewise.' She paused and took a deep breath. 'It would be wonderful if he could set up a school so that all the children in Ffobrecon and Blaenafon could learn to read and write. I would like nothing better than to help him in such a project.'

'Right. Well, if that is settled perhaps the main course can be served,' Tudor remarked, ringing the small silver handbell on the table in front of him.

Kate ate mechanically, her eyes downcast. Her outburst had drained her and, it would seem, had not achieved anything. David had neither supported her nor expressed any opposition to her opinions. Her dilemma had not been solved.

43

Kate and David were married at St Mary's church in Fforbrecon, ten days before Christmas.

It was a bright cold day. The sun shone and a thin covering of snow gave the occasion a touch of fairy-tale magic. Kate, wearing a gown of pale champagne velvet, edged with cream swansdown, looked regal as she stepped down from the ap Owen carriage.

Pale, but composed, she paused by the Lych gate, while Beth and Mary, looking delightful in their bridesmaid's dresses of peach velvet trimmed with white fur, stepped forward from where they had been sheltering to join her.

Then, very sedately, they walked behind her carrying the long train of Honiton lace.

Kate felt a frisson of fear as the waiting crowd of shabbily dressed men, women and children pressed forward. For one frightening moment she was back in Newport on the day of the Chartist rising, being pushed and jostled by an excited crowd. Her ears rang to the remembered sound of pistol shots ringing out over the heads of the thousands who had thronged Westgate Square. She shut her eyes to blank out the carnage that had followed, the agonized pleas and groans of the dying, the shrieks and screams of the injured.

She felt herself swaying and placed her hand on Sir George Sherwood's black-coated arm for support. Taking a deep breath, she steadied herself as they entered the church.

The past was over, she reminded herself as she heard the music peal out. Today was the beginning of a new life. She was crossing the divide; from now on she, too, would be regarded as one of the Gentry.

'There's still time to turn back.'

Her grandmother's voice filled her head, admonishing her, warning her to remember her place.

'There's they as must serve and them that has t'be served. Parson says we all 'ave our rightful place in life and your'n m'girl is to serve.'

It had been her grandmother's constant admonishment.

Serving didn't necessarily mean being a servant, she told herself rebelliously. As a servant she'd have no power to change things or help anyone. As the wife of a coalmaster her influence would be considerable and could be used to benefit a great many people. Surely that was a form of serving.

David wasn't a hard-hearted tyrant, but a man who was ready to listen to reason. He'd already admitted he couldn't be ruthless like his father. Given time, once he was in charge at Fforbrecon colliery, she was confident she would be able to persuade him to relax some of the harsh conditions imposed on the workers there.

The church was packed. Every seat was occupied. Titled personages and Owners, the Hanburys, the Baileys, Sir John and Lady Guest, the Thomases and the Hills sat alongside local dignitaries and tradesmen.

Kate saw them as a rainbow-hued collage as she walked down the aisle. Top-hatted, frock-coated gentlemen in fine-cut suits and quality calfskin boots, accompanied by their wives and daughters dressed in elegant gowns, their bonnets lavishly trimmed with fur, feathers and flowers.

Her eyes focused on David waiting at the altar steps. Although still thin and pale from his ordeal, he cut a handsome figure in his black cutaway coat worn over light grey trousers, an exquisitely embroidered satin waistcoat and a frilled white shirt.

Her heart thudded until she thought it would burst with expanding joy as she moved towards him. Her fur-trimmed, white kid slippers seemed to skim over the red carpet.

The strain melted from his face the moment he saw her

and she felt an overpowering surge of love and optimism as their eyes met. Whatever the future might hold she was confident that their love for each other would transcend any differences of opinion.

Tudor ap Owen, now fully recovered from his heart attack, stood at his son's side, straight-backed, autocratic, tight-lipped. His white beard stabbed the air, his sharp gaze missing nothing.

As they took their vows, the enormity of the step she was taking impressed itself on Kate. As her hands were joined to David's she felt a glow of supreme happiness. When they entered their names in the Register and handed the quill to Tudor ap Owen to add his signature as witness to their marriage, Kate had an inner conviction that she was fulfilling a pre-ordained destiny that was part of some greater scheme.

Solicitously, David placed a cream fur cape around her shoulders as they left the church and settled themselves in the open landau that was to take them back to Llwynowen for the Wedding Breakfast. She smiled up at him, grateful for the cape's warmth. Winter's bite was in the stiff wind that made the ladies hold on protectively to their feather-bedecked hats.

It would have been more sensible to have used a closed carriage for the three-mile drive but if they had done so then those who lined the road would have barely caught a glimpse of the Owner's son and his new wife.

Men, women and children, shivering in the keen December cold, doffed their caps, bowed or curtsied, their dark eyes devouring the splendour as Kate and David drove past followed by the rest of the wedding party resplendent in their furs and jewellery.

Although the Fforbrecon coalmine had not been completely closed down for the day, most of the workers had been given time off so that they could watch the wedding procession. And afterwards, when Tudor ap Owen's guests had driven back to Llwynowen, there was to be a grand celebration staged in the town's main street.

Free ale and a spread of food, more lavish than most of them had ever dreamed about, would be laid out on the tables set up there. Whole hams, a side of beef, meat pies, a truckle of cheese and as much freshly baked bread, butter and pickles as they could eat. A sumptuous feast which they would talk about for many years to come.

Their obvious enjoyment of the occasion delighted Kate. It added to her own pleasure that provision had been made for them all to be able to participate in the celebrations.

Once they left the crowd behind, the coachman whipped the horses to a gallop. With a sigh of contentment, Kate slid her hand into the crook of David's arm, silently vowing to enjoy herself and put her concern for the workers from her mind, for the rest of the day at any rate.

'Happy?' He bent his head and his lips rested fleetingly on hers. His arm slid round her waist, holding her even closer. She relaxed against him and for a brief spell it was as if they were floating through space.

Behind them, Coity mountain was a sheer white wall, without bush or tree, curving jaggedly across the horizon. To their right the massive outline of Blorenge in its snow-white mantle undulated against the skyline, while away in the distance the conical shape of the Sugar Loaf rose up white and gleaming as though polished for the occasion.

So much white, so much purity, it was hard to believe that hidden below the surface were the black gold seams of coal and veins of metal ore that claimed and maimed so many.

Back at Llwynowen, as they greeted their guests, Kate felt relieved that she had not insisted on inviting Morag and Iestyn. David was right, they would have felt uncomfortable in such a glittering assembly of Owners, country gentlemen, lawyers and judges. For a brief moment she felt lonely and vulnerable, set apart, as if she was merely an onlooker.

The feeling passed as she saw how much Beth and Mary were enjoying the occasion. Both of them had flushed cheeks and shining eyes and in their bridesmaids' dresses they looked extremely charming. They were her family now, she reminded herself, and she hoped Helen would let them visit her often once she was settled into Llwynowen.

Tudor ap Owen, too, seemed to be deriving pleasure from the proceedings. Seated at the head of the lavishly spread table, his keen eyes missed nothing of what was going on.

He was completely at ease, knowing his authority was undisputed, even though he was surrounded by the most important people in the whole of South Wales. The men deferred to him, the ladies appeared flattered and smiled readily if he spoke to them.

At the end of the celebratory meal, when the enormous wedding cake was brought to the table, he called for silence. Kate smiled up at David and he gave her hand a reassuring squeeze as they waited nervously for Tudor ap Owen to summon them forward to cut the first slice.

Instead he rose to his feet, frowning in a preoccupied manner as he looked round the hushed assembly. Kate felt suddenly apprehensive, then her fears abated as he began to make a speech welcoming her to the family and pronouncing his pleasure in the ceremony that had just taken place.

Suddenly, his voice changed. His tone became harder, his words biting. His eyes momentarily met Kate's then looked away, his gaze sweeping the room, commanding everyone's attention.

'My son's new wife has a very radical outlook on life,' he declared, pausing to look round the hushed room as though addressing a public meeting.

'While I lay on my sick bed she informed me that she doesn't approve of the way we run things here in South Wales,' he went on.

There were gasps of astonishment from all around her,

and Kate felt her face and neck flush with embarrassment.

'She condemns the way we treat our workers here in Ebbw Vale. Given a free hand she would insist that all children below the age of twelve years should not be sent to work but attend school so that they can learn to read and write!'

He paused. A titter of laughter slithered around the room.

'And this is not all! She would have shorter working hours even for men and women! And to compensate them for the loss of earnings this would result in she suggests we increase their wages!'

He held up his hand for silence as another wave of laughter erupted.

'That is only the beginning. She wants better living accommodation for them. A house for every family, if you please! Orphaned children must not be left to huddle together in the bricked-up archways beneath the tramways but be properly housed and some motherly body, paid for by the company, should be appointed to look after them!

'She also advocates that pregnant women should not work underground, that they give birth in their own beds, not down on the coal face, and that they spend four weeks at home after the child is born.'

Stroking his white beard, he waited until the guffaws and protests began to die down and then, once more, raised his hand for silence.

'As a marriage settlement, it was my intention to take David into partnership and to put him in complete charge of Fforbrecon colliery.' He paused dramatically. 'Having listened to his new wife's views, and been warned by my physician to avoid any kind of upset, I am in something of a quandary.'

'What's more to the point, you'd soon find yourself bankrupt!' a voice called out.

As laughter roared out on all sides Kate bristled with anger at the unfairness of the attack. How could

375

David's father expose her viewpoints so blatantly and with such mockery, she thought resentfully. It was utterly shameful. If he wanted to rescind the promises he'd made to David then surely he could have done it privately, not humiliate them both in front of their wedding guests.

Her face flushed, she sat up very straight, squaring her shoulders, struggling to hold her temper in check, determined to speak out the moment the laughter abated. David's restraining hand on her arm made her hesitate and the moment passed as Tudor ap Owen resumed speaking.

'That is a valid point but one which I don't intend to put to the test since, as I have already pointed out, I most certainly am not in a fit state of health to cope with any stress. So, with this in mind, I have decided not to give David a partnership after all.'

Tears of compassion glistened in Kate's eyes at the thought of how bitter and frustrated David must be feeling. Her hand found his, seeking to reassure him that she understood his disappointment.

'With my family and closest friends gathered here,' Tudor ap Owen went on, 'I thought it an appropriate time to announce my plans for the future.' He paused, picked up his wine glass and took a few sips.

'Early in the New Year,' he went on, 'I intend to start building more houses at Fforbrecon, a step which I am sure will please my new daughter-in-law.'

Kate lowered her eyes, embarrassed by the hum of comment all around her.

'I also intend to build a school and try out this idea of educating the children. This school, unlike the classes run by the chapels or the Circulating school in Blaenafon, will not just teach them reading and writing but give them a full education. It will be compulsory for all children under the age of twelve years. They can stay on longer if they have any aptitude for learning. David tells me he would rather be a teacher than a coalmaster, so he will be in charge of this new venture, although I have no doubt that Kate will insist on having her say in how things are run.'

For a moment the room swam in front of Kate's eyes. David was holding her in his arms and kissing her so fervently that she was breathless. Then, as he released her, it seemed to her that everyone in the room was shaking their hands, kissing her on the cheek, patting David's shoulder and extending their good wishes.

The buzz of conversation all around them was like the roar of the sea in her ears. She couldn't properly take in what was happening. She wondered whether the excitement of the occasion and the champagne she had been drinking were affecting her senses.

Over the heads her eyes locked with those of Tudor ap Owen. The gleam of understanding that passed between them, as he raised his glass of champagne and smiled at her, filled her with a sense of security and direction. She made her way over to him and she kissed him on both cheeks.

'I shall expect to see all those radical ideas of yours fulfilled, you know,' he told her.

'You will! A school is the most wonderful present you could possibly have given us.'

'It won't be easy,' he warned, gruffly. 'Many of those who are congratulating you at the moment will oppose the changes when you come to put them into practice.'

'It will take time and a great deal of hard work but the lives of the workers and their families will be enriched and Fforbrecon colliery must benefit as a result,' affirmed David.

'You're bound to have some antagonism to your ideas,' he reminded them again.

'Once they see it results in greater efficiency, an increase in output because the miners will work harder so that they can earn more and enjoy a better standard of living, they'll accept it,' argued Kate confidently.

'It's not going to be easy,' he frowned.

'I know. Together, David and I will do it, though. You'll see,' she promised.

'Yes, I think perhaps you will,' Tudor ap Owen agreed. 'Now, isn't it time you cut the wedding cake?'

After the toasts came the dancing which lasted late into the night, revelry greater than any that had been witnessed at Llwynowen for many generations.

Next day, David and Kate set out on the first part of their journey to Bramwood Hall. At Helen's suggestion, they were to spend the first week of their married life there.

'Make sure you come back in time to celebrate Christmas,' ordered Tudor ap Owen as they took their leave.

'I've told Helen that she and her family must stay on after Christmas so that we can all be together to usher in the New Year.'

1840! A new decade. What changes would it bring? Kate wondered.

She would soon be twenty years old and for her it would bring a whole new way of life, she thought exultantly.

There would be no more dreaming of the impossible, no more sighing for the moon, but the realization of all her dreams.

She and David would work side by side. They'd take up Tudor ap Owen's challenge, and establish a school for the children of Fforbrecon. They would help them to understand that there was more to life than grubbing black gold from the earth.

They'd also give Tudor ap Owen the grandson he yearned for. And, by the end of the decade, having fulfilled his personal ambition, David would be ready to accept responsibility for the management of Fforbrecon colliery and the Llwynowen estates; a willing custodian until his own sons were of an age to take his place.